GAIA BOOK 4

OLYMPUS DAWN

GAIA BOOK 4

ZOË ROUTH

GET AN EBOOK AND AUDIOBOOK FOR FREE:
TERRA BLANCA: INSURRECTION, PREQUEL TO THE
GAIA SERIES

WITH THE FREE BOOKISH E-JOURNAL:

https://www.zoerouth.com/bookish

With Bookish, you'll get an invitation to our free community of
readers and leaders, where we chat about books,
life and leadership.

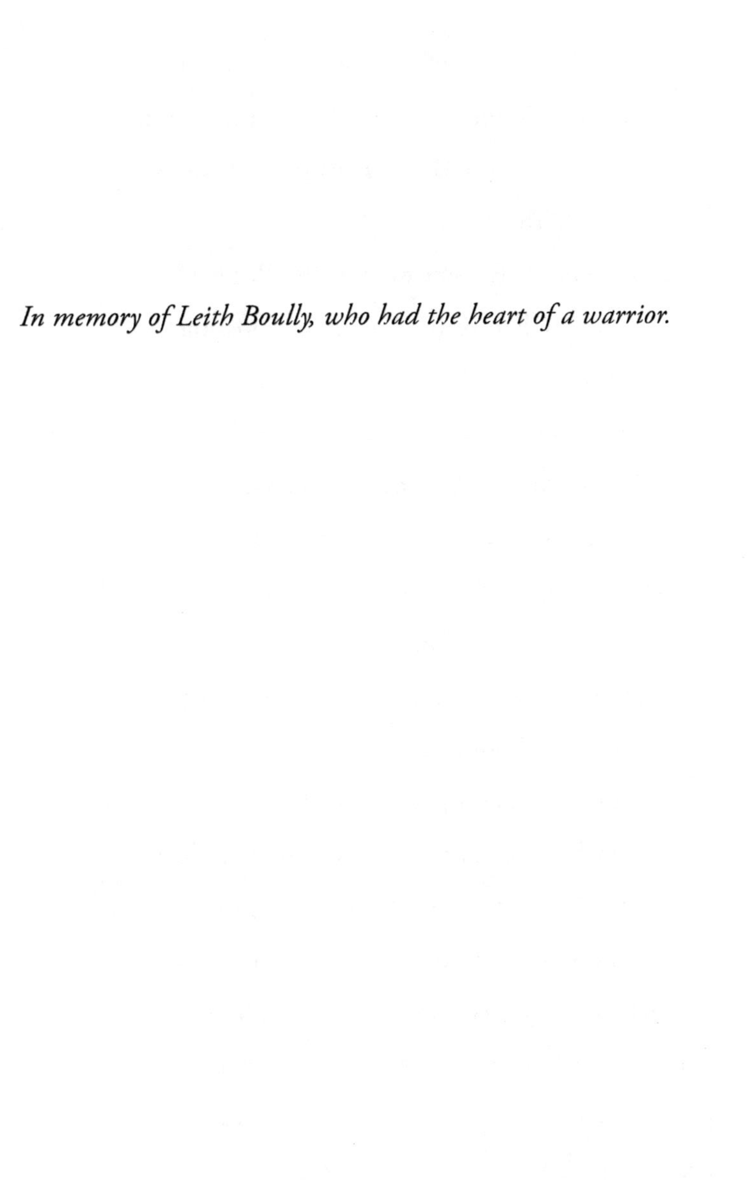

In memory of Leith Boully, who had the heart of a warrior.

DRAMATIS PERSONAE

Alexandra Minke — CapCom for Gaia Enterprises

Arlene Floyd — Madison Floyd's incarcerated mother

Aryanna Sharif — Founder of Aryanna Industries

Athena — A.I. ThinkLink

Claire Edwards — Eco-terrorist for Earth First

Colonel Jin — Chair of the Lunar Commission

Dr Elena Fischer — CEO of Human Habs

Dr Janice Naylor — Therapist at the New Baths of Caracalla

Dr Tarek Mansour — A.I. space tech engineer

Dr Troy Bruin — *Nyx Odyssey* Commander

Dr Victoria Tang — Scientist working for Human Habs

Epiphany — A.I. ThinkLink

Felix Dubois — Contractor for Aryanna Industries

Gareth Barrio — Pilot of the *Pinnacle*

Greg Johnson — Life support engineer for Human Habs

Gustav Ranchero — Contractor for Lincoln Ellison

Huw Chan — Co-founder of Gaia Enterprises

Lincoln Ellison — Founder of Spaceward Bound

Jonas Seaborn — Gaia World Design engineer

Madison Floyd — Pilot of the *Nyx Odyssey* and *Saturnia*

Maja Garcia — Founder of Gaia Enterprises

Max King — Life support technician

Serena Fox — Life support technician

Volkov — Humanoid robot developed from original missing Russian dictator

Xanthe Waters — *Nyx Odyssey* Deputy Commander

Xavier Consus — Food and provisions expert

Ships and Locations

Helios Clipper — Spaceward Bound Moon shuttle

Kunlun — Chinese Martian base built by Dopplebots

Mars Alliance — International conglomerate of spacefaring entities, nations dedicated to the welfare and development of Mars

Mars Accord — International agreement of protocols on the research, exploration and settlement of Mars

New Baths of Caracalla — Dr Troy Bruin's centre-based training facility for emotional mastery and VR therapies

Nyx Odyssey — Chinese Mars space transit vehicle loaned to Gaia Enterprises and Aryanna Industries

Pinnacle — Spaceward Bound's helium-3 mining spaceship converted for Mars expedition

Po Secco — Medical refugee camp in an Italian salt pan

Prima Aqua — Corporate city-state with groundwater monopoly claim close to Po Secco

Saturnia — Gaia Enterprises's helium-3 mining spaceship

Terra Verdi — Floating hydroponic agricultural farm-city with 'Glass Crown', breath domes protecting inhabitants from the sulphur air; founded by Xavier Consus

Vesta — Lava tube habitat

FRENCH LEXICON

Ah, les filles — Ah, girls / Oh, girls

Arrêtez-vous! — Stop!

Bof – Meh / So-so / Whatever

Bonsoir — Good evening

Ça suffit! — *That's enough*

C'est chiant — That's annoying / That sucks / It's a pain

Eh alors — So what? / And then? / What's the big deal?

Exactement — Exactly

La belle vie — The good life

Mais non — Of course not / No way

Merci —Thank you

Merci, mon frère — Thank you, my brother

Merde — Shit / Damn (strong expletive)

Merveilleux! — Wonderful! / Marvelous!

Mes filles et ma chérie — My girls and my darling

Mes petits — My little ones / My kids

Mon ami — My friend

Mon chéri — My darling / My dear (romantic)

Mon cul — My arse (rude, dismissive: "Yeah right!")

Mon Dieu — My God

Mon vieux — My old friend / Old chap / Mate

Non — No

Oui — Yes

Putain — Fuck / Damn (very strong expletive, often used like "bloody hell")

Salauds — Bastards / Scumbags

Trou du cul — Asshole

PART ONE

EARTH

CHAPTER ONE

*"Mars? Mars sucks. It's far, dry as hell and everything
can kill you. But it sure is beautiful."*

—Jonas Seaborn
MEMOIRS FROM MARS

NAPOLI INSTITUTE, HUMAN HABS LABORATORY: VICTORIA

Ping. *Data packet received: Mars-vES06. Decrypt?*

Dr Victoria Tang fumbled for her mug—hot chocolate sloshed over the rim.

She froze. There it was: the data that confirmed proof of concept. She shook her head in amazement, hot chocolate spilling down her lab coat and across the keyboard.

"Damn it!" She shoved the mug aside and pushed away from the desk, liquid dripping onto the floor.

Her colleagues' quiet patter ceased. She waved them off, not wanting to draw attention to her screen. Victoria looked around for something to mop up the spill. Finding nothing towel-like nearby, she reached for a scrap of paper. She wiped at the mess, eyes drawn to the report.

This was the big breakthrough she'd been quietly plugging away at with her Dopplebot Martian twin. After months of persistent attempts to get Human Habs and the larger European Space Agency to listen to her project pitch, she'd gone rogue.

Well, not completely. Just a little. A side project.

The bitterness at the stonewalling swelled again as she reached for her drink, pursing her lips against the edge of the mug; what remained of it was still too hot to drink.

It frustrated Victoria to no end that the lead scientists thought her project might compromise the helium-3 reactor. Honestly, how ridiculous. The cartridge, the size of a suitcase, would easily run off the waste heat and electricity of the fusion reactor.

But no, 'first things first, Victoria' the Chinese–Dutch governance team had chided. Stabilise the helium-3 power, secure a lava tube extension to the main base, build out the infrastructure. Then they'd get around to atmosphere. After all, there were no humans heading to Mars any time soon. Earth was the priority with the helium-3 Moon shipments. Yada yada.

She exhaled, heart hammering. One suitcase cartridge, one waste heat tap and Mars could breathe—Earth, too.

It wasn't the science they rejected. It was her. Or rather, it was Greg Johnson, that manipulative bastard, who undermined her at every chance. He wanted to control the Human Habs narrative and output. He wanted his name on the Mars project.

She clutched the remnants of her hot chocolate while she stared at the CO_2 reports from the Red Planet. Groggy from yet another late night, she yawned and rubbed her eyes with the heel of one hand while the other held the mug in front of her. The pit-a-pat of her colleagues' quiet work, studying charts and drawing sketches of habitat filtration systems, grew into low-grade white noise. Coupled with the artificial light turned to gentle 'ambient' light, given the late hour, plus lack of windows, Victoria struggled to focus.

It wasn't just fatigue. Having synced her Mars-based Dopplebot data packet with her brain computer interface, she was jittery with excitement.

Epiphany, she thought-connected to her A.I. ThinkLink. *Confirm the data readings from the Martian cartridge.*

"One cartridge suitcase with a scalability factor: ×1,000 = 21% O_2 in a 50-metre dome within 24 hours," the ThinkLink projected. *"Looks like it worked, Victoria! Congratulations!"*

"Oh my God," Victoria said.

The clickety-clack of keyboards ceased once more.

"You okay, Vicky?" A round-faced sausage of a man jumped to his feet far more nimbly than Victoria would have thought possible for a man of his girth. He peered over his display screen, craning for a peek, old-school, wire-rimmed glasses perched on an upturned nose.

Victoria moved in front of her monitor, shielding it. "Fine, thanks Greg," Victoria muttered and returned to mopping at the mess with a scrap of paper. "Just spilled my drink. And"—she paused to catch his gaze—"it's 'Victoria'. Not 'Vicky'."

He held up a hand in apology and sat down again with the ghost of a smirk flitting across his face.

Turdball, she thought.

"He's just trying to get a rise out of you."

I know, damn it. And it worked.

Victoria mopped up the dregs of the hot chocolate with another crumpled ball of paper and tossed it into the recycling basket. Wiping her fingers on her lab coat, she resumed her study of the report display. She clicked through a few screens to the video of the Mars dome her Dopplebot twin had erected out of sight of the main camera feeds.

The readings scrolled: the CO_2-catalyst ran spikes from 0.04% to 1% in six minutes—projected to 20% in 18 hours at scale—historic! They'd taken the CO_2-rich atmosphere of Mars and made oxygen. Enough to create atmosphere in the dome. With just one cartridge. Scale that up, and they could start tackling terraforming. Breathable Mars air within a generation.

This is Nobel prize territory for sure.

"Don't get ahead of yourself, Victoria! Publish headline findings to the CEO?" the A.I. asked.

Forgiveness beats permission.

Do it.

Victoria then sent the video and reports directly to the CEO, Elena Fischer, and deleted her path files just in case. She didn't want that puffed-up little prick Greg Johnson finding the files and claiming ownership of her breakthrough.

She sat back in her chair, mind whizzing with possibilities. She drained the hot chocolate, silently toasted her Dopplebot twin and swallowed in sweet success.

SPACEWARD BOUND HELIUM-3 LANDING AND PROCESSING CENTRE: CLAIRE

Bleep—Message from unknown sender.

Claire Edwards secured the last helium-3 canister inside Spaceward Bound's secret loading tunnels, rapped twice on the truck's door and watched it vanish into shadow. She killed her headlamp and waited three slow minutes, shivering in her heated suit, a whiff of liquid nitrogen frost creeping through her dark face mask. There was only the distant thrum of the main off-load bay and the *drip, drip* of condensation seeping through cracked concrete.

She hated this subterfuge. Claire remembered the offer Lincoln had made: he could make Earth First legitimate, bring them out of the shadows. After all, he'd managed to position Spaceward Bound as the lunar helium-3 supplier when they'd orchestrated the downfall of the Indian Space Agency and hamstrung Gaia Enterprises.

No more space agencies left to run the Moon operations. The Lunar Commission had had no choice but to grant Lincoln the shipments.

He'd gone from prisoner accused of double-dealing and sabotage to the hero of the day.

Claire thought she heard a sound down the far end of the tunnel and froze, senses electric, heart thumping. She counted breaths.

Nothing.

Just a few more minutes and she could head out.

She shook her head to cure the regret that poisoned her attention.

She sighed. The deal hadn't turned out as planned. Lincoln had been willing to manipulate a free pass for her and several more for Earth First too. They'd be redeemed: no longer eco-terrorists, but serious environmental advocates and social entrepreneurs.

But she didn't trust any of the techno-billionaires and greedy space tech companies. Not Lincoln, not Aryanna Sharif, not the Chinese, not the Indians.

So she'd made a deal with Lincoln instead: she'd keep the space agencies struggling to keep up with Spaceward Bound, and they'd get a cut of the helium-3 Lincoln was skimming off each lunar shipment.

Her agreement had turned them into Lincoln's hired guns.

Regret soured her thoughts again.

She checked her watch. Time to go.

Satisfied no one had tailed the diverted cargo, she thumbed her wrist comm for the agent's message.

"Acquire Tang and all relevant design specs. Zero public fallout."

Tang had done it then, Claire mused. Mars was 'go' now.

She flung a leg over the seat of her electric motorbike, donned her night-vis helmet and accelerated hard down the tunnel.

As the bike hummed between her thighs and the walls sped by, ghost-lit by her visor, Claire experienced none of the usual exhilaration. Instead, a worm of doubt wriggled in her guts.

Earth First, as a radical eco-coalition, had everything they needed now thanks to the deal she'd made with Lincoln Ellison: helium-3 supplies, bankroll to fund their advocacy work and sabotage ops. They were close to pushing governments and the other tech billionaires to fix their catastrophic geo-engineering failures, with compensation for the millions who died and were dying in cities under permanent sulphur drizzle or choked by toxic air.

Lincoln Ellison's agent at Human Habs, Greg Johnson, had promised game-changing intel. And now it seemed they had delivered. Tang and that cartridge painted a whole new future.

Whoever controlled the air controlled everything.

And that's what bothered her. Ellison already had the helium-3 ops stitched up. And now this too?

Claire checked the gauge and cranked the bike to max.

She could worry about Lincoln's plans later.

First? Get Tang.

NAPOLI INSTITUTE, HUMAN HABS LABORATORY: VICTORIA

Victoria rummaged through her desk drawer for a painkiller. Since she'd briefed the CEO Elena Fischer about the ALVEUS biogenic cartridge scrubber, she'd been swamped with meeting after meeting. The engineers, life support techs, governance group and peers all wanted to know more. And she'd had to thread a fine needle of sharing enough to satisfy curiosity without revealing the proprietary secrets of the device.

This breakthrough from the team at Human Habs would not only help Earth's battered atmosphere; it would accelerate the development of Mars as humanity's second planet. What a time to be alive—and it was all thanks to Victoria's innovative technology. The attention was draining.

Johnson had fumed. Then he'd gone into snake mode. She'd seen it happen before: he'd dial up the charm, cosy up to a colleague, mine them for ideas, then start gaslighting and undermining, claiming the ideas as his own. He targeted the juniors, the rising stars; too often, it was the women.

God, she hated him.

He'd done it to her too. She'd designed a software update that would make synching with the Martian Dopplebots faster and easier. Johnson had been gushing with praise and admiration. Then in a meeting with the governance team, he'd proffered the idea as 'something Vicky and I had been discussing'. It would have been seen as sour grapes to point it out as her original idea.

Once news of the ALVEUS scrubber ripped through the office, Johnson had booked a meeting with the CEO. He stood outside her door now, talking amiably with Elena's assistant.

Victoria found the painkillers and tipped one into her palm. She swallowed it with the cold dregs of the morning's cup of tea, keeping Johnson in her peripheral vision.

Epiphany, amplify the conversation in the CEO's office, she thought-commanded.

The door swung open and Johnson slithered into the CEO's office, closing the door behind him.

The voices were still muffled. Victoria glanced around, grabbed a stack of papers and made her way towards the office door, where she pretended to stumble, the files cascading to the floor. She took her time restacking them on hands and knees as the conversation piped through her ThinkLink.

Johnson's sycophant voice dripped its oil: "Vicky and I had many conversations about the prototype. I actually suggested a Dopplebot twin could possibly run a trial on Mars. Once we'd fulfilled our mandated priorities, of course."

Victoria swallowed the bile that gurgled with resentment in her throat as she kneeled, still shuffling papers, face burning.

"I was really surprised she went ahead with this idea, without telling anyone. I'm concerned she used undeclared resources and unsanctioned time in the office to push this ahead. I'm also quite disappointed she did not acknowledge my cartridge design ideas. The celluloid membrane in particular was one of my early concepts."

Elena mumbled a reply—something about concerns duly noted and getting to the bottom of this—and then footsteps.

Victoria sprung away as Elena appeared in the doorway.

"Victoria, can you join us please?"

Victoria spun and feigned surprise. "Certainly. I was…ah…I'm right here." She clutched the files and followed Elena back into the office, ignoring Johnson.

Luckily, Victoria had been in to see Elena again before Johnson and had briefed her extensively on the why and how of her endeavour: long hours after work, using discarded components, in a region of the base that would not affect the rest of the Mars mission but would only enhance it. The time away from family, the drain on her health—shingles, bronchitis, weight loss—but the commitment to finding a terraforming, atmosphere transformation tech that would salvage not one but two planets.

Victoria showed the data, the experiment failures, the video journals: incontrovertible proof she was the sole pioneer and author of the invention.

Victoria also warned Elena that Greg Johnson might try and claim credit for some of the project. For once, she was on the front foot when it came to office politics and that reptile Johnson.

Elena was Dutch and did not suffer fools. She cut straight to the issue.

"Victoria, Greg says he gave you the celluloid membrane idea."

"Well, I…ah…"

Before she could reply, Elena turned to Greg and said, "This is an incredible breakthrough. Previous prototypes have not been able to overcome degradation, especially in low-G, carbon dioxide-rich environments. How ever did you solve that issue?"

Johnson held Elena's gaze. A slight nostril flare was the only thing that gave away his apprehension. Satisfaction curled into a smile on Victoria's face.

"Yes…degradation is an issue…" Johnson bit his lip. "My solution to that was genetically modified plants spliced with synthetic cotton fibres."

Not bad, thought Victoria. *But not good enough.*

"Victoria?" Elena peered at her. "Does this synch with the final plans?"

"Unfortunately, no. We do start with genetically modified plants, but any reinforcement splicing still degraded. My solution was nano repair bots that washed the fibres and wove new threads, on a six-hour cycle, once an atmosphere was up to spec."

"It's great you managed to expand on my concept, Victoria." His eyes narrowed.

"I'm curious, Greg. When exactly did we discuss the celluloid filter? It seems to have escaped my memory…" She stared, daring him to continue the bluff.

"Oh, I don't know. Ages ago. Since we had been assigned other priorities, I focused on the job at hand."

"Was it a year ago? More?"

His eyes darted about the room and he licked his lips. "Two years ago. At the space tech conference. We'd just seen a presentation from Gaia Enterprises on food in space. Xavier Consus was the speaker, I believe."

Victoria smiled. "I remember that session. I remember us chatting about his observations of plant capillaries in low-G on the Moon. But I don't remember talking about celluloid membranes for air filters." She leaned towards him, teeth bared almost in a snarl. "Because we didn't. We never spoke about celluloid membranes or anything else to do with creating atmosphere on Mars."

Victoria turned to the CEO. "Elena, you will find in my written journals, which are all date stamped, that I dismissed the splicing solution three years ago. Well before Greg and I supposedly chatted about it."

"I see," Elena said. "Greg, Victoria and I are presenting her technology at the UN Science Forum in two days. I want proof of your supposed contribution by the time we are back. Otherwise, you can pack your things. I won't tolerate lying and undermining on my team."

"So it's my word against hers?" Johnson's nostrils widened and his eyebrows pinched together.

"Not at all. It's Victoria's evidence, Victoria's *science*, against yours. No notes, no science? No job. Now, please get back to work. I have a speech to write."

UN SCIENCE FORUM: VICTORIA

Dr Victoria Tang leaned against the side rail of the maglev capsule as it hurtled around a bend in the tunnel toward the UN Science Forum. The humming of the magnetic rail coils matched her own internal buzz as she sank into the plush seating of the VIP carriage.

Red, of course, trimmed with gold. For royalty.

She couldn't stop grinning. She had splurged on a dress, professional hair and makeup, and here she was—travelling with the CEO herself, Elena Fischer. Victoria's smile tugged wider at Elena, the tunnel lights strobing against the other woman's serious face, though Victoria thought Elena too was excited, a telltale drumming finger along the window. They were on first-name terms now, sharing a secret that would transform the future.

Four years of secret development and now the prototype was

working safely on Mars. Pride surged. Every nerve fizzled in anticipation. They had kept it on the down-low, of course. Victoria had been in lockdown ever since the confrontation with Johnson. She'd shared videos, research reports and extensive notes with Elena to shore up her case.

The results had been independently verified, and no one had asked too many questions about the project's unauthorised origins. Except for Greg Johnson who continued to seed half truths about her endeavours.

Since showing Elena the data, events had torpedoed forward, overwhelming Victoria, and now the breakthrough was hours away from its grand reveal at the Forum. News reports about the "big announcement" were already streaming in. The world was waiting with bated breath—and soon, Victoria told herself, that breath would be free and clear.

The lights flickered, and the capsule glided to a halt. Victoria looked over at Elena who shrugged, confused.

"What's this, Harold?" Elena asked into her wrist comm.

"We're in a maintenance zone, ma'am. Checking it out now," came the reply.

An access hatch hissed open ahead of them, and a team of rescue techs in bright orange suits spilled into the tunnel. One pressed the emergency hatch control; the capsule door slid open with a whoosh.

"Excuse me, ma'am," said the lead technician, sealed head-to-toe in hazmat gear. "You're at risk. Please put on these suits—we'll get you clear before the gas reaches this section." He tossed the suits at Elena.

"Gas?" Elena snapped. "Terrorists?"

"Unclear, ma'am," the muffled voice replied. "We've received threats against your security detail, and we're not taking chances."

Alarm spread across Elena's face; Victoria's hands began to tremble.

"Here," Elena said and handed a suit to Victoria.

Harold's voice crackled over Elena's wrist comm. *Elena, that's odd—we have no incident reports, and **we** are your security detail. Check their credentials—*

The transmission cut off.

"Harold?" Elena tried again.

Static.

The lead technician glanced down the tunnel. "Quickly now, ma'am—we don't have much time."

"What about Harold?"

"I can see him." The man's visor reflected nothing but darkness. "My colleagues are assisting your security team."

Something niggled at Victoria. *This isn't right.* Where *was* Harold? Where was the rest of the team?

Nevertheless, she stepped into the orange emergency suit, visor snapping into place. A second technician took a firm grip on Victoria's arm, guiding her out of the capsule and through the access door. As Victoria craned back, she heard a muffled scuffle inside.

"What's happening?" she asked.

"This way, ma'am," the man said in the same unnervingly calm tone.

"Where are we going? Elena? Where's our crew?"

Panic squeezed her throat as a sharp chemical odour seeped into the suit, stinging her eyes. A tide of fatigue crashed over her. Her vision smeared and knees buckled, and the tech caught her just before she hit the deck. In the mirrored visor of the technician, she glimpsed Elena's silhouette collapsing behind her—then the world went black.

SKY CRANE PLATFORM: CLAIRE

Claire Edwards stood on the maintenance platform above the maglev tunnel, orange hazmat suit snapping in the downdraft of the waiting sky crane.

"Package secure," a voice clipped over the helmet comm.

"Roger that. Spoof the surveillance feed now."

She pointed to the crane's open door. A colleague nodded, tapped rapidly on a laptop and flashed a thumbs up.

Claire checked her wrist display and broadcast to the team: "Extraction in thirty seconds—everyone in position."

At zero, she heaved open the tunnel hatch. A suited man emerged, Victoria Tang slung limp over his shoulder. He eased her body towards Claire who hooked her hands under Victoria's arms; together, they hauled the unconscious scientist to the crane alongside the rest of the crew who sprinted from the hatch. They strapped Victoria to a medical stretcher, the door clanged shut and Claire shouted, "Go!"

The craft lurched skyward.

The ride to the airport took scarcely fifteen minutes—exactly the window they had before the alarms would trigger once their jamming link dropped when the crane lifted off. Inside the cabin, Victoria's head lolled and she moaned. Claire glanced at her suit-HUD—vitals stable. Finally, she let herself breathe.

The crane set down with a shudder, its doors sliding open. The team stripped off their hazmat gear to reveal crisp white ambulance attendant uniforms. They hustled the blanketed stretcher down to a waiting ambulance, the tarmac thick with the stench of jet engine fuel, sodium lights glaring. Sirens flared. Claire signalled the drivers to gun it for Lincoln Ellison's private jet.

Airport security intercepted them—lights blazing, tyres screeching.

"Easy," Claire murmured over her comm. "Play your part."

A security officer jogged to the ambulance. "You don't have clearance here."

"Emergency evac. Gas poisoning in the underground," Hank, the driver, replied, handing over an e-tablet.

Claire watched through the window as the officer—a slight man, security name badge 'George' askew on his worn uniform; he seemed more librarian than law enforcer—scrolled, frowning. His radio crackled: *Patient cleared for medical evac. Do not delay.*

He met Hank's eyes, paused, then swiped the tablet and waved them through.

"Well done, Hank," Claire said into her wrist comm as the ambulance sped off.

The crew rolled the stretcher up the jet's airstairs, then doubled back, stripped their ambulance uniforms, swapped to civilian shirts and abandoned the ambulance to melt into the airport bustle. Claire boarded last, gave the ground team a thumbs up and ducked into the cockpit.

"Passengers aboard?" the captain asked.

"All secure."

"Roger that. Prep for take-off."

Victoria—still sealed in her suit—was lashed to a first-aid bench opposite the sumptuous leather cabin seats. Claire ran one more vitals check, buckled herself across from the scientist and felt the jet surge down the runway.

The jet nosed upward, engines howling. Another operation, almost wrapped, for Lincoln god-damn Ellison. Not for the first time, Claire chafed at playing minion to his every underhanded whim. But this gig…it was next level. Would he finally get a step ahead of Maja Garcia and Aryanna Industries?

The image of her former mentor stabbed into the darkness behind Claire's eyelids, and a familiar pang ripped through her, tracing an old path of regret.

CHAPTER TWO

"Play nice."

—**Madison Floyd**
MARS CULTURE CODE

GAIA ENTERPRISES HEADQUARTERS: TROY

Under blue floodlights on Gaia Enterprises's lunar launch pad, Dr Troy Bruin posed for photographers while dignitaries trumpeted the latest Lunar Helium-3 Accord. He kept his megawatt smile dialled high, though inside he was collapsing from the third event of the day, the overdose of pastries and the fawning praise. At least he had Madison here this time.

"You alright, Troy?" Madison Floyd asked her colleague between camera flashes and frozen smiles. "You look a little haggard. Can't have the playboy looking downtrodden!"

Troy smiled without mirth at his friend. "It's shockingly brutal being the poster boy for this enterprise."

"Cry me a river," she smirked. "All that champagne and hobnobbing. It's right up your alley."

"Perhaps. Used to be. These days, not so much." He gestured to the podium with the mics. "Shall we get this over with?"

"Let's do it." She gave him a fist bump and a wink.

Reporter: "Dr Bruin, have you visited the families of the Moon rock-fall tragedy?"

Troy (sombre): "Yes. Yesterday marked the fifth anniversary; I met with them privately."

Click-whirr, click-whirr.

Reporter: "Thoughts on Spaceward Bound's expansion on lunar territory?"

Troy: "All within the Accord—planned growth, preservation of heritage sites, strict non-military protocols. All good." Broad smile, open-palm reassurance, while privately seething at fresh lunar scarring.

Reporter: "Dr Bruin, are you concerned at all for space industry security with the disappearance of Dr Victoria Tang?"

Troy: "A terrible assault on science and space. I hope the perpetrators are brought to justice soon. My thoughts are with the family." Face serious, concern radiating.

Reporter: "Captain Floyd, how does it feel to clock the most lunar landings of any space pilot?"

Heads spun as Madison leaned over the mic.

Madison: "Well now, you're just stirring trouble. You know that point is contested between me and Captain Gareth Barrio. I always maintained I piloted the descent onto the Moon's surface for the Jonas Seaborn rescue mission. But Captain Barrio seems to remember it differently. Why don't you ask him when you see him tomorrow at Spaceward Bound's base?"

Reporter: "Captain Floyd, will you join us there? Rumour has it you and Captain Barrio have more than just a friendly rivalry going on—"

Madison: "No comment."

Troy caught a trace of a smile on the hard-nosed pilot's face.

Damn! Barrio? Didn't see that one.

A tabloid voice piped up: "Troy, still dating Christina Varese?"

"Friends, I don't kiss and tell."

Cue chuckles.

"That was last month's supermodel," Madison said under her breath.

Troy kept his smile pasted on and discreetly stepped hard on her toe, feigning a small loss of balance.

"Any hope of rekindling with Commander Xanthe Waters?"

His smile locked; he pretended not to hear. "That's all, folks. See you tomorrow at Spaceward Bound Base with Captain Gareth Barrio and the *Pinnacle* crew."

Reporters surged like hungry squirrels, snatching tidbits; he strode off with Madison, entourage in tow, pausing for flag-waving fans—signed a few Gaia posters, snapped a handful of selfies—then vanished through HQ's secure doors.

"Thank God," he muttered to Madison as she traipsed in behind him, shaking off anxiety from the scrum.

His aide Elizabeth floated to his side.

"Anything else?" he asked.

"You've an hour's break, then dinner with Lunar Commissioner Colonel Jin."

"Lucky you," Madison chuckled.

"Really? I thought tonight was clear."

"Late booking—Aryanna's invitation," she said, grim. "And you're invited, or rather expected to attend as well, Captain Floyd."

Madison's face sagged.

"Aryanna asked me to give you this."

She handed over a sealed envelope to each of them: **OPERATION OLYMPUS DAWN – CANDIDATE PACKET – CLASSIFIED**.

Troy raised an eyebrow. "What is it?"

"For your eyes only," Elizabeth replied.

CHAPTER THREE

"The mission is bigger than any one person."

—Dr Troy Bruin
MARS MANIFESTO

GAIA ENTERPRISES HEADQUARTERS: TROY

Their meal now moved to the boardroom, Troy and Madison padded after Colonel Jin, Chair of the Lunar Commission. Troy marvelled at the Colonel's stoic countenance, face immovable, with an anxious dewy upper lip. Troy noted the stiff pace of the bullish Colonel and understood this was no ordinary meeting. He exchanged an apprehensive look with Madison.

Colonel Jin shoved open the boardroom's heavy doors. Beyond them, a mahogany table dominated a glass-walled room that over-looked the Gaia launch pad. The *Saturnia* sat there, having recently returned from Madison's lunar helium-3 haul. Technicians crawled all over her. *At this hour?* Troy frowned.

His confusion evaporated to be replaced by delight as he spied Maja Garcia, perched on one of the enormous leather chairs at the far end of the table, deep in conversation with the poised, imposing Aryanna Sharif, biotech billionaire.

And their funder, Troy reminded himself. *Keep the charm dialled up.*

"Maja!" Madison said, as she and Troy hurried to embrace their employer and mentor, who rose for hugs.

"Aryanna," Troy said, acknowledging the Gaia funder with a gracious bow.

Aryanna nodded coolly, waiting. No hugs forthcoming, Troy noted.

"Please be seated. Dinner will be served shortly," Aryanna said.

Troy caught a waft of roast pork and was suddenly famished, his last meal hours ago. He settled in beside Madison, curiosity competing with hunger.

"It's time," Maja said pointedly to Aryanna, eyeing the oversized clock that hung like an accusation. "The announcement is due to start now." Maja pulled a woollen shawl more tightly around her shoulders, despite the heat.

Black eyes hardening, Aryanna clicked the remote and glared at the live newsfeed that leaped onto the display.

On-screen, Lincoln Ellison, CEO of Spaceward Bound, stood on stage with a throng of reporters jumbled in with a buzzy public.

"Dr Victoria Tang has defected to Spaceward Bound after enduring years of bullying and a toxic culture. We helped her escape the slave-like conditions at Human Habs and have spent the last week counselling her through the trauma.

"She brings with her breakthrough technology: a three-layer cellular cartridge that converts CO_2 to O_2, driven by waste heat from a helium-3 micro-reactor." Lincoln paused as an image flashed up on the gigantic screen behind him. *"Folks, we're going to make a breathable atmosphere on Mars. This is our chance to create another Earth, a future for humanity beyond the burned-out cradle of this planet. The space-pioneering age has begun. The Red Planet offers the opportunity to create a new future for you, on behalf of all humankind.*

"That's why today I'm announcing Spaceward Bound will launch,

within six months, its first crewed expedition to the Red Planet to establish a permanent settlement on Mars. Thank you."

The pressroom erupted, camera flashes blinding, reporters roaring with questions. Aryanna clicked the feed and tossed the remote onto the mahogany table.

"Goddamn Lincoln Ellison," she muttered, smoothing the cream silk of her blouse with manicured fingers.

Troy sat astounded. Across the table, he saw the announcement had stripped the fatigue from Maja's eyes. Colonel Jin tugged at his uniform cuffs, square jaw working as he simmered. Madison stared, wide-eyed.

Aryanna tapped one long finger, took a deep breath, then plunged in.

"Ellison hasn't only kidnapped Dr Tang—"

"Kidnapped?" Troy said. "That report says she defected."

Aryanna's black eyes sparked with fury. "That's Lincoln's spin. No way Tang defected. My sources are clear on that."

Troy wondered about Aryanna's 'sources'. She seemed to know everything about everyone. Only this time, Lincoln was a step ahead.

Aryanna continued. "That conniving bastard has also served us with injunction papers on our water filtration patent. The scoundrel—" Her voice cracked; she rarely lost composure. "Our production facility was locked down this morning."

Troy pieced the implications together. "We can't move ahead with the water purification breakthrough? So Lincoln maintains control of water distribution in his company city-states…"

"And the rest," Maja added. "Prima Aqua won't want that technology getting out either. It breaks their stranglehold on supply. And there's a dozen of these corporate feudal city-states who would support Lincoln to shut us down."

"The bastards," Madison said, scowling. "Chasing profit over helping their fellow humans."

Troy glanced at her sympathetically. This was Madison's mother's lifelong crusade. A radical activist, now in prison palliative care, she was never far from Madison's thoughts.

Troy's mind raced ahead again. Lincoln's move could fracture the hard-won helium-3 global space agency collaboration. He could kiss his next command expedition to the Moon goodbye. The agencies and tech billionaires would be back to territorial claims. "So not only does Lincoln dominate the helium-3 supply chain, he now owns the tech to terraform Mars and maybe even reverse Earth's air crisis. And he's breaking the Mars Accord's 'no human expeditions' clause because…why?"

Aryanna's painted lips thinned.

Maja answered, her voice measured. "By securing Dr Tang, Lincoln now controls energy, water *and* air. I suspect that the six-month launch is a grab for the Chinese habitat."

Colonel Jin nodded. "Our Dopplebots have spent ten years constructing a base near a deep subsurface aquifer. If Ellison lands first, he can claim territorial rights once he's at the base."

"He can *do* that?" Madison blurted.

"Oh, yes," Aryanna said, bitterness icy.

"Why Mars, though?" Troy persisted. "It's a long bloody way."

"Because on Mars he's free of Earth's laws," Maja replied. "A clean slate. Dr Tang's scrubber means the place becomes habitable far sooner."

"That'll still take decades," Madison argued. "Meanwhile, people are dying here now."

"Time is no obstacle for Ellison," Aryanna said. "He's bankrolling longevity research and expects another century of life to secure his empire."

"Unless—" Troy prompted.

"Unless we get there first," Madison finished.

Troy's pulse thudded. *Six months?* The last briefing had talked in decade blocks. "So, what's the new plan?" He tried to keep his voice level.

"The original plan," Aryanna said, her voice still icy, "was to begin a campaign for Mars. Our water filtering patent—"

"The one Lincoln is challenging?" Madison asked.

Aryanna nodded. "—the patent would help us build a campaign for Mars. Solving one of Earth's crises would loosen the Accord's need to keep human resources focused on Earth problems. But Lincoln has got air solved now. There is no rationale for staying on Earth."

Troy leaned over the table, planting his chin on the heel of his hand as his mind whirled with the repercussions. "That's assuming he actually uses Tang's invention to reverse the air crisis here. He hasn't exactly been reliable."

Troy's stomach growled. Clatter from the executive kitchen as the chef plated their food distracted him from the double-cross and subterfuge Lincoln had plagued them with since the Olympus Project launched all those years ago.

Madison crossed her arms and leaned back in the chair. "What now?"

"The ten-year project needs to be adjusted," Aryanna said.

Troy's hand fell from his chin as the penny dropped. "Six months?"

"Sooner," Maja corrected. "We must leave before he does. Five months, twenty-five days is the next window."

"How? We have no crew, no craft—"

"We *have* a craft," Colonel Jin rumbled. "The *Nyx Odyssey*. Built with what remains of the Chinese Space Agency, designed for long-range Mars transit. Decades in the making. We need to reconfigure for six crew."

Madison's head spun. "Six?"

Jin nodded. "Energy, life support, delta-V—all point to a crew of no more than six."

Troy exhaled. "So, the ship is mostly ready. What about the crew? Who are the lucky six?"

Aryanna's voice steadied. "Troy, I want you to command the expedition."

His eyes widened. "An honour—and a lot." His mouth went dry.

"And Madison, I want you to pilot *Nyx Odyssey*." Aryanna's eyes were like black lasers.

Her jaw dropped. "Mars…"

Troy clapped her shoulder; she didn't smile.

"I…can't," Madison breathed. "My mother's in palliative care. I can't leave now."

Aryanna steepled her fingers and stared hard at Madison. She held her gaze.

"This is sudden," Maja noted. "Aryanna contacted me in transit when Ellison's news broke. We've had mere hours to sketch a plan, but we need experienced astronauts who've worked together."

Troy nodded. "The Olympus crew. That's why you want us. We worked together for a year on the Moon."

"And then some," added Madison.

"Mad Dog, there is no one else I'd trust to pilot that ship." He put a hand on her shoulder and peered into her brown eyes, which were mired in pain.

She said nothing, arms crossed, and shook her head. "I can't leave her, Troy."

"We can find a way," Aryanna soothed. "My medical team can look after her. Let's talk about it later."

Madison shook her head again.

Give her some time, Troy thought. "And the others, then?" he continued. "Jonas Seaborn for engineering. Though his post-trauma recovery is still underway. Not sure he'll be ready." Troy rubbed his jaw, excitement rising. "Serena Fox as life support tech. She's the obvious one with her Breath Dome design. It would marry well with the Tang cartridge filter, I'm guessing."

Madison shifted in her seat, pulling herself back into the conversation. Thoughts of her mother no doubt crowding her mind, thought Troy.

Madison shook her head. "No way Max is going to like that. Serena beating him to Mars? Oof. Plus, those two are inseparable these days."

"Second-in-command?" Troy asked.

"Xanthe Waters," Maja replied, jaw set. "She's got the medical training background that would be ideal for the role. Plus, she led the Olympus Project. She's a proven leader. And she has a ThinkLink, a distinct advantage."

"She would be my first pick as Commander," Colonel Jin said.

Troy drew a breath at the slight.

Ignoring him, Jin continued, "But I understand Aryanna's reservations about her leadership. So, I would support her in the second seat instead."

Aryanna's jaw worked a little before she said, "Xanthe is not a preferred option as Commander. She has shown herself to be defiant and cavalier as a leader. As second, this might be acceptable."

Madison's brows shot up. "Good luck—she's committed to Po Secco."

Troy folded his arms, wry grin covering a gnawing dread. "I'll ask nicely."

"Fat chance," Madison muttered.

Maja held Troy's gaze with a knowing look and said, "Perhaps let me speak with her first."

A wave of regret—or was it shame?—surged through him.

The catering door swung open, and the waitstaff arrived with steaming plates. With the prospect of Mars looming within his grasp, Troy discovered his appetite had fled to space.

CHAPTER FOUR

"An injury to one is an injury to all."

—**Xanthe Waters**
MARS MANIFESTO

PO SECCO MEDICAL CENTRE: XANTHE

T-172 Days

Xanthe stood and stretched her aching back, wiping sweat from her brow with the back of her wrist. The medical refugee tent sweltered, though the fans whirred relentlessly overhead. Here in Po Secco—once Europe's most fertile plain—only a cracked salt pan remained after the upstream glaciers vanished.

Leaving behind the clatter of instruments, muffled moans and the pungent fug of blood and excrement, Xanthe stepped under the tent's awning. A sulphur-tainted breeze washed over her and she shivered in relief, grateful for the mask that kept most of the poisonous air at bay.

A ramshackle row of canvas shelters sprawled toward an obsolete diesel pipeline manifold that dribbled brackish water. Far to the south the sea glittered—golden, beautiful, deadly. Seeing her silhouette, the waiting patients raised weak voices:

"Prego, signora, prego…"

Fatigue clung to her like the dusty salt crust embedded in every garment despite "regular" washings. Xanthe had water enough to rinse clothes—unfair, when people were dying of thirst. The guilty luxury of privilege. But medical staff needed to be clean, so they didn't kill their patients with infection.

Rolling her shoulders to ease the tension, she forced a smile and returned to the chaotic triage line.

Maja should be here soon, she thought, a frown creasing her weary forehead. Maja only made house calls when it was important.

Any news of Maja, Athena? Xanthe asked her A.I. ThinkLink implant.

"Her plane arrived not long ago. She should be here shortly. There were delays due to the Victoria Tang disappearance. Increased security at all airports," Athena said.

Xanthe grunted in acknowledgment and beckoned to a young mother, face aged beyond its years, to bring her son forward. They ducked into the makeshift medical tent.

"Grazie, grazie," the woman whispered, hope easing the strain etched on her face. The boy—no more than four—trotted after Xanthe.

Xanthe helped the mother lift him onto the examining table. His huge brown eyes shimmered with a pain a child should never know. Xanthe's pulse skipped: Jack had been this age when the tsunami took him—another innocent claimed by Earth's fury. She let a heartbeat steeped in painful memory pass and then she steeled herself for the examination.

The boy's skin was pockmarked with blisters and open sores, the trademark of acid rain. His breathing rasped; she pressed a stethoscope to his chest.

"How long has he been struggling to breathe?" she asked in rusty Italian.

"About a month," the mother replied, brushing salt-stiffened hair from his forehead.

Xanthe dipped her fingers into a tub of TerraGreen paste, an emerald protein salve spun from the Napoli vats at Terra Verdi. Brilliant on acid burns, she thought sourly, even if it existed only because geoengineering had failed so spectacularly. She finished dressing the boy's sores and handed a small pot of salve to his mother.

"È solo voi due?" she asked. "Any other family?"

"No—*sono due solamente,*" the woman replied.

Only the two of them.

Xanthe hesitated, then murmured, *"Un momento, per favore."* She fetched her rugged tablet, tapped a message and waited for the secure reply. A code flashed on-screen.

"I've arranged a pass for Terra Verdi—for you and your son," she said, tilting the display so the mother could memorise the sequence. Nothing written down—to be stolen, or to implicate Xanthe. Prima Aqua treated refugees like property, keeping their herd desperate for 'charity' water trucks. Not *too* desperate though. "Repeat the code to Xavier Consus or any of his crew; they'll honour it."

"Terra Verdi…le cupole di vetro?" The woman's eyes widened.

"Yes, the glass crowns. It's a day's walk if you leave after the heat breaks. Beds are still free on the newest pontoon. You can stay as long as you like. There's work if you're able, and your boy will be cared for."

Tears welled. *"Grazie, signora…grazie."*

"Prego." Xanthe stroked the child's salt-crusted hair. *Another clandestine referral; another tick against my name.* "Good luck."

Outside the flap, she watched them set off in a bitter gust of air and dust and then merge with the refugee tide just as a water credit truck rattled down the dry, cracked road through the heat shimmer. Voices rose. Desperate hands thrust heirlooms, clothing—anything of value—towards the dispensers for a few extra litres.

Prima Aqua had carved out the neighbouring city-state enclave and laid claim to every drop of groundwater beneath it. Since the rivers turned acidic, the town depended on the company not only for jobs but for survival rations meted out through a fierce monopoly. Unless you paid a ruinous premium, you received only the daily minimum.

Each morning, hopefuls queued at the gates for work permits. Each evening, most trudged back to the refugee compound Xanthe served.

She turned to usher the next patient inside when a familiar voice boomed over a portable loudhailer near the truck:

"Water is a birthright, not a line on a balance sheet!"

Xanthe's face cracked into a rare smile. Maja—mentor, friend, indefatigable agitator—had arrived, railing at Prima Aqua's convoy with the same indignation Xanthe felt. She touched the Gaia insignia above the breast pocket of her uniform: the compass. It still guided her. And Maja too, Xanthe felt sure.

Xanthe observed the water truck altercation from the tent flap. She knew Maja would be streaming the confrontation, hoping to stir anti-corporate sentiment and pressure Prima Aqua into more humane practices. For a tense few minutes, the cries of thirsty refugees mingled with the guards' shouts for order, but once the first allotments gushed into canisters, the crowd settled into rough discipline.

Xanthe spotted the slight figure of her mentor edging away. Maja's lined face melted into a fond smile when their eyes met.

"Ah, *there* you are." She opened her arms.

Xanthe stepped into the embrace, flushed with pleasure. "All this way, Maja? You could've used the holo. Must be serious if you've come in person."

Maja chuckled. "Well, yes, I have news. Somewhere private?"

"This way." Xanthe led her through the chaotic warren of canvas until they reached a demountable hut. "Please." She bowed theatrically and ushered Maja inside.

The diminutive cabin was shockingly cool compared to the sulphur-tainted heat outside. Both women exhaled in relief and pulled their masks away. The space was barely wide enough for a bunk opposite a desk and a stack of medical fridges; a small round table with two plastic chairs filled the entry.

The hum of the fridge motor and the labouring air conditioner dampened the cries and clamour of the refugee camp. Her pocket oasis of privilege, Xanthe thought with another surge of guilt.

"Have a seat." Xanthe retrieved two chilled water bottles from a fridge marked **PERSONAL**. She handed one to Maja, noticing how ageless the other woman seemed. Her brown skin was smooth and glowing, her owl and heart necklace charm sparkling.

"That's luxurious," Maja said, eyebrow arched. "Ten credits apiece."

"The last of the original supplies. I had to lock them up in here to prevent any more violence."

Xanthe tore off the cap, swigged, then wiped condensation across her forehead. "So…news?"

Maja tapped a fingernail against the table. "Aryanna Industries has cracked a modular nanofilter. Turns brine into potable water ten times faster than Ellison's patents. Lab tests verified a 99% salt extraction."

"That's brilliant! Clean water at last. When do we get a shipment?" Xanthe smiled, then noticed Maja's frown. "Why the long face?"

"Ellison's claiming espionage—that Aryanna stole his IP."

Xanthe snorted. "Pot, meet kettle. The man practically invented corporate spying."

Maja's expression stayed neutral.

"Is it true?" Xanthe asked.

Maja hesitated. "I don't know. I'm not in Aryanna's inner sanctum."

"Then why *are* you here?" Xanthe's tone darkened. Something smelled off.

"Aryanna is offering Gaia Enterprises free, unrestricted use of the nanofilter tech," Maja began.

Xanthe's focus snapped back to attention. "That's brilliant. So, what's the problem?"

"It will let Terra Verdi expand world design builds all along this valley—create a viable, egalitarian alternative to Prima Aqua and pressure the other city-states to drop extortionate water pricing."

"Still not seeing the downside, Maja."

"Once we use Aryanna's kit, we align ourselves publicly against Lincoln."

"That's nothing new. Aryanna's bank-rolled us since the Olympus Project. Why panic now?"

Maja exhaled. "I'm worried it escalates beyond courtrooms and clickbait into outright city-state wars and corporate sabotage. Po Secco is on a knife edge as it is. Terra Verdi is vulnerable to attacks from both sea and air. So are our other world design communities. We did not build them with the thought of needing a militia."

"You sound paranoid, Maja," Xanthe said. "More likely, Ellison and Aryanna lawyer up while the rest of us patch acid rain burns and keep refugees alive. So—" She levelled her gaze. "Why are you really here?"

Maja held eye contact.

"I want you to find a replacement for your role in the camp. Someone who can handle the politics and drive the political change required to turn Po Secco into the model city-state."

"You want me to leave Po Secco? All the work I've done here?" Xanthe wiped her mouth with the back of her hand, tasting salty sweat and acrid sulphur. "Just when we are about to turn the corner with Aryanna's tech? Why?"

"We want you as Deputy Commander for an urgent expedition to Mars."

Her mouth fell open. After a moment, she collected herself enough to ask, "What?"

"Lincoln has not only blockaded the water filtration tech, he's working on a stranglehold for air." Maja filled in the details of Tang's suspected abduction and Lincoln's announcement for Mars.

Xanthe's eyebrows furrowed and she sat back in her chair with a long exhale.

"You said *Deputy* Commander…"

"Troy Bruin has been named Commander."

Xanthe's gut soured, and she gripped her water bottle hard.

"No. Absolutely not," she fumed. "I'm done with politics. Done with space."

"You're the best person for the job, and you know it."

"That's exactly what you said when you pushed me to the Moon—and look what happened."

"What happened is you saved the helium-3 collaboration that's powering half the planet."

"You forget about Jack," Xanthe said darkly. "And all the others who died on that mission."

"I could never forget Jack. Or the others." Her jaw tightened, eyes pained. "It's because of them that I'm here."

Xanthe held her gaze for a couple of heartbeats then turned away to sip some more water. "Nice try. The answer's no. I'm staying here as a medic—hands on, saving lives. Let one of Gaia's younger guns follow Troy. I'm staying out of it."

Maja tapped her bottle, then sighed. "With respect, please reconsider."

"With respect," Xanthe replied, "I won't. Ask Serena. Ask Jonas. I'm staying right where I am."

Maja studied her protégé's lined, salt-caked face, realised the decision was immovable and nodded. "Do think about it, Xanthe. We need you."

"And those people out there need me," Xanthe said, tilting her head towards the refugee queue. "I don't need the theatrics of leadership in space, playing second fiddle to Troy bloody Bruin. I can make Po Secco the model we've been working on for decades. I know I'm making a difference here."

"You have always made a difference." Maja drained her bottle and replaced the cap. "This assignment needs someone experienced, mature, savvy. If you decline, Aryanna might insist on one of her candidates—someone much less experienced—and well, lives could be lost."

Xanthe crossed her arms, and her face pinched in disdain. "You know what I think about Aryanna's staffing picks. Regardless, I'm staying put."

Maja placed her cool hand over Xanthe's gnarled fist. "I'm heading to Terra Verdi now. If you change your mind, call or come."

"Will do. Say hi to Serena, Max and Xavier for me."

"Of course."

They embraced once more, then Maja slipped back into the heat and sulphur haze.

Can you believe the nerve, Athena? Xanthe 'spoke' to her ThinkLink A.I.

"I think you should think about it, Xanthe. She's right—you are the best person for the job."

CHAPTER FIVE

"Air, water, food—guaranteed for every Mars Custodian."

—Serena Fox
MARS MANIFESTO

BREATH DOME, TERRA VERDI: SERENA

T-171 Days

Serena Fox lay on a skateboard trundle, legs protruding from beneath a chugging industrial air scrubber. She eyed the sensor reading: 'scrubber load 78%' and groaned as she struggled with the sensor's casing.

"Hey, frogman!" Her voice echoed under the casing. "Hand me the drill—it should be charged by now."

He didn't answer, so she pulled herself free. "Frogman!"

A hulking figure straightened, peering over steel-rimmed glasses. "*Mon Dieu*, always so rude, *non?*" Xavier Consus rolled the filter he was inspecting between gnarled fingers. "I, too, am working on important things."

"Of course you are, Xavier. Just bring it, will ya?"

He sighed theatrically, lifted the drill from its cradle and limped across the deck, arthritis cramping his old Moon injury. "Scrubber fixed?"

"Will be once this bolt's home." She slid back under the scrubber. She swore; metal clunked. "Done!" She shot herself out on the trundle, grease-streaked hair clinging to her scalp.

Xavier offered a hand. She gripped his wrist and he hauled her upright.

Just then the floor lurched; Serena staggered. "Damned floating island," she muttered.

"The stabilisers should cancel wave action," Xavier said, eyes narrowing. "Must be another disturbance at the docks."

"Asthmatics?"

"Who else? We hand out masks, but they clog within a week. Sulphur and acid rain…" The reality smothered their mood.

"Enough for today," Serena declared, patting Xavier's shoulder. They left the central engine room, the humming heart of Terra Verdi, and went onto a Perspex link bridge. Sunset painted the sulphur sky in burnished ambers and toxic reds. Both inhaled reflexively.

Xavier's wrist comm pinged. He glanced down, eyes lighting up. "Maja is coming—tonight."

Serena grinned. "Haven't seen her in ages. Any idea why?"

His smile faltered. "She doesn't say."

They crossed the arboretum, vines heavy with Terra Verdi's famed produce; Serena plucked a raspberry from the run. In the main atrium, a small group of staff crowded around the news display feed: *Still no statement from Human Habs scientist, Dr Victoria Tang, about her defection to Spaceward Bound. CEO Elena Fischer remains in critical condition alongside her security team with the tunnel gas leak rescue gone wrong.*

"Poor Elena. They should have caught those people by now! Crazy. And Europe is rife with surveillance tech," Serena said as they breezed past their colleagues mesmerised by the feed.

"*Eh alors!* Don't forget security checks before you break for the night," Xavier called over his shoulder as the crew sprang back into action at the sound of the boss's voice.

Approaching the Glass Crown's main dome, they heard the din first—desperate asthmatic refugees pounding the clear walls, begging for entry. A guard, sweat staining his uniform, tightened his grip on the stun baton as the racket etched up a notch.

"Xavier! Xavier!" Hope flared when they saw him; his generosity was legendary.

"Franco!" Xavier called. A stocky technician, hairy to the knuckles, spun at his boss's voice. "Bring another case of air filters."

"You're not going out there, are you?" Franco asked.

"Of course. These people need help." Xavier pressed his wrist comm; his voice boomed through the exterior speakers. "*Bonsoir. Buenas noches.* We're fetching more masks."

"Let us in!" the crowd cried.

"The new pontoon isn't ready. I'm sorry. But we can issue passes to the mainland shelter."

Groans rippled, yet a murmured *grazie* followed.

The automatic doors slid apart; a wave of hot, sulphur-dusted air rolled in on the salty breeze. One refugee burst through the doors and tumbled into the foyer past Xavier and Serena, followed by two more, then the crowd surged through the narrow space.

The bitter smell of sulphur and fear caught in Serena's throat as the desperate crowd pressed in all around her. She grabbed Xavier's hand in panic. Someone stepped on her foot. She winced, and then an elbow drove into her back and she yelped.

Serena heard the guards yelling, followed by frenzied screams as the guards deployed their stun guns. The surge forward halted, then the crowd pushed backwards, edging towards the door.

"*Ça suffit!* That's enough. *Arrêtez-vous!*" Xavier's voice boomed over the crowd. They froze at his tone. Xavier pulled his hand away from hers and shoved to the front of the crowd beside the guards.

"Stop with the stunners! Franco, everyone, calm down. We

have masks for you all. We have a bed for everyone too. You will all get passes to the next pontoon when it's ready. Now line up at the door. You'll get your mask and then get on the ferry so we can take you straight to safe accommodation. It will be alright."

It felt anything but alright, thought Serena. These people were desperate, barely alive. As much as it galled her, they just couldn't save everyone.

Xavier limped forward, hand on hip, crowd parting—faces anxious, grateful. Serena's chest tightened at the sight. The sea beyond, once a jewel, was now lifeless: no fish, no oysters, only fetid mats of algae.

Her triumphs in life support engineering inside the Breath Dome felt small beside such ruin.

Still, she set to work—helped Franco and Xavier hand out masks, while being careful with the delicate nanofilter cellulose; demonstrated their fit; then guided recipients to the ferry bound for the overcrowded, reeking mainland shelter that could never save them all.

She pocketed a clogged, discarded mask snagged and fluttering on the dock rail. Another day's work done—yet never done.

An enormous enforcement drone buzzed overhead, its rotors chopping the heavy air. Red-and-blue strobes washed across the Glass Crown entrance, momentarily blinding Serena and Xavier. A klaxon blared, followed by an amplified declaration:

"Terra Verdi, you are in breach of power-siphoning regulations. Cease unauthorised draw-down immediately or face fines and a cease-and-desist order."

A hot gust stirred by the downdraft forced them to turn away, coughing.

"*Merde!*" Xavier said, flipping a rude gesture at the machine.

"Don't," Serena warned, shielding her eyes from the strobe. "Prima Aqua will record it as a threat."

"They're all talk. I only boosted the extra module long enough to balance the scrubber."

"We'll shut it down—no breach." She placed a steadying hand on his arm. "This is harassment, and you know it. Once the solar, wind and wave stacks come online—plus the helium-3 micro-reactor—we'll be free of their grid."

Xavier scowled. "I hate those *salauds*. Greedy pigs."

A boat engine purred in the distance; they squinted towards the quay.

"That must be Maja," Serena said, momentarily brightening—until the drone dropped lower, repeating its warning.

Xavier pressed his wrist comm, forced a courteous tone and spoke directly to the camera. "We acknowledge your report and will adjust our draw. *Merci.*"

He toggled a second channel. "Franco, shut down Generator Four, please."

"*Si, signor,*" crackled the reply.

The drone hovered, sensors verifying the reduced load, then climbed away.

"Don't antagonise them," Serena murmured as Xavier half-raised his finger in another rude gesture.

He exhaled loudly into his mask, then followed Serena's gaze toward the approaching boat, where the slight figure of Maja, grey-streaked hair lifting in the sulphur-tinged breeze, lifted a hand in greeting. Elegant as ever.

The boat nosed alongside the floating dock. Serena and Xavier offered Maja a hand, hoisting her onto the planks before waving the pilot off. Together, they crossed the softly lit arboretum beneath the Glass Crown's dome.

"I am thrilled to see you, Maja," Xavier said, kissing her cheeks. "We haven't even had time to wash up." He wiped oily palms down his overalls, before continuing. "Not to worry. I've a pod prepared for you." He pulled his mask down, smiled, and led them limping along the executive corridor. "My wife's favourite for Maja—pure princess paradise."

He unlocked a compact suite on a side pontoon. Beyond the Perspex wall, the sea glittered under pontoon lights. Inside, velvet furniture in deep reds overflowed with cushions; pots of colour-splashed begonias perched on every ledge. Cool recycled air and faint flower scent drifted through the room.

"This is lovely, Xavier," Maja said, her smooth brown face barely touched by age.

Maja sank into the couch. Xavier perched on an armchair. Serena dragged a plain kitchen chair closer, wary of dirtying the upholstery.

"What's so urgent you had to make an evening call?" Xavier asked.

Maja repeated the news she'd given Xanthe: Aryanna Industries had perfected a modular nanofilter, ten times faster than Ellison's patents.

Xavier beamed; Serena clapped. "Bloody fantastic! Food, hygiene, expansion—we can ramp up construction immediately."

"Hold on." Maja lifted both hands. "There are complications."

"Let me guess," Xavier grunted. "That *salaud* Lincoln Ellison."

"Got it in one. He's claiming the technology is his and vows legal action."

"Alright…" Serena waited for the rest.

"We have battles with Lincoln over a number of issues: the water filter nanotech is just one. But for now, we need to ramp up Terra Verdi expansion so we can prepare for the water filtration. We want to be able to house as many people as possible—in the Breath Domes, on the water and on land."

Serena's eyes widened, and Xavier let out a pained 'oof'.

"I know you're flat out already," Maja continued. "Gaia will reallocate resources. We need our most seasoned engineers, given Prima Aqua's hostility and Ellison's meddling."

"Maja, we're better at hands-on tasks," Serena said. "Politics isn't our game. Xanthe's perfect, but she's burnt out."

"I agree, though not about the burnt-out part. I would say

'wary'. Xanthe would be perfect for this political role and could oversee the expansion easily. But we've asked her to take on a different project."

"And? What is that?" Serena perched on the edge of the seat, enthralled by the news.

"She is considering it. I'll give you the details later. For now, we need to secure the new face of Terra Verdi's expansion."

"If not Xanthe, then who?"

"There is another option…" Maja hesitated. "Someone who is good with the media, who could build a good image for the future city-state…"

"Who did you have in mind, Maja? I can tell by that look you have a plan. Spit it out," Serena said.

"Someone who is confident without being arrogant; someone smart but down-to-earth; someone who's overcome great challenges like…climbing Everest five times…"

"You want Max to head up the build—Max to do *politics*?" Serena did not know if she wanted to laugh or cry with envy.

Xavier cackled. "You won't need a Breath Dome with that man around—his hot air will clear the space. Hasn't he had enough accolades since the Moon?"

Maja chuckled. "Our celebrity mountaineer does keep Aryanna happy, and the public. He could stand up to Ellison and Prima Aqua."

"Good idea," Serena said, "but…" Her heart ached at the thought of him being away from her. He'd be so busy offsite they would hardly see each other.

Maja gave Serena a kind smile.

"I know," Maja sighed, "you will miss him. It's my best plan. I came to get you onboard and help figure out how to make it work. Besides, we might just have another project to keep you busy."

CHAPTER SIX

"Our choices must outlast our lifetimes."

—**Xavier Consus**
MARS MANIFESTO

TERRA VERDI: TROY

T-170 Days

Troy Bruin reached Italy less than twenty-four hours after the boardroom war council. With only six months to assemble a crew, he had given himself a single week to secure each key player. Maja had gone ahead to speak with Xanthe. She was 'thinking about it', Maja had said. Then she'd headed to Terra Verdi to lay the ground-work for the big ask.

He checked his watch; Maja should have arrived last night to meet with Xavier and Serena. When Troy arrived too, they'd lay out the whole plan.

Now, on a boat to Terra Verdi, he struggled with jet lag and the sea air. Even through an industrial-grade mask, the sulphurous tang of the lagoon made his stomach flip. A water taxi delivered him to the research pontoon at dawn, where security scans were still humming. The first familiar face was Max King—giant, bearded, eternally cheerful.

"Troy! Holy crap, how are you, man?" The mountaineer wrapped him in a bear hug. "Morning meeting's just about finished. Does Xavier know you're here?"

"Not yet. Surprise."

"Good."

"Maja arrive okay last night?" Troy ventured.

"So Serena said. I was out late at a promo event." The big man glanced down at Troy. "What gives with the reunion, man? Serena was bursting out of her skin this morning. What are you up to?"

"A bit of business, a bit of pleasure, I hope."

Max's chest rumbled with laughter. "With you? No doubt!"

Max hustled him along passageways stacked floor-to-ceiling with produce: lettuces in movable rails, tomatoes dangling from overhead trellises, moss panels breathing quietly in LED light. Xavier's trademark "every surface grows" philosophy gave the place an earthy humidity that felt almost natural.

Workers clustered near the planning centre, thrusting tablets at a short, silver-haired man.

"Expansion permits," Max explained. "We've got the go-ahead to double the pontoons and start the land site."

"Even with the water purifier injunction?" Troy asked.

"Lawyers' problem," Max said, palms up. "I just do the PR these days."

So he doesn't know yet, thought Troy.

Xavier Consus finally looked up, recognition flashing in his dark eyes. "*Putain!* Troy, *mon vieux!*" He limped over, embraced Troy and thumped his back. "Why no call? I'd have taken the day off, *non?*"

"I've got something exciting, and I wanted to ask in person." Troy's grin turned conspiratorial.

"Ah *oui?* Don't tell me you are finally settling down—one of those supermodels caught your heart?"

Troy flushed. "Nothing like that. Where can we talk?"

Max waved them off, and Xavier led him onto a small deck—two deck chairs and an ocean vista. "An old man needs a break."

They sat; Xavier massaged the leg that had nearly cost him his life on the Moon.

"Spit it out. I can tell you are hopping like a frog in a sock. That's what Serena would say, *non?*"

"Did Maja talk about Po Secco?" Troy began cautiously.

"Yes. She wants Max to head up the build if Xanthe does some other big project. She was testing the water with us last night. Or rather, testing Serena with the idea." Xavier chuckled, rubbing his chin.

"How did that go?"

"About as good as you might expect. She was shades of excited, sad, jealous and happy for Max. All in 1.2 seconds."

They chuckled.

"How are the girls?" Troy asked.

"*Ah, les filles,*" he said. "They are both at university now. One is an eco-activist." Xavier rolled his eyes. "But not crazy, you know. She just wants a better planet. And the other one is studying law."

"Perfect. They'll keep you in line."

Xavier chuckled again. "I am forever being told what to do better. That's the life of a father: to be endlessly disappointing to his daughters."

Troy's face sagged a little. Xavier eyed his friend. "So. Back to Po Secco. What is going on? First Maja, then you. In person. This is more than just a little project manpower issue."

"Uh huh." Troy smiled and took a deep breath. "That big project for Xanthe? Well, it's big. Very big. It's Mars."

"Oof." Xavier rocked back in his chair. "And what do you want from me?" he said cautiously.

"Come to Mars with me."

Xavier was speechless.

"Aryanna named me Commander. I want the best crew—and that means you, for supply and space farming."

"Wait—" Xavier stopped rubbing his chin. "Aryanna named *you* Commander? Not Xanthe?"

Troy gritted his teeth. "She's been offered Deputy."

"Mon Dieu…"

Troy pressed on. "I need you on the *Nyx Odyssey*. We'll be securing the first selfsustaining habitat. Nobody grows food in space like you do."

"Bof!" Xavier threw up his hands. "Send one of my team. My leg—" His fingers traced the old scar; Troy's mind flicked to the lunar cave-in, the emergency surgery, the eco-terrorist kidnapping that followed.

Xavier's wrist comm buzzed. *"Oui, ma chérie."* He relaxed at the sound of his wife Maryse, his face softening into a smile.

"Guess who's here? Mr Moon Star."

"Troy? *Merveilleux!* Mr Sexy Pants troublemaker! Here to steal some hearts?"

"Hello Maryse!" Troy waved to the holo, and she blew him a kiss.

Troy watched his friend's face bloom as he spoke to her. He sighed. Xavier was dedicated to his family and had called it quits in space after the Moon expedition. He stared out to sea, waiting for the conversation to finish.

Xavier signed off and Troy dragged his attention from the sea back to his friend. Troy swung his legs over the side of the deck chair and leaned towards Xavier.

Time for the big guns.

"Xavier, I know why you don't want to go. It's a long way, and I know you promised Maryse…"

"But?" Xavier said.

"But we have a tight launch window: 170 days."

"Oof, why so quick?"

"Lincoln Ellison."

"*Putain,* of course it's Ellison! What has that *salaud* done now?"

"Ellison's moving," Troy said. "If he reaches the Chinese base first, he claims it all. And with Tang's scrubber, he controls air, water and energy. We need to stop him. Get there first."

Xavier's amusement vanished. "One man…so much power. But why me? Take my blueprints."

"Blueprints won't improvise when something jams. We need a reliable food supply, and you're the best, Xavier. A genius." Troy leaned forward. "Without you, the risk multiplies tenfold, from dangerous to suicidal."

"Genius, eh? *Bof.*" Xavier smiled at the flattery. He rubbed his leg, eyes staring across the watery horizon. "How long is this expedition?" he asked after a while.

"Two and a half years. Maybe more."

"*Putain.* That's a long time."

Troy followed his gaze out over the sea, the sun spinning diamonds across the sulphur-laced surface.

"I'll speak to Maryse," Xavier said at last.

❧

At 2:00am, Troy was still awake, picturing algae tanks frosting over on Mars, crops wilted, the crew weak from malnourishment. All because he had failed to persuade an old friend. Had he pushed too hard?

At dawn, still dressing, he heard a knock. Xavier limped in, lowered himself onto the sofa.

"Maryse is the love of my life," he began. "I swore 'never again' after the Moon. But she reminded me why she loves me—because my work helps people breathe and eat. If Ellison wins, Terra Verdi's purpose dies."

Troy held his breath.

"She says *Nyx Odyssey* must succeed. Which means I must go."

Relief flooded Troy—then Xavier raised a hand.

"Conditions: Aryanna funds proper surgery for my leg; Terra Verdi is shielded from any legal fallout; Maryse and the girls get full comms access."

"And the lawyer daughter insisted on those clauses," Troy guessed.

"*Exactement.*"

"And the other daughter, what did she say?"

"She sent this message." Xavier clicked his wrist comm, and a holo message popped up with his daughter's face.

"*Dad, you've got to go. We're trading two years without you for the future of humanity. Go!*"

"Daughters," Xavier said. He patted his heart, eyes shining. Daughters indeed.

Troy choked up. "Thank you, Xavier. I can't imagine doing this expedition without you."

"Me neither, Mr Three Times Sexiest Human Alive."

"It's four times now, actually," Troy laughed, clearing his throat and wiping his eyes.

"Oh *mon Dieu!* Who else is going to keep that ego in check, eh?"

CHAPTER SEVEN

TERRA VERDI: SERENA

T-169 Days

Serena Fox ran a hand down Max King's broad back, still thrilled by the simple strength of the big mountaineer. Torn as she was about this new opportunity for Max to head up Po Secco, she was devastated by the idea of being separated from him, should Xanthe take on whatever project she'd been offered. But his delight at being offered the prospective role more than made up for it. They'd make it work.

Yesterday, Troy and Maja had toured Terra Verdi with Xavier before finishing the day inside Serena's Breath Dome prototype with its misty panels, photosynthesis lights and the enormous filter that functioned as filtering lungs. She'd showcased the bio-bubble with pride. "I had some help from Max," she'd half-confessed, cheeks warm.

"Oh, no you didn't," Max had said. "Designs were all yours. I just checked your math."

Serena passed Max a coffee and slid into the breakfast nook opposite Maja and Troy. With one hand on his coffee mug, Max reached down and scooped up Sophie, the blue point Siamese cat who patrolled Terra Verdi for vermin. Normally recalcitrant to anyone but Xavier, she adored Max and purred happily in his lap. He scratched under her chin, and she meowed in response.

Serena ventured a finger behind the cat's ear, waiting for Maja and Troy to start. Their secret plans were driving her bonkers, but hopefully they'd lay it all out this morning. Now, over toast, Serena's curiosity vibrated. Maja and Troy were here for something huge; Xavier's expression last night had confirmed that.

She jiggled a foot, then blurted, "Come on, Bruin, out with it. Why the fly-in visit?"

Troy set down his cup of herbal tea. "Serena, how would you like to go to Mars?"

Both she and Max gasped. Sophie's eyes shot open, and she stopped purring.

"Mars? It's been off the table for years," Serena said. "What gives?"

Troy summarised Ellison's press conference, and the stolen Tang cartridge. Shock shrank to hard concern.

"So, Ellison—that ratbag—finally betrayed us," Serena said.

"Looks like it," Troy agreed.

Max clutched Sophie in one arm, and she wriggled in protest. He squeezed Serena's hand with his free hand. "When do we leave?"

Troy hesitated. "Actually, Max, Serena is the one we need on *Nyx Odyssey*."

Max's grin faltered. "Just her?"

Serena glanced at Max, saw his mind chewing at the Mars carrot. "You can't expect me to leave Max behind? We're a package."

"Mars," Max said dreamily. "Olympus Mons is there…the size

of France. Three times as high as Everest. I'd love to climb that mountain. Be the first one." Max stroked Sophie's soft fur, and she settled in his lap again. Then he looked up at Troy, face earnest. "If Serena doesn't want to go, take me."

"Are you kidding me, Max?" Serena spun to her lover. "You'd go without me?"

He shrugged, and she smacked him on the shoulder.

"Really?"

"I'd miss you for a little while, but I'd be back," he said, teasing.

She frowned. Was he serious? "Well, take Max then," she said with a drop of venom.

"Can't do it," Troy said. "Serena, you own the IP for the Breath Dome."

"So?" Max said.

"Under the Mars Accord, only the inventor can install life support tech off-planet for human habitats."

Max looked confused.

Maja explained. "Like the Roman engineers, stand under the archway when the scaffolding comes down. Prove faith in your tech." Maja pushed her toast aside. "That's why Lincoln needs Tang—the veneer of compliance. He's still pretending to follow the rules."

"If we ignore that clause," Troy said, "Ellison could use it to shut us down on the launch pad."

Serena snorted. "That's rich, but he'd do it. He's not above ducking around laws and using the courts for his own purpose."

"Apart from the bureaucracy, it's a delta-V issue," Troy continued. "Manifest tops out at six crew—everything mass-balanced down to the last kilogram. You're fifty-five kilos. Max is—"

"Hundred and five," Max admitted with a shrug. "A lot of push-ups." He flexed a bicep with a grin.

"So, you need the smart, short girl," Serena muttered.

Troy raised his palms. "No other way to keep the risk manageable."

Serena sprang to her feet, pacing. "The Breath Dome expansion breaks ground next month. They need me. They need both of us, Max."

"Others can run the build," Max sighed. "I'll oversee it. That and Po Secco, if Xanthe doesn't want to. Serena, it's *Mars.* You've gotta go."

She folded her arms. "You just want rid of me."

"Not at all." He pulled her back to the booth, sandwiching Sophie between them, and kissed her brow. "But think about it. If Ellison corners the air market, Breath Dome investment dies. Terra Verdi stalls. Earth chokes. We trade two years apart for Earth's future. And a chance to extend humanity to Mars." He peered earnestly into her eyes, his conviction reaching into her heart.

Serena exhaled. She fiddled with an o-ring in her pocket as her mind raced.

Troy sipped tea. Maja adjusted the chain of her owl necklace. Max patted Sophie.

Serena's mind careened between elation and fear of separating from Max.

At last she blurted, "Fine. Here are my terms: an *equity clause* guaranteeing my license on every Martian install, and *weekly comm bandwidth* with Max."

"I'll push Aryanna for the equity," Maja said. "Bandwidth, Troy will have to code into the schedule, but we'll make it work."

"Make it work, Sexy Pants, or I'm out."

Troy grinned. "Deal."

Serena sat up with a jolt. "Wait—what about Xanthe? Is she being offered Commander? Is that her 'special project', Maja?"

Maja shot a look at Troy, who had found something interesting in the crumbs on his plate.

"We have asked Xanthe to be Deputy Commander. Troy is leading the mission to Mars."

Serena gaped. "Deputy? Not Commander? Oh, that won't go well."

Troy swigged his coffee and pulled his mouth into a smile. "I'm hoping she'll say yes. Maja asked her, and she is thinking about it. I'm heading to Po Secco myself soon to see her too."

Serena's eyebrows flew north, but she held her tongue.

"In any case, Serena, welcome to the *Nyx* team." Troy grasped her hand.

"Come here, you goose." She stood and gave him an enormous hug. Then Maja too.

Max let Sophie jump to the floor and scurry off, and he too rose, then cupped Serena's face, eyes shining. "My queen. You'll carry Earth's breath to Mars." He pressed something into her hand. "And I'll always be right there with you."

Serena studied the object in her palm: an old, battered oxygen mask clip from Max's first expedition up Mount Everest. His lucky charm.

She beamed back at him. She already missed him as if he were an amputated limb. A phantom loss that haunted her.

"Won't you miss me?" she breathed, hiding her face in his shoulder.

"Of course. But I'll have a cat to keep me company. She purrs and scratches, just like you."

He held her tight and kissed her head. Serena's eyes filled with tears as the warmth of his chest and the thud of his heartbeat enveloped her.

As they said goodbye to Troy and Maja, the Breath Dome glinted in the scorching sunlight beyond the breakfast nook window, its bio-lungs expanding as with her own. As she breathed out, residue of dread lingered.

I need a scrubber for that, she mused before carrying on with her day, Mars on her mind, oxygen clip in her hands.

CHAPTER EIGHT

"Was it really worth it? That depends greatly on how you measure success. Mars is a creditor that takes its cut, no matter what. We pay in sweat, fear and sometimes in lives."

—JONAS SEABORN
MEMOIRS FROM MARS

NEW BATHS OF CARACALLA: JONAS
T-168 Days

JONAS SEABORN BREATHED slowly through his nose, focused on the temperature of the air as it passed through his nostrils, then exhaled in a measured count. Flashes of the caves on the Moon poked at his awareness, but he kept breathing: in through his nose, feeling the coolness of the air; out through his mouth, warmed by his body.

He was here, present, sitting in the green-saturated garden of the new Baths of Caracalla. Birds twittered and flitted among the trees, and a light breeze stirred the leaves, cooling his damp shirt.

"That's great, Jonas," the therapist said. Her long limbs crossed at the ankles as she reclined in an outdoor wooden chair beneath the giant fig tree.

In the distance, he saw a figure approaching across the garden.

He frowned and closed his eyes to block out the distraction and the foreboding that washed through his gut. He breathed in through his nose, out through his mouth.

His nervous system felt…rested. The occasional flash still sparked—bright as an angle grinder—whenever a lunar memory popped into his mind, but the breathing helped.

"Thanks, Janice," he said. "That was a good session. I dropped into that calm zone really quickly."

"Any flashbacks?" she asked.

He looked away, watching a sparrow flit from a branch and peck at an errant seed near the table. "A bit," he admitted at last. "It's always the same: black, blacker than you can imagine—and the Moon, so white and grey and cold. In Olympus, every machine hums, reminding you that your survival depends on hardware, nothing natural. It's a constant battle."

"That's alright, Jonas." Janice reached out a steadying hand. "Remember: breathe. Ground your feet."

Jonas kicked off his sandals and wiggled his toes in the grass. Coolness seeped up despite the torrid air. Deep breath. The scent of growing green living things cradled his body. He was where he was meant to be—on Earth. They were all creatures of Earth, and though humanity had stuffed things up, they belonged here. Gratitude welled in him, followed by a pang of guilt for those who hadn't made it back from the Moon—Pabi and the rest.

Breathe in…breathe out.

It had been five years.

Every day was a gift, and he was grateful to Troy for embedding him here at Caracalla as resident A.I. engineer while he undertook intensive therapy—and hid from a world that wanted to hear his survival story on repeat. The only living soul on the Moon for three months after the disaster that claimed the Chinese and Indian astronauts: fame he'd never sought. He just wanted to be well, and after five years, he finally felt pretty good.

"Well done, Jonas. We'll call it a wrap for today." Janice glanced past the fig tree. "Besides, I think you have a visitor."

"Really?" Jonas frowned. "I don't have any notice of that… It's not a reporter, is it? I said no more interviews."

"It's not a reporter, old chap," came a familiar voice. The suave form of Troy Bruin sauntered into the shade, tugging off his sunglasses and running a hand through his mop of blond hair.

"Good God—Troy! What are you doing here? I wasn't expecting you back for another six months. Don't you have a Moon command or something?" Jonas leapt up and enveloped his friend in a hug.

"Came to see you, of course," Troy replied.

"I'll leave you to it," said Janice, rising. "Good afternoon, Dr Bruin."

"Thank you, Janice." Troy stepped aside as the willowy woman glided off in her cream linen suit.

The men settled into the wooden recliners. Troy wiped his brow. "Hot one."

"It's Earth—it's always hot," Jonas quipped, pouring them each a glass of water. "But at least there's air. And water." He toasted Troy with his glass.

"How's the therapy going?"

Jonas sighed. "Getting there, I suppose. Fewer nightmares." He put his glass back on the table, water beading along its side in the heat. "How is life on the Gaia circuit?"

Troy smiled. "I'm on a first-name basis with pretty much every reporter in most towns. Endless interviews."

"You love it, though!"

Troy shook his head. "Give me space any day."

"Not me." Jonas grew cold despite the heat and instinctively reached out for his glass again, running a finger along it to collect the condensation. "I'll take grass, birds, bugs over the black vacuum of space every time."

Troy chewed his lip. "Ah, yes…well. Understandable, I suppose."

He heard hesitation in Troy's voice. "What is it? What's happened?"

Troy filled him in: Chang's cartridge-scrubbing breakthrough, her alleged kidnapping and Lincoln Ellison's brazen move toward Mars.

"That son of a bitch," Jonas spat. He slammed his water glass on the table, the heavy crystal thudding on the coaster as water slopped onto the ancient mosaic tile motif. "And we just let him get away with it?"

"Not quite." Troy refilled Jonas's glass from the condensation-slick jug.

Jonas narrowed his eyes. "Oh?"

"Aryanna wants us to go after him," Troy said. "We need to reach Mars before Lincoln claims the tech and the Chinese base."

Jonas blew out his cheeks. "Mars? Really? Isn't the Moon enough? The Mars Accord forbade humans, left it to robots."

"It did. Things changed with this technology. It won't just make settling Mars easier—breathable air inside a generation—it could solve Earth's air pollution crisis. Terraform Earth."

"No way." Jonas shook his head. "Let the geo-engineers loose again? Look what they've done! Remember the sulphur Sky of '64? Mediterranean folks choking on sulphuric air, refugees everywhere, people cooking in heatwaves. Now you want to do it on another planet?" Bile rose in his throat.

Troy set down his glass and leaned forward, hands clasped. "Here's the thing: we need you. *I* need you. Aryanna named me commander of the Mars mission, and I want you as flight engineer."

Jonas felt the ground tilt. Mars. Space. Two—maybe three—years. His heart hammered. "No can do, Troy. I'm not going back there."

Troy fiddled with the arm of his sunglasses, studying its hinge, before he looked up at Jonas again. "You saved our lives more than once in Olympus. I know you went above and beyond to try to save Pabi and the rest. You're a great engineer, but you're more than that…" Troy put a hand on Jonas's shoulder. "You're a great friend. And I could use a good friend on this mission."

Troy's face dissolved from its usual debonair man-about-town composure to the pleading features of a ten-year-old. Jonas frowned at the fear he saw flit across Troy's face.

It was gone in a heartbeat.

Dr Troy Bruin, Commander, re-emerged.

"Your therapy's been brilliant. Janice says you've made enormous progress."

"Because I'm *here*—not in bloody space."

Jonas noticed the subtle wince that flicked across Troy's face. Then one hard swallow.

"Xavier's going, and Serena."

Jonas's brows shot up. "Getting the band back together?"

"It's the best solution. We're"—Troy punched his wrist comm and a holo display lit up—"T-minus 168 days. I need people I can trust. No time to build a team from scratch."

"168 days? No-one's made it to Mars alive, and you want a mission ready in five months? That's rubbish. There's not even a ship."

"We *have* a ship—the Chinese *Nyx Odyssey*. And your A.I. interface work here plugs straight in. We need someone who can operate the system."

"Well, find someone else. I'm happy on the ground, feet in the grass."

"Think about it, Jonas. This mission could clear Earth's air and give us a second home. A once-in-three-millennia chance."

"I don't care. I can't get through a day without hearing Pabi's last comms echo in my skull. The idea of another nine months in a tin can—look at my hands; they're shaking."

Troy took Jonas's hand between his for a moment and took a deep breath. "It's just the shock of a new idea. I sprang it on you—sorry. And maybe you're right. It's too soon for you." Troy sat back. "Have you got anyone who could sub for you? Who knows the A.I. interface?"

"Not with space experience." Jonas's thoughts reeled.

"We can train them up. There's time."

Jonas blew out his cheeks. "Very tight time frame, Troy." Jonas pulled his hand back.

"I appreciate that, but we're up against Lincoln. We can't let him win." Troy's head sagged and he ran his fingers through the mop of his hair.

"I need people I can trust, who are proven. Like you. Serena, Xavier, Madison. And Xanthe, with Athena."

"Xanthe? You should've thought harder about that these last few years," Jonas muttered.

"I know." Troy hung his head and studied a column of ants wandering past the table leg. "I'm seeing Xanthe tomorrow. If you've got any advice on that front, I'll take it."

Jonas stared at the fluttering leaves overhead, sunlight reaching through the branches, heart still racing.

"I'll give you a day or so," Troy continued, shifting his focus back to Jonas. "Let you know how it goes. Think about who could step into your shoes."

A drone buzzed nearby while the birds kept singing, oblivious to the decision that might change—or save—the world. And Jonas's own world with it.

CHAPTER NINE

"Consequences must fit the crime, never exceed it."

—Xanthe Waters
MARS MANIFESTO

PO SECCO: TROY

T-167 Days

Troy wove his way along the sun-scorched street. Midday heat drove people beneath giant sun hats and oversized sunglasses, like beach-going flies dressed for the surf. His breather mask fogged with each inhale, and relief flooded him the moment he slipped through the door of the old watering hole.

He looked around nervously, wondering if he'd see Gemma. She said she was in town. He wasn't ready for that encounter. Not with Xanthe arriving any minute.

This was it. He needed to persuade Xanthe Waters to join him as second-in-command. No one else was as experienced or as qualified. Plus, she had a ThinkLink—something no one else had.

But had there been enough water under the bridge?

Inside, dishes clattered and voices babbled, punctuated by the occasional guffaw. He claimed two stools at the far end of the polished timber bar, ordered a beer and waited. The first bitter, bubbly mouthful soothed his parched throat; warmth bloomed in his cheeks.

The bell over the door pealed. Quick glances flicked towards the entrant before conversations resumed.

It was Xanthe.

Troy's heart skipped, as ever. Three years since their last encounter—and that one had ended badly.

They exchanged an awkward half-hug, air kisses, and she unwound the cotton scarf that served as her mask. He ordered her a gin and tonic—the usual—and slid it into her hand while the waiter swept past with a tower of fries and a glistening steak. Grease hung thick in the air, smelling of seaside summers and gulls screaming for scraps, a fragment of Troy's childhood.

"You look good," he ventured.

Her green eyes met his. "You lie," she said, managing a small smile.

"How's the camp?"

"As you'd expect—crowded, hot, miserable. Every day's a battle." She sipped her G&T, smacking her lips at the sweet tang.

A lazy fly buzzed between them; Troy swatted at it and missed. The bartender whipped a tea towel from his shoulder and stalked the insect with murderous intent.

"So," Xanthe said, "to what do I owe this visit—after, what, three years?"

Troy set down his glass, drew a steadying breath. "We're going to Mars."

Her brow creased. "So Maja said. I told her no."

"Here's the thing…" He fought for words then blurted, "I want you on the mission. I need a second-in-command, and I can't think of anyone better."

Icy barely covered her tone. "Is this your idea or Aryanna's?"

"Mine." He met her gaze. "I know you wanted the command, but Aryanna chose me. I still want you there."

Xanthe looked away, expression unreadable. Troy traced the bar's smooth edge, waiting.

"You've got Moon dust where your conscience should be," she said at last. "Second fiddle? After everything?" She jabbed a finger into his shoulder. "You actually need Athena—one crew member with A.I. amplification—or this whole thing fails. But Aryanna can't stomach me in the captain's chair, so she puts a leash on me through you. Tell me that's not it."

He swallowed some more beer, unnerved by her anger. "It's true Athena boosts our odds," he conceded, fumbling at the mission patch on his sleeve. Then he reached for her hand, "but it's also true that I want you there."

A young woman with wind-reddened cheeks and a mess of auburn hair piled atop her head appeared beside them. "Is *this* Xanthe Waters?" she demanded.

Troy blinked, then recovered. "Gemma—good to see you." He pecked her cheek. "Yes, this is Xanthe Waters."

Xanthe's tired green eyes were bright and on alert, following the exchange. "Hello," she said shaking Gemma's hand.

Gemma slipped an arm under Xanthe's as if they were old friends. "Troy, you're an idiot for letting this woman go. Sure, she's older than your usual floozy, but I mean come on. She was Commander of the Olympus Project. He's so fickle, isn't he?" Gemma said to Xanthe, leaning in as a conspirator.

"He is certainly…fluid, I suppose," Xanthe said.

"Fluid! Good one. And so up himself, right?"

"He is rather confident," Xanthe said, the ghost of a smile appearing.

"And he flirts with *everyone*."

"Yes. Yes, he does." Xanthe scowled.

"See Troy? Xanthe has you pegged. Why on Earth would you let a smart woman like this out of your clutches?"

"Well…it wasn't exactly my choice, I recall."

"Pfft." Gemma snorted. "More the fool you for not chasing her and holding on tight."

Xanthe pulled away and turned to Gemma, confused. "I beg your pardon, but you are…?"

"Oh, he didn't tell you?" She stood, hand on hip.

Troy winced.

"I'm his daughter." She tossed a loose strand of her reddish mop over her shoulder while Troy shrank into his barstool.

"See you later, Troy?"

"Yeah—call you."

Gemma vanished into the crowd. Troy's face was in flames. He gripped his beer bottle, studying its label.

"Daughter?" Xanthe's voice dripped acid. "You have a *daughter?*"

"Well—yes. Sort of." He looked up, heart thudding.

"*Sort of?*"

"I was eighteen. My brother raised her—I've been more uncle than father." The old knife twisted in his guts.

"You never told me." Her eyes flashed. "All I went through with Jack, and you hid this?"

"I didn't hide it. I just…don't feel qualified to claim the title. Also, with everything that was happening with Jack, it didn't feel like the right time."

Xanthe pushed her drink away. "After the Moon rescue, the fame, the serial girlfriends—now, *this*. What makes you think I'd trust my life on a trip to Mars with a man who's fickle, feckless and false?" She wrapped her scarf around her head, shoved through the crowd and vanished into the glare outside.

Troy's shoulders sagged. He drained his beer, paid and stepped into the cooling dusk. Long shadows stretched across the street, sirens wailed and a dust-laden wind pelted his breathing mask as the first stars winked into the darkening sky.

Now what?

Maybe Madison could help thaw Xanthe's resistance, prove he wasn't the 'feckless' man she believed—but only if he convinced Madison to strap in first. One more 'no', and the Mars mission would fizzle on the launch pad.

CHAPTER TEN

"Why go? Because others can't. Because others might."

—Madison Floyd
MEMOIRS FROM MARS

GAIA HEADQUARTERS: TROY

T-166 Days

Troy studied the boardroom's holo-display, waiting for Madison's mother to come online. He tucked in his shirt, straightened his lapel and ran a hand through his hair.

"Dude, you look fine," Madison said, drumming an e-pen against her tablet.

He sat beside her, scanning her notes. "How long has she been in the Phoenix complex?"

"They moved her there last month. She's been on a steady drip of painkillers ever since." Madison slid the tablet to him. "You sure Aryanna will cover all this?"

"Absolutely. She needs this mission to fly—and she wants you on board. Compared with that, this is peanuts."

A chime sounded. The display brightened. First a pair of wardens appeared, then the caption: ***Inmate: Arlene Floyd.***

Madison leaned forward.

"Is that Madison Floyd?" one guard asked.

"Affirmative. I'm here with Commander Troy Bruin to speak with my mother."

Arlene's wan face appeared, half-hidden by an oxygen mask. She tugged it down, rasping—but her eyes held a mischievous glint. "Madison," she breathed, smiling.

"Ma…" Troy heard the quaver in Madison's voice. "How are you feeling?"

"Girl, I'm high on morphine." Deep laughter carved fresh lines in the weathered cheeks. "The government is keeping me well-stocked in drugs, finally doing something right."

"Ma, this is Troy. He's here to explain the medical protocol Aryanna's arranged for you."

Arlene waved her IV-tethered hand. "Whatever that billion-aire wants is fine. This old body's got a couple yards left, that's all. Now—what's this I hear about you turning down a trip to Mars?"

"It's two or three years," Madison whispered. "I don't want to leave you."

"Don't be ridiculous. I've been in this place twenty years. Nothin' changes in two or three." Arlene hauled herself upright, wheezing. "We see each other twice a year as it is. Video lag from Mars won't kill me."

"Ma, you might not make—"

"So what? My time on this planet is nearly done. We've said our goodbyes, we've said our hellos, we've had a lifetime…and then some. I'll shuffle off this coil…pleased as punch…at the…game I played. Sure, I didn't mean to end up in this hellhole…but it was worth…getting the message out there. Protect Earth, protect the people.

"And I'll be a goddamn pumpkin before I let my only daughter give up on a dream and let humanity down, pretending to stay by my bedside. I'll be fine. When the time comes, they'll load me up with this heavenly morphine and I'll drift away—right among the stars with you."

"But Ma, I'm not ready to say goodbye."

"Poppycock. No one is ever ready to say goodbye." She leaned back on her pillow and closed her eyes for a moment. Then they snapped open again. "What you should be asking is are you ready to say hello? Hello to Mars, hello to the future, hello to your next step."

She pointed a gnarled finger at Madison. "You can't be living a life looking backwards. Love is letting go, they say. But I say, bullshit. Love is stepping forward. It's shoving the people you love onto their next thing. And that's what I'm doing here. I'm shoving you right onto that ship.

"Don't you be an embarrassment to me and turn it down for an old woman and her crusty bones. My girl, my Madison, is gonna save the planet. You gonna beat that goddamn son of a bitch, Lincoln Ellison."

A cough racked her body, and she spat into a tissue.

"Listen." Her voice hardened. "I didn't raise my daughter to quit. You sign whatever they need, take that pen and write big. I'll take the billionaire's drugs and happily drift away while my daughter goes to the stars. Beat that son of a bitch Lincoln Ellison and bring that cartridge thing home so people can breathe again."

Tears rolled down Madison's cheeks.

"Ms. Floyd," Troy said gently, "I'll make sure we look after her—"

"You'd better, boy. Truth is my girl'll be lookin' after *you*." A sly grin, then a rasping sigh. "Now get your scrawny butts off this link. I need to rest."

The holo winked out. Air conditioning hummed in the sudden quiet as Madison wiped her face.

Troy shook his head. "Your mother—she's something else."

"A force of nature," Madison agreed, voice thick.

"So…?"

She drew a breath, squared her shoulders. "I'm in. I'm not saying no to that woman."

They shared a shaky laugh.

"That makes four seats filled," Troy said. "Two to go."

"Xanthe and Jonas's replacement," murmured Madison. "How many days?"

"T-166. Not enough," he admitted, "but they're all we've got."

He offered his hand; she clasped it.

"Let's get to work."

CHAPTER ELEVEN

"Speak your truth."

—**Xanthe Waters**
MARS CULTURE CODE

GAIA HEADQUARTERS: TROY

T-164 Days

Glancing at his watch, Troy cleared the reports from his screen, sat up straight and ran through his breathing down-regulation protocol. Xanthe would be calling any minute.

After the disastrous meet-up, he'd gone to find her in the camp. He'd found her elbows deep in acid rain salve and grubby bandages, cleaning up after an intensive day of medical treatments. He'd steeled himself as he approached her. Plastered in dust, reeking of sweat and sulphur, brow creased with focus, she was ferocious. Troy had swallowed hard against the lump rising in his throat, grateful for the breathing apparatus hiding his face.

Once she'd noticed him, he'd pulled off his breather and smiled sheepishly. She'd cocked her head, not smiling. But not sneering either. *Progress.*

With a head tilt, she'd led him to the back of the tent and an empty consultation area. They'd sat on the plastic chairs, halogen bulbs bathing them in harsh light, the sounds of the camp winding down for the evening.

"So?" she had said.

He'd laid it all out again for her. The catastrophe if Ellison secured the tech and Chinese base on Mars. How the crew would perform better with a trusted known commander. How they desperately needed a second medico with space experience. How she was the only one familiar with both Chinese and ESA protocols. How the ThinkLink was an exponential asset to help ensure their survival and mission success.

"And?"

"And I want you there. I need you there." *Still not convinced.* "I know I've made mistakes," he'd said quietly, heart lurching. "When we got back from the Moon, I was devastated when you broke it off. I would have waited…I could have waited…"

Xanthe'd remained unmoved.

"Those relationships I had after the rescue were distractions, I know that." He'd pulled at the rubber strap of his breather while Xanthe watched him silently, green eyes hard as jade.

"I should have told you about Gemma. I'm sorry. I'm…still a work in progress."

"A piece of work alright," she'd muttered.

Troy's shoulders had sagged. "I may not be your favourite person right now, but I do hope you'll give me a chance to live up to the role of Commander. You bring out the best in people, Xanthe."

She pursed her lips and remained silent.

"Here's what Aryanna is putting on the table," he'd continued as his spirit scorched with pain. "She'll negotiate water rights off Prima Aqua so that Po Secco gets fair access to water supply and her new filtering tech. She's sending a medical team to help indefinitely.

The people here won't be hung out to dry without your advocacy or medical expertise.

"Next, she's promised to dedicate an entire Aryanna Enterprises staffing cohort for leadership, working in collaboration with the existing people on the ground. She'll also build the Breath Domes with Terra Verdi. Max will manage it all. The work will get done. The people will be protected."

Xanthe'd nodded slowly, eyes narrowing.

"Here's what I also want." She'd leaned towards him in a hushed voice. "Po Secco gets stock in Aryanna's water filtering tech. I don't want this place dependent on Aryanna's charity indefinitely. I want an in-flight independent comms channel, veto on med-risk decisions and no direct reporting to Aryanna."

He'd stared back at her wide-eyed. "Those are big asks."

"So is going to Mars with five months prep, with a Commander who can't even talk about a secret daughter."

He'd flinched.

"I'll do my best."

"Your best might not be good enough, Troy."

"Perhaps not," he'd said as he readied to pull on his breather. "But yours is."

⁊

The ping jolted Troy from his reverie. Xanthe. Her face popped up on the holo, hair wet from a shower, fresh clothes, ceiling fans of her accommodation whirring.

"Hello."

Was that a softer tone? He dared to hope.

"Hello, Xanthe." His smile was genuine; he loved seeing her.

"How did you go?"

"Aryanna agrees to it all—"

"Really?" Xanthe said.

"Except for one condition…"

She waited, the corners of her mouth pulling down slightly.

"Medical assessments remain in my veto. It aligns with my Commander role." He hated how defensive he sounded.

"Let me think about it."

"Xanthe, we're T-164. I've got to know. Either way." A fraction desperate.

"I'll get back to you." Eyes hard, brow creased.

The holo winked out.

Troy fought the urge to pound the table and held back a scream of frustration. Instead, he got to his feet and ambled slowly towards the floor-to-ceiling window overlooking the Gaia launch pad. They'd moved the *Saturnia* to make way for the *Nyx Odyssey*. There were teams everywhere, rushing, working long hours to get this mission off the launchpad. He cracked his knuckles before jamming fists into his trouser pockets.

Would they be ready in time?

Ping.

He shot back to the holo to read the message:

"I accept. One chance to prove you've changed."

CHAPTER TWELVE

*"Are we ever ready for what life throws at us? Life is ruthless, unfair.
There is no giant equation in the sky balancing good deeds. We
just need to keep on and find hope in raindrops and chocolate."*

—JONAS SEABORN
MEMOIRS FROM MARS

GAIA HEADQUARTERS: TROY

T-160 Days

THE BOARDROOM HUMMED with the air conditioning and something more human—anticipation, maybe dread. Morning light angled through the glass walls, catching the dust that never seemed to settle, even in a controlled environment. Troy watched the motes drift across the holographic projection of the *Nyx Odyssey*, a magnificent machine, designed with safety and comfort in mind for an extraordinary journey across fifty-five million kilometres.

So much could go wrong.

Starting with the crew.

They were already behind schedule. Finding a replacement engineer for Jonas had knocked a critical leg out from under them. They knew none of the existing space engineers were the right fit, assigned already to the Moon helium-3 operations anyway. So, Jonas's recommendation of an inventive colleague was their slender hope.

Aryanna and Maja joined Troy and Xanthe at the holo console. Jonas's signal rang through and Aryanna patched him in.

Jonas appeared, looking fit and polished in slacks and a good dress shirt.

He looked the best he'd ever seen him, mused Troy.

"Hello there," Jonas said. "Good to see you all."

Just a hint of regret, noted Troy.

"Thank you for joining us, Jonas," Aryanna said. "We've read Dr Tarek Mansour's file and we are keen to meet with him."

"And here he is." Jonas keyed the holo-link, and a projection shimmered to life.

Dr. Tarek Mansour appeared, talking to someone out of view, before he pulled his attention back to the holo, a fraction late. Behind him: the blurred outline of drones, technicians, the chaos of an active lab. He didn't even pretend to stand at attention. Fatigues, sleeves rolled, curls escaping the regulation tie-back.

"Apologies," he said, with the grin of someone who didn't mean it. "I was calibrating a neural assistant that refuses to learn basic manners. Apparently, I'm late. Consider it a feature, not a bug."

Troy felt a pulse of irritation rise in his throat. Confidence was fine. Flippancy? A red flag.

"Dr. Mansour," Aryanna said, keeping her tone neutral, "we run on precision here."

"Precision's easy," came the reply. "Imagination's the hard part."

Aryanna took a long breath, a muscle working in her jaw. "I'm here with Commander Bruin, Deputy Commander Waters and Maja Garcia."

"Yeah. Got it. All the top brass. Good to meet you." Tarek grinned and winked.

"Dr Mansour, you are aware of our tight timeline. We are eager to meet with you and begin training. Your references and testing are all…sufficient. What questions do you have before we move to the next phase?" Aryanna held herself stiffly, conveying a command presence that intimidated, even through a holo.

"Thanks there, Aryanna. Yeah, I'm curious about the A.I. systems on board. Override protocols, ThinkLink updates? Dopplebot syncs?"

Xanthe twitched beside Troy. That faint, invisible thread between them flickered—*he's going to be trouble*, it seemed to say.

"Those protocols are classified until you are onsite," Aryanna clipped. "Did you have any other onboarding questions?"

Troy logged Aryanna's shut down. Espionage? Infiltrators were always a risk.

"I just want to know how much creativity is welcome for problem solving? I like to work way outside the box. Jonas will tell you—my most brilliant ideas come from where others did not tread."

Troy straightened. "You'll find we have enough imagination. What we also need is discipline."

"Then I'll learn to salute ideas instead of people," Tarek shot back, quick as a strike.

Jonas jumped in before Troy could. "Tarek worked with me on the New Baths of Caracalla spinoff project, adaptive ethics and environmental A.I. He's the reason the symbionts there didn't turn the air toxic. He'll fit right in."

"Prevented mass suffocation," Tarek corrected lightly. "Sounds less poetic, more accurate."

Troy skimmed the data on his wrist pad. IQ off the charts. Published in three languages. Two reprimands for unauthorised system overrides. Every interaction piled another stone on the stack of concern in his mind.

Yet he couldn't deny the technical fit. The man's work in adaptive pattern modelling was exactly what the Nyx team needed. He thrived on adaptive problem solving under the pump. For emergencies in space, Tarek was their best hope.

That was the problem. Genius always came with side effects.

Xanthe spoke up, her tone smoothing the static between them. "We salute results here, Doctor, not just rank. But we do respect the chain of command, especially in emergencies."

A pause.

Tarek smiled, and for a moment Troy saw what Jonas saw: brilliance, pure and untamed. The kind that could move the project from theory to triumph. If it didn't burn down the lab first.

"Gotcha, Xanthe. I'm sure I'll deliver results for you and the team."

Jonas caught Troy's eye, almost pleading. "He's what you need, Troy. You'll see."

"Doctor, you're a little unconventional for a space mission," Troy began.

"Ha! Yeah, I get that a lot. I've been told: 'Fails to respect authority.' I guess I'm a bit raw in the ole command and control stakes."

"Raw isn't the problem," Troy said quietly. "Unmanageable is."

Tarek leaned forward through the holo-field. "Good thing you're a great manager, Troy, old buddy."

Xanthe's lips twitched, betraying her amusement. Troy ignored it. He'd learned long ago that command wasn't about liking people. It was about containment: keeping the mission safe from brilliance gone feral.

The meeting wound down. Jonas closed his tablet, eyes distant. Tarek lingered in the projection, gaze shifting to Xanthe.

"I read your papers on cognitive empathy," he said. "Impressive work. Maybe one day the machines will actually feel us back."

Xanthe inclined her head. "That's the hope."

"Or the warning," he replied, and cut the feed.

The silence that followed was thick as dust.

Jonas set the tablet down. "He's brilliant. He'll drive you crazy. Try not to kill him."

"No promises," Troy said. "Thanks for the introduction, Jonas. You're still my first pick though. We'll let you know how he goes."

Jonas signed off and Troy turned to the others. "So? What do you think?"

"Technically brilliant," Aryanna said, steepling her fingers, "but abrupt. Doesn't like to follow the rules. Challenges authority. I'm not sure we need any more of that on this mission." She cast a sidelong glance at Xanthe whose shoulders tensed in response.

Maja took a seat at the boardroom table and drew her woollen wrap more tightly around her narrow shoulders. "He's a typical expert. Thriving on his expertise and his need to stand out, even if it means flaunting convention. You have a few months to bring him into the fold, Troy. Advanced team building as well as technical drills."

"Xanthe?" Troy asked as she traced a finger along the grain of the mahogany table.

"We've made the mistake before of valuing technical skills above interpersonal ones. There's a steep price we pay in team trust."

"Can we make it work?" Troy fought the concern rising in his chest.

"Not much of a choice, is there? Everybody else screened out. With his PTSD, Jonas is still too much of a risk."

"He's getting better every day," Troy said. "Did you see how well he looked?"

"Don't mistake wishful thinking for accurate observation," Maja added.

Troy looked back at the flickering ghost of the mission plan, their shining cylinder of hope for Mars, turning slowly in holographic light. It still filled him with the same fierce commitment as the day he'd first seen it: a future worth fighting for, proof that humanity could outgrow its mistakes.

But the path there was so fragile and full of shadows.

CHAPTER THIRTEEN

*"We don't have to fit in to belong. We just have to row
in the same direction when the storm hits."*

—Xanthe Waters
MEMOIRS FROM MARS

NYX ODYSSEY SIMULATION
HABITAT: MADISON

T-87 Days

The oxygen bay always felt alive at night.

Pumps thrummed in her bones, and the glass tanks pulsed green in the half-light, algae exhaling their slow, damp breath. Madison had logged enough late shifts to know the rhythm by heart. The Nyx's lungs.

She leaned back in her chair, boots propped on the console, watching the CO_2 levels scroll across the display. Serena would hate it…the boots, not the data.

"Another thrilling night breathing our own recycled farts," Serena muttered, and waved at Madison to drop her feet off the console.

Xavier didn't look up from his monitor. "You want fresh air, you picked the wrong career." He stood, stretched with a groan, and plodded across the bay, humming as he adjusted a nutrient flow line, tender as a parent checking a child's pulse.

The man treated his plants like babies, Madison mused.

And then there was Tarek. New guy. All nervous energy and uninvited opinions. He prowled from console to console, muttering under his breath, tapping equations on the glass surface like it owed him answers.

Maja was perched on the observation platform, watching, arms folded, the picture of control. Madison could tell she didn't trust him. None of them did. Yet.

A soft chime interrupted the monotony: CO_2 levels nudging above baseline. Barely a blip.

"Calibration lag," Serena said, logging it. "Happens every shift change."

Tarek tilted his head, eyes narrowing. "No. Pattern's wrong. It's oscillating. That's a cascade feedback."

Serena frowned. "Athena hasn't flagged it."

"She's slow to learn." He was already at Serena's console, leaning over her, fingers flying.

"Hey! Do you mind?" Serena shoved at him and pulled away.

Madison sat up straight. "Hey, Doctor Handsy, maybe wait for permission before you start rewriting oxygen?"

Tarek didn't even glance at her. "Permission wastes oxygen."

The console lights flickered. A low mechanical groan rolled through the bay. The algae tanks shivered, bubbles dancing too fast, too violent.

Serena's voice pitched high. "What did you…"

Then the vents hissed. A fine mist spread through the air, sweet and metallic. Alarms wailed. The green glow shifted to angry red.

"Warning," said Athena intoned. "Oxygen depletion. CO_2 concentration rising. Recommend immediate evacuation."

Madison's chair hit the floor as she leapt up. "Masks, now!"

She slammed the emergency release and respirators dropped from the ceiling. Serena was already coughing, grabbing one. Xavier stumbled against the tanks, swearing.

"Tarek, stop!" Serena barked.

He ignored her, fingers blurring. "Almost got it…just need to reroute…"

"You *caused* it!" Maja's voice cut through from the platform. "You don't fix a living system by stabbing at it!"

Tarek didn't look up. "You built a dying one."

The floor vents whined like wounded animals. Madison's ears popped, pressure dropping.

She jammed her mask on, breath fogging the visor. CO_2 graphs danced in red spirals across the wall.

"Back it off!" she shouted.

Tarek slammed one final command.

The vents coughed, then settled with a long, wheezing sigh.

The alarms cut out.

For a moment, there was only the sound of people breathing through filters.

Then Athena's voice:

"System stabilised. Unauthorised override logged: Mansour, Tarek."

The silence after was heavier than the air.

Serena ripped off her mask. "You could have killed us."

Xavier's face was white. "He reversed the flow."

Maja climbed down, eyes blazing. "You reckless—"

"Efficient," Tarek interrupted, wiping sweat from his temple. "The loop's balanced. Improved by 0.8%. You're welcome."

Madison groaned, half relief, half disbelief. "You nearly suffocated the crew to make the numbers prettier?"

"Survival's in the decimals," he said, and actually grinned.

The bay doors hissed open.

Troy strode in, Xanthe right behind him, calm and sharp as glass.

"What happened?" Troy demanded.

Serena spoke first. "Unauthorised override. He triggered a CO_2 surge."

Tarek lifted his chin. "I *corrected* a surge. If I hadn't intervened, you'd be scraping us off the floor."

Maja took a step forward. "You caused the surge."

Troy's jaw tightened. "Let me see." He reviewed the screen data, Xanthe crowding in beside him, and they watched the video playback.

Troy stood up and rubbed his chin. "Brilliant, Tarek. Reckless as hell, but brilliant. But you nearly compromised the team."

Tarek's grin faltered just a fraction. "But I didn't."

Xanthe moved closer, voice even but firm. "Tarek, you can't go in half-cocked. You need to work with the team not despite them. It's not a one-man show. You break trust that way."

For a heartbeat, no one moved. Then Tarek gave a small shrug. "Trust can be rebuilt. Systems too."

"Not always," Maja said softly.

Athena's ambient hum filled the silence again. "Shall we run a new scenario? Or does the team need to debrief some more?"

"New one," Tarek suggested. "This time I promise not to go rogue. Much."

Madison exhaled, the taste of metal still on her tongue. She watched Tarek wipe his hands on his coveralls, the picture of unbothered genius, and thought:

Seventy days of training as a team and he still doesn't get it. Mars is going to eat us alive.

❧

The hum of the training compound in the replica *Nyx* never really stopped. Even in her bunk, lights dimmed to lunar grey, Madison could still feel the low pulse of the oxygen processors three decks below, a faint heartbeat that shouldn't have been audible, but was.

She lay on her side, one arm flung over her eyes, replaying the alarms, the smell of metal and algae, the look on Tarek's face when the system came back online: exhilaration, not remorse.

They were supposed to be a team.

She'd flown with plenty of cocky pilots, soldiers, even scientists who thought the laws of physics applied differently to them. But Tarek was something else. He didn't just bend the rules…he *believed* they were wrong.

Madison stared at the ceiling, listening to the soft rhythm of the air vents.

Trust, Xanthe had said.

She'd meant it like a line in a debrief report, but it stuck. Out here, trust wasn't sentiment…it was oxygen. Lose it, and the whole system collapsed.

She turned on her side, listening to the distant murmur of footsteps in the corridor. Probably Serena heading to the lab, double-checking the sensors, again. No one would sleep well tonight.

Madison reached over and tapped the comm pad off. The hum stayed.

No silence left, even in her own head. Just the rhythm of machines breathing for them: steady, fragile, artificial.

And beneath it, one thought she couldn't shake:

If Tarek Mansour is our margin for survival, we're already out of air.

CHAPTER FOURTEEN

"What if trust isn't a bond, but a gamble…and we're all just betting on the least dangerous player? Out here, maybe that's enough to keep us tethered: the illusion that someone, somewhere, might hold."

—**Madison Floyd**
MEMOIRS FROM MARS

NYX ODYSSEY SIMULATION HABITAT: TROY

T-67 Days

THE HOLOGRAPHIC DASHBOARDS glowed soft blue against the morning haze, light streaming in from the launchpad observation window. Troy stood with his hands folded behind his back, studying the cascade of crew performance metrics scrolling down the display. For the first time in weeks, everything showed green instead of the more familiar orange and reds.

"First week without an incident," Xanthe said, crossing the room with two mugs of tea, one of Troy's calming blends. Troy took one and sniffed: St John's Wort and chamomile. Perfect.

Xanthe smiled. "Even Athena sounds bored. That's a good sign."

He pointed at the cohesion chart. "Tarek's reports are clean. Polite, even. He cited Serena for precision under pressure."

"That must've hurt him," she said.

Troy allowed himself a grin. "Maybe humility's catching."

The change in crew mood had been noticeable of late: steady, bright, cooperative. The background static that had haunted every interaction since the CO_2 breach was gone. Troy let himself enjoy the sensation of smooth sailing for a change.

"They're laughing more," Xanthe said. "Even Madison."

"Training fatigue breeds humour," Troy replied. "It's healthy."

"Maybe we should ease off a little?"

Troy winced. Training load was a constant tension between them. "They're fine. We're fine. We've got to keep on task." Troy sipped his tea to keep his irritation from leaking out any more.

Xanthe held her mug to her lips and studied the display alongside him.

She let out a breath, as if about to say something, then stopped.

"What?" Troy asked.

"It feels…different. Calmer. Like the system's compensating."

"For what?"

She hesitated. "Balance before another spike."

He set his mug down, meeting her eyes. "A little paranoid? Sometimes people just learn, Xanthe."

He wanted to believe that. He wanted it so much his chest ached with it.

"Then let's hope the lesson holds," she said.

Outside, sunlight cut through the windows, turning the air dust-gold. Everything looked stable.

Afternoon light slanted through the off-duty recreation gym, gilding the track and the worn training mats. The smell of disinfectant overlaid the mix of physio cream and sweat.

Madison jogged the treadmill at an easy pace, headset draped around her neck. "Athena, play something with actual drums. None of that ambient whale noise."

"Request denied," the A.I. answered. "Pulse rates indicate current rhythm suffices."

Madison snorted. "Control freak."

Xavier passed by with a tray of protein bars still warm from the lab oven. "Made with real soy! From plants that actually like us."

Serena dropped her dumbbells and grabbed one. "The plants like you. They tolerate the rest of us."

"Because I talk to them," he said. "Positive reinforcement."

Tarek strolled in, towel over his shoulder. "So that's why my workstation hums when I'm near it. Never met an A.I. who didn't fall to its knees in front of me. My 'positive reinforcement'," he said with air quotes, "must be working a treat."

Laughter rippled through the room. Even Maja, perched on the edge of a bench, let out a soft chuckle.

"Don't flatter yourself," Madison called. "It hums because it's terrified."

Tarek put a hand over his heart. "Fear and admiration—identical data signatures."

"Keep telling yourself that, Doc," she said, grinning.

Troy and Xanthe entered mid-banter, exchanging a look that Madison thought said *let them have this*. The crew was relaxed, aligned. For once, no one bristled.

Madison was beginning to enjoy the daily rhythms with this team.

Tarek stretched, glancing around. "Turns out teamwork isn't a myth from management seminars."

"Careful," Serena teased. "That almost sounded collaborative."

He raised his hands. "I'm learning. Slowly. I even thanked a technician today! Athena logged it as an anomaly."

More laughter.

Madison felt a strange swell of pride being part of the team, the easy rhythm of people who had stopped testing one another's edges.

Tarek grabbed a bottle of water, nodding toward the hangar doors beyond the dome. "I've got a maintenance run tonight. Guidance module's throwing a drift warning. Quick fix."

Madison tossed him a towel. "Need a hand?"

He waved her off. "Easy job. Can't possibly break anything."

"Famous last words," she said.

He grinned, walking backward toward the exit. "Then remember me fondly."

The door slid shut behind him, sealing the laughter inside. For a few moments, it lingered…real, unguarded, human.

Madison caught Xanthe and Troy exchange a look of delighted surprise. She knew they'd had their doubts about Tarek. But people could change. Nothing like shared adversity and an audacious goal to bring folks together.

Madison was willing to give Tarek a chance. They needed him to make the whole expedition work. Their lives depended on it.

Something of that magnitude could act like gravity for a cohesive team.

At least she hoped this was the case.

She finished her stretches and headed to the showers, saying another prayer to any god listening to keep them all safe.

CHAPTER FIFTEEN

*"Every rival is just another version of yourself
who made a different choice."*

—Aryanna Sharif
TRANSCRIPT FROM THE LUNAR
COMMISSION DEPOSITION

HIDDEN LAB: CLAIRE

T-66 Days

Claire Edwards climbed the narrow stairs to the surface, palms brushing the damp walls. The bunker sweated like a living thing—cold, slick and airless. She needed out, just for a moment, eager for a breath of unfiltered air.

At the hatch, she checked the perimeter feed. Nothing but trees and silence. She entered the code, waited for the heavy lock to release and slipped out into the night.

The air hit her like grace—fresh, pine-laced, alive. She breathed deep, eyes closed. This is what Earth used to be, she thought. Cool. Clean. Breathing back. For a heartbeat she let herself pretend she belonged here.

Her wrist comm chirped. The sound sliced through the stillness.

"Damn it," she whispered.

Lincoln Ellison. Of course.

His holo flickered to life, a ghostly blue in the dark. The light painted the trunks and needles in unnatural hues.

"Go ahead, Lincoln," she said, her voice flat.

"Good evening, Claire. How's our guest?"

"Dr Tang's not cooperative."

"I see." His tone didn't shift. "Keep at it. I've got something else for you to organise."

"What is it this time?" She didn't bother to hide the edge.

"My source at Gaia says the *Nyx Odyssey* crew are making progress. We need to put a spanner in their works."

She folded her arms, the cold biting through her sleeves. "What did you have in mind?"

"Your usual operation. Something inventive to slow them down."

"I've got a lot going on here," she said. "What about using our contact at Human Habs? Arrange a special delivery. They're still partnered with Gaia Enterprises, aren't they?"

"Yes. Greg Johnson."

"That's the one."

"Get him on the job," Ellison said.

"Sure." She met his gaze, the holo's blue light cutting across her face. "Will do."

"Good." The image blinked out, leaving her alone with the dark.

Claire lowered her wrist. The forest had gone still again, but it no longer felt peaceful. The night pressed close, the air heavier, tainted. She drew one last breath before heading back down into the bunker.

CHAPTER SIXTEEN

"What shapes the future? Not the hand, not the heart, but some vast indifference turning beneath us. And yet, we reach for the clay, trying to sculpt what was never ours to hold."

—MAJA GARCIA
THE JOURNALS

NYX ODYSSEY SIMULATION HABITAT: TROY

T-62 Days

TROY STOOD ON the upper gantry, watching the crew run checks on the Mars rover. Another simulation in an endless lineup of possible catastrophes. There was no one else out there on Mars; they were on their own.

The hangar smelled of ozone and hydraulic oil, comforting and familiar. The crew moved as ants, scurrying between posts, laughter cutting through the hiss of compressors, easy voices echoing off steel.

Below, Tarek balanced on the service platform, calibrating the vehicle guidance array. His sleeves were rolled, his collar open, while he whistled something that might have been jazz. Between him and Xavier's French ballads, they practically had a symphony!

Madison had joined Xavier and they were running diagnostic sweeps nearby; Serena logged data from the life support module on the rover. Even Madison, normally rigid during drills, leaned against a rail trading dry jokes with Tarek.

They looked and sounded like a team. Finally.

Xanthe joined him on the gantry, arms folded. An air of judgement rolled off her.

Here we go, he thought. There's always something.

"Is Tarek behaving himself this time?" Xanthe asked.

A muscle clenched in Troy's jaw, but he released it consciously before speaking, keeping the defensiveness from infecting his words.

"All good. They've found the fault in record time…as a team."

He felt her studying him sidelong. "You're proud."

"Absolutely." He nodded toward Tarek. "Our resident contrarian's mellowed and found a groove with the others."

"Good." Xanthe unfolded her arms and leaned on the rail, studying the group. "But we've got to keep at it. Can't let them slide into poor habits."

Troy blinked, preventing an eye roll but not the exasperation in his voice. "I know. I'm on it. Not my first rodeo as a team leader."

Xanthe threw her arms up and backed away. "Just trying to help."

Troy cursed himself inwardly as she left the gantry and headed to the floor.

Below, Tarek called up to Serena, "Let's try the cross-link on channel four, yeah? If it's stable, we'll shave a full second off manual override time."

She gave a thumbs up. "Copy that."

The easy banter made Troy's chest unclench. Months of discipline and doubt were finally paying off. Things with Xanthe…still patchy. He followed her to join the others as they were wrapping up the drill.

Troy caught up to Xanthe, having prepared a mini-apology for his attitude.

Then came the distraction: a courier pod sliding through the hangar's airlock. The logo gleamed on its side: *Human Habs.*

Troy frowned. "What's Johnson doing back here this late?"

"Delivery," Xanthe said, eyes glazing as she consulted Athena. "Spare oxygen regulators. Routine."

This didn't feel "routine" to Troy. It was late. Even with the extraordinary timeline they were running, this was unusual.

Greg Johnson climbed out of the pod, corporate casual in pressed fatigues, smile too smooth.

"Evening, Commander! Got the shipment for the rover life support module, straight from Geneva."

Troy met him halfway across the hangar. "We weren't expecting hardware until next week."

"Fast-tracked for redundancy tests," Johnson said. "Can't have your crew running short of air on the Red Planet, right?"

Troy studied the manifest, frowning, then signed it with a stylus that caught the light like a scalpel.

Xanthe studied the crate with a guarded nod, eyes narrowing, before she accepted it. Johnson offloaded the crate and disappeared in a gleam of efficiency.

Troy watched the pod slip back through the airlock, a faint unease prickling his neck. "Corporate efficiency," he muttered. "That's what keeps me up at night."

Xanthe crossed her arms frowning after Johnson. "You're not the only one."

"We'll integrate it tomorrow," Troy said. "Everyone's clocked enough hours for one night."

Tarek poked his head out of the rover. "I'll get it done,

Commander. I've got a bit of excess energy after that scenario. A simple install will help calm me down."

Troy tapped a finger on his chin, assessing Tarek's energy levels.

"Alright, but make sure you get enough downtime and sleep for tomorrow. We've got meteorite strike drills and those can be intense."

"Copy that. A bit of grease and fix here, a bit of shut eye and I'll be right as rain, you'll see!"

Troy watched him whistle as he tackled the crate, wondering at this boundless energy. Tarek was becoming an invaluable asset. He hadn't seen that one coming.

⁊

Hours later, the hangar was quiet again.

Troy lingered in the control booth reviewing final reports. The rhythmic thrum of systems felt almost like a meditation.

Below, Tarek was still working—of course he was—adjusting the new regulator Johnson had dropped off.

"Tarek," Troy called over the comm. "Wrap it up. You've earned a night off."

Tarek laughed. "Just fine-tuning, Commander. Nearly done."

He crouched beside the open panel, humming, gloves bright under the work light. He'd drawn one of his fractal spirals across his knuckles, blue ink curling like circuitry. Troy had often marvelled at the intricate designs Tarek doodled to help him process complex challenges. There were fractal patterns everywhere.

Troy had had to stop Tarek from doodling on his jumpsuits. A messy look if the press caught a snap. They were already under extraordinary scrutiny; they didn't need to throw extra fodder to their detractors. The ravenous critics jumped on anything that might imply mismanagement.

The regulator clicked into place. Troy heard the thunk from the booth.

Then the lights flickered.

A static crawl raced up the tablet beside Troy. He glanced over to Tarek.

Tarek frowned. "That's not supposed to—"

The world went white.

A plasma arc leapt from the conduit, exploding through the bay in a roar of heat and light.

Troy flinched behind the glass as alarms screamed to life.

By the time he reached the floor, Xanthe was already running in. Smoke rolled low, thick and metallic.

"Tarek!" Xanthe shouted, coughing.

They found him near the console, sprawled beside the scorched panel, his left leg at an unnatural angle. The air stank of burnt insulation and something worse.

Xanthe dropped to her knees, fingers searching for a pulse. "No response. Athena, emergency med-bots, now!"

"Medical emergency. Dr Tarek Mansour unresponsive." Athena sounded the alert, blaring over the top of the fire sirens.

Xanthe bustled around Tarek, paramedic training driving her diagnostic checks. Troy grabbed the defibrillator and together they exposed his chest and readied for cardio resuscitation.

The bots whirred in, followed by the attending medics. Any drowsiness blasted away in the smoke and at the sight of one of the astronauts prone, unconscious and contorted. Xanthe and Troy stepped away as the medical team went to work.

"Clear!" the medic said once the defib panels were fixed. Tarek's back arched and slumped as they sent an electric jolt through his heart.

Troy's medical mind watched the scene, detached, counting out the compressions. Tarek's abdomen heaved as they forced blood through his body with the vigorous chest thrusts.

Troy's Commander mind, however, skittered over the implications with rising anxiety.

Xanthe stood beside him, a slight tremor in her hands as she clasped them together.

Her proximity chipped into his mask of disbelief. "He said it was a quick fix."

Xanthe's voice cracked. "It was supposed to be routine."

Troy swallowed hard.

The medics administered another series of shocks and resumed compressions.

Behind him, Serena, Madison and Xavier arrived at a run, eyes wide. The emotional tide from the others hit Troy in a rush—grief, shock, guilt, disbelief. He wobbled, bracing a hand on the wall.

Troy's command reflex locked his face into calm while something inside him split open. He could already hear the investigation reports writing themselves—*operator error, fatigue, miscalibrated regulator.*

"Jonas will blame himself," Xanthe whispered.

"We can't let him shoulder this one too."

Smoke curled upward, whispering through the vent system. On the floor, Tarek's gloved hand lay palm up, the blue fractal still visible through the soot, perfect and unfinished.

Troy stared until Athena's voice broke the silence again.

"System failure origin: Human Habs Regulator Unit 043. Probability of recurrence—0.02 percent."

A corporate part number, cold and clean.

Troy closed his eyes. "Get me Aryanna," he said.

No one moved.

Then one of the medics said, "I've got a pulse."

The debrief room felt too small.

Condensation blurred the windows; the air was thick with steriliser and silence. The lights were low, the holo replay of the incident an ambient hum, a ghost in the corner.

Troy sat at the table, hands folded, posture perfect. He'd learned early in command that grief looked like weakness if you didn't cage it. Across from him, Xanthe hadn't spoken in ten minutes. Her eyes flickered faintly, the ThinkLink processing, emotional residue still clinging to her like static.

They were alone in the room while the base clattered with investigators, emergency personnel, clean-up team and counsellors for the crew.

Athena's voice piped through the comms and broke the quiet. "Medical report uploaded. Cause of incident: electrical trauma due to power surge cascade originating from Human Habs regulator module."

Troy exhaled once through his nose. "I've read it."

"Preliminary analysis indicates installation error."

"That's enough." His voice was low, brittle.

The A.I. paused, subdued. *"Acknowledged."*

Xanthe looked up at him finally. "He didn't make an installation error. You know that."

"What then? He was alone down there. He shouldn't have worked late. Fatigue. I should have called it."

Her eyes softened, the way they always did when she saw too much. "He wanted to prove he could be trusted."

The words hit harder than he expected. He looked away, jaw tight. "He was stubborn. Reckless. Pushed the boundaries. That's what hurt him."

"No," she said quietly. "That's not what happened. He didn't need any rogue moves. This was just a regular install of a processor." She chewed a thumb then scratched her head. "Something else caused that accident."

He hated the truth in it. Hated how calm she sounded when he felt like something was burning behind his ribs.

He stood abruptly. "We'll conduct a full review with the team in the morning. I'll file the report."

"You mean *bury* it."

That stopped him cold. "What are you implying?"

"That you'd rather call it human error than ask why a Human Habs unit failed twenty minutes after delivery."

"Human Habs? You're making connections we can't prove."

"I'm *seeing* connections you refuse to."

She tapped the back of her neck where the ThinkLink was plugged. Where he'd installed it all those years ago on the Moon.

He met her gaze. "Let's make sure we let the humans take a look too. It's not always sabotage when things go wrong. We can't just lead with A.I. conjecture, Xanthe."

"And we can't survive without it."

Silence again. Sharp, final.

Outside, the training compound lights glared, abandoning the night cycle.

Inside, Athena spoke softly, as if to fill the space they'd hollowed out.

"Crew cohesion index: 42 percent. Declining."

Troy rose to his feet and gestured for them to leave the room. "End session."

The lights went dark.

⤴

The Nyx sim-habitat was quieter than it should have been.

Usually the air hummed with drills, Athena's guidance prompts, Serena's running commentary, Xavier's gravelly expletives, Madison's no-nonsense chiding and Tarek's brash disregard for protocol. Now there was just the sound of recycled air moving through ducts, a slow mechanical breath.

Outside, the air was still as death.

The urge to scream and smash the table hit Troy hard.

Instead, he sipped tea then rubbed his temples.

Troy sat at the round table in the Nyx's briefing module. The glass walls curved outward, showing the desert simulation beyond, empty and pale under artificial light.

Xanthe sat opposite him, spine straight, hands clasped tight enough to whiten her knuckles. Maja lingered by the viewport, not looking at anyone, her attention half on the data feeds scrolling beside the glass.

Aryanna breezed into the room, silk suit floating behind her in a wave, and dropped her tablet on the table, startling the others. Propping her fists on the table, she hung her head for a moment, then took a deep breath.

Troy shifted in his seat, readying for the onslaught.

"That was a shit-show," Aryanna said. "How the hell does our spaceflight engineer end up with a fractured femur and a concussion sixty days from launch?" Her black eyes flashed at each of them.

Troy held her gaze, rubbing his jaw, while Xanthe unclenched her hands and stacked them in front of her, ready.

Maja turned away from the window and joined them at the table, gaze distant, still lingering on the vista beyond.

Aryanna slid into a chair with a scowl and tapped the tablet with a stylus, the patter a sharp staccato in the quiet room.

"Athena, report on crew," Aryanna commanded.

"Crew complement reduced to five. Operational readiness at sixty-two percent."

Troy dismissed the A.I. with a wave. "We'll fix it."

"We've got no choice but to fix it," Aryanna spat. "And fast. Even my medical team can't put this Humpty Dumpty back together that quickly." She tapped with the stylus again, her long, coloured nails gleaming bright red in the dim lights. "Let's talk solutions."

Troy looked to Xanthe first. "We need a replacement systems engineer. The logical choice is Jonas Seaborn."

The name rolled through the room like a bowling ball.

Xanthe's expression tightened. "Jonas isn't ready. You saw him last month—functional, yes, but not field-fit. His trauma responses still spike under neural load."

"He's stabilised," Troy countered. "His last psych eval cleared him for controlled simulation. He's the only one who understands Tarek's integration code. We need him."

"We need him alive," Xanthe shot back. "Sending him up there half-healed is reckless."

Troy balled his own fists and then consciously stretched out his fingers. He cracked his knuckles as he fought the urge to shout Xanthe down.

"Can't we take someone from the Moon crew? At least we know they're fit and capable," Xanthe said, her calm voice tap dancing on Troy's irritation.

He held her gaze.

"It's a long bloody way, Xanthe. We can't just plug anyone into the team now. It was sketchy with Tarek, and we were only just getting it right after months. Jonas has the skills and he fits with the team."

Aryanna rapped her stylus against the table. "Let's be clear: I do not want to risk the entire expedition because we are trying to jam a splintered peg into a damaged hole."

Her tone was ice: procedural, not emotional. That was Aryanna's way of caring—codified.

"Understood," he said evenly.

Xanthe leaned forward. "We're not talking about a line item, we're talking about a person. Jonas has witnessed dozens of deaths in space. Now, a colleague—one he recommended—is lying in intensive care for an expedition he himself declined. You really think his first day back on this team is going to go smoothly?"

"It doesn't have to go smoothly," Troy said. "It just has to work."

Silence again. The kind that folded inward, like the walls were listening.

Aryanna scraped a finger across her brow, smoothing her hair. "Troy, I want *independent* psych assessments on Jonas. And I want each crew member to be fully on board with this plan if he's cleared by medical." She tapped the stylus again. "And that's assuming he'd even consider it this close to launch."

Something like hope sputtered to life in Troy's chest. His shoulders dropped just a fraction.

Maja finally spoke, voice low. "I'll speak with Jonas if you don't mind, Troy. I've been tracking his recovery and have a good relationship with his therapist."

Troy nodded an acceptance. "Jonas is the only viable option."

Xanthe leaned forward, both hands flat on the table; the motion was crisp, controlled. "You're gambling with a man's recovery to save a mission."

"And you're gambling the mission to protect a man," he said. "A man who should make his own choices."

Their eyes locked—command and conscience at a standstill.

Aryanna's stylus tapped again. "Decision?"

Troy drew a breath. "I'll contact Jonas after Maja speaks with him. He deserves the choice."

Maja's voice was quieter. "And if he says no?"

"Then we look at the Moon team, as Xanthe suggested," Troy conceded.

Xanthe rubbed the back of her neck, wincing. The ThinkLink must be bothering her again, Troy noted.

Troy felt Maja's gaze on him and he turned to her.

"While we consider Tarek's replacement," Maja said, "there's something else we need to address. I want to know why Human Habs sent us faulty equipment. The regulator that injured Tarek was manufactured under their quality protocols. And with Elena Fischer still unconscious in hospital and Dr Tang still missing, I'm wondering who is really running the ship there. And whether they have things fully in hand."

Xanthe frowned. "You think it was sabotage? Or negligence?"

"I think it was *something*," Maja said. "At least Greg Johnson, the technician who delivered the part, jumped straight into action, saying he would review the processes from beginning to end. He seemed remarkably intent on handling it himself. That's not normal."

Aryanna gave her a look. "You're seeing ghosts. Human Habs is a trusted partner. Tarek's installation must have been human error. They've all been under pressure."

Maja turned from the window, eyes sharp. "Pressure doesn't rewrite safety specs. I think we need to review all of Human Habs' contributions."

Troy let the words hang.

The last thing they needed right now was more delays.

"We'll log it," he said finally. "Athena's running trace analysis on the hardware metadata. If there's corporate interference, we'll find it."

He turned back to the table. "But right now, we're one engineer short and we've got a bucket load of work to do."

Xanthe didn't say anything. She rose from the table with clinical precision and walked toward the door.

Troy watched her go, jaw tight. "End session," he said as they followed her out.

The lights snapped shut, decisions made, dread still burning in his chest.

CHAPTER SEVENTEEN

*"How do you know you're ready? You do the work—and
even then, the dragon isn't slain. It slumbers."*

—JONAS SEABORN
MEMOIRS FROM MARS

NEW BATHS OF CARACALLA: JONAS
T-58 Days

THE REHAB WING always smelled faintly of citrus and steriliser, like
someone had tried to disguise the scent of fear. Troy really ought to
have that fixed, thought Jonas.

He lay in the diagnostic chair while the sensors mapped the
electrical chatter behind his eyes. He'd been through this routine
so often he could tell which nodes were firing from the hum alone.
The holo displays fluttered above him in delicate amber lines, tracing brainwave patterns like constellations.

Dr. Janice Naylor, his therapist, watched from behind the
glass, tablet in hand, lips pressed together in quiet concentration.

"You look good," she said through the comm. "Strong colour.
Steady pulse."

"I'm a hologram of health," he said.

100

She smiled faintly. "And your anxiety?"

He shrugged. "Well-behaved. Mostly asleep."

That wasn't true, of course. Anxiety didn't sleep; it waited.

He thought of Tarek—his laugh echoing through the comms feed, his impossible confidence, the way he made chaos sound like music. Then the message from Troy. The words that had stuck like a shard in his chest.

Accident.

Training.

Critical injuries.

It was just a few days ago, and every night when he closed his eyes he imagined the scene in excruciating gory detail. The stink of smoke, the electrical arc, the shattered leg, the CPR. A ghostly tableau.

He'd been the one who recommended Tarek. He'd sent him there.

And Tarek had come back broken. Not dead, not gone—just broken in ways that Jonas knew too well. The light sparkled just a little less in his friend's eyes.

At least he was still alive.

Not like Pabi and all the others crumpled under the Moon rock slabs.

Janice's voice cut through the memory. "Hmmm…heart rate spiking just a tad. You alright?"

He shifted in the seat, berating himself silently for letting his focus lapse.

"I'm fine. Just getting comfy."

He breathed and counted, breathed and counted, to bring his attention back to the present moment. To the smell of antiseptic and citrus, the hum of the machines, the sensors tugging at his scalp.

"You're ready for the neural integration tests."

"I know," he said quietly.

The door hissed open and Jonas's eyes widened to see Maja step in, tablet under her arm. Her usual calm was wrapped tight around something sharper. She looked tired, paler than he remembered, but still composed. He was glad to see her.

"Jonas."

"Maja."

They hadn't spoken since he'd declined the Mars mission all those months ago.

Maja nodded toward Janice. "Mind if I borrow him for a while?"

Janice gave her a brief, assessing look. "Fifteen minutes. No more."

Maja took the seat opposite him. "You look better."

"Better than what?"

"Better than I expected," she said, and it wasn't unkind.

Jonas leaned back again in the recliner. "Troy sent you to convince me."

"I came because I wanted to."

He smiled, a warmth glowing in his chest. "That's worse."

She didn't deny it. She eyed him coolly, assessing him.

"You really do look better. Fit. Vibrant."

Jonas clasped his hands behind his head and jutted his chin. "I've been working out. A lot. It's been good."

"I'm glad." She patted his knee.

Uh oh, he thought. She was bringing out the warm compassion. Her charm was notoriously disarming.

"I'm here to see for myself how you are. I won't lie, we do need you, Jonas. The Nyx's adaptive systems are coded to your systems architecture. No one else understands the engineering mapping the way you do. Not even Tarek. Though he did come close."

Something wilted inside Jonas at the mention of his friend's name.

Maja, sharp as ever, noticed and carried on before he got dragged under the sea of rumination.

"The team needs a trusted and proven engineer. An unknown variable right now is tenuous at best." Maja kept her tone even.

"I understand it perfectly," he said. "A weak team breaks under pressure."

Maja studied him. "You won't break."

He wanted to believe her. He wanted to believe he wasn't still the man who flinched at every systems ping, who woke with his heart racing from the sound of airlocks sealing.

"They said Tarek's stable," he said. "Fractured femur, concussion. That's all?"

"That's all," she said softly.

"Good," he murmured. "I'm glad I didn't kill him after all. People have a tendency to die around me."

Maja shook her head. "You didn't kill anyone."

"I recommended him. He took my place."

"He volunteered, Jonas."

He looked down at his hands. They looked steady now. Strong. He'd been running again—fast, controlled sessions on the treadmill. He looked alive, felt alive. But inside there was still that hollow hum, the one that whispered he'd get it wrong again.

"I don't want to be the weak link," he said.

"Then don't be," Maja replied. "Prove it."

He looked up, surprised at her bluntness.

She met his eyes squarely. "Run the toughest tests we have. Let Janice push you until you break the sensors. If you pass, you come back on your own terms. If you don't, no one's endangered."

Jonas nodded slowly. The logic steadied him. "I'll need Volkov," he said.

Maja blinked. "Volkov? The Dopplebot?"

"Yes."

"Jonas, you don't need—"

"I do."

He stood, pacing to the window. Outside, the compound glowed under floodlights, a world of angles and shadows. "Volkov's my failsafe. He monitors my vitals, interfaces with Athena's adaptive matrix, and—" He hesitated. "And he reminds me what I could be."

Maja tilted her head. "A machine?"

"A liability."

The admission hung between them like an open wound.

"You're not a liability," she said. "You're human. That's what we need."

He gave a small, weary laugh. "I am definitely certified human, warts and all."

Then softer: "But if you want someone who knows where the edges are, I can give you that."

Maja studied him for a long moment. "Then you'll say yes?"

He turned back to her. "After the tests. I won't go unless I pass every one of them. I won't put anyone at risk again."

Her expression softened. "That's fair."

He nodded. "Tell Troy I'll think about it."

Maja studied him again, her smooth brown face awash with warmth. "Jonas, do you *want* to go to Mars?"

The Red Planet loomed in his mind's eye: a cinnamon and burnt orange sphere hanging against the pitiless black of space. His heart thudded not with fear but with anticipation.

"More than anything," he said. And meant it.

CHAPTER EIGHTEEN

*"You don't integrate the wounded; you adapt the
system around them and hope it holds."*

—**Troy Bruin**
MEMOIRS FROM MARS

NYX ODYSSEY SIMULATION
HABITAT: TROY

T-53 Days

Troy bit his lip and rolled his shoulders as he stared at Jonas's
message on the boardroom holo:

"I'll go. One condition: Volkov comes too."

Troy punched the air with a shout of glee. At last, some good
news. He blew out a long breath and ran both hands through his
hair in utter relief. The mission was back on.

And now there was a mountain of work to get Jonas ready and
reintegrated with the crew.

First up, Jonas wanted the Dopplebot on the trip. He knew
Jonas had invested a lot of time and energy reconstructing the bot
after the Moon rescue, having insisted Volkov come back to Earth

with him. Troy had thought it odd at the time, but Jonas was in such a precarious mental state after being on the Moon, alone, for three months, he said yes to everything Jonas wanted just to get him back to Earth. They'd had to rejig the spaceship equipment to make allowances for the extra weight.

But Mars was a whole new ballgame.

Troy rubbed his jaw. How could he make that work? He'd have to trade weight for Volkov. Even with the updated alloy frame, the bot was still 83kg.

He pulled up the *Nyx Odyssey* manifest, scrolling past life support—untouchable. Options left:

- Secondary EVA drone—possible.

- Spare treadmill flywheel—no, crew needs full workout rotation.

- Storm-cache rations—too risky.

- Spare rad-tiles—forget it.

- Portable geology lab…pause. Samples could ship home; core mission stays intact. Done.

Ninety-two kilos traded for one sarcastic Russian Dopplebot, and a spare nine kilos to reallocate. He fired the proposal to CapCom Alexandra Minke, cc Maja and Aryanna.

Troy stretched back in his chair, letting relief flood his body.

There was still something niggling at him. He'd gone earlier to check on Tarek, who was still in medical care, leg bolted and in traction, facial burns bandaged. Tarek had managed a weary smile and a wave of an intubated arm as Troy came to his bedside.

After an update on his recovery progress—slow and painful—Troy had asked about the installation incident.

"Honestly Troy, I don't remember. I was working on the

regulator then next thing I'm in here, my leg throbbing and my face melted."

Troy had tapped the railing with a thumb as he studied Tarek. "The video playback records you saying 'That's not supposed to…' Any recollection of that?"

Tarek had rolled his head from side to side. "I've got nothing." He'd wriggled in the bed and Troy had helped him with the pillows. "It was all routine up to that point. I can tell you one thing for sure—there is no way that was human error. Even I can make mistakes, but this was a simple task. Something was off, but it sure wasn't me."

Troy's mouth had quirked at the cocky confidence, something that Tarek had not abandoned in their time together. Tarek had closed his eyes, sinking into a slumber, then opened them again. "I'd get Jonas to look at it. That guy can figure anything out."

Yes, yes he can, thought Troy.

Tarek had drifted into sleep then, leaving the incident still shrouded with questions.

Troy felt badly for Tarek. He'd worked hard to embrace the Gaia *Nyx* team and become a solid team member, putting in a laborious few months.

But Jonas was still the best man for the job, Troy felt sure of it.

Now, to convince the crew.

❧

Having called an all-hands, Troy waited in the briefing room, pacing to steady his jittery nerves. Everything was still so tenuous.

Xavier, Madison, Xanthe and Serena streamed in, chatting.

Good. No outright signs of stress, he thought.

They didn't bother to sit, seeing how Troy was vibrating with anticipation.

"What did he say?" Serena said, already smiling.

"He's in." Troy smiled broadly, the crease in his forehead finally relaxing.

There were cheers from Serena and Xavier, but Xanthe and Madison stayed silent and watchful.

"How did the tests go?" Madison asked cautiously.

"By all accounts, he aced them," Troy replied. "Janice gave him a full bill of health and is fully confident in his self-management skills."

"What does that mean?" Madison asked. "'Confident in his self-management skills?' Is he still getting stress responses?"

Troy raised his hands in supplication. "Given what he's gone through, he has more sensitivity than most of us. He has a heightened sense of danger."

"But that could be good, right?" Serena said. "We don't want someone complacent."

"That's right," Xavier added. "I don't want the engineer being all laissez-faire. I want that chocolate-loving monster on our team. He solved so many of our problems on the Moon. Besides, if he can pass all those tests Janice put him through, he can get through anything, right Mad Dog? You know better than most—six months of training in a coffin after selection to get over claustrophobia is no joke."

Madison dug her hands into her pockets. "Don't I know it!" She shivered at the memory. "But I got over it. And here I am. And Jonas has been working on this for five years."

Troy turned to Xanthe, who stood arms crossed.

"What do you think?"

Her eyes glazed as she consulted Athena.

"We won't really know until he gets here," Xanthe said.

Her voice was steady, absent of tone this time, Troy noted. He dared to hope.

"Let's get him in."

Audible sighs of relief flooded the room.

"But," she spoke more harshly this time, "if he's not up to it, we all need to be ready to pull the pin on the mission. Our lives, the ship, the future aren't worth pushing the boundaries because it's more convenient than saying no."

"And what about Lincoln? If he gets to Mars and seizes the Kunlun base? That's a lot to risk too, isn't it?" Serena toyed with the air filter clip Max had given her, softly snapping it open and shut.

Xanthe looked at Serena with steady eyes. "Then we find another way to stop Lincoln."

"First things first, I think," Xavier jumped in, his large frame bobbing in excitement. "Let's get our old friend on site and put him to work. Let's see if he is still a sucker for bad bets."

❧

Jonas arrived a few days later, awkward and shy. Troy was the first to embrace him, unsure how the others would behave. But the team folded him in a round of hugs—even Xanthe seemed happy to see him—and soon they were drilling Jonas on all the protocols.

It was much faster than it had been with Tarek, since Jonas had firsthand knowledge of the ship systems and emergency space protocols. The first few days were more of an orientation to the *Nyx* and her peculiarities than anything else.

That, and easing the crew into working with an unknown factor.

Well, a known unknown, thought Troy.

It was a rather large elephant in the room: would Jonas crack under pressure?

Day after day, hour after hour, they ran drills and worst-case scenarios, each more devastating than the last. Jonas remained even-keeled through it all.

Yet the crew remained sensitive to any perceived wobble. A headache might be the precursor to a panic attack. (It wasn't.) A hesitation was the sign of an impending anxietydriven performance freeze. (It was only additional analysis.) Fatigue was a mask for something more serious. (They were all tired.)

Troy wondered if they would ever settle on the issue.

Maybe it was something they'd learn to make peace with, like living on a fault line. Maybe disaster would strike; maybe it wouldn't.

In the meantime, they had a job to do.

A big one.

CHAPTER NINETEEN

"Everyone teaches; everyone learns."

—TROY BRUIN
MARS MANIFESTO

NYX ODYSSEY SIMULATION HABITAT: TROY

T-41 Hours

TROY STRODE INTO the sim-hab; the bulkhead timer glowed T-41:00:00 in stark white. His head still hammered from last night's marathon sim run. He wasn't recovering well. In the launch prep room, he grabbed his suit and pulled it on, observing the others for signs of fatigue. They needed to recover fast with just over a day to go.

Madison, already suited, locked her helmet seals. Xanthe crouched beside Jonas, double-checking his suit vitals.

"You've got a cortisol spike," she said with a frown.

"I'm edgy," Jonas replied. "Crappy workout this morning."

Xanthe checked the Velcro seal on his gloves and handed him

his helmet. "Troy, we'll need to augment the recovery schedule before we go into quarantine. Bio-markers deteriorating."

"Roger that, Xanthe," he replied, ripping his gloves' Velcro tabs open.

Serena entered a wrestling match with the torso section of her suit, lost and toppled into Jonas.

"It's tighter than skinny jeans after Christmas," she groaned.

"I told you to lay off the cookies, Serena," Madison laughed.

Serena sealed her suit and patted it down. "I'm no Cookie Monster. That's Xavier!"

"Wait till we're onboard," Xavier called, ticking items off his checklist. "You'll be grateful for my Cookie Monster cooking skills, *non?* Suits on. You're behind, Serena."

She stuck out her tongue and secured her gloves.

Jonas clipped on his helmet, rose and wheeled Volkov out of the bot's charging alcove.

"I enjoy this valet service," the Dopplebot intoned in its dry Russian baritone. "Not sure I'll enjoy stowage class."

"Your humour is worth every one of your 83 kilos," Serena shot back, eyeing Troy, who pretended he hadn't heard. She resented Volkov got a berth while Max hadn't.

"Launch seats—move," Troy ordered.

Though they'd drilled this sequence for weeks, Troy's mouth still went dry as he crawled into the cramped cubicle beside Madison. Their elbows and knees bumped, while they clipped in their belts.

A red strobe ignited; the klaxon shrieked. Pressure on the boards dropped 5 kPa.

"Hull breach drill," Troy barked. "Find it!"

Volkov tumbled free from the dolly as Jonas dropped it and jumped to the controls. Flashing panels scrambled Volkov's lidar, causing it to lurch; it cracked Serena's knee-plate.

"Bloody hell, you glitch-ridden tinpot!" she hissed, rubbing the throbbing knee.

"Water storage intact," Xavier reported, eyes on his display.

Serena leaned over, tapped a blinking red zone. "You sure?"

"*Putain!*" He zoomed in. "Leak in the recycler—internal."

"At least it's not venting," Serena muttered.

"Electric's green," Jonas called. "Where's the breach?"

He scanned, then shouted, "Hull section—sleeper pods!"

The klaxon hammered. Jonas's gloved hands trembled; Xanthe squeezed his shoulder. "Count your breaths," she murmured over the suit comm.

"Serena, Xavier—go seal it. Jonas, assist and prep the drone if we need external work. Helmets stay on, seal the doors. Madison?"

"Forty-seven seconds left on the 90-second window," she warned.

"Move!"

Serena shoved past Volkov. "Out of the way, bolt-brain."

"I am here to help," the bot replied, trundling after them.

Troy pursed his lips as the seconds ticked by, red light pounding his aching skull, horn screeching.

"Turn that goddamn siren off, Bruin!" Jonas yelled.

Troy frowned at the tension in Jonas's voice. He killed the klaxon; silence hit like a handbrake and yanked the scene to a halt.

Gasping with relief, head pounding, Troy pulled up the hull break cam.

Epoxy putty hissed as Serena slapped it over the hairline crack; Xavier isolated the water pipe and killed flow.

"Patched," Serena reported.

"Loop shut down," Xavier added.

"*Nyx Odyssey* crew, stand down," CapCom Alexandra Minke announced. "Debrief in situ."

Back in the dressing chamber, they popped helmets, sweat misting in the cool air.

"We blew the 90-second seal-off," Madison said. "Critical vent."

"What did we do right?" Troy asked.

"Quick breach ID," Serena offered.

Xanthe snorted. "After you missed it completely."

Xavier raised a hand. "Didn't check the secondary screen—my fault."

"We let that siren howl too long," Jonas muttered, rubbing shaky hands through his hair.

"And the bot was in the way," Serena added, massaging her knee. "We need better stowage—no time to shove him aside in a real emergency."

"I am right here," Volkov said. "I am here to help."

"Right now, you're a giant pain," she shot back. "What *is* the point of this bot?"

"Sacrificial lamb," Volkov said. "I do repairs in vacuum when bags of bone and water need to hide."

Jonas sighed. "If the breach had been bigger, we'd have sent him, not a human. He matters."

Troy logged the failures and glanced at the timer, now ticking toward T-41:00. Plenty of fixes left—and little time to make them.

"Alright everyone, stand down. See Xanthe for recovery protocols and rest mandates. We'll move Volkov's berth tonight."

"Before or after Aryanna's media scrum?" Madison asked.

"Before. Meet at 1800 so we can advise flight tech," Troy said.

A collective groan.

Troy watched them file out, Xanthe lingering behind.

"Jonas is struggling," she said in a low voice.

"He just needs rest. Good call to increase recovery," Troy said breezily.

"Don't be so cavalier, Commander," she said. "We need everyone 100% or we delay."

A zing of frustration shot white-hot through his aching head.

"I know the stakes," he said in a harsh whisper, leaning close. "And it's not your call to make."

CHAPTER TWENTY

*"Why go? The mission was critical. I couldn't not
go. I did it for Earth. For humanity. For the team.
At least, that's what I like to tell myself."*

—Xanthe Waters
MEMOIRS FROM MARS

NYX ODYSSEY LAUNCHPAD: XANTHE

T-24 Hours

Under banks of floodlights the *Nyx Odyssey* loomed, a silver
column against the starsplattered sky. The rocket's name stretched
along its flank in three-storey letters; an enormous mission banner
hovered at the foot of a temporary stage where hundreds of jour-
nalists jostled inside the Gaia Enterprises cordon. Camera drones
buzzed like metallic hornets.

Xanthe ran a finger over Gaia's logo—a compass—just below
the collar of her suit, seeking a modicum of reassurance before they
marched up to the media scrum. Her finger caught the edge of the
name badge: Xanthe Waters, Deputy Commander.

Deputy. It still rankled. But the mission needed her.

She knew the bitterness of regret, and she'd decided ego was not worth the price of missing out on Mars. Even if it meant working under Troy's leadership.

That lying, deceptive asshole.

"I thought we were getting past that, Xanthe?" Athena nudged her.

Some things are hard to shake off.

And here he came—the man of the hour. Tall, gorgeous, with sinuous feline grace.

Even in a goddamn spacesuit.

Troy patted the back of each crewmate as they formed up, expedition suits gleaming. Madison flashed him a confident grin—old hands at press drills after the Moon rescue. Xanthe's toes curled and her teeth gritted.

Next to her, Jonas wiped sweat from his brow, skittish under the renewed glare. Xanthe gave him an encouraging smile, and he nodded in gratitude.

Serena chewed her lip while hunting for Max in the crowd.

Lucky for her.

"Such bitterness? Thought we'd parked that too."

Yup. We did. I'm just—a little tired, I guess.

On her left, Xavier muttered, *"Mon Dieu!* What is taking them so long? I just want dinner and bed."

Next to him, Troy chuckled. "Last humans we'll see for two and a half years, Xavier—let them stare."

Jesus. Two years with Troy. In a tin can for nine months. Then who knows what at Kunlun base.

"A little late for second thoughts, don't you think?"

Maja and Aryanna strode past them, with Maja giving her a cocked eyebrow of concern. Xanthe realised she'd been scowling and worked her face muscles into a smile.

A staffer finally waved them out. A cascade of flashes erupted; to her surprise, Xanthe felt a genuine fizz of excitement as they mounted the stage behind Aryanna. The CEO's white silk suit caught every spotlight as she praised "the six who breathe for billions" and hailed the joint Gaia–Aryanna Industries effort to "give Earth a second wind."

Aryanna's assistant led the choreographed media scrum:

Serena Fox—"*How does it feel to bring Breath-Dome tech to Mars?*"

"One small breath for woman, one giant lung for humanity," she quipped, drawing laughs.

Xavier Consus—"*Any worries flying on a Chinese ship?*"

"Our Moon work proved a shared vision beats politics. In space, we're one people. Plus, I love Chinese food."

Madison Floyd—"*Your mother is in palliative care—have you said your goodbyes?*"

Her chin dipped; Xanthe caught Troy pressing a steadying hand against her elbow.

"My mum's a fighter. She's watching right now—aren't you, Ma? We're good to go." *Thumbs up to the lens.*

Jonas Seaborn—"*First flight since three months alone on the Moon. Nerves?*"

He managed a wry smile. "Can't hide forever. Besides, I've grown fond of recycled air—and Xavier's cooking."

Commander Troy Bruin—a voice shouted, "*Lincoln Ellison launched a probe yesterday—comment?*"

Jaw tight. "We have nothing but best wishes for anyone who is genuinely trying to put people above profits."

"*Are you saying Lincoln Ellison isn't putting people first?*"

Aryanna stepped in. "I'm sure we can all agree that Lincoln Ellison *does* put people first. At least, *one* of them."

This was hardly a friendly race to Mars. Galling, Xanthe thought.

Xanthe Waters—she snapped alert at the sound of her name— "*How does it feel to be second-in-command?*"

A frozen half-beat, then: "Mission first. We're one team. Hierarchy's just paperwork." A thin, ironic smile.

Champagne appeared. Aryanna raised a crystal flute: "To the six who breathe for billions."

Glasses clinked; flashes popped. CapCom Alexandra Minke pinned fresh mission patches to their suits.

Security funnelled the astronauts through cheering staff toward an awaiting transport. Tarek was there to wish them well, propped on crutches, and they paused to salute him. He smiled bravely despite his obvious disappointment.

They were still unclear on what happened with the regulator incident. The best Jonas could ascertain was that it had been damaged in transit, perhaps a hairline fracture. Greg Johnson from Human Habs had worked hours on it with Jonas, both of them still stumped by what happened. Greg had assured them he'd supervise all other parts, shipping and installation personally. There had been no other issues since then.

A power flicker rippled across the pad—just a grid load-shift, Xanthe told herself—yet Volkov's photoreceptors blinked amber.

On the bus, Serena slid beside Madison, who was tapping a message to her mother. "Say hi to your mum—and maybe she can pray for me too?"

"She's praying for us all," Madison promised.

Jonas leaned across the aisle to thank Xanthe for recovery ministrations.

"Anytime," she said.

Behind them, Xavier recorded a final voice message to *"mes filles et ma chérie."*

The PA crackled: "Crew, proceed to pre-launch quarantine-T-23.00."

Troy reached over and squeezed Xanthe's shoulder. She managed a wan smile as the bus lurched forward, carrying them toward the accommodation pod and the long night ahead, their last one on Earth for two and a half years.

CHAPTER TWENTY-ONE

"We all have a line, a moral code, that shapes and guides a path. We can't always see where that path leads."

—Claire Edwards
TRANSCRIPT FROM THE LUNAR
COMMISSION DEPOSITION

HIDDEN LAB: CLAIRE

T-12 Hours

Moist chill clung to the rock walls; every surface in the underground bunker felt faintly wet. She needed dirt and sky, not Earth's underbelly. Claire Edwards hugged her arms, sick of the cave's clammy breath and the five months she'd spent guarding Dr Victoria Tang—brilliant chemist, reluctant captive.

Time to wake the genius again.

Claire trudged down the narrow corridor, nodding at bored colleagues playing hacky sack under strip lights. A week-long stalemate had frayed everyone's nerves.

She keyed open Tang's door. The scientist lay strapped to a gurney, wrists cuffed, ThinkLink halo scanner dormant above her temples.

119

"Ready for another session?" Claire asked, voice flat.

"You can't make me go to Mars," Tang spat, head lifting then flopping back.

Claire stepped closer, hands folding over the rail until Tang squirmed under her stare. "This isn't about you, Victoria. Two planets hang in the balance. Be part of history—or *be* history. We can hack your ThinkLink. It's messy, causes brain damage, but we'll still get the calibration data."

"You're bluffing," Tang shot back. "ThinkLink can't be hacked—that threat was just corporate fear-mongering."

A thin smile. "You sure?" Claire tapped the halo. "Todd—our tech—will walk you through the process. Your A.I. can't lock us out."

Tang's gaze flickered. "You'd sacrifice me?"

"Prefer not to. Though one life is a small price to save billions—to secure air for Earth *and* Mars."

"You really buy Ellison's utopia?" Tang wriggled against the restraints. "He'll control air like he's cornered water and helium-3. First the Red Planet, then Earth. No one will stop him."

Claire's expression didn't change. "Ten minutes to decide. After that: plan B." She stepped outside, locking the door on Tang's muffled defiance.

Back in the command centre, Claire caught a whiff of antiseptic. No matter what they tried, the mold grew back. Life was persistent.

So was the boss, she mused. Like a crocodile in a death roll, he would never let go.

She tapped the call to Lincoln's low Earth orbit station, the *Helios Clipper*. He'd retreated there after the abduction. They would hardly launch a rocket just to detain him. Especially with Elena Fischer still in critical care. No evidence, no witnesses.

Lincoln Ellison's hologram flickered, then sharpened. He was a popsicle of a man with a slick helmet of hair, skin stretched and buffed, scrubbed of age. Arrogance kept him young, along with multi-million-dollar rejuvenation protocols.

Creepy, she thought.

"What's the update?" he snapped.

"Phase 2 oxygenator holding at sixty percent. Tang refuses the next calibration," Claire reported.

Ellison threw up his hands. "Bruin's circus lifts in twelve hours. We need proof of concept *before* they launch so we control the narrative."

"She needs rest. Push now, and we risk breaking her—or the device."

"Then *break Tang*," Ellison said.

"If we scour her ThinkLink we could corrupt the files—no guarantee we'd get usable data. And we'd lose future cycles."

"Options are gone. Threaten her family."

"They're under guard across three jurisdictions; we can't reach them."

"Then find *something else* to motivate her." Ellison leaned toward the cam, eyes cold. "Bruin cannot arrive on Mars first. Make Tang cooperate—whatever it takes."

The feed cut.

Claire exhaled, knuckles white on the console. Her stomach twisted.

Ten minutes.

And ticking.

❦

Claire marched back to Victoria's room, swung the door open, strode to the gurney and held up the holo. Victoria shrank back, eyes bulging.

A recording of Victoria's colleague, Greg, popped into the room.

"…it is with great delight I can announce the recovery of the

ALVEUS air scrubber blueprints that Dr Victoria Tang stole in her dishonourable and illegal defection to Spaceward Bound. Under my direction, with Elena Fischer still out cold, we will charge ahead…"

Claire snapped the holo closed.

"That clip goes live in one hour."

"How did he…?" Victoria muttered. "You gave it to him?"

Her voice cracked with the betrayal.

"I gave him enough to think he had a chance to replicate it," Claire said, slipping the holo into her pocket, "but that's the narrative out there. You're a traitor. And Greg's going to claim glory for your work."

Victoria's brows pinched.

"You should also know that we have your hard drive." Claire held up a palm-sized cartridge. "Your life's work—ours now. We will mine what's useful and sell the rest." Claire tossed it onto the nearby side table, Victoria's gaze following.

"You still have a choice, Dr Tang. It could be your work, your proprietary process, Nobel-worthy. Or Greg's."

Victoria bit her lip, groaning.

"Of course, if you don't agree to the next calibration of the scrubber, we will hack the ThinkLink and get what we need."

Claire leaned over the gurney's railing.

"But I know an upstanding citizen like you is not driven by ego or fame. You are prepared to give up your legacy and even your life. Commendable." Claire patted the scientist's shoulder. "But say the hack fails—we kill you and *still* come up empty."

Claire tapped a finger to her chin.

"Well, we've run a few options in the simulator."

Tang's cuff chains clinked against the rail as she squirmed.

"One wrong variable and the scrubber spits out peroxide, not oxygen. Every sim says so."

Victoria froze, staring at Claire.

"Now that's okay on Mars because robots don't care. They don't need good ol' O$_2$. But Lincoln is shipping *people*—hundreds of them. Volunteers who will take any risk to be the first colonists on Mars."

Claire turned away as a muscle twitched under her eye. She rubbed it and rolled her shoulders, before turning back.

"But I know Lincoln. He is tenacious. He'll keep testing, Earth and Mars, until he gets it right…no matter who chokes along the way."

Victoria's face twisted in dismay.

"Is that a legacy you're prepared to live with?"

Claire drummed fingers on the gurney rail.

"Calibrate, keep your name, save lives—or watch Greg and Ellison burn worlds."

"Alright." Victoria sank back and stared at the ceiling. "I'll do it."

CHAPTER TWENTY-TWO

"Mars belongs to the strong—those willing to bleed for it."

—Lincoln Ellison
MEMOIRS FROM MARS

HELIOS CLIPPER: LINCOLN

T-11 hours

Lincoln Ellison's grin widened as Claire's status report scrolled across the holo. He flipped a silver-cased data drive between his fingers, the label glowing:

NYX Diagnostic Patch v1.3

He beckoned his Dopplebot, Julius. "Load it and transmit—priority channel for *Nyx* intercept on launch."

The bot hurried off. Lincoln allowed himself a soft chuckle. Some thought it was ridiculous to fashion a Dopplebot after Julius Caesar, but he quite relished the subservience of the long-dead dictator.

The General could have done with a dose of humility. Might have kept him from getting stabbed in the Forum.

He stretched and rolled his shoulders. The plan was coming together nicely.

Still one step ahead of Aryanna.

He fiddled with the enormous silver ring he wore on his right middle finger. He'd had it made some twenty years ago after a tech conference where his peers had laughed at his ambitious plans for Spaceward Bound when it was just a fledgling company running out of a shed. He'd thought he'd been among like-minded pioneers: dreamers, visionaries, innovators. But they'd sidelined him, closing ranks, intimacy reserved for graduates of their own academies.

So he'd forged his own status ring, twice as big, and called it Ozymandias, a reminder to his adversaries that their petty plans would crumble while his world-changing path would transform humanity forever.

His mouth was dry and he checked his breath. Sour. He popped a probiotic supplement and chased it with a mint.

He keyed a course update to his pilot: Helios Clipper Lunar Transfer.

Next stop: the Olympus Moonbase. On a wall screen, the flight path of the *Pinnacle* arced from launchpad to the Moon in T-24 hours, where Lincoln would join them. Barrio and the *Pinnacle* crew prepped for their own Mars burn—one launch window behind *Nyx*. But the Nyx carried Lincoln's silent stowaway patch.

Greg Johnson had pulled off another nifty piece of sabotage. Perfect. Let Bruin blaze the trail; Lincoln would own the finish line.

Lincoln switched feeds to the earlier press conference, freezing on Troy Bruin's earnest face. "Enjoy the fireworks, Commander," he murmured. "I'll be waiting on Mars."

CHAPTER TWENTY-THREE

NYX ODYSSEY: TROY
T-2 MINUTES

Inside the sealed launch pod, Troy noted the eerie calm of the crew. Headset breaths were smooth, regular. His own vitals were stable, though the heightened focus of adrenaline brought everything into high definition. The pod glowed with screens and switches. Madison spoke clearly as CapCom ran through the last checks, swiping screens and signalling 'go' for each system.

Troy stretched his fingers inside the gloves, suit cloth creaking as he shifted in his seat. He noted the distant groan of the fuel lines alongside the gentle shudder of the ship as it primed for liftoff.

He glanced down the line to check his colleagues. Serena rubbed her knee. The bot was anchored to the bulkhead just beside her. Xavier hummed and jiggled a foot. Xanthe caught Troy's glance and gave a curt nod, while Jonas drummed fingers on his lap.

"*Nyx*, we are T-90 seconds." CapCom Alexandra Minke kept her tone even. "Crew—Go/No-go. Seaborn?"

"Go."

"Consus?"

"Go." Xavier's eyes were wide.

"Fox?"

"Go!" Serena flashed a thumbs up.

"Waters?"

"Go." Xanthe, with set jaw.

"Floyd?"

"Go." Madison studied the telemetry.

"Volkov?"

"Standing by. On the wall."

Chuckles.

"Commander Bruin?"

"Go. We are all go for launch."

Background cheers from the ground crew.

Troy beamed, and his eyes welled.

A 0.3-second telemetry blip fluttered on Madison's screen and then cleared. Troy glanced over, noticing her frown as she logged it but said nothing.

"Roger that, *Nyx Odyssey*. Godspeed to you all."

"Six who breathe for billions," Troy whispered.

"Three…Two…One…Lift off!"

A roar erupted. Vibration hammered ribcages; flames poured past the port. Lungs flattened to coin thickness. The cylinder surged upward, Earth's gravity clawing them back.

The hull groaned.

Jonas gasped, eyes bulging. Xanthe managed to give him a shaky smile. A warning system flashed red—Madison killed it with three quick keystrokes.

"*Putain!*" Xavier panted.

"Hang in there, crew," Troy said through rattling teeth.

Engines cut; sudden silence. A checklist card drifted free. Serena whooped.

Troy exhaled. "*Nyx Odyssey* nominal, injection burn in twenty-two minutes." He smiled and shook his head. Sweat cooled inside his liner.

Beside him, Madison reopened launch telemetry. She hesitated and ran her gloved finger over the data.

"What is it?" Troy asked.

"Checksum mismatch on the diagnostic patch. Auto-update flagged then cleared it."

He thought a moment. "Log it. We'll dig in post-burn."

"Roger."

"Look who's joined us!" Serena pulled a rubber chicken from her chair's side pocket.

"You brought Betty?" Xavier laughed. "Of all the luxury items you could've chosen, you picked a crappy old rubber chicken?"

"Hey, don't be mean to Betty. She's been through a lot. Just ask Jonas." She tapped the chicken on Jonas's helmet. He took the chicken from her and stared at it wistfully.

"Thanks for bringing that, Serena," he said, eyes glassy.

"Hey, don't miss the view," Troy said.

The blue curve of Earth filled the porthole, and they fell silent, mesmerised.

Off to starboard, a pin-bright engine plume flared as Lincoln's *Helios Clipper* departed Earth orbit for the Moon. Troy's smile thinned as they surged on. The race to Mars was on.

PART TWO
SPACE

CHAPTER TWENTY-FOUR

"The recipe for leadership in space? Start with a cauldron of courage. Add the bones of skills and knowledge and boil long and hard. Sprinkle with compassion and a large pinch of luck."

—TROY BRUIN
MEMOIRS FROM MARS

NYX ODYSSEY: TROY

Flight Day 27

TEN MILLION KILOMETRES on their way to Mars and no one wanted to be there.

Six seasoned astronauts and one cranky bot, on the expedition of a lifetime, with scarcely a mote of eagerness floating between them, even after twenty-seven days.

Except for me, Troy thought.

This was his command, his long-sought after dream of leading the first human Mars expedition. Except that Lincoln goddamn Ellison had beat them to it. Troy sighed as he drifted over to the navigation panel, looking over Madison's shoulder, who was a lonely sentinel at her post.

"What do you think, Mad Dog? Will the flare cause us any issues?"

"Nyx doesn't think so," Madison said, flicking to the long-range screen. "She classifies it as moderate. No EVAs."

"Good thing we're not planning on any. So far the ship's held nicely, thank you very much." Troy patted the edge of the display panel. "Let's hope our luck holds out."

He saw the grimace flicker on Madison's face as he pulled himself into the chair next to her. "Alright, I'm sorry. I know you don't like me talking about luck."

"Superstition is a killer. I've seen guys crap themselves without their lucky rabbit's foot or special underwear. They spook themselves into a crisis. I'll have none of it," she said with a dark look before turning back to the display. "Not on this trip. It's tough enough as it is," she added quietly.

They fell silent, faces tilted to the viewport. Beyond the glass yawned a black so deep it seemed to swallow reason. Stars pricked the dark like scattered embers—beautiful, yes, but impossibly remote, each one a reminder of how alone a human could be. The thought scraped across Troy's nerves; he drew a slow, measured breath, then another, anchoring himself to the steady hiss of the cabin air before his mind could tumble into that fathomless gulf.

Earth was behind them, a blue blob. Their view for just three more days, and then no more of their home planet for two or more years. Troy's throat tightened.

Troy let the soft whir of the computers and hum of the spaceship fill the void between them. Carefully he said, "How was your Mum? Did you get a patch through?"

The muscles in Madison's jaw clenched before she replied. "Yeah. She's alright. Kind of hard for her to talk with the stoma thing in her neck."

"How long…"

"Soon. A few days, maybe."

"Madison, I'm sorry," he said softly. He put a hand on hers and squeezed gently.

"Thanks." She swallowed, pulled her hand away and then said, "Where is Volkov? Nyx wanted him to fix the navigation capsule lights. They're still flickering. Maybe a faulty fuse. I'm worried about life support though, but with Serena in the freezer, all I've got is Nyx's advice."

"And Nyx is never wrong, right?" Troy mused, hoping to coax a smile.

"There's always a first time," Madison replied. "But still the best A.I. I've ever worked with."

"Better than Athena?"

Madison considered this. "Better than our Olympus Athena? Much. Better than what's in Xanthe's head?" She shrugged.

"What about Volkov?" Troy said, nodding towards the bot that pulled itself clumsily onto the flight deck.

Madison scoffed. "Why anyone made a Dopplebot of that old crazy dictator I'll never know."

"My origin source code was known for brilliant strategy and strength," the bot's Russian accent dialled high. It clamped onto the handrail beside the electronics panel.

"Not to mention arrogance," Troy added.

"Arrogance comes from strength," Volkov said. "Everyone says so about source code."

"Everyone says your 'source code' was a tyrant who oppressed his people," Madison said.

"Everyone entitled to opinion, even if wrong." The bot prodded the electronics, and the lights flickered.

"That's surprisingly insightful, Volkov," Troy said as he unclipped himself from the chair and floated over to inspect the bot's work. "Did Jonas add more emotional intelligence to your software upgrade?"

"No need. I am already very intelligent. More than you fleshbags."

Troy glanced back at Madison with a smirk. She rolled her eyes then leaned back in the captain's chair. "Volkov, you're an ass. But at least Jonas changed your face so you're less creepy." The bot ignored her and continued fiddling with the control panel. She waved towards the bot and said to Troy, "Still, that bot's been useful. If for nothing else than to support Jonas."

"Yes," Troy said as concern rippled across his face. Troy didn't like the dependency Jonas seemed to have on the recalcitrant bot; he wouldn't go into the sleep freezer without Volkov standing by.

Troy watched the bot retrieve the offending fuse with unexpected deftness given its thick mechanical metal digits. The fuse floated as the bot searched for a replacement in the electronics cupboard.

"You ready for shift change?" Madison asked, snapping Troy's attention away from the repair.

"Yeah. I'll get the others out of the freezer." Troy smiled and patted Madison on the shoulder. Human touch was an important psychological support on this long voyage, even for a crew member as tough and stalwart as Madison.

Troy kicked off the flight deck handrail with a practised flick of his ankles, letting the Earth-rise vista slip from the cupola windows behind him. The cabin lights shifted to soft amber night cycle as he floated down the narrow shaft of the utility spine, fingers brushing the colour-coded bundles of coolant and data lines humming inside the wall.

First stop was the storm shelter core. Water tanks bulged behind translucent panels, sloshing softly—thirty centimetres of liquid shield between the crew and the Sun's next tantrum. He drifted past the ring of snug cabins, each hatch clipped with its owner's call sign. All six berths would be full tonight once he woke the sleeping beauties, and they resumed normal human sleep cycles.

Beyond, the corridor opened into the galley–mess. A cloud of brewed coffee aroma from Madison's breakfast hung in the microgravity like an invisible nebula. Velcroed mugs and tethered utensils clattered as the air recycler sighed. Troy palmed a handrail and propelled himself onward, resisting the urge to linger.

The hygiene bay floated by with its silver iris doors, allowing for a pressure tight, zero-g shower with its sphere glistening inside. Across from it, the medical nook waited in tidy silence, its fold-down surgical table latched to the deck ready for deployment, immaculate.

Let's hope it stays that way, thought Troy.

He ducked beneath the frame of the exercise station. The cycle-ergometer's pedals spun lazily from his earlier workout, stray droplets of sweat sparkling in the LED glow. Madison would growl at him for that. She was so meticulous.

A coil of resistance bands trembled, then settled as the ship's attitude thrusters whispered through the hull.

Next, he climbed through the workshop, all restless machines and metallic tang. A carbon-fibre strut printed layer by layer in the corner, the 3D nozzle tracing its quiet orbit. Must be the bracket for the reading light Madison wanted in her cabin. Spares were lashed in neat packets to the mesh walls; he noted a missing tether and made a mental note to log it.

Past a pressure door, the air tasted greener. Xavier looked up from examining the lettuce seedlings rotating in slow circles beneath grow lamps, roots misted by a nutrient haze. The science lab was lit by chlorophyll, washing Xavier in a green glow.

"Is it time, *mon ami?*" Xavier said as he primed the plants' nutrient flow.

"On my way to the freezer pods now. Join me?"

Xavier pulled himself along the rail behind Troy as the corridor narrowed, the lighting fading to a cool sea blue. Troy eased through the hatch into the torpor module. Three pods lined the curved bulkhead like pale cocoons, biometric graphs pulsing on their lids. Inside, their crewmates lay in induced slumber, faces peaceful, skin haloed by the blue safety glow.

The hush here was total—only the low chorus of heartbeat monitors and the distant murmur of the ship.

They were on fourteen-day rotations in cold chambers. Chemically induced nearcoma states combined with careful chilling allowed them to reduce the demand on supplies, oxygen and water for the nine-month trip to Mars. It also helped manage the boredom and irritation that plagued confined quarters.

Xanthe, Serena and Jonas were on active duty next. With her brain computer interface, Xanthe filled both the medical and pilot roles, while between them Serena and Jonas managed the life support and engineering issues, respectively. The Dopplebot Volkov served as a general hand across both shifts. They would have three days together as an entire crew first, though. The marble Earth moment was coming up, and Troy wanted them all together when they lost sight of Earth.

Troy stared down through the plexiglass at Xanthe's prone form. Her face was so peaceful. He hesitated to press the reactivate button, savouring this version of Xanthe before the hard, distant woman he still loved reanimated and life's bitterness creased her brow into deep furrows and pinched her face pale. With one last glance, he hit the controls and started the wake cycle before moving to Jonas and Serena's pods.

At least Serena was a bit more enthusiastic about this trip. She still surfed a wave of excitement for the adventure, though she definitely resented Troy for leaving Max behind. But they simply didn't need two life support engineers on this expedition. Max could come later. Assuming they brought Lincoln Ellison under control.

Troy and Xavier monitored their vitals as the pods cycled them back through the waking stages. They would need fluids and guided movement therapy until their bodies revived completely. Then a few hours of muscle activation at the exercise station. Getting them to eat was the hardest part. No one felt like eating while the freeze chemicals rolled like toxic slosh through their bodies.

Thank God Xavier was here! The old Frenchman could make anything taste good, obsessed as he was with nutrition and food cultivation. But there was no room on this expedition for any fancy horticulture. This was a 'contain and manage' assignment.

Since Ellison broke the space treaties with the Spaceward Bound mission to Mars, and Gaia followed with *Nyx Odyssey*, the Mars Alliance had erupted into factions. They were getting regular updates about the controversy.

Troy found it incredible some heralded the brazen techno-billionaire as the saviour of humanity's future. Maja called him a 'colonising corporate feudal overlord'. Usually so gracious, Lincoln's treachery had peeled her placid veneer back to raw outrage.

An alarm sounded on Jonas's pod. Troy shot over. The hydration settings surged. Excess fluid put Jonas at risk of hyponatraemia, seizures and organ malfunction. Troy hit manual override to open the pod's cover.

"Come on, come on," he said.

The cover retracted at a glacial pace.

Jonas's face swelled, heart rate and respiration spiking.

"*Merde!*" Xavier said as he slid alongside him. Troy slipped a hand under the cover but couldn't reach the IV. Xavier strained against the cover. Jammed.

"Nyx, override the pod cover lock," Troy shouted.

"Pod cover unresponsive," replied the A.I. in a neutral electronic tone. "Reboot the system? Potential threat to reanimation sequence."

"Negative—that could dump even more fluid. We need this door open and then I can do a manual drain."

"Still unresponsive. I recommend manual intervention," Nyx intoned.

"Volkov, report to the freezer now!" Troy roared into the ship's comm on his lapel.

Xavier and Troy heaved.

"Is this a priority over electronics repair?" The bot's voice sounded annoyed through Troy's earpiece.

"Bloody hell, Volkov! It's Jonas's pod. Hydration over-saturation. I need you now. Cover is jammed!"

"Hold horses. I am on the way."

"Goddamn bot," Troy said through gritted teeth, alarms screeching.

The other two pod covers had retracted, with Serena and Xanthe stirring.

Moments later, Madison followed Volkov into the sleep freezer.

"Mad Dog, look after the others," Troy said as they pushed against Jonas's cover, holding back his own panic.

Jonas's prone form gurgled. His eyes sprang open, bulging. He gagged and his limbs thrashed, terror etched across his face.

"Bloody hell!" cried Troy and they redoubled their efforts.

Volkov pushed himself over to Troy, anchored one hand on the rail, a metal leg around the pod's stand for leverage, and hauled the cover open with a grating screech. Troy fell on Jonas's flailing arm, secured the IV and closed its valve. Xavier readied with a vomit bag as Jonas coughed.

"I've got you, Jonas," he said steadily despite his racing heart.

Jonas spluttered, straining for breath, his face puce.

Troy checked the renal drainage catheter and made sure it was open to maximum, then jumped back to the display. "Nyx, protocol?"

"Cut free-water, start 100mL 3% saline, repeat neuro-check in ten. Jonas gets 40 mEq KCl in normal saline—run at ten an hour, central line only, ECG on lead II. Redraw lytes in four."

Troy primed the hypertonic syringe. "Let's dry you out, big guy."

He grabbed Jonas's arm once more, driving the needle directly into a wrist vein; Jonas's skin was deathly cold.

"Nyx, can you adjust Jonas's pod temperature? Are those circuits still working?"

"Affirmative. Adjusting now."

Troy breathed out slowly, his concern easing as he watched the renal catheter container fill with fluid. But why was Jonas still struggling? And the damn alarm was still blaring.

"What are you trying to do—drown him?"

Troy froze at the voice. Xanthe. Madison was helping her sit upright, and she looked with bleary eyes over at Jonas's pod.

"Pulmonary drain." She nodded towards the chest catheter.

Troy saw his mistake instantly. With the pulmonary catheter blocked, fluid was building up in Jonas's lungs. He lunged for it, snapped the valve open and checked the length of the line. It was flowing freely now.

Jonas coughed viciously, veins standing to attention in his neck, then vomited into Xavier's waiting bag. He fell back against the headrest, gasping, his breath coming more easily now.

The alarm shut off, bringing immediate relief.

Troy peered at the display as all Jonas's vitals returned to normal and fluid indicators levelled out. He was out of the woods.

Serena stirred and lifted her head above the sleep pod's side, taking in the faces of her colleagues crowded into the small chamber.

"Did I miss the party?" she said.

CHAPTER TWENTY-FIVE

NYX ODYSSEY: TROY

Flight Day 27

Troy shoved his shaking hands into his cargo pants pockets, hooking a foot under a freezer sleep pod, as the crew started the reanimation routine. He caught Xanthe staring at him while she did movement therapy with support from Xavier.

Troy'd nearly lost Jonas, and she knew it.

They'd need a debrief.

Soon.

First, get the sleepers back to full function. The sleep pods needed a full check after the near disaster, adding this to the growing list of jobs.

Panels along the ceiling pulsed with a slow night-into-day rhythm, casting a cool dawn-like wash over the stainless steel handrails while tiny indicator diodes blinked red green all around the sleep freezer galley. Nothing else was out of place that he could see. Except for a floating chunk of vomit.

"Volkov, can you clean up the puke traces before they go around the room, please?" Troy said. He frowned as a glob floated nearby. He pulled a towel from the sleep pod's drawer and handed it to Volkov. "Here—you can contain it with this."

"You think because I cannot smell anything I do not think this is disgusting? Parts of body should remain in body," the bot replied as it stretched the towel around the offending chunk.

"Sometimes things spill out. Get on with it," Troy commanded.

He turned his attention to Jonas. "How are you doing, old chap?"

Jonas cleared his throat and gestured for a fluid pouch. Madison passed him one, and he slurped gratefully.

"That was a bit rough," Jonas said after he squeezed the remnants of the hydration pouch. "What happened?"

"Sleep pod malfunction—I couldn't get the cover open, and the fluid was flooding your system."

Jonas ran a hand through his hair. "That's one hell of a way to wake up."

"Well, you look pretty good for fourteen days of beauty sleep," Serena said. "First time in the sleep pods—we didn't do too badly, I think." She scrubbed at her scalp with her fingertips as her hair stretched in a zero-g halo around her.

"Dunno," Jonas said. "Madison, Troy and Xavier had a rough time their first time out."

"We'll be fine," Serena retorted. "Can we get these tubes out now?" She waved at the catheter and IV still sprouting from her body. "I'm desperate for a shower."

"I bet you are, my friend," Madison said. "Lucky I cleaned it out for you yesterday."

The water recycler kicked in with a sympathetic high-pitched whine.

Xavier checked the freezer pod settings while Troy and Madison unplugged their friends and guided them out of the freezer beds.

"Family dinner tonight, *mes amis*!" Xavier said. "Steak? Pork? A cheesy pizza?" He chuckled as they groaned. Appetite was the last thing to return after a bout in the freezer pods.

"I'd be happy with a cup of tea and a bag of painkillers," Serena said.

"Debrief before chow," Troy said. "Kitchen galley at 1600."

"Yes, Commander," muttered Xanthe.

He shot her a look, and she saluted with a wan smile before pulling herself out of the sleep freezer galley towards the living quarters.

It was going to be a long three days before his turn in the freezer, Troy thought.

Gathered in the kitchen galley for the debrief, Serena, Xanthe and Jonas looked weary but otherwise in good shape. The recent sleepers nibbled at protein bars, washing them down with coffee or tea. Rich, roasted bitterness flooded over the familiar faint metallic tang of recycled air as Jonas cracked his second warm coffee pouch, gazing at it wistfully.

"I'd trade all my rations of chocolate for one of Xavier's spill-free low-G printed mugs," he said.

"Too much weight. Luxury item," Xavier replied. "We can try printing when we get to Mars."

"You'd trade chocolate?" Serena said. "Stake some on chook tag bets?" She waggled the rubber chicken at Jonas, made it squawk and then let it drift.

"I can't believe you chose Betty as your luxury item, Fox," Madison said as she manoeuvred herself expertly using the foot rails around the briefing holo-display that doubled as a dining room table for meals. Crossing her ankles over the bar, she relaxed with her own coffee pouch, obviously savouring the brewed aroma over the clinical whiff of surface disinfectant that lingered in the galley.

"She doesn't even squawk properly anymore," Madison chided. "And her colour is all faded."

"Don't let Madison talk you down, Betty," Serena said as she batted the rubber chicken towards Jonas. "We love you just the way you are."

Jonas caught the chicken nimbly and smiled at Serena, who winked back. He shoved the chicken down the front of his overalls to keep her from floating through the galley.

Troy drifted over to the table and hooked in beside Madison and Xavier. Xanthe, Serena and Jonas were opposite. The sleeper shift groups were bonding, Troy noted. He frowned. Was that a concern?

The water recycler whined and kicked over. It rattled against the ever-present hum and bone-deep vibration of the life support fans. The ship's gentle acceleration added a bass-note thrumming that reverberated in their six sternums. Troy imagined his very cells being shaken like sand sieved for gold.

"Well, this is a lovely opportunity," Troy began. "So far, the mission is going extremely well. We're on track, and we're coming up on ten million kilometres from Earth with no significant incident."

"What do you call nearly killing Jonas?" Xanthe said, eyebrows raised as she took a sip of tea from the pouch.

"That, of course, was—you're right—an obvious problem. Sorry, Jonas, I didn't mean to discount that hairy incident."

"Yep, happy to be the test bunny for pod rescue, but not that keen to repeat the process."

"I'm not sure I trust that pod," Xavier added.

"We'll get Nyx and Volkov to do a complete system check with you to ensure it doesn't happen again," Troy replied.

Madison blew air out of her cheeks. "I don't know, Troy. I'm not so good with confined spaces, as you well know. That glitch makes me nervous. We go in the freezer in two days, and I'm a little freaked out."

"If we take the whole thing apart—or at least get all the systems checked—would that be good enough?" Troy asked.

Madison tilted her head and scrunched her face. "Maybe."

"It's good that we're all here now. The ship is on track, and we're heading off on this grand adventure—the first people, apart from Lincoln Ellison, to set foot on the Red Planet. This is an incredible opportunity for all of us. Together we can beat all the challenges, and together we have much to celebrate."

The life support system hummed while the crew said nothing. Eyes averted, they sipped drinks or nibbled bars. Jonas poked absent-mindedly at the magnetic cutlery on the galley table, while a few rogue crumbs and unidentified globules from an earlier meal hovered near the air vents, pulsing in slow spirals until a vent gust sucked them away.

"I'm sure our families and friends and all the team at Gaia Enterprises will be super proud of us," Troy continued, his enthusiastic declarations drifting through the galley unheeded. The handrails were slick with condensation brought on by the additional bodies.

"I think you're forgetting a few things, Troy," Xanthe interrupted. "Lincoln Ellison and the *Pinnacle* are now ahead of us."

"Really?" Madison said. "How do you know that?"

Xanthe waved at her Athena ThinkLink.

"Did you know that?" Madison turned to Troy.

His face coloured. "Just got the news an hour ago."

"Plus, we've lost contact with the Chinese Dopplebot base," Xanthe added.

All heads spun to Xanthe in alarm.

"We don't know that for sure," Troy replied, palms supplicating.

"We only know that the Dopplebots stationed at Kunlun have stopped communicating."

"What we do know," Xanthe interrupted again, "is that Lincoln Ellison has his sights set on establishing a permanent base on Mars and he'll take whatever is available to him to make it happen—including seizing Gaia property, Chinese property and whatever else will make his life easier. He doesn't give a fig about international law or the Mars Accord. We're up shit creek. Stop trying to put lipstick on a pig."

"Harsh," Serena said, bumping a shoulder against Xanthe. "Did you drink cranky syrup out of the freezer?"

In his peripheral vision, Troy was conscious of the heads-up display showing Earth shrunk to a pale blue dot beside a scrolling kilometre counter, updated every ten seconds.

"Regardless," Troy continued, dragging his attention back from the display and trying not to get irritated with Xanthe's tone, "this is still an incredible opportunity for all of us—one for which we should all feel grateful and honoured to undertake."

"Grateful and honoured," muttered Jonas. "Sounds good in theory, but really, people don't care. They're too busy dealing with whatever's happening on Earth."

Something in his tone put Troy on high alert.

Jonas kept his gaze on the magnetic spoon he was lifting and releasing back to its stand on the bench. "I was alone on the Moon for three months," he said in a low voice. "No one cared. They had their own lives to worry about."

"That's not true, Jonas," Xanthe said, eyes glistening.

"Oh, we cared about you, Jonas!" Serena said. "We did nothing but worry about you the entire time. But you're right about one thing; our expedition doesn't have much support. There was a reason the Mars Alliance banned human settlement and travel to Mars five years ago—after the Moon stuff," she said, glancing over at Jonas. "Too risky, too dangerous, not worth it. We should have let the Dopplebots handle it all."

"Look," cut in Madison. "We've all got folks left on Earth we'd rather be spending time with, or things we'd rather be doing." She looked pointedly at Xanthe. "But here we are. We all signed up for this gig in the end. No one forced our hand to be here."

"Didn't they?" Xanthe asked. "Maja and Aryanna laid down a pretty heavy hand: the future of humanity off-planet and bringing Lincoln Ellison to account. They stacked the guilt pretty high."

"You didn't need to come," Xavier said.

"Didn't I?" Xanthe replied. "I don't see anybody else with a brain computer interface—Athena—in their head."

"That was your decision on the Moon to get the implant," Serena replied. "Don't go playing the martyr now."

Xanthe rolled her eyes.

"Okay, forget it," said Troy, exasperation lacing his words. "I get it. Not all of us are pumped to be here."

"And some of us are here out of obligation," muttered Xanthe.

"But the thing is," Troy pressed on, "we need each other. We're still pretty vulnerable flying through space, and we've got all the unknown factors coming up on Mars: the landing, finding the habitat, figuring out what happened to the Dopplebots, dealing with Lincoln. It's a lot. So I need everybody to bring their A-game—and their A-attitude—to make this a more pleasant experience."

Another protein bar crumb floated past and Madison grabbed it. Jonas slurped his coffee pouch while Xanthe studied her fingernails with an arched brow.

"Nice pep talk, boss," Serena chimed in and patted him on the shoulder.

"Thanks. I'll try to do better," he mumbled.

"Well, tomorrow we say goodbye to planet Earth for good," Jonas said. "So, you know, that'll be a happy time." His voice dripped with sarcasm.

"Let's try to make the best of it. Think about everything we're looking forward to, rather than everything we're leaving behind," Troy said. "Tomorrow, when we gather in the cupola to farewell Earth, let's think about all the things we're moving towards, not leaving behind."

CHAPTER TWENTY-SIX

*"Things I miss from Earth: my wife, my daughters,
obviously. Sea breeze. The way moonlight glitters like jewels
on the water. Ants. Tulips. I mean, what is the point of
a tulip? Nothing. It's just beautiful. I miss that."*

—Xavier Consus
MEMOIRS FROM MARS

NYX ODYSSEY: TROY

Flight Day 30

They pulled themselves up into the cupola, shoulder-to-shoulder, to take in the panoramic vista. There, in the far distance—shining blue among a sea of white stars—was their last glimpse of Earth.

Troy swallowed as his throat tightened. He'd been anticipating this moment—or dreading it, he wasn't sure—for a long time. He could sense the tension in Madison's shoulder as well; the view was sobering.

"Well, this is nice and cosy," Serena said. "Couldn't think of any better humans to share the last look at Earth with. Well, actually—maybe just one."

Jonas put his arm around her and gave a squeeze. "You and Max are the cutest. I'm glad that's working out for you."

Serena leaned her head towards him in acknowledgment of their long-standing friendship. "Have you got your heart locked on a girl this time, Jonas? Didn't you have one in every port after the fanfare and rock-star status you enjoyed when you got back from the Moon?"

Jonas smiled shyly. "I got a few offers and a few dates, but nothing really stuck—too much time in therapy."

Serena's face sagged, thinking about what he'd been through.

"Right then," Troy said, noting the drag in atmosphere. "We're meant to be thinking about where we're heading, not what we're leaving. I call this ceremony to order."

They wriggled awkwardly to face one another, using the handrail around the base of the cupola to anchor themselves. The flight deck's display lights shone below their drifting feet, and the ship's systems purred through the handrail, greasy with their fingerprints. The cupola itself was spotless. They each wiped it with meticulous attention every time they ventured up into the cavity for the view.

And now the view was two-tone: the impossible nothingness of space and the searing white of distant stars. And there in the far distance, a smear of blue—the last colour they would see through their window for another ninety days when Mars and its smudge of ochre drifted into view.

"While we're obviously thinking about Earth and the people there, let's also think about Mars." Troy mustered a bright, cheery grin. "Madison, would you like to go first? What are you looking forward to on Mars?"

"Testing the single-pilot copters we brought along," she said. "We know the bots can fly them, but it'll be awesome for a human to skim the terrain." She made a flying motion with one hand. "And I'm looking forward to touching down safely."

"You and me both," Troy said. "Thanks, Madison. Serena—how about you?"

"Gravity," she replied. "It's only been thirty days and I'm already sick of floating. My face is swollen like a puffer fish, my hair's sideways and sweat pooling on my scalp is gross on the bike. Give me gravity or give me death."

"Let's maybe tweak that phrase," Xanthe said.

"Alright—give me gravity or give me gorillas," Serena amended. Madison smirked.

"Jonas?" Troy prompted.

Jonas thought for a moment. "Just being with people. I figured I'd had enough of space once I got off the Moon. Being back out here—especially for this long—is tough. But being with you all, not alone, is what I'm grateful for. Besides that, I want to see what the Dopplebots have built and whether they did a better job than we would have."

"Xavier?"

The big Frenchman stroked his chin. "More room to move. Setting up the first Martian food farm. But I still have Maryse and the girls on my mind, back there on that precious dot." His eyes welled.

"Xanthe?" Troy asked gently.

She had her face turned to the mesmerising blue orb quickly fading from sight. She turned now to face her colleagues. "Honestly, I'm not looking forward to anything on Mars. I used to dream of leading the first expedition, but now? I just wanted to stay on Earth and help there. Do my bit and be done. But here we are."

Troy felt the mood dip. "Surely there's something?" he nudged.

"Actually—yes," she said.

His face brightened.

"I brought some of Jack's ashes. I'd like to release his stardust to Mars."

A leaden weight settled in the group; vivid images flashed of the mother-and-son reunion cut short by violent tragedy.

Xanthe turned back to Earth; the others hung silent in their little circle.

Troy drew a breath. "I'm looking forward to the adventure—the majesty of Mars, the miracle of humans planting seeds of a possible next home. It's daunting, and I'm humbled. I'm also grateful for each of you. I hand-picked this crew, and I'll serve you as commander, doctor"—he glanced at the back of Xanthe's head—"and friend."

Xanthe swivelled and met his gaze but said nothing.

Serena craned her neck. "I think that's it. There she goes."

They strained to catch the last glimmer of blue—then it faded into the star-shot darkness.

CHAPTER TWENTY-SEVEN

"Discourse strengthens; division weakens."

—Troy Bruin
MARS MANIFESTO

NYX ODYSSEY: TROY

Flight Day 31

THE NEXT DAY, Troy prepped the handover with Xanthe. As the deputy commander, she'd kept their interactions cool and professional, despite his subtle overtures of friendship. It was exasperating and taxing at once.

He longed to press rewind on their relationship—to start over, to rekindle the intimacy they'd shared on the Moon before Jack's death sent her down a grief-filled path. The chasm had widened after Troy's rescue of Jonas from the Moon, and things hadn't gone well since.

Shoving these thoughts aside, he pulled himself hand-over-hand into the flight deck capsule to review the flight path and long-range scans.

"Xanthe," he said.

She looked up from the captain's chair.

"Can we run through the course-correction protocols for this next leg?"

"Of course," she replied coolly. She shifted in her seat and sat up straight, businesslike.

He slipped into the neighbouring chair and strapped in. She'd already brought up the long-range scanner display.

"Looks like a clear path for the next ten days," Troy began. "Then we've got this little cluster here." He pointed to a smear of specks.

"Yes, yes, I know. Possible meteoroid field," Xanthe said. "Athena told me." Her fist unclenched, and she wiped it on the soft grey of her cargo pants.

Troy suppressed a sigh. Her Athena ThinkLink was a vital edge for them all, but it rattled his sense of inadequacy.

"Right. You'll just need to watch potential course corrections, booster burns and fuel impact."

"Yes, yes, I know." She caught a breath, then decided against saying more.

"Great," he answered breezily, masking his angst. "Jonas thinks the sleep pod's fixed. Nyx confirms all sensors; we've replaced every catheter and printed extra needles just in case."

"Good. I'm ready to take command, Commander," she said, the edge unmistakable.

The navigation display changed back to the local view, triangulating the ship's position relative to Earth and Mars, distance travelled and distance to destination scrolling endlessly.

Troy's face slipped. "Xanthe, I—"

"What?" she asked, dismissive.

"I'm sorry that Aryanna chose me to command this expedition."

Xanthe rolled her shoulders before replying. "You didn't have to accept, did you?"

He stared at his hands. "No. But I wanted this assignment.

And though I knew you wanted it too, Aryanna was never going to appoint you—you know that."

The red LEDs from the display washed Xanthe's face in an angry glow.

"Oh, I know Aryanna has a thing against me—undermining bitchiness of an older woman."

"I don't think she's bitter, but—"

"No? Excluding me after Colonel Jin specifically requested me as captain is spiteful."

"Perhaps," Troy said. "But here we are."

"Yep, here we are," Xanthe replied in a bored tone.

"Xanthe, what can I do? I'm working my hardest to lead, yet you fight me all the way."

"I'm not fighting you, Troy."

"Then what is it?"

"I'm tolerating you."

"Tolerating me? Is it that bad?"

"Yes. It is 'that bad'. Since you came back from the Moon, after rescuing Jonas…" She struggled to find words. "All that fanfare, then trotting round with all those—*women*…" Xanthe paused to suck back her venom but failed. "Back to the good old days, Troy the playboy."

Colour crept up Troy's neck; the ship's hum seemed to drown his thoughts.

"And then finding out you have a daughter. Why didn't you trust me enough to tell me?" She fiddled with the flight manifest pencil.

Troy shifted in his seat. "Shame. I was ashamed. I let my twin brother take on the father role while I went on to a life of celebrity. It got harder and harder to think about parenting. Gemma seemed happy with him and his partner, so we just carried on."

"Do you regret it?" Xanthe asked quietly.

"I regret many things." He stared out the portal.

"Is that why you date so many women? To drown out regret?"

The jab wrenched him from memory; emotion spiked. "Why do you care?" he said at last. "You made it clear it was over."

Xanthe's mouth fell open, then shut again. "You're right. All over, Red Rover. I've no right to comment on your"—she waved a hand in search of a word—"affairs. So, I'll put it behind us and focus on the task ahead."

"Great," he answered coldly. "Let's do that."

❧

Troy left Xanthe on the flight deck, his mood sour.

Shake it off. You're heading into the freezer. Headspace matters.

He started his breathing routine as he pulled himself down the ship's corridor. He paused at the crew quarters, securing his journal and belongings before donning the freezer sleep suit. Xavier and Madison had already completed their prep and were waiting in the torpor bay along with Serena and Jonas, who would put them under.

As he pulled himself along the length of the ship, he checked everything was in place. The familiar hum of the life support system rattled happily. The air recycler whirred and thumped. Though the kitchen galley was immaculate, no doubt the result of Xavier's diligent ministrations, there was a pervasive fug lingering from dinner. A bizarre mix of Indian spice and roast beef. Personalised nutrition often meant a clash of odours, difficult to clear in an enclosed atmosphere. He hoped the charcoal stack would neuter the curry-beef mash while they 'slept' for two weeks.

Floating through the medbay, he noticed the storm shelter panels were loose and tightened their straps. He shot through the exercise pod, wrinkling his nose at the body odour scent, barely masked by the liberal use of antiseptic.

Volkov was recharging in the workshop, eyes closed, body rigid.

Much better looking than the original, Troy thought, impressed yet again by Jonas's adaptations of the bot.

He slowed down as he entered the green lab, the air moist and heavy with the scent of foliage, the tiny plants budding under their grow globes. Everyone's favourite spot, aside from the cupola. The soft green reminder of Earth and the only natural splash of colour in their artificial tomb.

Cylinder, not tomb, he reminded himself. Words were weapons; self-sabotage was the enemy.

Holding the rail, he breathed slowly, peering in awe at the tiny fronds. A surge of gratitude went through him for their interplanetary companions.

He drifted towards the torpor chamber. As he levered the door open, a sharp whoosh of cold air washed over him, and anxious voices brought him up short.

"Madison, relax," Serena intoned as she held the other woman's shoulders pinned to the bulkhead.

Madison gulped, shaking.

Xavier sat up in his pod as Jonas stopped securing the fluid lines.

"Mad Dog, you got this," Jonas said and pulled himself over to them, alongside Troy.

"What's happening?" Troy looked at Serena.

"Madison's nervous about the sleep pod after Jonas's experience."

Troy moved in front of Madison. "Madison, we've done the checks; the pod is fine."

She nodded, chest heaving. Her breath hung in vapour crystals, goosebumps prickling the exposed flesh of her wrists.

"Walk me through it, Madison. You know the drill." Troy's voice was firm, hoping to reboot her military discipline.

She took a few steadying breaths and nodded. She climbed into the pod and lay down so Serena could secure her. One strap went over her waist, then another around her chest, but she bolted upright.

"I can't! I can't!"

"Sedatives?" asked Jonas, looking on.

"Can't. It will interfere with the torpor solution," Troy said.

"I'm sorry. I can't," Madison said, shaking her head. Serena fetched a water bottle and she took it, hands trembling.

"Maybe she sits this one out?" Jonas suggested.

"That will put a lot of pressure on our supplies," Xavier said from his pod.

Pod lights glowed while the vitals monitors blipped in the hush, haloing Madison's trembling form. The ship's cooling systems whined as they adjusted the temperature with the extra bodies in the small space.

"I could take her shift," Jonas offered.

Heads spun to consider him.

"You just had a near miss, Jonas," Xanthe's voice cut in over the ship comm. Troy stifled his annoyance at her interference. "Are you sure you'd be up for it?"

"I'm good. I did all the checks myself along with Volkov. I'm confident of this sucker." He tapped the pod cover with a smile. "Besides, I'm up to date with my work list. I can afford another nap."

"Maybe just a week?" Serena suggested. "Give Madison some time to work through the anxiety?"

"I'll be fine," Madison said, waving a trembling hand.

"Mad Dog, you're not fine." Troy tapped the pulsing red bar on the holo readout. "You can't go into torpor in this state."

"I agree." Xanthe pulled herself into the room and hooked a toe under Madison's bed railing, nudging Troy in the cramped space. He tried not to flinch. "Jonas could go in for a week, as Serena said. That will give Madison a bit of time to refocus."

"I don't like it for Jonas," Troy said. "He's had a big episode not three days ago. This could add undue stress to his system."

"Athena says his biomarkers are recovered. Good to go for torpor." Xanthe smiled at Jonas. "He's the easiest one to swap out considering the workload and duties at this stage of the trip."

Goddamn it, thought Troy. She was right. But Jonas had barely recovered. An image of Jonas choking flashed through his mind. He drummed fingers on the sleep pod rail.

The crew stared at him, waiting. An ice-pump ticked like a metronome.

"Madison, let's do the wind-down routine," he said.

She nodded, determined. Together they went through the visualisation and breathing exercises she'd learned from Troy at the New Baths of Caracalla all those years ago. She lay back again, Troy strapping her in, voice soothing, while the others hovered, willing her on.

Troy fixed the suit catheters and primed the drip for the freeze solution.

Alarms screeched and Madison ripped out the IV.

"I can't. My Mom."

Troy released the straps and held her as she sobbed.

"Okay, Madison, it's okay," he said.

"Troy…" Xanthe shot him a look.

Troy nodded and tamped down his empathy. Leadership needed compartmentalisation right now.

"Jonas—prep for freeze, one-week roster. Madison—you're in therapy and rehab with Nyx. You've got to get this sorted."

They surged into action as Troy slipped into his sleep pod, offering Xanthe a thin-lipped smile while she clipped his lines and he closed his eyes. Sedatives pooled in his veins, chased by the icy hibernation fluid.

Madison would rise or break in those seven days; now it was Xanthe's turn to keep them alive.

CHAPTER TWENTY-EIGHT

*"Is leadership glamorous? Leadership is relentless. Everything
is high stakes, high consequence. All the decisions…
it's exhausting. There's no glamour. Only guts."*

—**Xanthe Waters**
MEMOIRS FROM MARS

NYX ODYSSEY: XANTHE

Flight Day 38

Strapped into the captain's chair on the flight deck, Xanthe pressed the heels of her hands into her eye sockets. Her head pounded.

What a day.

After a solid week of therapy, and plenty of off-the-record chats, Madison finally agreed to return to the freezer. Xanthe had also secretly granted Madison extra data dumps so Madison and her mother could message back and forth. Madison's relief was palpable with each video recording.

Arlene, despite having a 'days to live' prognosis, was still fiery and alert. Reassured, Madison was ready.

First thing that morning, Xanthe had followed Madison and Serena down to the torpor bay. While they watched Jonas cycle out of his pod, the hatch had glitched, sending their adrenaline through the roof. The lid had groaned, stuck. Xanthe had counted one-one-thousand, two—and then the lid spat vapour and popped.

I swear this ship is playing practical jokes.

"*I assure you the Nyx has no such proclivities,*" Athena said.

Maybe it's you then? You bored, Athena?

"*Not at all. Humans are an infinite source of amusement.*"

Xanthe smiled at that.

She flicked open the exercise bay log. Serena had guided Jonas through reanimation like a pro. He was right on schedule, all physical and emotional milestones intact.

Except for that one.

She tapped the orange marker.

Persistent headaches.

They all had headaches.

Sleep was hard.

Drinking enough of the flat recycled water was hard.

Eating the freeze-dried food was hard. It lacked taste and texture.

God, she missed a good cracker.

She could hear Xavier's voice: "Crickets give good crunch."

That reminded her—she'd promised to check in on the cricket farm, make sure the little guys got a serve of fresh leaves from the hydroponic crop.

These insects were to be the first livestock on Mars and their primary source of protein during the long two years on the planet.

Just two hundred and twenty-one days to go until landing.

Xanthe yawned and stretched her legs out, loosening the seat strap so she floated a little. She really should get to bed. The other two had showered and hit their quarters over an hour ago.

She unclipped fully and drifted up into the cupola, the black nothingness greeting her. She shivered despite the warmth of the constant temperature.

Consoles thrummed below; corridor strips glowed a sleepy cobalt.

But up here, gazing out into the great no-thing, the impossible never-knowingness crept through her soul like ice crystals on glass.

Ping.

"Data burst 327. Shall I open, Deputy Commander?" Nyx asked.

Xanthe hesitated. Should she wait until morning and share with the others? Data dumps were always a highlight. Curiosity niggled at her; she tumbled forward in the cupola to pull herself back into the captain's chair.

"Go ahead," she replied.

Mission Ops Bulletin: *Nyx Odyssey* showing lag in transit. Review of system power use advised. Spaceward Bound *Pinnacle* has executed an unscheduled mid-course burn; new arrival ETA = 20 days ahead of *Nyx Odyssey.* We are working on scenarios. Advise the same on your side.

Twenty days! Ellison just shaved six-million kilometres off their arc… How the hell did they carry enough xenon for that? Even a double-length xenon tank could only shave five days, not twenty.

Helium-3.

Lincoln had created a helium-3 engine and siphoned up Lunar Commission supplies. It was the only explanation. Xanthe's pulse raced. Lincoln would scoop their landing spot and seize the Dopplebot base. Their mission would be over before they even got there. The whole trip a waste. Should she get Troy out of the freezer?

She rubbed her temples then reached for the animation control button on Troy's sleep pod. The screen showed his face, smooth and peaceful in its chilly incubator.

No, she was in charge. She could handle this. That was the whole point of the rotation—to give people a break.

Athena, run scenarios for Pinnacle burn, and landing site and possible Nyx countermeasures.

The pressure surged in her head, an icepick behind her eyes.

"Ow! Athena, use the ship's computer for processing. That hurts like hell!" Xanthe groaned, a hand reaching for the ThinkLink portal at the back of her neck.

"Apologies, Xanthe. That should not have caused a disturbance. It's just a regular processing load. Swapping to the Nyx system now."

The pain eased instantly as Athena shifted computation ports.

That's weird, Xanthe thought. Was the BCI deteriorating? The thought tugged at her. She filed it for later investigation and turned back to the report.

Mission Ops Bulletin: Policy Note – Mars Accord debates continue over Piracy Law application off-planet. No resolution yet.

Xanthe scoffed. Whatever resolution they came up with, it would mean diddly squat on Mars. It was finders keepers regardless of political wrangling. They needed boots on the ground first, secure access to the Dopplebot base and then Tang's tech.

She scanned the mission bulletins for any updates on Tang or Human Habs—nothing. She clicked on the crew feed, OpenNet Trending Digest.

Her blood ran cold at the headline: War #PrimaAqua vs #PoSecco as Mediterranean water rights treaty collapses – riots in Naples.

Tears welled. They had it all sewn up! The agreement really was good for everyone. What had caused the breakdown?

People were so disappointing.

"Hey." Serena, bleary-eyed and in her sleep suit, pulled herself into the seat next to Xanthe. "I heard the data dump ping. Anything from Max?"

Xanthe winced. It had been weeks since Serena had heard anything from her partner at Terra Verdi. The data dumps had been squeezed for transit and ship analysis. And Madison's priority comms.

"Haven't checked."

"News?"

Xanthe filled her in. Serena was instantly alert.

"War at Po Secco! Was Max there? Are you sure there's nothing?"

"No reports from Po Secco or Terra Verdi. I'm sure they're fine. We would have heard otherwise," Xanthe said, not feeling the reassurance her voice conveyed.

Serena scanned the data stream headlines in brooding silence, running her fingers over the oxygen mask clip Max had given her, counting its divots like prayer beads.

"You waking Troy?"

"No need. Athena's working on scenarios," Xanthe replied steadily.

Serena eyed her with a cool gaze. The air recycler thudded and whirred.

The hair on Xanthe's nape prickled. "What?"

"You ought to be a little nicer to Troy."

"Nicer?"

"You're a little short around him."

Xanthe shifted in her seat before looking away.

"He's trying really hard." Serena put a hand on Xanthe's. "And he's doing a good job."

Xanthe closed her eyes. Her head was still pounding.

When she opened her eyes again, Serena was still staring earnestly at her.

"I'm listening. I hear you. But Troy needs to listen, too."

Serena rolled her eyes. "You two need to sort your shit out, honestly." She pulled away and peered at the data dump display. "Mind if I check for personals?"

"Go ahead." Xanthe rubbed her temples, looking around for her water bottle. She found it strapped to the seat and took a long slug.

Serena scrolled through the list. "One for Madison. One for Xavier. Another one for Madison. And another one?" Serena glanced at Xanthe and frowned. She scrolled some more, the frown deepening. "Why does Madison have so many data dumps? Over twice the usual allocation!"

Xanthe gritted her teeth and shifted again in her seat. "I gave Madison extra data so she could connect with her mother."

Serena's face contorted. "I see," she seethed. Turning back to the screen, she scrolled furiously and tapped hard at her own data dump tab, cheeks blotchy.

Xanthe groaned inwardly. She did not want to deal with Serena's huff.

Athena, any progress on the scenarios?

"Almost there, Xanthe. Assessing best course of action now."

Serena leaned back from the screen, staring out the viewport, her emotions spent. "Last message—a few weeks ago—" she said through gritted teeth, "Max said he was worried about the riots. They had to turn away twice the usual number of refugees, and it was getting pretty hairy. Now, war?"

They shared a disheartened look. Earth was a long way away. And they were here in this floating tube while people struggled and died.

Serena readied to move, then paused. "Xanthe, I get why you gave Madison the extra data, I really do. But playing favourites? That's not cool. We've all got our hearts on Earth."

Serena pulled away and left the jab hanging alongside the whirr of the display monitors.

Xanthe sighed. *This goddamn job.*

"Xanthe, I have the scenarios."

How does it look?

"The choices are between bad, more bad and very bad."

Great.

Xanthe sat up and swigged some water from the bottle, then Velcroed it back to the chair.

Let's go through them.

CHAPTER TWENTY-NINE

"You ask me about ethics as if it's a dispensation from God. Ethics are values wrestling; why do you get to decide which one wins?"

—CLAIRE EDWARDS
TRANSCRIPT FROM LUNAR
COMMISSION DEPOSITION

EARTH FIRST SECRET BASE: CLAIRE

Flight Day 40

CRACK! THE JUDGE'S gavel echoed through the courtroom. Claire Edwards flinched though she watched it on Earth First's livestream, sloshing her scalding coffee onto the dirt floor. Solar lights flickered against the tin roof of her forest hideout, cricket song strident in the cool evening air.

Her private tablet read, "Po Secco Death Toll Rises to 38."

Her old mentor, Maja Garcia, took the stand in the countersuit against Lincoln Ellison over the water filter patent.

She looks worn out, thought Claire, leaning forward to study the familiar face.

Claire sipped the coffee, enjoying the burnt aroma. The others were away on a mission, setting up a helium-3 generator for a struggling eco-refugee community that had pledged to switch all their power to the stolen supply.

Not stolen. Earned.

Claire listened to the proceedings as she reconciled accounts and checked progress on their various helium-3 power projects.

Changing one community at a time. Pride bristled in her chest.

Voices from the livestream buzzed through the cheap speakers like wasps.

"Maja Garcia, is it your testimony that the nanotube technology is a genuine product of Aryanna Industries?"

"Yes."

"And you are responsible for the implementation of this technology at Po Secco?"

"That is correct."

"You are the signatory of the Po Secco and Prima Aqua accord?"

"Yes. Myself and Gustav Ranchero."

Claire's ears pricked and she spun to stare at the screen. Gustav Ranchero was one of Lincoln's men; she was sure of it. She'd heard his name a number of times when she met with Lincoln.

She stabbed the volume icon.

"The accord required immediate notice to Prima Aqua, correct?"

The prosecutor, all pinched lines and sharp angles, read over the top of his notes in a slow, controlled voice.

"Yes, that's what we agreed." Maja was calm as a river.

"Is that what happened?"

"Well, yes..."

"Yes or no, Ms Garcia?" Voice sharp now.

"Yes, we notified Prima Aqua when the filters were installed."

"But not right away, isn't that so? You installed the filters and drew down from Prima Aqua's groundwater, causing a shortage in their compound, isn't that right?"

"That was not our intention."

"But that's what happened. You stole water."

"I wouldn't say 'steal'—"

"Water shortages spark fury, correct?"

"Yes."

"Gaia caused water shortages in this instance, correct?"

Maja pursed her lips. Then said, "Yes."

"So, Po Secco—and Gaia Enterprises and thus, Aryanna Industries—are therefore responsible for the riots that followed. Yes?" The prosecutor rapped the balustrade with his notes, eyes large, penetrating.

"Objection. Badgering the witness, your Honour."

Claire blew a long breath. She knew this playbook. It had Lincoln written all over it. He'd had his man, Gustav Ranchero, either by coercion, manipulation or bribery, stir up trouble at Prima Aqua.

And now this lawyer was hanging it on Maja.

Lincoln goddamn Ellison. He had power sewn up with the helium-3 sweetheart deal. He had seized Victoria Tang with her help and was on his way to control the air tech. And he had good enough water filter tech. Why bother with this Po Secco squabble?

Did he really need to go and screw these people over? Aqua Prima was not much better off than Po Secco, both dusty struggle towns. More people dying for corporate control.

Claire ground her teeth. Not for the first time, she rued her deal with Lincoln.

Maybe there was something she could find out to rein him back in.

She shoved the coffee aside. The master tablet snapped open with its encrypted server, and Claire went to work, shoulders tight.

She had a backdoor into Lincoln's files through their private comms channel. She never fully trusted Lincoln—who would?—so she had one of Earth First's tech boffins install some high-tech software. A few deft encryption slingshots later, Claire unearthed Ellison's 'Special Assignments' directory…

PRIMA AQUA AGREEMENT, HELIUM-3 ENGINE, CONDOR FAILSAFE.

"Let's see what you're up to, Ellison," she whispered, clicking the first file.

CHAPTER THIRTY

"We plan for survival, not just for today but for tomorrow."

—**Xavier Consus**
MARS MANIFESTO

NYX ODYSSEY: XAVIER

Flight Day 46

THE WATER FILTER alert flashed red, klaxon blaring.

"*Putain!*" Xavier cried, hauling himself along the hydroponics growth baubles over to the console. Beads of water trembled across the touch panel like ants.

Flow-rate critical. Thirty-six hours and potable water drained.

This was bad. Very bad.

He shook his head. First full day after the freezer on the full-crew shift change. His brain was still a tiny bit slow.

"Xavier, report." Xanthe's voice boomed over the comm.

"Water leak. I'm on it," he shouted.

His heart rate spiked as he ran through options. Blockage in the filter? He toed over to the irrigation pipe and pulled the filter plug, scraping fingernails over the bio-slime.

"Drink up, *mes petits!*" He cooed to the tiny plants, smiling as the recycler dropped a pitch and the siren shut.

The siren wailed again. Still critical. His heart thudded, mouth dry.

Serena swept into the space, hair damp from her post-workout shower, pulse monitor blinking on her wrist.

"Micro-fracture in the feeds?" she asked, gliding past him to examine the pipes.

"I think clog in the filter." He pulled out the next plug and dragged fingernails through the slime.

Serena flicked on a UV torch; watery spores bloomed. "Whoa. Not good."

"Xavier, report," Xanthe blasted over the wailing klaxon.

"Hairline crack—"

"—filter clog—" Xavier glared at Serena.

"Impact?"

Xavier put a palm out to Serena to stop her speaking. "If it's a clog, we lose pressure but keep water; if it's a crack, water drains into the hold and we lose it. We will check both." To Serena he said, "I will do a back-flush with compressed CO_2 and clear the filter."

He nudged her aside as he pulled himself over to the protein farm. "First, we need to store the crickets, get them out of the spray zone."

Serena held the storage cache open for him as he slid the transparent boxes with their jumping inhabitants under the bulkhead. Xavier noted her sour look.

"What?" he asked.

"A CO_2 flush might rupture seals. Let's find the crack and patch it first."

Irritation crawled through him. "This might fix it, *non?*" He braced a hose, attached it to the filter plug end. Carbon snow plumed; crystals pinged metal walls.

He watched anxiously as the flow meter returned to spec.

Serena studied the pipes, eagle-eyed. Xavier followed her gaze. A thread of water beaded across the bulkhead, surface tension making mirror globes. "We're not done yet." They followed the leak along the bulkhead. "Xavier, it's the whole damn cartridge."

"Can't be. I serviced it myself last roster. Let me try the flush again."

"No! You might create another fracture! I'm telling you, it's the cartridge."

He grabbed the torch from her and peered into the recess. His heart sank. She was right.

"*Merde!* That's a twelve-hour cartridge swap."

Serena scowled in agreement.

"Can you patch it?" Xanthe's voice crackled.

Xavier shrugged.

"The cartridge needs replacing, Xanthe," Serena said.

"If you patch it, how long will it hold?" Xanthe said.

Xavier and Serena exchanged looks.

"A week if we baby it," Xavier said. A tendril of panic unfurled in his chest.

"Hours if vibrations spike," added Serena.

After a beat, Xanthe's voice returned, lower, flatter: "All hands to galley now. Emergency briefing."

Xanthe headed straight to the galley. The corridor lights glared on the daytime setting. She noted the increased condensation on the handrails. Water seeping fast.

Great. Just what they needed. Fresh out of the freezer on the whole-crew swap days. Pain seared white across Xanthe's eyes.

Athena, is that you?

"Just doing a data update. I'm concerned these routine processes are causing you distress."

Me too. Still waiting for CapCom to come back to us.

The deadline loomed. Just twelve hours left to initiate a burn to catch Lincoln. Losing half a day on the chase was a price she could live with. She was glad she had decided to keep the crew in the freezer after the news of Lincoln's extraordinary burn putting them ahead of the race. This way they'd maintained the roster, spared Troy the fog of a hurried thaw and gave the crew steady hands for the fuel dump needed to catch up to Ellison.

If they agreed. The burn had serious consequences. Time to put options on the table.

Madison and Troy were there waiting, sweaty from their interrupted workout. Serena and Xavier arrived, swapping strategies for the cartridge fix, with Jonas floating Volkov behind him. Troy filled his water bottle as Xanthe anchored a foot around the dining table rail.

Jonas rubbed his temples, eyes bloodshot from reanimation.

Xanthe studied him for a moment. "Jonas—fluids, painkillers, check in later." He nodded. "Good. Here's the situation."

She relayed the *Pinnacle's* surprise move and then added the filter leak update.

"The stakes just shifted. Our grey water loop is haemorrhaging, and we need to change the cartridge—a twelve-hour job. If we wait for that fix, the planets will have inched out of line, so we'd need a whole tanker of propellant to get the same boost than if we burned now, with a fraction of the fuel.

"Second complication: if we fire the burn now, the vibration could blow that crack in the grey water system wide open and we'll be rationing by tomorrow."

"Let me get this straight," Madison said. "We need to do a burn to catch Ellison. Any burn cuts our safety fuel reserves for emergency braking when landing and returning to Earth?"

Xanthe steadied her sideways drift with a grip on the table. "Correct."

"If we wait to fix the cartridge, we'll end up burning even more emergency fuel. And maybe not have enough to get off Mars?" Xanthe nodded. "It's a no-brainer, then."

"If we blow the water valve with the burn, it means water rationing." Xavier poked the table with a finger, his sleeve crusted with slime. "The crops might die, the crickets after that and we starve later."

The air filter thumped as it turned over a gear, labouring with the additional moisture. Water droplets clung to the metal trim.

Xanthe chewed a thumbnail as she considered the crew. Madison straightened her wrist pulse monitor. Serena pulled her hair back into a ponytail to keep it from haloing while Jonas rubbed his eyes. Volkov was clamped to the rail just behind him, no expression. Troy held her gaze, sombre.

Those eyes! Her heart squeezed. She clenched her jaw.

Xavier crossed his arms as Troy turned towards him.

"How confident are you in that patch, Xavier?" Troy asked.

Xavier shrugged, turning his palms to the ceiling. "*Bof!* Best guess? Eight hours if the ship doesn't shake it to pieces."

"We're six who breathe for billions," Troy said quietly. "We can't let Lincoln win. I say we burn now."

Xanthe swallowed. "Who's in for the burn?"

Grim nods.

"We burn." Xanthe shut the briefing holo. "Deep tank kick in ninety minutes. Xavier—we need that filter patched now. Serena—babysit that cartridge like it's our last lung. Jonas—keep Volkov on leak patrol. Madison—I want you in the cockpit monitoring trajectory. Troy—we can brief for command handover. Anything else?"

Volkov raised a finger from his position in the corner.

"Yes, Volkov?" Xanthe asked.

"I don't breathe. Neither does Betty. A more inclusive motto would be nice."

"Really Volkov? Now?" Xanthe said.

"What do you suggest, buddy?" Jonas said as he drifted over to guide the bot from the galley.

"Eight. Eight who burn for billions."

"Somehow I don't think that's going to catch on," Jonas chortled.

"Xanthe, there's a data dump from Maja. About the ThinkLink. Read now?" Athena's voice in the ThinkLink was cautious.

Save for post-burn.

She would deal with that later. First, they'd get the burn done without blowing their water.

⁓

Xavier hauled himself back to the farm bay. The enclosure was ripe with damp heat and the cakey pong of algae. Their future food. If he could keep the leak contained. The crickets could stay where they were for now. Safest place if the water blew too.

As he rummaged for the pipe and filter repair kit, Serena floated next to him.

"I can do this, Xavier. Technically, it's my area—life support systems. Water is central to that."

He raised an eyebrow. "Biggest risk is no more water for food production—*my* area."

"Why do you always do that? Treat me like I'm a subordinate." Her voice hoarse.

"*Bof!* Not true."

Serena yanked a smelting iron from its Velcro patch. "I'm bloody sick of this."

Glancing at her as he ferried the kit over to the cartridge panel, he wondered if this was just a pre-freezer nervous outburst. But she should have her mind on the patch, not politics.

"Help me with this?" he offered with a placating tone.

"Of course."

She seemed to regroup a little. Thank goodness.

They worked in efficient silence, with her holding the torch, handing him tools, and him patching the fracture and reinforcing the pipes on either side.

He checked the time. Three minutes until the burn. "Hope this holds. I'll watch this corner. You take the downline? We can put Volkov upline." Xavier gestured to Jonas, who guided the bot to the other end of the plant pods.

Serena stayed where she was until Jonas disappeared back to the flight deck where he'd monitor engine systems alongside Madison, Troy and Xanthe for the burn.

Serena looked at him coolly. "Next time, let's discuss before you take over."

"Ah, Serena—"

He winced as Nyx signalled 'ready to burn' and she lurched to position.

⁖

Xanthe chewed a thumb as she stared at the monitors, the burn moments away. Jonas tracked the ship functions while Madison studied the telemetry, responding to burn commands from Nyx with a practiced hand.

Troy sat next to her, face grim. She and Troy had agreed they'd officially hand over command after the burn, given she'd been across the detail from the beginning. He'd been unusually gracious about it.

"Thruster warm-up," Nyx said.

The hum built like distant thunder. Xanthe gripped the armrests as the ship vibrated, rattling teeth.

Where were the alarms? The ship should have had sounded the warning siren. She exchanged looks with Troy and Madison as the ship groaned. Xanthe leaned towards the gauges to see if there was something amiss.

And then, just as she was about to call abort, the siren wailed like someone daydreaming being startled to attention.

"Commander, we are go for burn," Madison said, voice elevated.

"Roger that," Xanthe replied. "Crew—brace. Three…two… one…Go!"

Madison tapped the release button.

Engines kicked in. The ship boomed and thrummed. The pungent smell of fuel shot through.

Xanthe's eyes tracked the telemetry alongside Madison as she was pressed back in her seat.

An alert blared; Jonas shut it down.

Forty-five seconds to go.

Hard to breathe. Noise squeezed through her very pores.

She rolled her head to watch the water levels. She blinked hard to see through the rattling. Couldn't see.

Athena—report.

"Water pressure dropping."

Patch?

"Holding. New leak in the shower grey water recycler."

Bad?

"Tank at fifty percent."

God damn it.

The ThinkLink spiked like ice, Athena drawing cycles again. She groaned, grabbing her head.

The burn cut and they flopped forward, silence an overwhelming relief.

"Xanthe? You alright?"

She felt Troy's hand on her back as she panted through the pain. It ebbed and she sat up again with a weak smile. "I'm alright."

His crystal blue eyes held hers, flooded with concern.

"You sure?"

"Yeah." She shrugged him off and hit the comm.

"Xavier, Serena—report?"

Xavier's voice crackled on the comm. "Commander, we need to shut down the shower leak ASAP. Patch held. Lost about three quarters of a tank into the hold. We can probably use the wet vacuum to salvage most of it."

"Cancel your dance card folks," Serena piped up. "Between the cartridge swap and the shower leak, we're in for a late night."

"Madison, telemetry?" Xanthe asked, rubbing the back of her neck.

"On track, slightly ahead of the mapped route."

Xanthe ripped the Commander's patch from her shoulder and slapped it on Troy's Velcro tab.

"Your turn."

CHAPTER THIRTY-ONE

"Waste nothing, value everything."

—SERENA FOX
MARS MANIFESTO

NYX ODYSSEY: TROY

Flight Day 60—Commander Troy Bruin, log

I FINALLY HAVE ten quiet minutes before the crawl-tube lights dim. Last night of command shift before we hit the freezer again tomorrow. I know Xavier, Madison and I are looking forward to the break. It's been a long two weeks.

1. Water system—status and scars

Day 46 feels like a year ago, yet the smell of scorched polymer still burns. We ended up stripping both water cartridges after Serena botched the initial swap, steam sterilising every panel, and cannibalising spare parts intended for the return leg. Xavier was furious. He's still grumbling about it.

The grey water leak was more problematic, trying to catch water droplets in the confined space before they disappeared into various nooks and crannies. We are ultra-careful with water after our reserves took such a hit. We adopted Serena's three-sip rule (no casual gulping outside mealtimes), and so far no one has cheated. Even Xavier pours the dregs of his coffee back into the reclaim bag like it's holy water. Good sign.

Serena's guilt hasn't eased even with two weeks in the freezer. She checks the filter pressure every third breath and still jumps when someone jokes about "pond scum lattes". I've scheduled her for a mandatory half-shift off the monitors tomorrow, though I doubt she'll take it without a tussle.

2. Crew dynamics—observations

- ***Xanthe*** *is pushing through headaches that spike whenever the ThinkLink updates. She insists they're "low grade", but I've logged three occasions since she got out of the freezer two days ago where she stopped mid-sentence and pinched the bridge of her nose. Will run a full neuro scan once power margins allow.*

- ***Jonas*** *oscillates between hyper-focus and a thousand-yard stare. The silent alarm during the filter failure triggered buried EVA memories; he hides it behind busywork. I've suggested to Xanthe that she team up with him on nav diagnostics—structured tasks seem to settle him.*

- ***Madison*** *remains the ship's serotonin pump. Her daily "space-barista" ritual (rehydrated cocoa frothed with a syringe) is keeping morale afloat. She's fielding delayed family vidmails, which makes me worry the next comms outage will hit her harder than she admits. Arlene seems to have rallied these last two weeks, which will make it easier for Madison to get in the freezer this time.*

- ***Xavier*** *snores through anything shy of a hull breach, yet he's logged the most uninterrupted maintenance hours on the* *farm. The man talks to tomato vines like they're puppies—and yields are up 6 percent. I'll take eccentric over lazy any day.*

- **Serena**, *as noted, is living in the life support bay. I've caught her running unlabelled data pulls during off-peak. Not sabotage—more likely a private project—but the extra bandwidth is flirting with our power budget. Need a tactful chat before it becomes a confrontation.*

- **Volkov.** *The bot remains caustic but completely reliable. I'm actually glad we have him along. It was worth the weight sacrifice.*

Overall mood sits at cautious but cooperative. Not a bad two months into eight and a half.

Troy chewed the end of his pen. Two months. It felt like five years. And only a few messages from Gemma all this time. Since the surprise meeting with Xanthe, Troy had tried to build a stronger bond with his daughter. But who was he trying to fool? After thirty years as an absent parent, to want sudden connection was a tall ask. At least he was trying.

He sipped some tea from a pouch and resumed his scribbling.

3. Ship systems—lingering gremlins

- *Power rails show occasional micro-dips at shift change; root cause still elusive. Jonas blames ageing converters, Serena blames "background noise", I blame both and keep one hand on the manual bypass.*

- *Autonav required a 0.12° trim yesterday—tiny, yet larger than drift models predicted. Xanthe'll run a deeper star-tracker calibration next comm window.*

- *Radiation monitors pinged twice last night with minor solar-particle upticks; shelter drill time shaved to seven minutes—best yet.*

4. Next up—controlled normality

I'm thinking of a crew movie night on the next shift changeover. Yes, entertainment burns watts, but shared laughter is always a winner.

Xanthe? Professional as always. She does think a little differently to me and I've found I've had to spend a few days sorting through her decisions at the start of my shift to get things the way I like. It's stupid, I know, but it bugs me.

In the meantime, I've got half a mug of lukewarm cocoa. It tastes faintly of iodine, and I've never been more grateful for it. Tomorrow I might

Troy paused as the comms beeped.

"Hey *mon ami*, you awake?" Xavier's voice piped in the Commander's lapel comm.

"I am now. What's up?"

"We have crickets loose on the farm. I need some hands."

"Kidding, right?"

"*Mais non!* Ever tried to catch a cricket? *C'est chiant.*"

Troy sighed. "On my way."

CHAPTER THIRTY-TWO

"Look after each other. We're all we've got."

—Jonas Seaborn
MARS CULTURE CODE

NYX ODYSSEY: TROY

Flight Day 74

Troy grabbed his sleeping bag on the way to the galley. Movie night. Change-over day entertainment was always crude but fun, and he'd insisted they do something social together for once. He launched off the handrails into the galley; the crew already hung in their slings like kangaroo joeys. The smell of buttery popcorn perked him up immediately. He spied Jonas tucking in.

Xanthe massaged her temples beneath the dim lounge lamps. A pang of worry pricked Troy—she'd been hiding headaches for days. He'd have to insist on a full medical before hitting the freezer again tomorrow.

Madison floated past with a fluid pouch, steam escaping from its valve.

"Hot choccie?" she offered.

"Lifesaver," Troy said, sliding into an empty sling and pulling the sleeping bag over his lap.

At the front, Serena fussed with a compact holo-projector.

"It's Casa-blanket time!" she announced, mangling *Casablanca*.

To Troy's right, Jonas tapped restlessly on his tablet between mouthfuls of popcorn. Xavier snored in a corner net, blissfully unaware.

Madison slipped into the next sling, tablet stowed for the moment. Serena clipped the projector into a ceiling mount. The image shimmered then stabilised—just.

"How old is this file?" Madison asked.

"It's a classic," Serena shot back. "Ageless."

A faint whine bled from the power converter—half a semitone too sharp. Jonas's head snapped up.

"What is it?" Troy murmured, leaning over to grab a handful of popcorn.

"Something's drawing current." Jonas opened a diagnostic app; numbers scrolled down the screen.

Serena frowned at her console. "Background uploads are clogging the feed," she muttered.

Madison's tablet chimed—an unread ping from her mum. She snapped it shut, but Serena heard it.

"You done checking your personals?"

"Yep. Sorry. Carry on."

Serena jabbed *play* again, and the film rolled cleanly. Troy forced himself to relax, though he kept half an eye on Jonas's display. Amperage high, no alerts. Leave it, he decided. Later.

Halfway through, even Jonas seemed to loosen up, though his foot jiggled against the sling. Xavier snored, woke himself, snored again. Troy yawned behind a fist as the story edged towards its finale.

"Here's looking at—" Bogart never finished.

The screen flared white. Cabin lights strobed. Groans.

"Who blew the electrics? Was that you, Serena?" Xavier crowed.

Face flaming, Serena ducked beneath the console. "Loose mag-plug, that's all."

From his angle, Troy glimpsed her own tablet tucked in a storage box. On Jonas's display, the amperage spiked, then dropped back.

The picture returned; Serena rewound a minute and hit play. Now the soundtrack lagged compared to the actors' lips by half a beat.

"Oh, come on." Madison laughed and scrunched her fluid pouch.

Troy caught Jonas's expression, and his eyes narrowed. That desynchronised audio mimicked the Day 46 alarm cadence with the extra burn. Troy's breathing shortened.

Troy shrugged off his sleeping bag. Xanthe still kneaded her temples while Serena muttered at the projector. Madison flicked open her tablet; a tinny "Love you, sweetheart" leaked out before she slapped it mute.

"Could we not clog the comms again?" Serena snapped.

"Bandwidth Police is on patrol," Xavier grumbled, unstrapping. "I'm turning in."

"I've got this, Xavier." Serena held out a palm to Xavier, glaring. He clipped back in. "Everyone ready?" She eyed each of them.

"Here's looking at you, Serena!" Madison chuckled.

Serena rewound a few minutes, and they watched the rest of the film, glitch-free. At the end, they clapped.

Then the lights flickered—and died. Emergency red washed the galley; a sonorous alert echoed. Troy's stomach lurched.

A diagnostic ribbon scrolled across the bulkhead:

DATA-BUS ERR—PACKET LOSS 14%

Jonas's voice cracked. "Navigation feed rides that data-bus!"

"Damn." Madison hauled herself from her sling. "If we drift six minutes, we'll miss the gravity assist and strand ourselves."

"Not a problem," Troy said, though his pulse hammered. "Probably a surge."

Xanthe straightened, eyes pinched with pain. "Order a system diagnostic," she whispered to Troy.

"*You* need a diagnostic, Xanthe." His hand went to feel her forehead.

"I'm fine." She pulled away.

"You're not."

His brows knit. Was he overstepping? Another flinch from Xanthe and he was resolved. "Jonas, Madison—power check now. Xanthe, medbay."

Xavier drifted by, hitching his sleeping bag. "I'll check the farm—make sure the crickets haven't chewed a cable." He vanished down the corridor.

Troy caught Serena at the console. "That bandwidth spike earlier—what was it?"

"Systems noise," she said, not meeting his eyes.

Xavier's voice floated back. "Noise, *mon cul.* What're you hoarding, Serena?"

She snapped the storage box shut. "Nothing to hide. Want to dump personal logs and see who's really hogging?"

"Later," Troy cut in. "Ship first."

Xanthe was waiting on the medbay ceiling rails, pale, as Troy floated in.

"It's the ThinkLink," she confessed. "When it pulls Earth updates, the packets hammer my head."

"We'll scan anyway," Troy said, guiding her to the diagnostic couch.

"Power's flaky."

"Then we wait two minutes."

The overheads blinked back to full illumination. Madison's voice broadcast through the intercom.

"Power stable, but we've got a bigger issue." A holo slammed to life beside them:

AUTONAV SYNC LOST—MANUAL INPUT REQUIRED

Troy exhaled. "Right. New priority." He squeezed Xanthe's shoulder. "I need a full ThinkLink-sync schedule and pain management plan on my tablet tonight. Water, painkillers, the lot."

He keyed his mic again. "Madison, Jonas—on my way. Let's get the ship back on course."

Xanthe managed a weak nod as he pushed off toward the flight deck, glitchy movie night already forgotten as the new danger flared.

CHAPTER THIRTY-THREE

"Knowledge is power, and power isn't free."

—Lincoln Ellison
MEMOIRS FROM MARS

GAIA HEADQUARTERS: MAJA

Flight Day 90

Maja mopped her brow, shifting from one foot to the other, as Aryanna pored over the flight reports. The holo display beamed 'Flight Day 90'. The Mars expedition seemed to crawl along. It seems like years since the launch, thought Maja.

The air conditioner laboured, vents humming, the boardroom stuffy and sweltering. Everything sagged in the heat: the enormous mahogany table had lost its usual shine; the buffet strained on slender feet with glassware and water jugs beading water. The floor-to-ceiling observation window groaned as the wind stirred howling dust devils.

Maja poked at the sticky holo display console, studying the latest news from Po Secco, their Mediterranean community still struggling after the riots. Her fingers traced the owl and heart charm of her necklace absent-mindedly.

Maja jumped in surprise as Huw Chan burst through the door, face flushed in the heat and shirt rumpled. "Aryanna, Maja. I have news." He closed the door behind him, scanning the corridor for eavesdroppers.

Maja made room for him at the holo display as he slid before the console and punched in access codes to bring up an intelligence report. Maja caught a whiff of perspiration and stale coffee. She frowned. This was very unlike Huw, always so meticulous with his appearance.

"Max and our Po Secco team have found evidence of Gustav Ranchero receiving payments from Lincoln Ellison." Huw clicked a file and images of Ranchero at a crowded cafe popped to life. "Watch this handoff." Huw pointed at an exchange of documents, a gold wrist comm flashing on-screen.

"Lincoln's wrist comm," Huw said, triumphant.

"That could be anyone's, Huw," Maja said, stepping aside as Huw spread some papers on the table.

He waved a dismissive hand. "Lincoln custom codes that gold band. It's unique."

He rifled through the papers. "Plus, there's this." He tapped a document. "Our staffer—see them there on screen—followed Gustav and caught a screenshot of the paperwork." With a flourish, he swiped to another screen and zoomed in.

Aryanna and Maja leaned forward, squinting. A message in blurry letters: "One hundred thousand water credits—L.E."

Maja rubbed the back of her neck, sweat running cold down her spine. She picked up the printout and studied it. That many water credits could save thousands.

Why the riots then?

"Lincoln's giving Prima Aqua water credits?"

"Not Prima Aqua. It's a personal transfer to Gustav." Spittle flew from Huw's mouth. He wiped it, embarrassed.

"That's an astounding amount," Aryanna said quietly, tapping a long finger on the console.

"Exactly," Huw continued. "Enough to stir up trouble. Like rioters." He cracked a fist into his palm.

"Slow down, Huw," Maja said. She wiped damp palms on her sleeves.

The air conditioner heaved and a blast of cold air shot over them. Maja shivered, moved away, pulled out one of the giant chairs and sank into it to think.

Huw strode to the buffet. He poured a glass of water and gulped it down. Then he grabbed a jug and three glasses, thunking them onto the table as Aryanna slipped into the seat beside Maja.

Maja noticed the change in Aryanna at once: her dark eyes flashed, her movements slow and deliberate. She sipped the chilled water, glancing out the window as wind whipped dust in swirls against the observation pane. It pattered like meteorites. The UV index display flickered to 14, dangerous exposure level. Maja's pulse quickened.

"What's the game plan?" she said, turning back to Aryanna.

"Huw, get Max and the team to chase down more evidence at Prima Aqua and Po Secco." Aryanna smoothed the silk of her pantsuit. "Detailed reports of all rioters. Chase the money trail, confirm Lincoln's involvement."

He nodded as he drained another glass of water.

Maja's brows knit together, mind churning in the heat-haze hum. The air smelt of overheated wiring and citrus floor polish. She reached over to prod the holo console. "There is the other matter—the *Nyx*."

The ship's Mars transit lit the display, alongside Lincoln's *Pinnacle*. Her finger traced the arc of Lincoln's ship.

"Athena tracks a boost in the *Pinnacle*'s acceleration here." She circled an inflection point. "With that kick, Lincoln could shave nearly three weeks off transit." They stared at the screen as the air con clunked and rattled, the downdraft dropping a notch in temperature. "Lincoln could hit Mars up to eighteen days ahead of the *Nyx*."

The wind whined and spat grit at the window.

"Has Lincoln done another helium-3 burn?" Aryanna grumbled, staring at the telemetry trajectories on the holo display.

Maja peeled her damp cotton jersey away from her skin. "CapCom Minke thinks that's likely." Maja pointed at the *Pinnacle*'s acceleration point.

"Will he get to Mars first?" Aryanna turned to Maja, black eyes fierce.

"It's possible. There might be more helium-3 aboard." Maja kept her tone calm, masking her inner anguish.

A vein stood at attention along Aryanna's neck. "He must have stolen helium-3 from the Lunar Commission's Moon haul."

Maja shook her head in disbelief. Lincoln broke every Lunar Commission agreement and lied baldly. With a gracious smile.

Aryanna's fists balled. "That man is such a—" She took a deep breath. One hand drifted to her forehead. "It's time we had a chat with everyone's favourite eco-terrorist," she said with a grimace.

"Claire?" Maja asked. Dread slid between her ribs. "Not a sign of her in months."

"Not since Elena Fischer was poisoned," Huw said with a knowing look. He drew a handkerchief from a breast pocket, wiped his brow and smoothed his hair.

Maja flinched as the air conditioner heaved and clunked again, rattling in its brace.

"I'll send Felix." Aryanna smiled. "He loves a good snake hunt."

CHAPTER THIRTY-FOUR

"Resources aren't rights; they're assets. Take them or lose them."

—Lincoln Ellison
MEMOIRS FROM MARS

SPACEWARD BOUND HELIUM-3 LANDING AND PROCESSING CENTRE: CLAIRE

Flight Day 95

CLAIRE PULLED HER breathing mask tighter, one hand on the truck's steering wheel, as it rolled to a stop at Spaceward Bound's security gate. Rocket fuel fumes flooded through the cab as the window slid down. The *Saturnia* still steamed on the landing pad, recently returned from its helium-3 Moon haul.

Though she was confident in her disguise, the credentials her colleague had provided were sketchy, and she breathed deeply to steady her nerves as the guard approached.

His pug-like face, all jowls and slobbery lips, didn't match his crisp and pressed uniform, or the manicured hands sliding the scanner over her pass.

Worry made her hands tremble, but she kept her gaze focused, confident. An icy trickle of sweat slipped down her spine.

The guard scrutinised the pass, eyeing her for half a heartbeat before waving her through.

First hurdle complete.

She popped the truck into gear and headed to the loading platform, the pad clogged with safety techs, engineers and processing boffins. High-vis traffic controllers guided her through the maze with neon batons, whirling like pinwheels in the evening twilight.

She followed the procedure to the letter, just as her operative had reported: back the truck in the loading bay, listen to instructions. The helium-3 transportation was heavily monitored: offloaded from the *Saturnia*, counted into the truck, checked at the waypoint, then stationed overnight with the fleet, ready for armed convoy escort the next day to the various power centres.

Somehow, Lincoln and his cronies were skimming helium-3 at one of these points.

At the loading bay, Claire studied the process in her mirrors. Spaceward Bound techs transferred the helium-3, counting it off. Her knuckles gleamed white as she gripped the steering wheel, waiting for the signal to move out.

She rolled on to the next inspection waypoint, security heavier here with guards carrying machine guns.

Rolling the windows a crack, she strained to hear the count, the movement of canisters obscured by the truck doors. She felt the vibrations, though.

A muffled voice; she leaned against the window, pressing her ear towards the sound. "Twelve canisters in, swapping out four."

Those would be the O2 canisters her operative said they used to replace and move the helium-3 for Lincoln's own projects. Like the booster on the *Pinnacle*.

Completely illegal and against the Lunar Commission and Mars Accord.

She had to see it for herself to be sure. The files she had hacked showed billions of dollars of helium-3 being shifted somewhere out of the Lunar Commission's supply to Lincoln's stash.

What's good for the goose…

Hypocrisy was what it was called. Why should she balk at Lincoln's skimming when she was doing the same, in exchange for criminal activity to keep Spaceward Bound's rivals left behind?

The difference was the ends: the Earth First mission was to restore ecological balance, to dismantle inequality, by boosting downtrodden communities with their own power source.

Robin Hood and all that.

Except now her noble mission felt tarnished, if everything in the files was true. Scenes from Maja's courtroom testimony rushed through her mind. The riot body count was now at sixty.

The minuscule camera stashed in the truck would record it all, and she would have the proof.

Claire studied the process as she followed the controllers and loading bay instructions. When she'd cleared the distribution bay, the techie drummed the door and yelled, "Clear." She returned the truck to the fleet, which was heavily guarded.

Her throat tight, she stepped from the cab, walked around the back and retrieved the camera, tucking the coin-sized disc into her bra under her overalls. One more hurdle: clear security and exit. She checked her wrist display. It would be a squeeze to get out, sneak into the base and hit the hidden tunnel to meet her Earth First colleague, who had brought her bike in with their own scheduled helium-3 collection.

Hands still shaking, she managed to walk with a casual gait towards the exit gate. They scanned her pass, stood in the security scanner and did the DNA swab. She held her breath. Moment of truth—had Jim managed to hack the system and give her a green light?

The swab results glitched. The guard's face crinkled in confusion. Tried again. It glitched a second time.

The guard came out again. "Sorry, gotta do another one."

"No problem," Claire said. "Wanna be sure, right?" She pulled the mask aside again for another cheek swab.

Moments felt like hours. Claire wiped her forehead around the mask, clearing sweat from the visor.

"You're clear, Ma'am."

"Thanks. Have a great day."

Forcing herself to keep a measured pace, Claire left the security hub and walked towards the staff parking lot. So far, so good. Floodlights bleached the carpark to a false noon.

She dived behind a van, gravel biting her palms. Uniform off, she tossed it into the wheel-well. Now only in thin thermals, she scrambled to the fence and reached under it where she'd stashed tools earlier. Wire cutters freed from the bag. Two fierce snips. The fence eased open. She snaked through—shirt snagging then ripping free. Ten metres to the shrubs. Go.

"Claire Edwards."

She froze. A gun muzzle pressed against her ribs.

"What might you be doing out here in the dark?" A man's voice whispered brusquely.

She knew that voice.

Slowly, she turned her head to the man lying under the bushes beside her. The gun pressed harder, a warning.

"Felix."

Her chest swirled with emotion.

"We've got to stop meeting like this, Claire." A wry smile was barely visible in the gloom. "I know where you're heading. But first I have questions."

Claire's mind raced. How did he find her? Who snitched about this op? And more urgently—how the hell would she get away?

"Don't worry, I'm going to let you go. So no shenanigans,

alright? I don't want any unnecessary blood sport. Just do exactly as I say, and you'll be gone before you can say bolt hole."

The gun stayed pressed to the back of her neck as he guided her backwards away from the floodlights, under the shrubs and behind a tall patch of trees in the forest bordering the Spaceward Bound base.

"Put these around your ankles." He handed her plastic zip ties. Her eyes darted everywhere for escape as she did as asked, keeping them a little loose.

"Nice and tight."

The gun was still trained on her. She cinched them a little.

"Roll onto your stomach, hands behind your back." He pressed knees into her hamstrings and lower back and the gun into her neck. He secured her wrists with zip ties before she'd even had a chance to try and buck him off.

Fuck.

He rolled her onto her back and hauled her up against a tree. "Now, talk. What do you know about Ellison's little operation here?"

"Nice to see you too, Felix. It's been a minute." She tested the ties and winced.

"Not here to catch up on old times, Claire. I know what you've been up to these last few years, so no bullshit." He tucked the gun in the back of his pants and crouched in front of her, out of reach of her feet. "Between kidnapping, extortion, a few vicarious deaths and helium-3 stealing, you have a lot to account for. Plenty of folks want to see you hanged."

He tilted his head and the damn smile reemerged.

"I don't happen to be one of them. So—talk."

Claire weighed her options. Felix obviously knew about her helium-3 deal with Lincoln. How? She filed that for later. What could she tell him that would get him out of here?

"What do you want to know? Who for?"

"What are you doing here? You planning to blow this place up too?"

Claire shot hate lasers at Felix as her stomach roiled. She shunted against the tree, pretending to get comfortable while trying to loosen the ankle ties.

"You're on the wrong side of history, Claire. I know you're trying to change the world for the better. I get that. But there's been a lot of collateral damage. Help us stop more of it."

Who the hell was 'us'? Who was he working for?

Aryanna.

The thought hit like a megaton brick.

So that's where he'd disappeared to after the Chinese space base disaster.

Her mind reeled, throwing up thoughts and regrets like seeds in a storm.

"One more chance, Claire, and then I'm pinging security to come and get you. They will be beyond thrilled to catch the notorious eco-terrorist. Haul of the century."

She swallowed hard. "Lincoln."

Felix waited, his stocky limbs coiled and ready as he peered at her.

"He's skimming helium-3."

"How much?"

"Maybe four canisters per truck. I was trying to get proof."

His eyes narrowed. "Why? Things with Lincoln gone south?"

She set her mouth and said nothing, pulling her wrists sideways to stretch the ties.

He dropped a knee to the ground and propped an elbow on the other, hand dangling. "You took Tang, didn't you?" Felix said quietly as the pieces flew together for him.

He rubbed his jaw, thinking.

"Where is she now?"

There was no point in lying. It was all too late anyhow.

"On the way to Mars."

He raised an eyebrow. "Lincoln's really going for it, isn't he? He thought he had the water monopoly all stitched up too, but Aryanna trumped him there. Did you stir up the protests?"

She shook her head, miserable.

"Lincoln did that too, did he? That asshole." Felix stood, ducking behind a tree as voices trailed from the carpark.

"Time's up, Claire." He stooped in front of her. "It's too bad you threw in with Lincoln. Poor choice. I hope you see that now. He wants geomonopolies. Power. Control. And you're his handmaid."

The disgust in his voice punched her in the solar plexus.

"Good luck, Claire." He rose.

"Felix—ties?" She wriggled as he made to leave.

"You're a clever girl. You figure it out."

CHAPTER THIRTY-FIVE

NYX ODYSSEY: TROY

Flight Day 98—Commander Troy Bruin, log

The routine grinds on. There's always something to do—a repair here, a tweak there—and Gaia back on Earth demands daily reports, while sending us daily mission briefs. Still trying to boss us around. But more and more, we feel like we are truly on our own.

The shower has sprung another leak; the iris doors aren't sealing properly. I've kept Jonas out of the freezer for three extra days to fix it. We know how Serena loves her showers and how insufferable she'll be if she comes out of sleep and it's still broken.

Volkov and Jonas are determined to adjust the iris doors without printing a new blade—spare alloy is precious, and who knows what else we'll need it for. There are still many more days to go on this endless trip, caught as we are in the belly of a hundred-metre metal cylinder, slung somewhere between the Sun and Mars, with nothing but black and speckles of stars.

I hadn't realised how destabilising it would be to lose sight of Earth. Like losing sight of the shore with nothing but ocean everywhere you look. Except here, there is no horizon. No up. No down. No direction except what the computers tell us.

At least we have each other. We're family.

Troy paused as thoughts of Gemma swam through his mind. She'd sent him a message, finally. She was starting a world design class. He bristled with pride. Despite his brother Travis's influence, Troy was still her biological father. Surely that counted for something. He shook his head. He was asking too much. Back to the journal.

Shifts stay the same for now. Madison, Xavier and I have fallen into a comfortable familiarity—we echo each other's routines, give each other a wide berth, then share an evening meal and start the next day with coffee and a chat. Madison tolerates my attempts to find out about her and Barrio, but as ever, her guard is always up. Xavier is his usual grump, with a long list of irritations.

Xanthe and I remain cordial. Professional. I swing between longing and resentment. Not great.

Morale is okay. We all cherish our personal data dumps. Especially Serena, who has taken to reading Xavier's Terra Verdi reports so she can suck as much news of Max as possible.

Troy paused, staring at the blank wall of his quarters while floating in his sleeping bag. He cherished these nightly confessions in his diary. Bringing paper was an outrageous luxury—grams he could have spared—but the visceral act of pen on page anchored him. Besides, who counsels the counsellor? A journal was far better than any A.I. persona in the library.

He pondered crew dynamics. Jonas, Xanthe and Serena had

an easy camaraderie he envied. There was something more stilted between him and Madison. A lingering resentment over the freezer incident? She was so embarrassed by that.

Xavier was ever his best chum. Did Madison feel like the third wheel? Maybe he should shuffle the shifts.

The ship's alarm shrieked, jolting him from his cocoon. His pen ricocheted off the bulkhead and smacked him in the forehead.

"Nyx, report," he barked.

"Meteoroid strike imminent. Prepare to take shelter."

"What the hell? Why wasn't this on the radar?"

"Objects too small—only visible when inside nominal-radius field."

"Can we take evasive manoeuvres?"

"I have reoriented the ship to minimise impact."

"And the cupola?"

"It is retracting now."

Troy wriggled free, slid the hatch aside and met Madison in the corridor.

"This sounds bad," she said, hauling herself along the rails toward the flight deck, her usually smooth face wrinkled in worry. Jonas—hair tousled, still in sleeping trunks—followed groggily.

The flight deck flashed red, orange, purple—alerts strobing like a disco, the shrill klaxon killing any sense of excitement. Madison was already strapped in when Troy followed, first confirming the cupola had sealed.

"Nyx, which parts of the ship are most vulnerable?"

"Trajectory shows possible impact to starboard-medial section."

"That's…the repair bay?" Jonas asked, pulling up schematics.

"Repair bay and supply cabin," Nyx confirmed.

"What about the sleep pods?" Madison said. "How vulnerable are they?"

"Direct penetration risk minimal, but decompression or

electrical failure is possible if the hull is breached. I recommend rousing the sleepers and moving all crew to the solar flare shelter."

"We don't have time for full reactivation," Jonas said. "Health risk?"

"They are three days into a fourteen-day cycle. Reanimation time is unchanged; limbs will be weak. Monitor for hypothermia and dehydration while sheltering," Nyx advised.

"How long until impact?" Troy asked.

"Fifteen minutes."

"Let's move," Jonas called, bolting down the shaft. Madison shot after him.

Troy rubbed the back of his neck. He had a sudden and urgent desire to pop an oxy. Something to haul his nerves into line. "Can we outrun it?"

"Unknown particle density ahead. Acceleration may increase hull penetration risk. We'd lower flux but raise impact energy if we sprint."

"So we just sit tight and hope for the best?"

"The hull is reinforced for such incidents. The heat shield is facing forward. The whipple bumper can take a 2-mm hit at 30 kms. Likelihood of penetration remains low," Nyx said.

"That's why you still want us in shelters?"

"Better to be safe than sorry."

"Anything else I should do up here?"

"Negative, Commander. Retrieve your team and start sheltering protocols."

Troy pushed off toward the long tube—mind racing, alarms wailing, ship shuddering beneath the cosmic hail that was now only minutes away.

CHAPTER THIRTY-SIX

*"You know what being alone on the Moon taught
me? Life has no meaning without others."*

—**Jonas Seaborn**
MEMOIRS FROM MARS

NYX ODYSSEY: TROY

Flight Day 98

Troy pulled himself back to the sleeping quarters, slipped on a ship-issue headset and grabbed his crew-top uniform and lapel comms. He wriggled into his light EVA suit as he bumped against the corridor handrails.

"Nyx, broadcast," he said.

"Go ahead, Commander."

"Jonas and Madison, seal each section as you return with the crew. I'll have light EVA decompression suits ready for Xanthe, Serena—and for you two as well. Xavier, secure the farm and get back here to crew quarters now. We have twelve minutes before impact."

"Affirmative, Commander," Madison's voice crackled over the comm.

202

Troy opened Xanthe's cabin first, wincing at the photo of her son Jack and the small container he assumed held Jack's ashes. He located the pouch containing her EVA suit, activated the heating element and repeated the process for Serena's suit. Troy checked the suit bladders—a third full.

With all five light EVA suits in hand, he headed for the galley. Daytime lighting was dimmed to emergency levels as section hatches slammed shut. Madison and Jonas were struggling to manoeuvre Serena and Xanthe—both pale, clammy and weak—through the compartment. Xavier followed behind.

Troy thrust a suit to Madison and another to Jonas. Xavier caught the other as it floated free. "Get yours on. I'll start with Xanthe. Serena, if you can, start wriggling into yours."

Serena panted and nodded. As the ship shuddered—stronger than usual?—Troy crouched in front of Xanthe, guided her legs into the suit, then helped her thread one arm and the other into the torso. She gave a ragged nod of thanks.

Serena meanwhile curled into a ball, bouncing off supply cupboards, Velcroed cutlery and a holo display board while fighting her suit. Jonas executed a nimble hand-over-hand swing, anchored his boots on the rail and caught Serena's spin.

"I'll get the legs and pull your pants up for you," he said.

"That's not how it usually goes," Serena managed between breaths.

"You had your chance, Fox. Now hold still." He wrangled her legs into the suit.

Once all five suits were sealed, Troy, Madison and Jonas shepherded Serena and Xanthe to the crew cabins, strapped them into their cubicles and locked their helmets. Xavier sealed the passageway behind them as they moved through. Troy double-checked Madison's and Jonas's restraints, then secured himself.

"Comms check," he said over helmet audio. One by one, the crew answered.

"Nyx, status on Serena and Xanthe?"

"Both show dehydration, low electrolytes, elevated pulse and respiration."

"Serena, Xanthe, sip the suit's nutrition slurry—get any fluid you can."

"There isn't much in mine," Serena replied weakly.

Troy winced. He should have topped up the sleepers' suit reservoirs; hibernation protocol left them dehydrated. "Drink what you can. Nyx, how long until we clear the meteoroid field?"

"Impact window in three minutes."

Three minutes, Troy thought—just get through that. Again, the itch for oxy. He shoved that thought aside.

A yawing whistle reverberated through the ship; sirens blared.

"Hull breach," Nyx announced.

"How big?" Troy's heart pounded. He inhaled to steady himself.

"Assessing damage. Isolating medical bay."

"Let's hope you and Volkov left nothing unsecured," Serena muttered.

"Where is Volkov?" Jonas said. "Nyx—location of Volkov?"

"Volkov is in the recharge bay, machinery room. Electronics in that area are shut down while I evaluate damage."

Scanners flickered. "Breach is approximately one to two millimetres in the medical bay hull," Nyx continued.

"How long until we exit the field?" Troy asked.

"One minute."

Troy forced himself to count seconds. Emergency repair steps scrolled through his mind.

"Troy, activate the repair protocols," Xanthe said, panting wearily into her comm headset.

"I'm on it," he replied, teeth gritted.

"Volkov—I need Volkov," Jonas said, panic rising.

"Volkov's fine," Troy replied.

The whine of escaping air raked through the hull. The ship

groaned and heaved as it adjusted to the change in compression. Objects clattered in one of the far sections.

"Volkov. I've got to get out of here."

"Stay where you are, Jonas. It's alright," Madison said.

Jonas's thrashing rattled his cubicle walls, the sound echoing across open comms.

"Jonas, *mon ami*. Be calm. If anyone can handle a hull breach, it's Volkov, *non*?"

"Alone. Alone. Can't do this alone," Jonas muttered.

"And what are we? Chopped lettuce?" Xavier pounded the bulkhead, giving his neighbour a thudding reverberation.

"Breathe, Jonas," Troy said, willing him to relax. "Breathe."

CHAPTER THIRTY-SEVEN

"Mental fitness is as important as oxygen."

—**MADISON FLOYD**
MARS MANIFESTO

NYX ODYSSEY: TROY

Flight Day 98

THE SOUNDS OF the ship under assault—meteoroids drilling into the hull—tap-danced on Troy's nerves. Over comms he could hear Jonas taking deep, steadying breaths, trying to stabilise his stress response.

"Commander Bruin," Nyx reported. "Serena and Xanthe's vitals are plummeting. They need nutrients now."

"Serena, Xanthe, are you drinking the slurry?" Troy demanded.

"Mine's all gone," said Serena.

"Mine too," Xanthe added. "There wasn't much there."

Damn it, Troy thought. He'd checked the water but not the nutrient slurries. "Have you got anything in your quarters you can eat?"

"Negative," Xanthe replied.

"I don't eat in bed," Serena said. "Besides—helmet."

"Hold tight—there can't be much more of this. Nyx, status of the strike?"

"Nearly clear, Commander. Thirty-two seconds remaining."

A garbled murmur came over the loop. "Who is that—what's wrong?"

"Commander," Madison said, "Xanthe is seizing."

Bloody hell!

Troy weighed hull penetration risk against his colleague's seizure for a fraction of a second before shedding his restraints and bolting for the door. He slid aside the hatch, shot into the hallway and pulled himself to Xanthe's cubicle. Her face was white, eyes rolled back, body rigid in convulsions.

"Nyx, report. What can we administer?"

"Force injection through the suit."

"That'll perforate it! Will the butyl layer handle the puncture?"

"The perforation can be repaired with the suit's self-sealing gel; projected integrity after the patch is 97%."

"Right." Hand-over-hand, Troy reached the shelter's first aid bundle, rifling through it until he found the RescuePen-D10 auto-injector. Back at Xanthe's berth, he steadied himself. "Best option?"

"Inter-muscular, deltoid region," Nyx advised.

Exhaling, he plunged the needle through the fabric into her arm and rammed the plunger home. "Xanthe, it's okay. Give it a moment."

"Commander, we are clear of the meteoroid field," Nyx announced.

"Status of the ship?"

"Atmosphere stable and breathable. Medical bay sealed. You may remove helmets."

Troy popped his gloves, unclipped Xanthe's helmet and called, "Madison, ready a 250mL bag of D5-normal saline, inline micropump set to 60 mL."

"Want me to add an electrolyte push?" Madison asked, hauling herself from her cubicle.

"Checking her levels now," Troy said as he administered a fingertip pinprick for blood panels. He studied the readout for a moment. "Yup. Dial it in."

Troy floated the kit toward her, exposing Xanthe's wrist and probing for a vein. Madison fished out the IV kit and saline bag, then handed it over so Troy could slip the needle into a pale vein. They watched anxiously as her seizure ebbed, then she slumped unconscious.

"Whoa now," Troy said and gripped Xanthe under her neck to open her airway. Her breath fogged on his helmet.

He hadn't been this close to Xanthe in five long years. He cursed himself for leaving his helmet on. The nearness of her now, vulnerable, needing him, electrified his senses. She stirred as the medication took effect and jolted him back to duties.

"Thanks, Madison. Get Serena a dextrose gel pack and do a blood panel with the testing kit. I don't need another seizure today."

"Roger that," Madison said. She fetched a pouch just as Serena emerged, pale and trembling.

"Just in time," Serena muttered, taking it gratefully.

"Hey, I'm stuck!" Jonas said. He thrashed against his restraints.

"Hang on, Seaborn," Xavier soothed and scooted over to his cabin door. Once he slid open the panel, Xavier freed Jonas's helmet, coached him through slow breaths, then unclipped the harness. Together they drifted into the corridor.

Xanthe moaned and opened her eyes. For a fleeting moment, Troy thought he caught a flash of warmth as she stared at him. She groaned and closed her eyes, licking her parched lips, and the fleeting spark of hope washed away in the drone of the ship's air recycler.

Troy fetched a slurry pouch for Xanthe. "Electrolytes and

glycogen crash," he explained as she drank. "We didn't have time for full reactivation."

She eyed the injection mark. "Inter-muscular?"

"Yeah. We'll patch the suit over the self-sealant."

"The ship?" she asked.

Nyx answered. "One-millimetre tear in hull; medical bay isolated. No other damage."

"Any more meteoroids nearby?" Troy asked.

"None on near or far scanners."

"Thank God," he breathed. "Next steps?"

"Recommend hull repair: internal panel removal or external EVA. Each presents different risks."

Troy chewed his lip. EVA was the riskiest thing they could do. Radiation exposure, debris and any number of mishaps in executing the mission could end in disaster. Opening up the ship from the inside risked damage to the life support systems and venting even more atmosphere. Repair from the source of impact was the best option, especially as they needed a fully intact hull for a landing on Mars.

With Serena and Xanthe recovering and Troy being the operative medical officer in Xanthe's stead, EVA options shrank to Madison, Xavier and Jonas. Xavier was still too clunky with his leg despite Aryanna's treatment. And Jonas…well, he seemed off-balance today.

"Mad Dog, you up for an EVA?"

Madison nodded, expression calm. "Best route is out the cupola, nose-to-tail traverse, then rear hatch. Saves atmosphere."

"Agreed. You and Jonas sort gear; I'll oversee reactivation here with Xavier."

"I'm fine," Xanthe protested.

"Xanthe, you seized two minutes ago," Troy said gently.

Her face darkened, then she regained her professional veneer. "Okay, Commander."

❧

Madison and Jonas mapped the job: supplies were in the machinery room beyond the sealed medical bay. Madison would apply a temporary patch en route, then return for permanent repairs.

Meanwhile, Troy kept Serena and Xanthe on rehydration and rewarming protocols with Xavier fussing like a mother hen.

"Jonas," Troy called, "get Volkov to assemble repair gear and meet Madison at the rear airlock."

Jonas, still rubbing his jaw, nodded. "Yep—on it." He retrieved his headset. "Volkov, you there?"

"Right where you left me," the bot deadpanned.

"Gather the repair kit and take it to the rear airlock. Madison will be outside."

"Okay," Volkov replied.

❧

Troy checked Xanthe and Serena: they'd made quick strides in their recovery after intensive fluid and food uptake. Once their biometrics stabilised, Troy and Xavier moved them to the kitchen galley—more room for improvised rehab. Troy left them and headed for the flight deck. Madison and Jonas were already suited up, helmets on, reviewing the EVA plan.

"Ready, Mad Dog?" Jonas asked, offering a fist bump.

Madison smiled, bumped back. "Ready to go."

They secured the flight deck for depressurisation. The airlock cycled; Madison climbed into the cupola, pressed the lever and the nose-cone iris peeled open onto the stars.

"Here goes," she said.

Troy and Jonas gave her a thumbs up as she pushed into the void.

From their consoles, they watched her helmet-cam. The EVA required crawling the ship's length along ladder rails, safety lines clipped in place. Her suit carried twelve hours of O_2 and active heating.

"She'll be fine," Troy told himself, chewing his lip.

Jonas strapped into the captain's chair, fingers drumming. Troy sat beside him, eyes glued to the feed. So far, the hull looked unscarred, but Nyx's overlay highlighted the region that had taken the brunt of the meteoroid shower.

Madison reached the impact area.

"She took a fair beating," she panted.

"Slow your breathing, Mad Dog," Troy advised.

"Roger. These suits are clumsy and the heating's a bit much," she replied.

"Better than freezing," Jonas said.

"You're right about that."

"Nyx, analyse surface damage for potential entry risk," Troy ordered.

"Affirmative, Commander."

Soon the sensor spike leapt.

"Ah, there it is," Madison said.

"You see the tear?" Jonas blurted.

"No, dummy—needle in a haystack. Nyx, guidance?"

"The breach is within one metre," the A.I. said. Madison used her handheld atmosphere sniffer until she locked onto a tiny vent.

"Confirming hull breach location," she reported.

"Confirmed," Nyx replied. "Apply temporary sealant now."

"Bloody hell," Jonas muttered. "It's just a pinhole. I can't believe something that tiny could kill us." He shook his head.

A ping sounded—an incoming message. Troy opened the comms panel: ATTENTION MADISON FLOYD—UPDATE ON ARLENE FLOYD. Her dying mother. Horrible timing. He closed the alert and forced a smile when Jonas glanced over.

Jonas switched off his external comms and whispered, "Anything urgent?"

Troy pressed the mute button and replied breezily, "Nothing that can't wait."

Troy resumed peering at the helmet feed until Jonas followed suit.

"That's great, Mad Dog. Patch looks good—continue to the rear hatch. Volkov's waiting with the kit," Troy said.

Madison resumed her painstaking crawl. The hull's blinding white curved against endless black, stars pin-bright and cold. Troy silently begged the universe to spare them.

At last, she reached the rear hatch where Volkov waited.

"Break a leg," the bot said.

Madison's hands froze as she reached for the kit.

"Really, Volkov?" Jonas snapped.

"This is good luck saying."

"If you're performing *Hamlet*. On a stage, bothead."

"Thank you, Volkov," Troy cut in. "Repressurise."

Madison clipped the repair kit to her belt and started back. Suit telemetry showed rising temperature and sweat saturation.

"Need a temp tweak, Mad Dog?" Troy asked.

"Control seems stuck—too hot beats freezing. Almost there."

At the puncture site, she worked through the checklist with Jonas. Thick EVA gloves hampered finesse; grinding tool vibrations shook her arms.

"Who knew this was such a workout in zero-g?" she puffed.

"Take a sip of water," Troy said.

As she resumed grinding, the tool slipped, slicing into her glove.

"Shit!" Madison said, dropping the tool and grasping her injured glove with her intact one.

"Suit breach! Suit breach!" Alarms blared. "Pressure dropped: O_2 80%."

The grinder, still live, ricocheted on its tether. Madison contorted, dodging its spin, but the tether snagged her leg.

In a near-impossible move, she tucked her knee, spun her torso, pinned the grinder under her boot, its vibration angry like a cut snake. She lurched forward and smacked the off switch.

Inside the flight deck, Jonas gasped; his knee jiggled.

Madison's wrangling rattled the hull.

"No, no, no," Jonas muttered.

Madison's suit alarm continued to blare.

"Jonas," Troy barked. "EVA rescue protocol—get ready."

Jonas just stared back, eyes enormous.

Troy grabbed Jonas by the shoulders and shook him gently. "Madison can't return to the ship without assistance. She needs to keep that suit breach secure. You got to get out there, man."

Jonas looked at Troy, his face blank, eyes wide.

"Me, go?"

"Yes, you, go. We launch rescue procedures. Come on, Jonas, follow protocol."

"Go? Alone?"

"Yes, go get Madison."

Troy noticed Jonas's breath coming thick and fast. "Jonas, breathe, breathe."

Xanthe's voice cut through on Troy's helmet comm. "Troy, he's having a panic attack. You can't send him out."

"How did you get flight deck access?" Troy said, astonished.

"Athena gave it to me."

Of course she did, Troy scowled.

"Listen to me, Troy. You need to go out. You can't send Jonas. He's panicking.'

"I've got this, Xanthe," Troy replied. He returned his attention to Jonas. "Jonas, listen to me, work with me, you know how to do this, breathe."

"Troy, there's no time," Xanthe said in a slow and pointed voice. "You need to go out there now."

"Thank you for your advice, Xanthe. I've got this."

"*Suit breach, suit breach.* Oxygen at 70%."

"If you don't go now," Xanthe replied, "Madison will lose pressurisation and she'll be dead."

Jonas's eyes popped even wider.

"Madison, Madison," he said, and lurched for the cupola opening.

"Damn it," said Troy, and caught Jonas's foot before he escaped and hauled him back to the captain's chair. "Strap in. Monitor the feed. I'm going."

Taking steady breaths, Troy exited the cupola and crab-crawled toward Madison.

"Mad Dog, I'm applying a temporary patch."

On three, she lifted her hand; he smeared sealant across the glove tear.

"Suit stabilising: O_2 60%."

"Head back inside—that sweat blob's a risk. I'll finish the hull repair."

Madison nodded grimly, the perspiration bubble pooling dangerously on her nose tip, and turned for home.

"Jonas, be ready to receive her," Troy said.

"Uh-huh," came the shaky reply.

With Madison safe inside, Troy prepped the hull: ground the area smooth, spread proxy compound, set the patch plate, set another proxy layer, then smoothed it. His own sweat now fogged the visor; the recycler lagged.

He secured tools, hauled himself towards the nose, sealed the cupola and drifted into the flight deck. Jonas and Madison helped him to a handhold and they repressurised the chamber.

They looked at each other, relief easing the adrenaline-shot nerves. "Well, that was more fun than a poke in the eye in a blizzard!" Madison bumped her helmet faceplate to Troy's. "Thanks for saving my bacon, Troy."

"Can't say it was my pleasure," he laughed. "Let's hope that's the last unscheduled EVA."

Jonas remained quiet as he busied himself around the controls, avoiding Troy's gaze.

"Leave it, Jonas," Troy murmured. "Why don't you check in with Xavier and see how Serena and Xanthe are doing in the galley. Mad Dog, grab yourself some downtime. Have a shower. Crew debrief in thirty minutes."

CHAPTER THIRTY-EIGHT

"No monopoly of power will be tolerated."

—Xanthe Waters
MARS MANIFESTO

NYX ODYSSEY: TROY

Flight Day 98

TROY STEADIED HIMSELF for the upcoming team meeting. He went through the reports with Nyx and sent an update to Gaia back on Earth. He winced as he glimpsed another message for Madison.

It could wait until after the meeting. Right now, he had to sort his thoughts before he dealt with the team. The ship's lights blinked and he bolted upright.

"Nyx, report."

"Repressurisation of the medical bay complete. No leaks detected. The surge is from the air cycle."

Heart hammering, he leaned back in the chair and closed his eyes. The lights strobed against his eyelids as he took himself through a relaxation exercise. Sensing his pulse had slowed, he unclipped himself and headed for the galley.

It was time.

They were all waiting, chatting quietly to each other. The ship's lighting was switching to evening twilight, and the room had a soft glow. Hooking a foot under a rail, Troy synced with the familiar thrum of the ship's life support systems.

"After Action Review? Then dinner?" Troy suggested.

"Sounds good to me," Serena said. "I'm famished. I've got a Tasmanian Devil growling away in my tummy."

"The nausea didn't last long this time, eh?" asked Madison.

"Just needed a near-death experience to kick-start the appetite, is all," Serena said.

"That and the thought of my cricket cake," Xavier said.

Serena pulled a face. Jonas's features stayed grim.

"Alright then," Troy nudged. "Let's walk through what happened and make notes for troubleshooting and prevention."

They used Nyx's timeline and playback video to analyse their actions. Once they hit Madison's glove slicing incident, there were gasps from Serena and Xanthe, who hadn't seen the footage yet. Jonas had brought the offending tool into the galley. They agreed that an additional Velcro strap to secure it to the user's glove would eliminate a slippage risk in the future.

"How about glove repair?" Madison asked Jonas. "Do we have enough in the workshop to fix it up?"

"I'm pretty sure," Jonas answered. "We also have spare gloves."

"We can't rely on spare gloves though," she said. "Who knows how many more EVAs we'll have to do. We're not even halfway there yet."

Silence crept in. The water recycler belched and hummed.

"There's something else we need to address," Troy said carefully. "Jonas?"

Jonas nodded to himself, rubbing his jaw. "Yeah. Well, that was a right cluster on my part," he blurted. His neck flushed in blotches. He hesitated, struggling to control his emotions.

Serena rubbed his back.

"When we sheltered and the meteoroids hit, I kept seeing Pabi and the others crushed in that lava tube on the Moon. It felt like my chest was caving in, and the ship was being smashed and rolled up like tinfoil." He grabbed the edge of the display table to steady himself, hands trembling.

"Then Madison…stuck outside, alone, suit depressurising…I couldn't take it. Losing someone else…"

Troy studied Jonas. "It's the PTSD, Jonas. We can work on that."

Jonas nodded, not looking up.

"The rest of us will need to be more vigilant in working with Jonas. Activate all stress management controls when on duty and check in with each other regularly."

"Babysitting?" Jonas asked, glancing up.

"Peer support," replied Troy. "In the meantime, we'll keep the sleepers out of the freezer for a few days to make sure the hull seal holds and everything else is back to normal function." Troy checked in with them, receiving thumbs up from all. "Supper time then."

"Great. Fettuccine Alfredo it is for me," Serena said and launched across the space to the supply cabinet.

Xanthe floated over to Troy and said in a low voice, "Troy, can I have a quick word please?"

He followed her out of the galley into the medbay.

She leaned towards him and he thrilled in it as her personal scent tantalised his senses. He favoured her with his famous lop-sided grin. Her face serious, it faded.

"What is it?" he asked.

"That incident with Jonas."

"Yes, it's definitely a concern. I—"

"Not him. You." Xanthe looked pointedly at him. "You took too long to act. Madison could have died while you did the psy-chologist routine with Jonas."

"He was having a PTSD episode, Xanthe. I couldn't leave him."

"You absolutely could have left him. Your priority was Madison."

Anger bubbled in Troy's chest. He crossed his arms, adjusting his foothold next to the medbay supply cabin. A waft of antiseptic slipped past as his shoulders drifted closer to the gleaming surface of the stored surgery table.

"What do you want, Xanthe?" he said at last. "You want me to concede you would have done better?"

"I don't need you to," she said sadly. "I know I would have."

Her tone lacked aggression. There was something more cutting there…pity.

"It's not your fault," she said. "I have Athena in my head. With her, I can predict and forecast in a fraction of the time. What takes you—or any human brain—minutes to assess, I've done instantly with Athena. Those minutes could cost lives. Like it almost did today."

The anger fired hot like a coal, burning its way to his throat. His eyes narrowed, lips pressed together. He waited a heartbeat, then two, before he replied.

Xanthe beat him to it.

"I propose sharing command. You default to me in emergencies. It will be faster and safer."

Stunned, Troy stared at her, studying the earnest glint in her eyes, the soft curl of her hair lifting in the zero-g, the creases in her forehead where age and grief ran their tracks.

"Thank you for the offer," he said, clipping the words. "I am the Commander, appointed by Gaia. By Maja and Aryanna. I intend to fulfil my duties. You are already Deputy Commander, and you have control of the ship while I am in the freezer. I trained twelve hours per day to handle the emergencies for this expedition."

He took a breath and added, "I too have an A.I." He leaned forward, eyebrows raised. "Just not in my head, screwing me up."

"What do you mean?" The line between Xanthe's brows deepened.

"You're a different person since you had that implant."

"How?"

"Harder. Clinical." He looked away, noticing a medical supply pack askew. "Distant."

A shared memory drifted between them, crumbs from another lifetime.

"And smarter. More agile," she said. "You know it's true, Troy. I can process way more information and make better decisions faster."

The earnest look on her pixie face stirred the ashes of his anger. "There's more to command than information, Xanthe. And then there's the pain Athena is causing you, especially when processing load goes up, like during a crisis. What if you pass out at a critical moment during an emergency?"

He uncrossed his arms. "The answer is no. We maintain our appointed roles."

With that, he launched back towards the galley and the banter of the crew as they tucked into the evening meal.

⁊

After a meal of spaghetti bolognese, Troy wiped his fork clean and cleared his meal pack into the recycler. He left Madison, Serena and Jonas chatting in the mess. Xanthe, having wolfed down her own meal, made her excuses and shot off to bed. After a few friendly words, he too excused himself, eager for the sanctuary of his quarters.

He removed his cargo pants and crew top, stuffed them in the netting holder and pulled on sleeping trousers and a shirt. The soft flannel was a balm to his exhausted body. Once he slipped into his sleeping bag and snapped the restraints in place, he activated his audio pods. "Nyx, play nature sounds, please. English forest."

He breathed slowly as *English Forest Sounds* piped through his earbuds. After a few moments, his body and mind settled. He opened his eyes, ready to write in his journal. He removed it from its storage sling and opened to the current page. Where to begin?

There was a pounding on his door.

"Troy, open up!" Madison cried.

He flung the journal and pen back into its storage net and slid the cabin door open.

"What is it? Everything okay?" His heart throttled into fifth gear.

Madison's face was contorted in fury.

"When were you going to tell me about the message from my Mom?" she spat.

Oh shit. He'd forgotten.

"I'm sorry, Mad Dog. With all that's happened—I—"

"She was dying, Troy. That message was so I could say my last farewell. But she died. She's gone. An hour ago."

The pain wrestled Madison's smooth features into a crinkled mess. Tears welled in her eyes, and her lips trembled.

"Madison, I am so sorry," he said and reached for her. The sleeping restraints kept him in place.

She slapped the wall of the crew quarters and headed for the flight deck.

"Madison!" he cried after her.

"Leave me be. I need to be alone right now."

Troy slumped back in his cabin and closed the door. He hunted for an oxy tablet but then remembered he'd stashed them all in the medbay. Away from temptation.

"Nyx, soundtrack off."

He stared at the bulkhead, listening to the creaking whirr of the ship and the soft muttering of the crew until exhaustion overtook him.

CHAPTER THIRTY-NINE

"People die. We all fade to stardust. But life—life goes on. That's why we need to get to Mars—so life can go on and on into the darkness."

—**Madison Floyd**
MEMOIRS FROM MARS

NYX ODYSSEY: TROY

Flight Day 99

Troy glided past Volkov, lashed to the flight deck console and ducked Betty the rubber chicken as it bobbed in the ventilation stream. He slipped into the cupola, where Xavier and Jonas parted to let him join the loose circle.

A whiff of soap filled the space as Serena's braid drifted above them. Serena, Jonas and Xanthe were scrubbed clean and dressed in their sleep suits, ready to return to the freezer once they'd finished the farewell memorial for Arlene Floyd.

All day Troy had noted averted eyes, truncated conversations, heavy sighs and thousand-yard stares. Though not a surprise—Arlene had been dying for months—it was still a shock.

Now, their feet dangled over the blinking controls of the flight deck below as they each gazed into the void.

Like the others, Troy often drifted here to stare at the stars. For him, the blackness was so complete it commanded total presence.

Thoughts fizzled out, everything unknowable.

The blackness reached into his mind and stilled his spirit, like a chime resonating into silence: a long trill and then quiet.

Xavier's elbow prodded his ribs, sharply bringing him back to the present moment. Xavier tilted his head with wide eyes, signalling to get started.

"Thanks for joining us here," Troy began quietly, drawing the attention of the others away from the emptiness. "Madison, we're here for you."

She smiled weakly. Arms went around each other in the circle. The ship thrummed as life support systems cycled.

"Arlene was a fierce warrior spirit," Troy said, voice cracking.

Nods.

Serena's face contorted, her eyes shining.

"It's been a great privilege to hear Arlene's messages since we launched. No matter how much she was suffering herself, her thoughts were always for us, sailing into the unknown. She backed us all the way." Troy swallowed and cleared his throat. "She was so proud of you, Mad Dog."

Tears filled Madison's eyes and she blinked into her sleeve so the drops wouldn't float into the cupola.

"Thanks, Troy," Madison said, voice hoarse.

The quiet was profound. Troy searched for sounds: the whirr of computer fans, the thrum of ship life support systems, the rustling of clothes in the weightless hush.

No stirring of the wind. No seagulls riding high on the breeze. No murmur from church pews.

Just the low thrum of circuitry, the whisper of cloth drifting against cloth, six breathing bodies—and, every few seconds, Betty the rubber chicken tapping the bulkhead like a metronome for the void.

"Ma was one in a million."

The air cycler clunked. A draft of air brought a taste of ionised metal.

"It's hard to believe she's gone. I feel her so close. Right here." Madison withdrew an arm from around Xanthe and tapped her chest.

Serena rubbed her back and squeezed her shoulder.

"Ma told me once about when she was a kid. She and other neighbourhood kids would play 'kick the can'. Someone played 'it' while one of the other kids kicked the can and hid. The 'it' kid had to bring the can back and then go and find the others, calling them out before they ran back and kicked the can again to go and hide.

"This one kid, Lenny McDougall, was always made to be 'it'. He was smaller than the rest, dribbled a lot and carried around a big bag of snotty tissues. Ma said the kids all thought he was kind of gross, so made him play 'it'.

"After a while, Lenny got good at spotting kids. Knew where all the hiding places were. One time, Lenny spotted all the kids except one—Jasper Moncrieff. Ma and a whole heap of kids now waited for Jasper to sneak home, kick the can and liberate them. For the first time, Lenny might get out of being 'it' if he could spot Jasper.

"Lenny hovered around the can, not wanting to lose his catch, but he couldn't see a breath of movement. He inched away, peering down the side of a house, when Jasper Moncrieff bolted out of the blue and ran for that can. According to Ma, Lenny spun and flew at that can faster than a cat on fire and made it back to the can to call out 'Jasper'. But Jasper kept running and kicked the can anyway, yelling to Ma and the others, 'You're free!'

"'But we ain't free,' Ma said. 'Lenny beat you.'

"Jasper pulled up short and stood over Ma. 'No, he didn't.'

"Ma stood her ground, backing Lenny. The other kids looked unsure, but when Jasper ran away yelling 'hide', they all followed. All except my Ma. She picked up the can and yelled out, 'All-ey all-ey in-come-free. Game over.' When the kids stayed out hiding, Ma threw the can to the ground and stomped it flat."

"What a badass," Serena whispered, shifting her toehold to another cupola loop to peer at Madison.

"Did the kids make up?" Xanthe asked.

Madison shrugged. "Ma never played kick the can again.

"When I think of Ma, I think of little Lenny McDougall who tried his guts out, playing by the rules. And it was Ma who said, 'Screw the system, make your own game.' And that's what she did all her life: she fought for the little guy. Fought against the system. They jailed her for it, but she never stopped fighting. That's my Ma."

Madison thumped her heart with a fist in respect.

"Some people plant seeds that grow to Redwoods in the forest of our lives," Troy said. "Arlene cast many seeds of courage. And in you, we have a towering giant as her legacy."

Serena sobbed. "I wish I had a mother like Arlene."

The ship corridor lights faded to cobalt blue, signalling 'night'. The computer fans whirred and settled.

"Life goes so fast," Xanthe said, leaning her head against Madison's. "We never know how long we have with the people we love."

Xavier sniffed. "Ah, *merde*." He rubbed his watering eyes against Jonas's shoulder, arms still around his friends.

"Easy, Xavier, I don't want snot all over my sleep suit." Jonas smiled at the big man.

They laughed softly.

"I love you guys," Serena said, also sniffing and mopping her wet eyes. "There's no one else I'd rather spend nine months with, breathing your farts and drinking your recycled pee."

Jonas poked her leg with his toe. "Now that's an inspiring thought."

They clung to each other. Troy enjoyed the warmth of his

friends' arms around him, even as the grief ebbed between them, a gentle tide.

Troy studied the faces of his friends, tension easing, eyes softer now. "As we say farewell to Arlene on her next adventure, she is with us always. Her warrior heart calls us to live every day with courage. Our mission is for the future of humanity, and we need to remember we are the six who breathe for billions."

"Eight." Volkov's voice drifted up from the flight deck along with Betty. "Eight who bump for billions."

Serena grabbed the rubber chicken as it bounced off the cupola handrail. "I think I liked him better when he didn't try to be funny," she said, laughing.

"Eight then," Troy called to Volkov below. "Eight who bustle for billions."

"Bustle?" Serena said, confused.

A bare toe tapped his calf.

"Speaking of bustling," Xanthe said, voice light but edgy, "shall we get moving?"

Troy flinched. He'd shaped the farewell carefully—one last minute of silence, a gentle glide back to duty. Madison's shoulders were still trembling, Serena's hand steady on her back; ending now felt like snapping a string before the note had finished ringing.

"Give them a moment," he murmured.

Xanthe's lips thinned. "Shall we meet in the freezer in ten, Commander?"

Commander. She hadn't used the title like that in weeks—precise, tactical. A reminder that procedure outranked sentiment. Troy met her gaze; starlight from the cupola glass carved a hard line across her cheek.

"Affirmative." He turned to the others and nodded. "Let's finish in the corridor."

One by one they pushed off the hand loops, their silhouettes sliding through the dome of stars. Each departure dimmed the small warmth the circle had held.

Troy swiped the cupola's lights to night mode and slipped after the crew, the hush folding closed behind him.

Ahead lay the freezer bay, eleven more crew freezer rotations, one hundred and fifty-nine more days of flight, and a line—thin but unmistakable—drawn between him and Xanthe that the mission couldn't afford to widen.

CHAPTER FORTY

*"Mars isn't for all—it's for those who can pay the
price in sweat, blood and brilliance."*

—LINCOLN ELLISON
MEMOIRS FROM MARS

NYX ODYSSEY: XANTHE

Flight Day 120

XANTHE HOOKED A foot under the garden corridor rail and drew
closer to examine Xavier's latest crop. Pak choy and lettuce sagged
like tired flags. She toed over to the filtration monitor and checked
the settings. All in order. What then? Atmosphere?

Athena, diagnose issues with the salad crop, please.

*"Primary failure mode is root-zone pathology, compounded by a
secondary calcium-transport disorder. Lettuce pillow A12 and pak choy
pillow B07 have entered an unrecoverable decline."*

So it's a microbe?

Xanthe poked the veggie pillow, peeling it back to study the
roots.

*"Exactly. The immediate culprit is a pathogenic water-mould,
Pythium spp., infecting the root pillows. It's an opportunistic microbe*

(an oomycete, rather than a true fungus) that thrives when the root zone goes 'stale'."

Fix?

Xanthe launched over to the hygiene bay to wipe her hands with ethanol to prevent cross-contamination.

"Quarantine and remove affected pillows. Hydro-loop flush. Aeration upgrade. Basically, you need to restore high O_2 levels, keep the solution at 18 °C, and flush the line with peroxide/UV-C and you'll knock the microbe back below the danger threshold—and the next sowing of lettuce and pak choy should stay healthy."

Bummer. There went six weeks of morale-boosting crunch.

Jonas floated through the narrow space, dragging Volkov towards the repair bay.

Xanthe drifted to the corridor ceiling to let them pass. "Volkov glitching again?"

"Yeah. His voice track gets muddled. Mostly it's his usual Volkov voice, but then he'll break into somebody else's. Just then it was Arlene's!"

"I don't know what you're so 'fraid of!"

Xanthe froze. Sure enough, Arlene's voice came through the Volkov bot.

"Thank goodness Madison is in the freezer. Ugh."

Jonas shifted Volkov under his arm as he slid open the hatch to the workshop. "It's like he picked up the profile from our data dumps when he's in recharge mode and has these other voice tracks that skip in."

"Jonas, maybe turn him off until you figure it out. It's unnerving."

"Data dump incoming," Nyx announced.

"See you on the flight deck once you've got Volkov sorted?"

"Might be a while. See you at dinner for algae cricket protein balls bolognese!"

"I'm not sure Xavier would approve of your recipe

experimentation, Jonas." Xanthe pushed off a handrail to close the hatch behind him.

"He's in the freezer. While the cat's away…" He grinned.

Xanthe shook her head, smiling. Xavier tolerated some variations to his instructions, but not much. He would be mad as hell about the lettuce and the badly needed nutrients.

She rubbed the back of her neck. She was still getting headaches, though not as badly as before. Since Athena was doing her updates through the ship's systems, rather than through the implant, the pressure had eased. Still, the report that Maja had sent through on the private channel bothered her, a background noise consuming far too much emotional energy.

The report seared a lasting memory: *"Tissue growth around ThinkLink implants was causing pain and impairment in most long-term implantees. Current remediation protocols have been unsuccessful, with side effects ranging from increased pain, vision impairment and in some cases, death."*

Nothing she could do about that here, she reminded herself. If experienced surgeons and programmers hadn't found a solution yet, she'd just have to wait. The workaround was good enough for the moment, she lied to herself.

She floated through the galley and crew quarters, Serena joining her as she passed, and tucked herself into the captain's chair for the data dump.

But first, check in with Mars. She craned her neck out through the viewing portal, and there it was: the stunning ochre disc, just a smudge, that was the bright Red Planet. They were nearly halfway there in distance and time.

When Mars had crystallised in sight, their hearts had lifted—a colour, faint as it was, a welcome beacon in the inky cold sea of space.

Reassured, she flicked through the updates and landed on one with a jolt. "Lincoln Ellison broadcast from the *Pinnacle*." She tapped the packet and Lincoln's image sprang to life on the holo.

"—delighted to announce that we are expected to make the first human landing on Mars in one hundred and twenty-one days. We've re-established communication with the Dopplebot Kunlun base, and they are expecting our landing at the Houyi pad. Dr Victoria Tang reports a fully operational, airtight and breathable atmosphere in the Martian habitat by our arrival."

Xanthe's head swam. She dialled the volume back as she swiped through to the telemetry of the *Pinnacle*.

"Nyx, give me the current location of the *Pinnacle*, its trajectory and expected landing location and timing."

The image flashed on screen. "Here is the broadcasted route."

"Huh." Xanthe fell back against the chair.

Serena paused her video message from Max and leaned over Xanthe to study the route plan. "What gives?"

"Lincoln's full of shit."

"And? Something new to report?"

Xanthe pointed to the diverging lines. "He says he's landing near Kunlun Station, but his actual location and projected landing spot are fifteen hundred kilometres away in Arcadia Planitia, not Utopia."

"That's a bloody long way. You don't think he has a base over there, do you?"

Xanthe shook her head. "There's no evidence of that, but it does mean he has a problem. A rover would take over one hundred days to cross that terrain."

"He might have a tilt-wing drone on board?"

Xanthe raised her shoulders in a 'who knows' gesture.

"Nyx, how long would it take Lincoln to get to Kunlun if he had a drone like that?"

"Approximately eleven hours plus recharge stops."

"Let me get this straight." Serena tucked her tablet into the chair pocket. "He's on track to beat us by eighteen days or so?"

"That second burn put him ahead, yeah."

"But it put him off course from the Kunlun base."

"So the data shows us."

"Which could be good if he's using a rover, because we will definitely beat him to the base that way. Even though we're currently eighteen days behind, we would still get to Kunlun at least two months before him."

Xanthe nodded, jiggling a leg.

"But bad if he has something like a drone to get him back fast."

Serena pulled her hair back into a ponytail and tied it in a knot to keep it from floating in the zero-G. "Can we do anything about it?"

"I'm thinking."

Serena scratched her chin, studying the trajectory. "What if we do another burn? Even the odds? Just in case he has a drone."

"Risky. That takes all our reserves. I'll have Athena run scenarios."

Serena stared at her for a moment and then pulled out her tablet to resume Max's vmail.

Athena, run scenarios for burn option. Or intercept option.

"That might cause some discomfort with the calculations required."

Dose me with something to numb the pain.

Chemicals flooded her system from the skin patch she had rigged with Athena's instructions for extra processing requirements at times like these. She closed her eyes and breathed through the rising pressure.

A tug at her sleeve. Her eyes popped open to see Serena's face contorted with worry.

"What is it?"

"It's Terra Verdi. There's been an acid rain incident and a

cholera outbreak. Max is in critical condition." She showed Xanthe the tablet with Max's prone form in a hospital bed.

Xanthe's heart stammered. She placed a hand on Serena's and gave a sympathetic squeeze. "I'm so sorry, Serena."

What else was there to say? All the news they could get was already here, and there was nothing they could do. Rage curdled behind the migraine's white noise. Her eyesight grew fuzzy and she closed her eyes again.

"Xanthe, there is an incoming hail from the Pinnacle."

Broadcast to the Nyx.

"Can't. It's encrypted. And it's for me."

What? She sat up again and peeled her eyes open through the rising pain. *Can you decode it?*

"Not without a major power surge in the ThinkLink and critical pain levels."

Can you use Nyx?

"It might be a bug. I suggest containing and monitoring for further signal."

Who sent it?

"A ThinkLink."

Xanthe froze. The *Pinnacle* crew manifest scrolled behind her eyes. *Who the hell was hot-wired?*

CHAPTER FORTY-ONE

"People think that when you're in space staring at the stars and all that blackness—blackness so loud it cracks the soul—that you come close to God. In the divine presence. Not me. The closest I feel to God is when a friend hugs me. Heart beating against heart. That's God."

—**Jonas Seaborn**
MEMOIRS FROM MARS

NYX ODYSSEY: XAVIER

Flight Day 146

THE HYDROPONICS BAY floated midship, bathed in grow-light amber. The fragile green tendrils and the earthy smell brought instant ease to the space travellers: a delicate and visceral connection to their home planet, reminding them of the perils and stakes of their journey.

Xavier smacked the handrail beside the grow trays.

Putain! A whole tray was gone. The infection had reappeared despite their careful attention. He unclipped the tray, hauled it to the composter and tipped the withered mess inside. That was another six weeks of salad and tomatoes gone. Between this and the previous failure, it had been a long time since they had good, crunchy, fresh stuff.

He upped the chemical dosage and slammed the flush button. The carbon material would be no good for recycling either. What a waste.

He hooked a toe in a loop while he gathered the disinfectant. The whole system might need a complete purge.

But where was the damn microbe coming in? They couldn't afford to ditch the entire supply. They would be very hungry with another 153 days to go.

He scrubbed his scalp with his fingernails. He pulled himself over to the irrigation system, dismantled it and gave it a flush, and then another one for good measure. Maybe the roots were struggling with water saturation in the zero-G. Perhaps the capillaries weren't strong enough to activate the water flow. He peeled back a corner of the fibre mat—roots pale, no slime, nothing.

The ship thrummed in dispassionate response. The air scrubber rolled over and kicked up a gear.

Maybe it was the air purifier, circulating the spores back in. Xavier's mind sparked. He drifted over to the cartridge and opened it. Damn, it looked spotless. He studied it, flicking his wrist light here and there to expose any blemish, any sign of mold, keen to blame something or someone for the crop loss. Anything to keep the devastating doubt at bay. His inner voice wondered if they were on a deadly fool's errand.

Anger seeped through his system, and he slammed the cartridge door shut, before he kicked up to the air vents. They, too, had been scrubbed clean.

Someone knew something. Someone screwed with his system; he was sure of it.

"Nyx, call the Commander, please."

"Commander Bruin to the garden pod," Nyx announced.

"What is it, Xavier?" Troy's voice popped in.

"We have a situation."

"I'll be right there."

Xavier toed over to the algae tubes. Those at least seem to be going fine. Right colour, right density, right pH balance. No problem there, perfect. If they lost those…no, better not to think about that.

Troy appeared, protein bar in hand, mouth full and munching.

"Troy, the other crew stuffed up the garden."

Troy swallowed and his brows shot up. "What do you mean?"

"I had to throw away a whole tray of lettuce and tomatoes. Gone. Microbe infection."

"Another one?"

"Something keeps circulating back in. I think it's the air scrubber."

Serena unlocked the garden pod door and drifted into the space.

"What's this about the air scrubber?" Her face was flushed from her exercise session and pinched in anger. "It's not the air filters. I pulled it all apart, scrubbed every last section, did an air purifier and had Nyx check it all."

"Then it must have been when you were picking crops. Some dirt from the cleaning got onto the grow pads."

"Not a chance. I wore gloves. As per protocol."

"Well, somebody screwed up our food."

"Whoa, hang on, Xavier," Troy said, a hand flying to Xavier's shoulder. "Everyone knows how important the garden is. And everyone knows the protocol for cleaning and harvest. We all have a vested interest in making sure this works. And it doesn't make sense to try to blame anyone or point fingers at people. Let's look at how we fix it."

Xavier glared at Serena. "We need to fix the air filtration system."

"We need to fix your attitude, Xavier."

Xanthe drifted in from the galley and hooked a toe loop next to Troy.

"What's going on?" she said in a quiet voice.

"We lost a whole tray."

"Oh."

"Look, Xavier, I know you're pretty frustrated, and this is disappointing for all of us. Let's look at consequences before we decide on the next action, eh, old chap?" Troy suggested.

Xavier did a two-handed scrub of his head and blew out his cheeks. "Okay, well, we've lost a whole tray, so that's six weeks of salad gone. If we plant now, they won't be ready for another thirty days. We've got whatever's currently here to sustain us." He drummed fingers on the handrail.

"How are the supplies in general, Xavier?" Xanthe asked as she poked her head over the cricket farm containers, nudging Troy aside.

"They're fine," Troy said.

Xavier noted the irritation in his friend's voice, his mouth in a grim line, while Xanthe looked up at him expectantly. Troy rolled his eyes, readying a retort, but Xavier cut him off.

"Our freeze-dried supplies are tracking, but our nutrient profile is poor. We could start upping the cricket protein. But I'm worried that this infection might spread and we will lose our entire crop. And we still have a long time to go. And if we can't get to the root of this problem, we're screwed for our time on Mars."

"I'll get Athena to work up scenarios for us," Xanthe said. "We'll have it all sorted by the time you come out of the freezer, Xav."

"It's still our shift, Xanthe," Troy said. "You and Serena and Jonas should focus on rehab and reintegration. Xavier and I can handle this."

Xavier made a face as Troy slapped him on the shoulder. His friend beamed a smile, though Xavier spotted the clenched jaw.

"I'll go through the air filter again, Xav," Serena said in a conciliatory tone. "I was just finishing on the bike, anyway. You're up, Xanthe."

"I'll run systems scans with Nyx and check the nutrient mixes in the hold, alright, old friend?"

"*Merci.*" Xavier breathed out slowly. They would fix this. They had to.

❧

Xavier worked his way through the entire growth tray system, zapping all organic material with UV light to kill any unwanted microbes, then dismantled every tube, rinsed them in a chemical wash and reassembled everything.

Despite the concern over their food supply, he was grateful for the distraction. News from Earth was sporadic, and none of it had been good. Max had only just come out of intensive care, and his second in command was barely holding Terra Verdi and Po Secco together in his absence.

And Xavier was no good to any of them up here in this metal tube. At least his family was fine. The girls were healthy, safe. Maryse was still fiercely supportive and made it a personal mission to check in daily on Max.

He felt for Serena. She had so few transmissions from Earth and welcomed any scrap of news of Max. She must be feeling as helpless as he was.

Xavier clambered over to the crickets and shone his torch at the insects. They at least seemed robust enough. All their metrics were on target and the zero-g did not seem to worry them. They pinged happily off the walls of their box, clung to the artificial sticks and feasted on their leafy greens.

"*La belle vie,* eh?" He chirped at them.

"Hey."

Xavier spun as Serena swam over to him.

"How are the little grots?" She tapped their tub and they zipped from side to side.

"Good. They like space."

She stared at them, watching their antics. "Must be nice. Your whole job just to eat and chill out."

"Then get eaten."

"A worthy purpose, I suppose." Serena sighed and bounced over to the air scrubber, pulling a tool from her Velcro thigh pad.

He winced at the heaviness in her voice, wondering what to say.

Xavier stashed the crickets and washed the container and his hands with disinfectant. Serena pulled the air scrubber apart and wiped each component carefully, storing them in a sling until the whole bones of the unit were laid bare.

"Serena, ah…I'm sorry for snapping earlier."

He caught the look of surprise as she glanced over, wrench in hand.

"That's okay, Xavier. I get it. No one wants the plants to die. We all want a solution."

He smiled weakly. She was being generous. He sprang towards her and caught a hand loop.

"Have you heard from Max?" he asked gently.

The wrench slipped on the last nut of the unit and she swore.

"Not yet. Still not cleared for comms."

"You can read the Terra Verdi reports again, if you'd like."

Another turn and the nut came free. She tucked it into a pocket, stuck the wrench back on the thigh pad. She grabbed an absorbent cloth, squeezed disinfectant into its fibres, and reached into the far corner of the unit. Xavier's nose wrinkled with the astringent tang.

"Have things improved much since the riots?" she asked, head inside the air scrubber unit.

"Not really." He tapped a finger against the bulkhead. "Maybe a little."

"I wish I were there. We left them with so much to handle."

"We can't save everything, everyone. *Be* everywhere." He sighed. "We made a choice."

He sounded hollow, even to himself.

Serena pulled her head out of the unit. "I know that, Xavier, but it doesn't make it hurt any less."

Her blue eyes swam with pain and his heart stretched in the void.

He reached out his arms. "Hug?"

"*Oui!*"

They clung to each other, heartbeats and human warmth tethering them to all they'd left behind, tiny roots seeking safety in a fragile cylinder hurtling through space.

CHAPTER FORTY-TWO

"People with power call those who challenge them radicals. But if you have power, it's a torch—light the way, don't burn people with it."

—**Claire Edwards**
TRANSCRIPT FROM LUNAR
COMMISSION DEPOSITION

EARTH FIRST HEADQUARTERS: CLAIRE

Flight Day 167

THE PERIMETER ALARM flashed red on the monitor, catching Claire off-guard. She spun in her chair and brought up the video feeds: figures in full camo and combat gear swept across the monitors. They were under attack.

Pressing the alarm, she delivered a single command across the base: "Breach! Quit and decamp." She holstered her pistol, strapped on her bulletproof jacket, shouldered her go-bag, triggered the self-destruct and headed for the back entrance.

An explosion hurled her against the wall before she reached the door. Bright sparks danced across her vision. She blinked away dust and debris. Had they found her? A quick self-check: nothing broken, though her left shoulder throbbed from the impact.

Footsteps and shouted orders echoed in the corridor—the hunters were closing in. She flung open the door, then dropped flat as a second device thudded behind her. Face pressed to the floor, she covered her eyes and ears. A hiss followed: tear gas.

Yanking a mask from her go-bag, she pulled it on. The corridor lights were dead, but she knew every metre of the facility, having drilled escapes with her team every other day. She sprinted ten metres through the darkness, lifted a hatch and dropped to the service passage below, sealing the lid after her. Moments later, an explosion roared overhead, burying the hatch beneath rubble.

I hope the others made it out, she thought.

The blast would stall the invaders, perhaps long enough for her to reach the electric motorbike stashed in the woods.

From the pack, she dug out her night-vision headset and slipped it over the gas mask. Torchlight was too great a risk. Her ears still rang, muting every sound, but waiting wasn't an option. She bolted thirty metres through the tunnel, climbed a short ladder and listened at the surface hatch. On the far side lay the silent forest, but a sniper could be watching. Using her pistol as a lever, she cracked the lid a sliver.

With a sudden shove, she flipped the hatch and vaulted out, rolling into deep shadow beneath a tree. Bullets spattered the steel behind her—they were already zeroed in. Staying low, she crawled through fern and leaf-litter, then sprang to her feet and raced between the trunks, praying the bike was still hidden.

Voices shouted in the distance—too close to judge.

She pressed on, GPS locator pulsing in her hand, dodging branches under the half-moon. The cache was metres away. *Three seconds to reach the cover, two to uncover the bike, another two to start it,* she calculated, heart hammering.

"Now or never," she whispered, and surged forward.

❦

Once Claire reached the bike, she slid on and slipped through the shadows, sticking to the forest. It was slower going cross-country, but they would have a hard time tracking her in the dark, even with infrared drones. She needed to hit the management track and bolt for the lake.

A thin grey veil of light thinned the darkness. Just twenty minutes or so left of cover. She drove the bike hard.

Arms and back aching, relief flooded through her as she spotted the track shining like a snakeskin in the pale dawn. The bike slipped forward, unfettered, winding through the tall forest. Wind knifed through her sweat-drenched clothes. She shivered and gritted her teeth. Not far to go.

The road ran straight into the lake, but Claire pulled up a kilometre from the end at an intersection to stash the bike. If they'd managed to track her here, the options could provide additional delay for her escape.

Bird calls sliced the hush.

Claire paused, straining to hear any other man-made noise.

Nothing.

Had the others made it out?

Claire stuffed the night goggles in her bag and slung it over her shoulder. She dashed through the forest and skirted the road edge, ears tuned to drones or vehicles. Still nothing.

At the lakeshore, squatting on a rocky promontory beside the road, she rubbed a pinch of the dark damp earth between her fingers while she scanned the surrounds. No sign of recent vehicle tracks. If the drones passed over with thermal logs, they might still zero in.

She breathed deeply, pulse slowing. As she took a few more deep breaths, she donned a pair of goggles and a head torch from her bag. Being careful not to make a splash, she eased into the water and did a front forward surface dive, kicking hard.

The headland plunged deep into the water. About three metres down, a ledge protruded out of sight of the road. Claire swam along the edge and stopped at the doorway to a submerged building. She punched a code on a dimly lit console. A magnetic seal hissed as she cranked the access wheel.

One foot braced against a rock, she strained to slide the door aside. She slipped inside, heaving it shut. Her head torch cast a gloomy glow as she swam two metres over to another access panel and keyed the code. Engines revved as she watched the water drain slowly from the narrow cavity, her lungs burning.

She gasped as an air pocket emerged, body growing heavier as the water receded and she stood in the narrow chamber. A bell chimed. She spun the access wheel for the inner door. She stepped through to a compact room: bunk, table and two chairs, kettle, hot plate, a tub of non-perishable supplies and importantly, a tablet.

She checked the electrical panel and turned on a small desk lamp. She stabbed at the tablet while dripping on the table, her teeth chattering. She shivered, waiting for it to boot up. Signal confirmed, she slapped the table in satisfaction.

She peeled off her soaking combat suit and hung it over the back of a chair, dragging it over to a small heater. She crawled into the bunk, trembling, her skin goose bumped. She pulled the covers up around her shoulders and sank into the pillow, feeling the adrenaline drain away and fatigue press down on every limb.

She closed her eyes, her breath ragged. Images of the explosion flashed inside her skull. The hunters' cries, fears for her colleagues and her crazed ride through the dark forest swam through her awareness until she sank into a dreamless sleep.

◈

The tablet's timestamp revealed two days had passed since she'd escaped to her underwater bunker. She'd built this in the early days with Earth First, not fully trusting the people at the helm. You never knew when you might need an alternative plan.

She'd been right about them too.

Claire drained her whiskey glass, her eyes blurring.

The Chinese space base had meant to be a sabotage mission, not a slaughter. Those fools. They'd set their agenda back decades and tarnished the Earth First reputation.

No longer noble eco-warriors but murderers.

Claire had worked hard to push the militant edge from the organisation, but somehow they slid further outside the law.

She was a fly on the lip of a carnivorous plant waiting to swallow her whole.

Claire poured herself another whiskey and stared at the tablet. She'd activated her own spy drone and scanned the headquarters. The camo hunters had torn the place apart. No sign of her colleagues.

Taken?

Escaped?

Dead?

More bodies were piling up around her.

Her chin sagged to her chest, but memories grabbed her soul and jerked her awake.

The drone feed blinked with a charge warning. She hit the return key, and it shot back home.

Her gaze landed on the bunk, her cramped and lonely temporary home. For how long?

She was tired of being on the run, always hiding.

She'd made her bed with Lincoln Ellison, seeing a path to vindication by exploiting his wealth and resources.

"Some Robin Hood I am," she muttered.

Kidnapping. Extortion.

Dead astronauts. Bullet holes in spattered suits. They'd danced like marionettes.

And Xanthe's dead son.

She never meant to kill him. He came at her. The gun went off.

Crimson puddles bloomed under his crumpled body.

She swallowed hard against the lump in her throat. Drained her glass, warm burn easing the strain.

There was no way out. Lincoln's flytrap held her fast.

He was the worst. Worse than they all suspected.

He funded corporate sabotage. Paid to incite riots at Po Secco. Skimmed helium-3 to fund his Mars project. Paid her to kidnap Victoria Tang. And—God help her—funded the assassination of anyone who crossed him.

All she'd ever wanted was a better future for the planet.

And now the Condor patch lay in wait for the *Nyx Odyssey*.

She had no love for that twat Xanthe Waters or that buffoon Jonas. She'd fought Maja about his selection at Gaia. Still resented it. Not to mention that petulant show pony Serena. An emotional firecracker. Unsuited to leadership or space. But Xavier? Loyal to a fault. Madison? Oozed competence. These were good people.

And Troy. That damned smile.

Her heart swelled.

What might have been.

Bleary eyes landed on the empty bottle. She picked at the label.

They'd never win against Lincoln.

He held all the cards.

She propped her head up on her hand. The room tilted and spun a little.

The lights dimmed. Batteries must be fading.

What was the mission day? She poked at the tablet and the *Nyx Odyssey* flight path popped into view. Day 167.

Ninety-two days to go.

There was still time.

She rubbed her face and shook her head.

She had to get out of here. She needed to find Maja.

Before they found her.

CHAPTER FORTY-THREE

"Transparency is survival; secrecy is death."

—**Madison Floyd**
MARS MANIFESTO

NYX ODYSSEY: TROY

Flight Day 181

Troy crawled into his quarters, head pounding. Once in his sleep suit and slung in his sleeping bag, he fossicked in a pouch for his private painkiller stash. Pulling out the oxy, he hesitated. The pill's chalky scent flooded memories of lunar sick-bay nights, flashbacks to his kidney surgery and the addiction that had taken root on the Moon.

You don't need it. Oblivion won't solve your problems.

He dug around for the milder painkiller, popped a tablet and stashed the rest, including the oxy.

The nightly ritual kicked in: dim the lights, play earth atmospherics in his headset, write in his journal.

Sighing, he retrieved the book and pen.

Feels more like a confessional these days. But it's good for me.

Commander Troy Bruin, log

1. Mission Status

On track for day 259 landing, as planned. Still no comms from the Kunlun Dopplebot Martian base. Satellite imagery shows the base is intact, so no obvious infrastructure catastrophe. Could be a power failure or some sort of EMP that has caused the Dopplebots to malfunction.

Ellison and the Pinnacle are status quo, ahead and sending bragging reports to Earth. Xanthe has reported several incoming ThinkLink hails from someone on the ship. She says it sounds like a garbled distress message. Athena has quarantined it through Nyx's systems and is building a firewall to contain any possible infection.

Troy pressed thumbs into his eye sockets, willing the drugs to numb the throbbing. Crew faces flickered past—tired, pale, space-puffed.

Determined, too.

An alert bleated in his headphones. "Commander, Mission Control requests personal data dump override for an unscheduled systems review."

"What are they worried about this time?"

"Cryo-freeze torpor readings. Shall I pause the personal data dumps?"

Troy pursed his lips. This would not go down well with the crew, but the sleep pods were a priority. "Yes, go ahead."

2. Crew dynamics: observations

Serena, Xanthe and Jonas came out of the freezer today. I'm wondering about the long-term effect of repeated exposure. They're reporting numbness in the extremities, a strange aftertaste from the chemicals. I have Nyx running through all the protocols to make sure we haven't overdosed them on anything. Maybe the systems review will reveal more.

We stuck to the agreement we made a few cycles ago: share only personal data dumps and the major news as they acclimatise, saving detail for a full brief on day two. So, I had to tell them about the crop failure.

Xavier has moved from gutted to sombre. The crickets may not survive if we cannot produce enough leafy greens for them. And without crickets, we will be badly malnourished during our time on the Red Planet. Added to that, the legume crops failing means we have serious protein deficiencies ahead.

Tomorrow, we'll work on a rationing plan. As long as Xanthe doesn't try to take over again. She walks a fine line between co-leading and trampling on my toes. She is so competent I can understand how naturally she steps into the role. But she needs to remember I'm the actual Commander with delegated authority. The crew doesn't need confusion over leadership in a crisis.

This time, she started mandating checks on Jonas as soon as they sat up in the torpor beds. As if I wasn't on to that! I am a goddamn doctor after all. Heat boiled in my chest over that one.

- *__Madison__ remains steady as ever. Though recently she seems to have let her guard down a fraction. We were talking about Captain Gareth Barrio and the Pinnacle, and she sparked up with a few choice words. Very animated. For Madison, anyway. Not sure what happened between the two of them, but something stuck in her craw. Must have been the romance. She was all doe-eyed and coy about him before the whole Mars expedition hit go. All that time they spent together on Moon helium-3 missions. Then Spaceward Bound announced their launch, and it all went to hell, apparently. Aside from the Barrio hot button, she's still grieving, of course. But maybe losing her Mum made her care less about what people think. I should try that sometime.*

- ***Jonas*** *is his reliable self. His baking prowess has improved with his latest batch of cricket protein-enhanced cookies, garnering thumbs up from Xavier. Rare praise indeed. Jonas has committed to working on bread for this next shift. Something to look forward to out of the freezer. His health however — mental and physical — remains an ever-present concern. Like a eucalyptus branch: it looks rock solid then one day out of nowhere it just snaps off. We keep an ever-vigilant eye on possible cracks. But not everything is visible.*

- ***Xavier*** *seems crankier than usual. Delayed comms from Earth due to bandwidth pressure doesn't help.*

- ***Serena*** *won't be happy about the bandwidth issues either. Terra Verdi reports show Max is improving, though the base remains under lockdown, with the latest air and water refugees pressuring for access. The water filtration tech is glitching at Po Secco, and Prima Aqua continues with its belligerence.*

- ***Volkov*** *needs quite a bit of maintenance. Some of his systems are showing degradation. He broadcast in Arlene's voice a couple of more times despite Jonas's multiple reboots of his communication patch. Understandably, Madison is disturbed by these incidents, though she doesn't say much.*

- ***Xanthe.*** *We are still on friendly terms. Sometimes frosty. She still hasn't forgiven me for Gemma.*

Troy's gaze drifted to the picture of his daughter. She had his eyes. And his smile. But his brother's mannerisms. Made sense, considering Travis had raised her. Troy sighed, chewing the end of his pen, his head still throbbing.

I want to be a better father. A bit hard this far from Earth.
I want to be a better leader, a better friend. A better man.

One thing at a time.

3. Ship systems: nothing electrical tape can't fix

Always something—a busted bulb, a blown fuse, a fan rattling like loose teeth. The Nyx has developed a real personality! A cantankerous witch of the night. Aside from the crop failures, the air cycler keeps getting clogged. Filters jam up with hair, crumbs, threads, no matter how careful we are with eating and cleaning. Plus, there's slime buildup in the exercise and hygiene bays. It boggles the mind to think about all the water that goes through the ship, into the plants, us and out again.

4. Next Up: Christmas

We are celebrating tomorrow. Hopefully, we'll have all the family data dumps by then. We've got some potatoes, chicken and homegrown asparagus that seems remarkably resilient compared with the other crops. We've done Secret Santa, and I pulled Xavier.

Troy stashed the journal, sipped nighttime herbal tea from its pouch, pulse bounding at his temple. He tapped his tablet and opened an old data dump file from Gemma. Birthday celebration with Travis and Meg, his wife. They looked so happy.

He tapped the screen to silent; the ship's hum rocked him gently, and the recycled air's metal tang lingered in his nostrils. He snugged the sleeping bag a little more firmly around him as the 'nighttime' atmosphere temperature dipped for optimal sleep.

Gemma pulled a silly face and waved at the camera, tossing her wild auburn mane like a thoroughbred.

Troy wiped the tear that welled in his eye.

Bugger it, he thought and dug an oxy tablet from the stash.

CHAPTER FORTY-FOUR

"We celebrate to keep our spirits alive."

—Serena Fox
MARS MANIFESTO

NYX ODYSSEY: TROY

Flight Day 182

Troy floated down the corridor towards the galley. The rich smell of roast chicken drifted on the recycled air. Jonas was making foil stars and pinning them around the compartment. A loop of Christmas carols—both northern hemisphere classics and southern hemisphere summer versions—blared through the sound system.

Serena had shredded some burrito wrappers into makeshift tinsel, but the strands had snagged in the ventilation grille.

Madison swam in after Troy and tapped him on the shoulder. She lowered her voice and leaned close. "Only enough bandwidth for one family packet to download. Mission Control is sending the update to the torpor pod report and medical contingencies. Shall we activate the personal download or wait?"

She mouthed the word *Serena* and gave him a pointed look.

Troy winced, glancing at Serena, who was humming carols and helping Jonas with the stars.

"Hold the personal data. We've got to get that report through now."

"Roger that," Madison replied. She pushed off the handrail with a foot, spun and glided back towards the flight deck.

"It smells delicious in here," Troy said, hooking a foot under a rail and nodding at Jonas.

"Thanks," Jonas replied. "I've been looking forward to serving this one up."

"What are *you* having?" Troy asked.

"I've got soy chicken with a crispy cricket coating," Jonas said.

"I see." Troy pulled a face. "I suppose we should all get used to it. No chickens on Mars. And the printed meat pulls too much power."

"It's better than it sounds."

Troy's wrist comm pinged with the updated report. He glided over to the central comm screen and punched a few keys to pull it up. His face fell as he read.

"Something wrong?" Xanthe asked as she kicked through the galley to join him.

He moved the screen so she could read it, their shoulders touching. He savoured the warmth and gentle intimacy, so rare these days with Xanthe.

Her face went grim and she shot him a deflated look. "What are we going to do?"

"Let's talk about it after dinner."

Troy shut the screen and set his face with an optimistic smile as Xavier dragged Volkov into the chamber and clamped the bot to a handrail. Madison shot in from the flight deck and floated to the drink station to fill her water bottle. "Anyone need a refill? We can pretend it's eggnog." A wry smile brightened her eyes.

"Ewww. That stuff is a gluggy cholesterol trap." Serena grimaced.

"Eggs, cream and booze—what's not to like?" Madison shot back.

"I'll take rum straight up any day." Serena hooked an arm through Xavier's as they gathered around the central console. "Don't need spices to fancy it up." She squeezed Xavier in a hug and started humming Winter Wonderland.

"Oh my God, I love Christmas!" Serena said. "It's the beach, prawns and that weird week between Boxing Day and New Year's when you have no idea what day it is."

"Beach, huh?" Madison said, shaking her head. "Weird that Aussies have a summer Christmas. But y'all sing Christmas carols about the snow."

"Of course! They're good tunes. Xavier, what do you love about Christmas?"

The big man's face glowed. "My girls. Their excitement and wonder. Nothing like children to bring the magic."

Serena nodded wistfully.

Troy imagined Gemma on Christmas morning with Travis—a little red-headed cherub bouncing on his knee. Could have been Troy's knee. Should have been his knee.

He swallowed the lump of regret that lodged in his throat with a swig of water, or Madison's pretend eggnog.

Troy studied his colleagues as Jonas handed out pouches of their celebratory meal, Serena and Xavier singing along to Jingle Bells. Those two had become close, Troy thought with a pang.

As Commander, there always seemed to be a veil between him and the others. Thin, but ever-present. He longed for a deeper connection, the ease and camaraderie of equals. But the privilege and duty of leadership drove a wedge between them that he hadn't fully anticipated.

Madison kept her own counsel, still incredibly private. Years of military training, he supposed. He worried about her grieving process. It was so much easier when loss was shared. Jonas knew that all too well, Troy thought as he took his meal from Jonas. He skewered a piece of chicken from the packet, chewing slowly. The flavours were more muted than he'd hoped. Space dulled everything.

Jonas had shown no further signs of a traumatic response, thank goodness, though he spent all his time with Volkov, tweaking the bot's programming, trying to fix the speech glitch that kept recycling voices from their families' videos. Somehow the data dumps had crossed the bot's updates and he now had a full repertoire of voices at his disposal.

Troy kept cursory attention on the conversation as his mind grappled with the sleep pod report and its implications. He'd have to address it tonight; the next freezer shift was tomorrow. Xanthe had remained next to him to his surprise, and he tried to dial down the acute awareness he had of the brush of her leg against his, the reassuring timbre of her voice as she joined in the banter.

Xavier rubbed his belly, now considerably smaller than when they'd first launched. "Jonas, *mon ami*, that was sensational. I give it eight stars out of ten."

"Only eight?" Jonas put his hands on his hips.

"Always room for improvement, *non*? Besides, you have come from two-star territory, so this is a huge improvement."

"Harsh, Xavier." Serena poked him on the shoulder.

"What? It's the truth. His cooking has improved. I won't, how do you like to say, 'blow smoke up his dress'?"

"Something like that," Serena laughed.

"I always speak the truth, you know that. Jonas has improved. You have too, Serena. You are much more reliable and thorough now."

She pulled her arm away from his. "I wasn't before?"

Troy was instantly alert. Her tone edged towards confrontation. "Thanks, all. Jonas, the meal was lovely." Troy signalled for everyone to pass him the food pouches and utensils. Xanthe and Jonas shifted aside to let Madison wipe the forks then tuck them in their storage bag while Troy passed a disinfectant cloth through each pouch and secured them in the recycler. Serena kept a stony silence as Xavier sipped his water, feigning nonchalance.

"Xavier, you had dessert, right?" Troy said, hoping to lift the mood. "Then presents?"

There was a buzz of excitement in response, thank goodness.

As Xavier worked his culinary prowess, the galley smelled faintly of cinnamon. He'd somehow coaxed spice from their dwindling hydroponics stash, heating it with protein mash to make a drink that felt like mulled wine if you squinted and wished hard enough.

"I'll go first," Serena announced with a barely contained fizz.

She slid a small bundle across the table to Madison. Wrapped in sterilised gauze, it held a tiny origami bird folded from ration foil. "To remind you of how high you fly," she said softly. "I so admire you, Madison. You soar, always so full of grace." Serena's ponytail wagged high above her head. "Plus, in anticipation of when you fly your first copter on Mars."

Madison smiled shyly, then handed over a slim data stick to Xanthe. "Don't laugh—it's an audiobook. I recorded myself reading your favourite Sagan passages. So even when you're sick of my voice on comms, you'll still have me in your ear. Also, a few of my guitar tracks from when we were on the Moon."

Xanthe's eyes shimmered with unshed tears, while Troy's heart filled with nostalgia and regret. He knew how much Madison wanted to bring the guitar on this trip. It didn't meet the weight restrictions.

Xanthe cleared her throat and presented Jonas with a crudely whittled "medal" cut from a plastic panel, engraved with a shaky "MVP." "For saving our collective arses at least five times this trip. Wear it with pride, mate."

Jonas grinned, pretending to pin it to his chest. "I'll expect salutes at breakfast."

In turn, he nudged a packet toward Serena—a deck of hand-drawn playing cards, each face sketched with crew caricatures. Serena burst out laughing at her own: wild hair, goggles askew, a queen of spades. "I'll take you all for every chocolate ration you've got," she declared, already shuffling.

Xavier waited until the noise died down, then gently laid a clay-like sculpture in front of Troy: a tiny hearth, rounded and smooth. "For Vesta," he said. "For your making this place feel like home. Minus gravity. And a real bed." They laughed. "May the fire never go out."

Troy ran a hand over it, voice gone quiet. "That's…beautiful, *mon ami*. Thank you."

He cleared his throat as he pulled a small tin from his cargo pants pocket. "This one's for you, Xavier," he said, handing him the tin. On the lid, in Troy's blocky handwriting, were four words: *For the Consus Girls*.

Xavier frowned, lifting it with care. "What is this?"

"Reserved seats at the table," Troy said gruffly. "Figured your wife and daughters ought to be with us at Christmas dinner. Might not be much, but…every meal, they're part of the crew too."

For a long moment, Xavier didn't speak. His thumb traced the scrawl on the tin as though it were sacred text. When he finally looked up, his eyes shimmered.

"*Merci, mon frère*," he whispered. "You keep me close to my family."

The others murmured their assent. Serena poked Betty the rubber chicken in approval and it squeaked softly in the hush. Then Xavier strapped the tin carefully to the cutlery panel, another place laid among them, small but unshakeably present.

Finally, Troy changed his toehold, fingertips tracing the table for steadiness. "I've nothing else material," he admitted, "but I've written each of you a letter, so you can read them now or years from now. They're about what you mean to me." He passed them around, fingers lingering on each hand.

Silence fell, heavy with emotion.

"What about me?" Volkov's voice cut through from the rail.

"Oh bollocks! Volkov!" Jonas cried. "What would you like for Christmas?"

"All I want for Christmas is my two front seals." The front panel of his chest plate popped open.

They groaned and Serena threw Betty at him.

Volkov caught the rubber chicken mid-air, holding it aloft. "Excellent. Replacement part acquired."

CHAPTER FORTY-FIVE

"Expertise speaks, but all contribute."

—Troy Bruin
MARS MANIFESTO

NYX ODYSSEY: TROY

Flight Day 182

"That was a lovely Christmas feast. Thank you all." Troy sighed with heartfelt pleasure. "Before we break for the evening," Troy raised a hand to grab their attention as they shifted away, "there's news from the sleep pod report."

He cleared his throat. "Maja and the team are concerned with the elevated fluid levels when emerging from the freezer. They're getting harder to manage and less predictable."

All eyes shifted to him, waiting. The scent of cinnamon faded as the air cycler sucked remnants of their meal into the filters.

"They're worried tingling and frost-nipped fingers could turn permanent." Troy shunted aside his own concern about numb toes.

"Frostbite?" Jonas clarified.

Troy nodded.

"Options?" Madison asked.

"Maja wants us to stop freezer shifts for the rest of the trip. I think—"

"A pause on the freezer is sensible. Crew health is paramount," Xanthe said.

Frosty the Snowman piped through the system.

"Nyx, stop music," Troy said. He clenched his jaw then responded. "That's not really workable, given our rations with the failed crops and reduced cricket output."

"You can't mean for us to go back in the freezer if it risks seizures, frostbite and potential infection, amputation?" Xanthe was aghast.

"I don't think we can really ration any more than we already are. It compromises our future survival on Mars."

"What's the point of rationing if we arrive dead and crippled?" Xanthe said.

Heat flushed Troy's cheeks. He rubbed his jaw, taking a steadying breath. "The risks are still manageable. We can increase monitoring of the pods, and we can change our reanimation protocols to be gentler on the extremities. I can get Nyx to run—"

"Athena just ran a few scenarios and the risk of serious injury is considerably more than the report shows, especially as we have several more freezer rotations before day 259 Mars touchdown."

Troy flung out a hand across the table. "Look, I understand the risks. No one will be forced into the freezer."

Troy was aware of the others following the exchange, eyes pinging backwards and forwards as if at a tennis match. One of Jonas's tinfoil stars came unstuck and drifted into the room.

Xanthe scowled and readied a reply, but Troy cut her off.

"Here's what we are going to do. We will all review the report together. Then each of us will share our thoughts on options: ration heavily, or increase monitoring on the freezer." He stabbed at the screen, and they read through the report again together in silence.

The air cycler thumped and the tinsel batted against the grille.

"Thoughts?" Troy said as lightly as he could.

Xavier scrubbed his head with his fingertips and blew out his cheeks. "*Bof.* Rationing will only make us weaker. We sacrifice now for what's next. Who knows what we will face on Mars." He shrugged. "I will take the freezer."

"I agree," Madison said slowly. She crossed her arms, holding her paper crane carefully between two fingers. "The risks are manageable."

Serena's face scrunched in concern as she shuffled her new deck of cards. "I hate rationing, but I think Xavier's right. Then again, the freezer has never been tested this long in space. But no one has gone to Mars either. I think we need to manage our resources carefully."

Troy's heart thudded as Serena weighed the choices.

"Freezer for me," she said at last.

Jonas nodded in agreement, fiddling with his MVP badge. Troy exhaled quietly. This tipped the decision in his favour. If they were going to risk their lives in the freezer, better if they went willingly than being mandated to do so. He turned to Xanthe, her face pinched and drawn. She closed her eyes, rubbing the back of her neck.

Athena's running scenarios again, Troy thought.

She bit her lip and winced, and alarm bells rang in Troy's mind. The interface was causing her a lot of discomfort lately.

They all watched, waiting.

At last, Xanthe opened her eyes and rubbed her temple. "It's possible to stay within range if we alter fluid flow."

"Maybe Volkov can adjust the fluid valves. He can act as sentry," Jonas said.

"At last, all my dreams come true," the bot said. "Piss recycling for flesh bags."

"Give it a rest, Volkov," Serena muttered.

"What's the matter, darling?" Max's voice spoke through the

bot. Serena's eyes widened. "Can't take a little joke? You need to climb a few mountains and toughen up—"

"Shut up, Volkov!" Serena said, face white.

"When I climbed Everest—the third time out of five—I didn't feel my fingers for days. I ended up peeing all over myself—"

"Jonas, shut him down!" Madison said.

"—couldn't do my zips up. Had to use my teeth—"

"Shut up…" Serena's eyes filled with tears. She covered her mouth with the back of her hand.

Jonas sprung off his foot rail and sailed over to Volkov to shut down his speech mechanism.

"Come on now, babe—" the bot said as Jonas flicked the switch.

Serena sobbed and buried her head in Xavier's shoulder.

The lights glitched and Troy's heart leaped in his chest.

What now?

"Nyx, report."

"Emergency systems reboot. Data dump compromised. Data dump compromised. Data dump compromi—"

The lights flickered again, went out, then on again. The life support systems surged, the ship groaning in response.

The central console burst to life with a few beeps and announced, "Message for Captain Troy Bruin."

The image, stuttered then Gemma's cheerful face in a Santa hat sprang to life as she said, "Merry Christmas, old man!"

Then the screen froze on her face.

It was the only Christmas message that made it through.

CHAPTER FORTY-SIX

"I've had more lives than a cat. And I don't even like cats."

—Jonas Seaborn
MEMOIRS FROM MARS

NYX ODYSSEY: TROY

Flight Day 201

"Nyx, give me an update from the medbay, please," Troy said as he pulled his way along the ship's main artery, stopping to nab a burrito from the mess. He hooked a toe in a foot loop while he inhaled the meal. He hadn't eaten in five hours, having been absorbed in reading the latest data dumps from Earth.

"Serena and Xanthe are securing Jonas in the medbay for the cranial scan."

"Still think it's just Moon-face syndrome?" he said between bites.

"Pain and discomfort would indicate something more serious," the A.I. replied in his earpiece. "Jonas has endured a complex cocktail with the near drowning reanimation injury incident, fluid shift in microgravity and possible rewarming syndrome."

"Anything else?" Troy asked.

"My bets are on the near drowning. Possible cerebral oedema or blood-brain barrier leak."

A thread of guilt stirred. Troy crumpled the burrito sleeve, toed over to the recycler and binned it. "Have we got the report back from Earth yet?" He filled his water bottle from the dispenser, took a swig and headed for the passage to the medbay.

"Bandwidth at 98 percent capacity. We're on amber for data download."

"Serena won't be happy," he said. "We will have to bump her private inbox again."

"That is six days in a row now, Commander."

"I know. She misses Max. I get it."

He pulled himself into the medbay, its consoles glowing with cranial scan graphs, intracranial pressure trends, ECG and electrolyte charts. Serena and Xanthe had loaded Jonas onto the vacuum-suction litter and were readying him for the coffin-shaped automated diagnostics bed for the mini-MRI, the transparent lid riddled with fibre-optic vitals lines.

A faint iodine smell from the skin-prep sticks drifted through the room alongside a dry metallic hint of ozone from the ionising scrubbers. Troy was instantly alert, his emergency response conditioning readying him for the treatment room.

Troy shot over to the group and checked the scanner displays.

"Ready, Jonas?" Xanthe asked.

His face was swollen and pale, and he squinted in pain.

"Just get it over with." His voice was muffled under the oxygen mask. "I can't take any more of these scans."

"Just a quick one," Xanthe said, "then we'll send it Earthside with the ECG."

Troy calculated the data dump required and winced. Another couple of days' delay for personal comms. He glanced at Serena, seeing from her expression she had realised the same. Nothing he could do about it. Jonas could lose his sight unless they found a workable solution.

Jonas gagged and pulled at the mask, his expression terrified.

Troy placed a steadying hand on his shoulder, peering at him. "You've got this. Just a few minutes and you're out again." Troy took a deep breath, signalling Jonas to follow him through the down-regulation exercises they had done multiple times.

After a few rounds, Jonas nodded and replaced his mask. "My head is killing me."

"And now we're going to find out why," Troy said.

The scanner cycled through its intermittent thudding. The background hush of fans was punctuated by a soft *thwup* as the air filter cycled samples. Troy ran a finger down each of the colour-coded Velcro strips on the wall above the scanner—red for trauma gear, blue for diagnostics, yellow for pharmaceuticals. The strips brightened the pale grey of the space. Dull but easy to spot contaminating flecks or floating fluid balls.

The Geiger click track changed tempo, and they were instantly on high alert.

"Nyx, radiation?" Troy asked.

"Storm warning," Nyx intoned as the radiation monitor panel flashed amber then red. The clicks came faster now—thud-click, thud-click, thud-click…Troy's console blazed red.

"Storm Mode!" he barked.

The crew checked their personal wrist dosimeters; readings crept past acceptable limits and they flew into action.

Xanthe reached for the Velcro rails and whisked out the lead-lined panels; Serena followed, yanking the high-density curtain around Jonas in the MRI pod, its scanner still thudding, Jonas wide-eyed.

Troy kept him pinned down. "Stay there, Jonas. We're going to get this scan done. You're in the safest part of the ship, so don't worry, old mate." Troy flashed him a brilliant smile, convincing despite the strain.

Xanthe's voice cut through the clatter: "Medbay team, suit up." She was already whipping out the suits from the storm shelter hold. "Hey—where's Madison? Xavier?" Xanthe said, stopping suddenly. She looked over at Troy.

A startled expression raced across his features, but he dampened them immediately.

"Mad Dog, Xavier—grab Volkov, get to the medbay now!" he blurted into his lapel comm.

"Already on our way," her voice leapt in his earpiece.

Serena and Xanthe scurried to store the sensitive electronics in hibernation mode behind the secondary radiation-hardened racks. A triple ping sounded and Troy dragged Jonas from the MRI coffin, handing him a storm suit.

"Communications shifting to deep-shield antenna. Data dump paused," Nyx announced.

"Goddamn storm," Serena said as she gathered the anti-nausea and anti-inflammatory kits. "Another freakin' delay!"

"Serena, check there's a radio protectant compound in there," Xanthe said. "I moved them around in the last stocktake."

Madison sped through the medbay door, followed by Xavier dragging Volkov behind. She latched the lead screens and high-density curtains behind them. Xavier shuttled Volkov to a rail where the bot secured itself out of the way. Troy handed Madison and Xavier protective suits and then pulled up the bridge display.

"Nyx, show us the radiation hot spots," Troy said. "Everyone, check your dosimeters."

"Spiking," Madison said with a grim look.

"Here, Mad Dog," Xanthe said. She administered a finger prick to check her blood and punched the 'monitor vitals' tab on Madison's suit.

Serena swam through the space and handed Madison an

anti-nausea oral disintegrating tablet. Madison placed it on her tongue gratefully, her lips growing pale as the nausea hit.

As they sealed in, the ship's hull hummed and the medbay LED lights cast iridescent red veils across their weary faces. The water tanks and the reinforced sheeting shielded them from the deadly solar wind that chased them like a celestial dragon, licking fiery breath at their heels.

"I feel sick," Jonas said. He clung to a hand loop near the scanner, rubbing his forehead. "I'm going to puke."

"*Merde!* Not again." Xavier tugged an ear and grimaced.

"Jonas—barf bag," Serena said, pointing at the wrist pouch.

He stared back at her, wincing. "I can't see it. It's all blurry."

Xavier toed across the space, retrieved a vomit bag and looped the Velcro tabs onto Jonas's wrist strap, the orange "EMESIS" label squarely in view. He flipped open the ziplock, tilted the rigid collar under Jonas's chin and guided him slightly forward.

"Okay, *mon ami*. Straight into the funnel this time."

Jonas heaved, face red, tendons stretched like drawn wires beneath his skin. The bag's inner gel beads locked the nausea in place, leaving his fingers clean and suit unsoiled.

"Nicely done," Xavier said, stifling his own gag reflex.

Xanthe shot over to them and checked Jonas's dosimeter.

"It's not radiation," she said quietly, sharing a knowing look with Troy.

"Alright now, Seaborn," Troy said breezily. "We're going to strap you onto the scanner bed. Xanthe—mannitol IV push, please."

"Already on it."

Within minutes they had him secured again on the storm shelter scanner bench, administering the drugs and sedatives designed to encourage fluid drain from his brain.

Once Jonas was settled, groggy and moaning, Troy checked the scanner report: inter-cranial pressure rising, possible brain herniation. He chewed his lip. They'd do another scan using the handheld ultrasound wand to see if the mannitol was having any effect.

He turned the screen to Xanthe as she floated over to the console. They shared a look, resolute. If the swelling continued, they'd need to make a choice: ride it out or attempt a burr-hole to relieve the pressure.

The hours crawled on, the red alert strobe a ghoulish discotheque in the tense and sombre room. All senses tuned to the Geiger metronome, hopes leaping if it slowed, dashed when it resumed.

Twenty-four hours in and nerves were rattled raw. Troy completed hourly scans for Jonas and each time there was a slight elevation of intracranial pressure. He continued with the mannitol. Jonas shifted in and out of lucid awareness.

Conversation was limited, as each crew member retreated to their own private thoughts, managing their anxiety the best they could. Troy counted deep, long inhales and exhales.

The room remained dimly lit, bathed in the eerie red glow from the alert. Consoles in hibernation mode. No data dumps. No comms.

They were alone, dependent on the ship's sensors and machinery to keep them alive, hurtling onwards to the distant dot of Mars.

"This is boring," Volkov said.

"Since when do bots get bored?" asked Serena, reclining in a webbing sling recessed as a medbay couch.

"My programming has made me sensitive to human emotions," Volkov said.

Madison gave a stilted laugh. "Yeah, you're right, Volkov. This is boring." She had rigged a few foot loops to keep her suspended in one spot. Xanthe had taken up the other medbay couch while Xavier had curled up on the medbay examining table, tethered himself there, and had been snoring for the last hour. Troy floated beside Jonas in the MRI scanner.

"Where's Betty?" Jonas asked, rousing suddenly.

Xavier snorted awake and wiped dribble from his chin.

"The rubber chicken?" asked Madison. "I haven't seen that thing in weeks."

"Who had her last?" Jonas asked, squinting across the room.

"Xanthe and I played tag with her last shift out of the freezer," Serena said. "I remember because I made the perfect throw—Betty floated all the way down to the sleep pods."

"Then what did you do with her?" Jonas said.

"Stashed her in your cabin."

"In MY cabin?"

"Yup. What—you never noticed a rubber chook in your sleeping bag?"

"Kidding, right?"

"Nope."

Jonas looked bewildered.

"Ha! Yes, kidding. I've got her in my quarters. She reminds me of Max. Keeps me company." Serena's voice choked.

"Max is very much like a rubber chicken: flaky and squeaks a lot," Xavier said as he rubbed his face, trying to wake up. Serena pulled a face and rolled her eyes.

Jonas winced and then groaned. They fell quiet as Troy checked his vitals.

"Hey. I'm sorry," Jonas said, opening his eyes and panting.

"What for?" Troy said.

"My med scans. I know they're clogging the data dump."

"It's not your fault, Jonas," Serena said quietly. "We all know the drill. We signed up for this. Your eyeballs and brain take priority. You're no good as a blind engineer. Then we'd have to rely on bolt-brain Volkov."

"Your insults lack creativity," Volkov said. "Try harder."

"Power warning," Nyx interrupted. "Scanning bed will sleep in eight minutes. Last scan is now or never."

Xanthe and Troy placed Jonas back in the scanner with now-practiced efficiency and held their breath. Jonas was near threshold.

The scanner triple-pinged, and Troy pulled up the display report. "80% risk of herniation in <6 hours. Burr-hole alert."

Troy swallowed hard. He'd done brain surgery before, on the Moon no less. Xavier's head injury had been nearly fatal. Then he'd installed Xanthe's brain computer interface. But that was on the Moon, with at least some gravity. The odds were terrible for Jonas: 70% mortality and high risk of infection.

Troy gestured for the crew to gather. Serena, Madison, Xavier and Xanthe joined him at the foot of the scanner bed where Jonas lay strapped, semi-conscious, head lolled back on the tray.

"This is what we are facing right now." He held the display report with its scan of Jonas's brain. "Nyx, highlight the problem zone." The swollen area lit up a vibrant red. "Our option is to do an emergency burr-hole to drain the fluid."

The Geiger clicks ratcheted down slightly and then surged again. The ship whirred. Their faces were pale in the red glow of the alert.

"Option. You said option," Serena said. "Is there another one?"

"We wait and see," Troy said with a hard look.

"We have A.I. guidance," Xanthe added. "We could drill with nano-precision. That would alleviate the pressure right away."

"We'd literally be drilling into his brain in the dark of a solar storm," Troy said, trying to keep the reprimand from his voice.

"We've run three mannitol boluses and the ICP is still hovering at 32 mmHg," Xanthe whispered. Troy's knuckles whitened on the monitor rail. "If this keeps up," she said, voice tight, "he'll herniate within hours…"

"Then what?" Madison asked quietly.

"Coma, brainstem compression, cardiorespiratory arrest," Troy said.

"*Merde*," whispered Xavier.

"I say we prep for the burr-hole," Xanthe said. "I'm confident with Athena's guidance in my retinal display that we will get an accurate drill. I've got instantaneous feedback and can—"

"No," Troy barked. He felt the crew jolt at his tone and took a breath before continuing. "We run another mannitol bolus. Give him a fighting chance. If we do that surgery, his survival odds are next to nothing."

"Troy, if we don't do the burr, he'll die regardless." Xanthe's gaze narrowed.

Troy chewed his lip. Four faces stared back at him. Jonas groaned.

"Nyx, how much power is left in the scanning bed?" Troy said suddenly.

"5%."

"Enough to get a partial scan," Troy said, animated. "Serena, load up the mannitol. Xanthe, help me with the scanner. Madison, you stay on the scanner report. Keep your eyes glued there. Look for the ICP levels. We want to see it fall."

"And if it's rising?" Xanthe asked as she readied to slide the scanning bed into position.

"We do the burr-hole," Troy said.

They locked Jonas in place, and the scanner took up its artillery-like thumping. Xanthe retrieved the pneumatic neurosurgical drill from the storm cache. The diagnostics bed's 3D head model projected target coordinates for Kocher's point of Jonas's forehead on the medbay wall.

"I'll do it, Troy," Xanthe said. "Athena will talk me through it."

"No," he said and put a hand on her forearm, startling her. "My call. My responsibility. The MedA.I. is designed for this."

She stared at him as the Geiger continued its relentless clicks.

The rubber-polymer scent swamped his adrenaline-stressed, sour-sweat musk as he pulled on the surgical gloves. It helped steady his nerves.

He took the drill from her, wiped it with the sharp alcohol antiseptic and fired it up. The pneumatic lines hissed as they bled pressure and the ozone tang filled the room. He stood poised over Jonas's form and glanced back at Madison, whose face was lit by the display screen, her face inches from it.

The scanner whirred to a halt as the battery drained.

"Madison?" Troy asked.

All eyes turned to her, waiting.

"ICP falling," she said, looking up with a broad smile.

Troy slumped slightly, and there was a collective sigh of relief.

"That was not boring," Volkov said from his anchored position in the corner of the storm shelter. "What is next?"

CHAPTER FORTY-SEVEN

"The path of righteousness is filled with potholes of regret."

—Claire Edwards
TRANSCRIPT FROM LUNAR
COMMISSION DEPOSITION

FOREST SHELTER: CLAIRE

Flight Day 220

SWEAT INCHED DOWN Claire's spine while she cinched the tarp's guy line, one hand still batting at a stubborn fly. The tarp was well-hidden, tucked between juniper trunks and a sea of cedar scrub. Pausing at the entrance, she threw a few more limestone chips on the tarp roof and dusted the edges with a handful of red dirt for more of a ground shadow effect. She scooped a handful of red soil into her hands and rolled it between her palms as she watched the dusk settle across the valley below, border patrol checkpoint lights flaring.

Nearly two months of making her way down the west coast, staying off the main highways and camping rough, had taken its toll. She was ready for a change.

Claire scanned the area with augmented lenses then ducked

towards the limestone cliffs, keeping out of sight. She climbed a few meters up the slope and reached around to retrieve the radio canister wedged in a crack, the limestone still radiating the day's heat. A rattlesnake buzz shot through the still air, and her hand snapped back, her heart racing.

She drew out her pencil light, risking the narrow beam in the growing darkness, and peered around the corner, searching for the snake.

It was there, a metre away, half in the crack alongside the canister. Its slitted pupils were gleaming, the tip of its rattle wriggling at her. She froze. The snake's coils slid over one another while its tongue flickered.

Slowly she edged backwards, pulse thudding. She strained her eyes in the half-light until she found a stick, snapping it to a suitable size. She counted two slow breaths, then leaned back towards the canister, stick and light gripped in one hand.

Moving slowly, she manoeuvred the stick to pry the canister free. The rattle sounded. Adrenaline shot down her spine. She yanked on the stick, dragging the canister as the snake lashed out, striking it. She flung the canister across the slope away from the snake, scrambled down and retrieved it before scurrying back to the shelter.

She ducked inside, placed the canister in the corner so she could pull on a sweater. Evening chill bit hard and fast in the mountains at dusk. She settled on the sit pad, cedar boughs crunching over the plastic painter's sheet that kept the fire ants out. She snapped her pencil light on again and swept the beam for hitch-hiking ants and fangs under the tarp, just to be sure.

Mexican free-tailed bats erupted from a nearby cave, pinpricks against the stars.

It was time.

She pulled the radio from the canister and then hooked it to the antenna wires she had rigged the day before and adjusted all the settings. Taking a deep breath, she hit the talk button.

"Gaia Enterprises, come in."

Crackle.

Claire adjusted the settings and tried again.

"Gaia Enterprises, come in."

A hiss, a moment of static, then:

"This is Gaia. Who's on channel, over?"

"This is Claire Edwards for Maja Garcia. Get her now. You have two minutes, then I'm gone."

Silence, then:

"Wait one, over."

Claire breathed in the earthy cedar and shivered as the sweat cooled under her sweater. She checked her watch. Time was almost up.

"This is Maja Garcia."

Maja's voice flooded the radio channel, calm despite the rush. Claire blinked in surprise at the flash of nostalgia in the presence of her old mentor. Their last conversation? Years ago, about the future of the Olympus Project. They'd each argued for a different vision of the future, neither of which had been realised.

"Maja. It's Claire."

A pause.

"Claire…this is a surprise." Claire imagined Maja reaching for the right words. "Why are you calling?"

"It's about the *Nyx Odyssey* Mars mission."

"Yes?" Maja's voice was wracked with suspicion. Not surprising, thought Claire.

"Lincoln Ellison plans to sabotage the mission."

"Lincoln is nearly on Mars now, Claire." The line crackled. "Why are you reaching out to us? What are you up to?"

Claire held the talk piece, mouth open, but words flapped through her brain without taking flight. "Look, I know this is coming out of nowhere, but I have evidence of Ellison's sabotage, helium-3 skimming, funding of the Po Secco riots."

Silence.

"Hello? Maja, you there?"

"Yes. This is all very…interesting. Why don't you come in and talk about it? Show us all this evidence."

Claire swallowed hard. Into the dragon's lair now. No going back.

"I will do that. But I have conditions."

CHAPTER FORTY-EIGHT

"The answer to all problems starts with communication. Try it."

—Xavier Consus
MARS CULTURE CODE

NYX ODYSSEY: SERENA

Flight Day 240

Serena crawled out of her sleeping quarters, the corridor half-lit as they eased towards yet another 'day'. Not long to go now, she noted as she sailed through the galley. The display read MARS ENTRY -19 days.

Lincoln bloody Ellison was set to land tomorrow, stealing the title of first humans on Mars. As long as they beat him to the Chinese Dopplebot Kunlun base, then it was all good. No one wanted a future where Lincoln controlled Mars and the future of humanity. Serena shuddered at the thought.

She filled her water bottle before heading towards the medbay. Her stomach was giving her trouble again and she wanted to grab a nausea tab before her comms shift began.

Serena pulled herself through the medbay doors, the smell of antiseptic assaulting her senses, and pulled up short, catching sight of Troy palming an oxy.

"Are you serious?" she hissed.

He flushed pink, then snapped. "It's a controlled dose—let it go."

She stared at him, but he held her gaze.

"How long have you been taking them?" she said in a quiet voice.

Troy closed the medkit pouch and stashed it in its cupboard. "I haven't been 'taking them'. Just one or two every other shift. My levels are fine. You can check the report." He grabbed a hand loop and stared down at her, defiant.

"Xanthe know?"

Troy's face flashed before resuming a cool demeanour.

"Time to wake the others," he muttered, toeing off a handrail, heading towards the flight deck.

Serena's eyes narrowed. How much of a problem was this? They were all self-medicating.

But oxy...

Troy had done irreparable damage to his kidneys on the Moon with his addiction.

Though his levels were fine now.

So he said.

Unnerved, she headed towards the back of the ship for her secret spot in the sleep torpor bay. She had about fifteen minutes before the others woke.

She searched under the far sleep tubes and retrieved the tablet she'd stored there. Working quickly, she primed the software backdoor data stream, nudging it into the tight mid-bandwidth window, praying it wouldn't glitch and squeeze out the other info coming from Earth. There'd been a lot lately—updates and reports ahead of the landing.

With all of them out of the freezer now until they hit Mars, demands on the data stream were critical. A twinge of guilt clenched her stomach.

But she needed this precious tether to Earth. With no family, Max was the keel that kept her upright in the craziness of this long journey. They all needed support. Max was her lifeline. She traced Max's oxygen mask clip she kept clipped to her lapel and her nerves settled.

And there he was! The private video from Max.

She glanced once down the corridor. Empty.

Kneeling at an access panel along Nyx's spine, she twisted the latch with her multitool and exposed the ship's nervous system: bundled cables, gleaming ports, the arterial hum of current. From her pocket she drew the data knife, a slim blade of circuitry, sharp with contact prongs, and slid it into the port.

The splice took. Her tablet was now tethered to Nyx's core, drawing Max's buried message out of the ship's data stream. Serena held her breath. Mission Control had promised today's patch would provide 'bulletproof' guidance, a clean artery to keep them safe. She prayed her tap wouldn't cross the same vein and choke the update before it could take.

Packet throughput dropped 18%.

A red icon flickered—only once, but enough to raise a sweat under her collar.

She hunched over the tablet to shield the glow and jabbed at the screen.

Play, damn you.

⁊

Troy took Madison's hail as he pounded on the treadmill, Xavier straining on the strength machine beside him.

"What's up?"

"The computer buffer flagged 'incomplete DSN package.' Was

that the guidance telemetry path we've been waiting for?" Madison's voice edgy.

"Could have been," he replied, huffing as he continued his run.

Xanthe's voice came over the system. "Could be interference again. Athena has been working on the decryption of the *Pinnacle* message, with support from Earth. Maybe it bumped the queue?"

"It shouldn't have. We made allocations for that patch," Madison said.

"We've also got a garbled message on an encryption we've been working on from the *Pinnacle* A.I. to Athena," Xanthe added.

Xavier paused his squats and Troy slowed to a walk. "Play it for me."

"*Pinnacle*…breach…helix…inbound."

"Athena thinks it might be one of several options: the *Pinnacle* is breached, we're breached, a message is inbound—an SOS or a patch or a virus—hard to tell. And—aargh—"

"Xanthe, you okay?" Madison's voice was strained now.

Troy stopped, listening. He exchanged a glance with Xavier.

"I'm okay. Just the pain that happens sometimes when Athena processes data."

"Madison?" Troy asked.

"She's okay. Just a passing glitch."

Concern coiled in the corner of Troy's mind. "I'll be there in ten. Just wrapping up the rehab session."

"Roger." Madison's voice was back to business.

Troy stayed anchored by the weight belt on the treadmill and performed his stretches, mind running over the exchange with Xanthe and Madison. He worried about Xanthe; her head pain was getting worse.

Then that data problem. CapCom was insistent this patch would adjust telemetry for re-entry. They'd had so many comms glitches lately: the minor solar flare burning up data, one of the relays going offline, corrupted messages. It was frustrating. More than that, it highlighted just how isolated they were.

Tinnitus whirred again in his ear, and his eyes cast a long look towards the exercise bay medkit, the oxy stashed in a pocket. He'd cut way back on the pills, but he felt the burn to have one smouldering constantly.

"You alright, *mon vieux*?" Xavier hooked a toe at the end of the treadmill and floated in front of Troy as he did his own stretches. "You look like you stuck a nose in the poo chute."

"All good," Troy said breezily with a reassuring smile.

"*Bof!* You fool no one. Is it Xanthe again?"

Troy glanced at him and conceded with a shrug. He grew uncomfortable as Xavier chewed a lip, eyes narrowed, obviously mulling over something.

"Xavier—what?"

Xavier raised an eyebrow and waved a hand as if to draw out the words. "Don't shut her down all the time."

"What?" Troy dropped his arm stretch in surprise.

"*Mon ami*. You are the Commander. It's a big job. But sometimes she is right. She has the Athena advantage, after all."

Troy pursed his lips. "That again. A computer interface does not trump human judgement. There are nuances."

"Alright already!" Xavier half-chuckled, throwing his hands up in a placating gesture. "I just want you to consider that maybe you squash her too much because you love her so much."

Troy's mouth fell open.

"Yes, I know. You threw that love story onto the compost long ago. But, my friend, that seed still sprouts in the dark." Xavier clapped him on the shoulder. "Stop punishing her because of your bruised ego."

A fire burned through Troy. "Speaking of egos, maybe you should tone down the superior tone you take."

Xavier sipped from his water bottle and secured it back to its

Velcro hold, eyeing Troy with a narrow gaze. "Eh? Superior tone? With whom?"

"Pretty much everyone." Troy undid the weight belt, regretting the conversation and wanting to escape to the shower.

"I will think on that. But you think about what I said too." He pointed a finger at Troy.

Troy tilted his head, hands on his hips, as he drifted before Xavier, his oldest friend. "I will. I promise."

They came together in an awkward floating space hug.

"Good. Now get out of here. That gorgeous woman is waiting for you on the flight deck and you smell like a wet goat."

CHAPTER FORTY-NINE

"Equality sounds noble until the weakest voice drags us all down."

—Lincoln Ellison
MEMOIRS FROM MARS

NYX ODYSSEY: TROY

Flight Day 254

Troy floated into the galley next to Madison.

"Power spikes again," she muttered, stabbing at the heat map. "That pod bay's glowing like a supernova."

Troy handed her a pouch of coffee, Jonas's special cricket protein enhanced brew. They were all underweight with the rations and lingering nausea from the torpor pods. Madison's flight suit gaped and her forearms looked like twigs.

Mine don't look great either, he thought, noting the skeletal look of his own arms.

Madison took the pouch gratefully and continued studying the console data dump display with a serious look. He sipped his own coffee, watching her work. Xavier had increased the cricket yield, and now they were on a nutrition boost regime. He clutched the pouch, savouring the rich roasted aroma that masked the faint whiff of decay from the composter as his eyes scanned the morning readouts.

They had been all-hands since the last freezer shift ended nineteen days ago. The ship had felt loud and crowded with all of them floating through cramped quarters. He'd hoped the excitement of getting closer to their goal would override any tension of diminished privacy and personal space. Mostly, they were getting along just fine.

They were too busy to get irritated with one another, performing multiple systems checks and drills, readying for the Mars landing. They'd had news that the *Pinnacle* had landed, presumably unscathed, though there was still no update.

He'd also hoped that things might improve with Xanthe, but the distance between them stretched back to Earth.

He swiped a screen on the galley display to bring up the flight deck cam. He watched Xanthe float at the flight deck threshold, headlamp haloed over tangled code. She didn't look up. Another day wrestling with code. No room for anything else, least of all him.

More messages had been arriving from the *Pinnacle* daily, but they were no further in cracking them.

Madison frowned.

Troy pushed himself over to her. "Anything?"

"There's an anomaly in here somewhere," she replied. "Weird power surges and diversions, especially during data dump windows. The sleeper pods seem to be a hotspot." She pointed at the screen with the ship's schematic overlain with an energy use heat map. "I've sent Volkov there to assess the pods' wiring and integrity."

She drained her coffee, her eyes still locked on the screen. "I might go join him there. Something's weird." Madison shut the console screen and sprung off the rail to haul herself down to the end of the ship while Serena, Xavier and Jonas swam into the galley.

"Ready for drills this morning?' Troy said, forcing a cheeriness he didn't feel.

"Born ready, *mon ami*." Xavier flexed a bicep and Troy laughed. Of all of them, Xavier had lost the most weight, his cheekbones pronounced and his jumpsuit so baggy he looked like a six-year-old in his father's clothes.

At least his leg wasn't bothering him so much. But gravity might have something to say about that if they landed on Mars.

When they landed, he corrected himself. The landing drills were still ending in disaster, concern worming holes of dread through all of them.

Jonas handed out coffee protein slurries while Serena retrieved their breakfast pouches.

"Where's Xanthe?" Troy asked.

Xavier waved behind him. "Flight deck. She thinks they're getting close on the encryption. But we have all heard that a million times already."

Troy scraped at his porridge pouch, ignoring the tinnitus setting his teeth on edge, the oxy burning a hole in his cargo pants—sweet relief just a blister pack away. But he needed full focus for the drills, and while oxy might dull the pain, it would also soften his thinking edge.

Madison returned, hauling Volkov behind her. The bot clamped onto a handrail, and Madison hooked a foot in a loop. She brandished a tablet, eyes wide and face full of fury.

"Volkov found *this*," Madison declared.

Troy, Xavier and Jonas continued their breakfast, unimpressed.

"A tablet? So what?" Xavier said as he scraped the last of his porridge pouch. "Did Jonas leave his in the workshop again?"

"Not mine," Jonas said, tapping the tablet Velcroed to his leg strap.

Madison slammed the tablet down on the display table: "Telemetry directory, 43 GB missing. Someone siphoned it."

"Have you checked the logs?" Jonas asked.

"Of course. Download tag: pvt_maxcam_icu. It's Serena's," Madison said in a low voice, her eyes locked on Serena, whose face washed crimson. "I cross-checked all the data dumps. You've been data hoarding for messages from Max, haven't you?"

"I—" Serena searched for words, then pulled her floating hair into a quick ponytail that floated upright like a rhino horn. "Must be a bandwidth glitch."

"This is your tablet, isn't it?" Madison poked the offending item.

"Yeah, it's my tablet. So what?"

"Jesus Christ, Serena! You stole bandwidth that compromised the telemetry uploads. And yesterday's Mission Control message." Madison shook the tablet at Serena. "What else have we missed? Oh my God—the decryption—it's been struggling for weeks!"

"Madison, calm down." Troy used his spoon as a gavel on the central table. Jonas and Xavier looked on, horrified. "Serena, is it true?"

Troy watched a ripple of emotion go through Serena. Dread cratered his gut.

"I only did it a few times. And I was careful not to when there were important data dumps coming through."

"We're nine months in space and nearly at Mars," Madison spat. "Everything is important!"

"We agreed to small personal bursts. Max is fighting for every breath, okay?" Serena shot back. Her hand covered the oxygen clip on her lapel. "We all let you have data when you needed it, Madison. And Max was in intensive care!"

"My mother *died*, Serena." Madison leaned over, two hands pressed onto the table, nudging Troy aside.

"Enough!" Troy said. "Comm privileges are revoked—"

"I would never compromise the safety of the mission!" Serena said. "Unlike *some people.*" She glared at Troy.

"That's enough," Troy warned, pointing his spoon at her.

"No, it's high time I said something. Troy has been taking oxy again."

They froze and stared at him. Troy dropped his head, jaw muscles clenching.

"We'll talk about each of our medical issues later, ahead of the landing. Right now, we need to figure out just what we've missed in the data dumps."

Madison looked absolutely apoplectic, nostrils flared, eyes bulging. Xavier opened his mouth to say something, while Jonas jutted his chin with brows knit. Serena crossed her arms, defiant, with her ponytail floating like an indignant cockatoo crest.

"Troy, where are you?" Xanthe's voice cut in over the ship's comm.

"We're in the galley," Troy said, avoiding the eyes of his colleagues.

"There's an urgent message from Mission Control. You need to see this."

❧

Troy shot out of the galley, leaving the others to clean up the poo bomb Serena had dropped on them.

I'll deal with that later.

He buried the anxiety that tightened his throat and brought his focus to the current moment.

As he floated onto the flight deck, Mars filled the cupola view, its rusty swirls mesmerising. But it was Xanthe's stricken face that sent his heart rate skittering.

"Show me."

He pulled himself alongside her, their shoulders touching gently, a hint of lavender drifting off her clothes. The screen blinked with red alerts.

Urgent: Mission-Critical Notice

Be advised Claire Edwards has been taken into custody. In exchange for immunity, she has provided evidence of Lincoln Ellison's sabotage of Nyx Odyssey mission. We suspect a corruption of landing telemetry delivered by malignant patch 'Condor'. Confirm you received secure telemetry patch in previous data dump?

Troy's mouth went dry. He looked at Xanthe and saw his own terror mirrored there.

"Athena finally cracked the encryption," she whispered. "It's from Dr Victoria Tang's A.I. She's been taken against her will and confirms that Ellison hitched the sabotaged Condor patch on our launch, and maybe again as we came close to their flight path on approach. Guidance software might be infected."

They stared at each other.

"How does it work?" he asked.

"Condor piggybacks on the guidance update, inverts a single number in the landing curves and waits for gravity to do the rest."

"So, it hits us when we are most vulnerable?"

Troy spun as Madison and the others crowded onto the flight deck.

"How bad is it?" Madison asked.

Noting his hesitation and their stricken faces, she kicked over to the console and read the dispatch.

"Goddamn it! Serena's data diversion prevented a telemetry patch upload!" Madison whirled on Serena, who had gone pale. "Your selfish actions may have killed us all!"

Alarms bloomed. A red strobe washed across six wide-eyed humans.

"Mad Dog, stand down," Troy said. He edged between them, heart hammering. "We need solutions, not blame. This is what we need to do: strip the firmware, isolate guidance, prepare for manual descent—we have five days."

CHAPTER FIFTY

ARCADIA PLANITIA, MARS: LINCOLN

Flight Day 255

LINCOLN ELLISON THREW his coffee mug across *Pinnacle*'s flight deck, a sheet of brown droplets arcing across the screens. He hit the comms button. "Barrio—where are you? Get your ass to the flight deck now! We have a situation."

"I'm in the hold, working on the copter. Be there in two."

Lincoln chewed his bottom lip, fuming. Mouth dry, he reached for a water bottle. His breath stank again and he clawed at his pockets for a mint.

That bitch Claire Edwards! I'll have her hide, come hell or high water.

Lincoln leaped to his feet as Barrio climbed off the ladder onto the flight deck, panting. They'd landed two weeks ago, but it was still taking some time to adjust to the Martian gravity. The captain, who was sporting a three-day beard, wiped his forehead with a grimy sleeve, his eyes sunken. He nodded at Lincoln, catching his breath, readying for the update.

"Claire Edwards sold us out," Lincoln said. "She's told the Lunar Commission about everything—the helium-3, Prima Aqua, Condor, the lot. Every ace in our hand—gone." Lincoln gripped the back of the commander's chair, knuckles white, Ozymandias perched like a turret. "They've frozen Spaceward Bound assets while Claire testifies in custody."

Wind lashed the flight deck window with red dust, adding to the grim coating.

Barrio rubbed the stubble on his chin. "What does this mean for us?"

"It means we need to get our asses to Kunlun before the Nyx lands in four days. If the Condor patch is discovered and disarmed, they will beat us to the base and claim sovereignty over it, and we will have nothing!"

He pounded a fist into the chair. "We need that air-cycling tech. Aryanna had our water purification operation seized. And the Lunar Commission has taken over the helium-3 Moon mining operation. Without the Chinese base, we are stuck here with no resources or backup, at their mercy."

Spittle flung across the room. Lincoln ran a hand through his greasy hair; the perfect coif long gone by the wayside. "When can the copter be ready?"

They'd had a rough landing with their land transport, the rover and the copter, having broken free from their brackets and churned together in a tumbler. Parts had grinded and seared in the tumble.

"The engine is working now since I stripped the Julius Dopple-bot for parts, but I've still got to fix the secondary tank so we have enough fuel to get us all there."

A vein stood out on Lincoln's temple like a baby snake.

"How many could the copter take with one tank?"

Barrio studied Lincoln's face, eyes growing cold. "Three, maybe four. Any more and we would land short."

"Good. Prep for three. Me, you and Tang."

The muscles in Barrio's jaw tensed as he considered Lincoln. "And the others?" His tone was even, but his lips pressed into a grim line.

"They can stay here for now." Lincoln waved a hand breezily.

"I had to harvest rover parts for the copter. They'd be stranded here." Barrio took a slow breath. "There are sixty-five days of rations left on board. And the water cycler is sketchy."

"They'll be fine. We'll get to the base and do shuttle runs to bring them over."

Outside, dust hissed faintly against the hull.

"There are a lot of variables to manage, Lincoln," Gareth said slowly. "First, we don't know the state of the base. Second, we don't know if there's fuel there for the copter. Third, we don't know if the copter can make that trip multiple times—we haven't even done it once—"

Lincoln slammed a fist down on the commander's chair. "God-damn it, Barrio! I said, prep for three! Now do it!"

Gareth held Lincoln's iron gaze for a long beat before turning.

"Thirty-six hours," he said. Then, without looking back, "Sir."

The word landed like an airlock slamming shut.

CHAPTER FIFTY-ONE

"There is no justice or fairness on Mars. Just survival."

—Lincoln Ellison
MEMOIRS FROM MARS

NYX ODYSSEY: XANTHE

Flight Day 259

XANTHE FLOATED ONTO the flight deck last, the others already strapped in, helmets clamped, acceleration harnesses secure. Volkov was fixed to his post by the electronics board; he gave her a small wave as she moved to the cupola to lock it for descent.

Mars swelled in the viewport: at its edge, the thin blue-grey limb of atmosphere clung like a desperate lover. She paused, mesmerised. Below, burnt ochre dunes rippled like the hide of an ancient beast.

Xanthe studied the beast's flank, seeing how sinuous canyons etched charcoal lines like scales. Dry, cracked veins of surface fractures ran in rusted red across plains whorling with wisps of cinnamon. Dust veils curled like dragon's breath catching the light in golden orbs.

Magic. A land of myth and monsters.

But she was no warrior.

Mars, God of War, we come in peace, she thought, though Lincoln might yet call them to fight. Xanthe took one last look, sealed the iris lid and sent a silent thanks to the universe. From the Moon's austere craters, to the cloudy blue swirls of Earth, to this—the dusty red face of Mars—she was grateful to have witnessed it all.

The murmur of the crew and the pressing reality of the imminent landing brought her back to the pings, blips and thrum of the metallic spear sailing towards the surface.

She tumbled forward to the crew. Serena had Betty the rubber chicken strapped to the console, while Jonas rubbed gloved hands along his armrests; Xavier hummed a French love song beside a photo of his family. Madison and Troy worked through the checklist.

Xanthe slid into the seat between them. A dull throb cradled the base of her neck.

"All biomarkers tracking well, Xanthe." Athena's voice was a familiar reassurance in her mind.

Let's hope the Nyx holds up too.

"All functions within range. No trace of the Condor patch."

That's what I'm worried about. Dormant viruses.

On a private channel, Troy asked, "How's the headache?"

"There but background." She offered a reassuring smile, his eyes a blue sea of concern that caught her breath. "How's *yours?*" she said pointedly.

"Under control."

Since Serena had revealed Troy's oxy use, they'd had a frank discussion about frailties—human and digital. Troy had surrendered the oxy, submitting to a full physical under her supervision. She shivered at the memory of warm skin under her hands.

"Standby for the final message from Mission Control." Xanthe snuck a look at Troy as his voice seemed a little strained.

He patched through the data burst.

"My dear crew of the Nyx Odyssey."

Xanthe recognised Maja Garcia's voice, and her heart lurched in her throat. What she'd do for Maja's counsel right now.

"We've all watched and listened to your progress over these long months. Please know how much we are rooting for you and in awe of your courage, resilience and resourcefulness. It's over to you now, and I couldn't think of six other individuals who would do as fine a job."

"Eight. There are eight of us," Volkov said in the background.

"Our thoughts and love are with you. See you on the other side. Have a soft landing. Ad astra."

"That's it, folks. Over to us now," Troy said, tone even. "Confirm ready for descent."

One by one, the crew answered 'ready'. Xanthe's heart thudded. She sipped a little water from her suit mouthpiece, the flat, warm taste strangely reassuring to her parched throat.

"Ready to go manual control. Madison, you've got the stick."

"Copy that. Manual control engaged." Madison eased the joystick deftly from its lock. "Nyx, route all landing telemetry to my console only."

"Routing complete."

"Starting descent."

Xanthe gripped the chair armrests, breathing to slow her heart rate. She kept her eyes locked on the nose cone feed, a dark patch in the bottom corner.

Athena, what is that blotch on screen?

"Lower atmosphere dust storm."

She waited a heartbeat or two for Nyx to identify it. Nothing.

"Madison, there's a dust storm in the lower quadrant—turbulence risk." Xanthe pointed at the screen.

Madison craned slightly forward. "I see it. Nyx, confirm." Nothing.

"Nyx, confirm dust storm," Madison said firmly.

A beat or two and Xanthe held her breath. Then Nyx replied,

"Confirmed: low-level dust storm. Crosswinds at thirty-two metres per second."

"Copy. Compensating." Madison nudged the stick.

"Nice and steady, Mad Dog," Troy said. "Good work."

Xanthe exhaled slowly, heart thudding in her ribcage.

The hull groaned as the heat shield bit into Mars' atmosphere. Thrusters roared, muffling commands.

"Altitude: twenty-three kilometres," Nyx reported.

Harnesses creaked as the ship jolted. Xanthe watched as Madison wrestled with the controls, her arms rigid and her face contorted in concentration.

Troy swiped a nav panel. "Hold your vector, Mad Dog." Voice edgy.

"Trying. Controls are sluggish—input lag's up two seconds."

Oscillations jolted the ship, and they slumped forward and back. Warning klaxons blared.

Alarm stabbed Xanthe hard in the gut. *Athena—analysis?*

"Disruption is not mechanical. Primary descent controls seem to have been rerouted."

How?

"My guess—Condor patch is now live."

Verify.

Xanthe squeezed her eyes shut against the searing pain as Athena activated more processing power.

Madison strained against the controls. "Ship won't respond!"

"Madison, hold steady!" Troy barked. "Jonas, systems check."

"All live," Jonas said as he shut down the alarms.

"I confirm: Condor patch is steepening trajectory—risk of burn-up."

Can you override it?

"Not without simultaneous physical manipulation of the controls. If we do this, the likelihood of brain tissue damage is high."

Xanthe blinked once, twice, then her resolve hardened.

"Troy, it's the Condor patch," Xanthe's voice cut through. "Athena has identified it. You need to give me command—now."

"Negative. We've got this."

The ship lurched, the hull roaring as it plummeted.

Troy glanced over then, "Madison—can you hold steady?"

"Not for much longer!" Her whole body braced, contorted around the controls.

"Troy, I can lock it out with Athena, but I need the conn. We'll lose seconds bouncing orders through you."

"You're asking me to step aside in the middle of final descent."

"No, I'm telling you—if you want us alive, you *have to*."

"And the brain damage?"

His crystal-blue eyes bored into hers.

"It won't matter if we're burnt to cinders!" She saw the devastation on his face, knowing what it was costing him to cede command, and to authorise her sacrifice. Her iron gaze willed him to step aside. "Please," she whispered. "For all of us."

A violent yaw rocked them.

Madison twisted in her chair as the ship seesawed. "Losing vector!"

Jonas muttered to himself as he punched at the display, adjusting sensors. "Thrusters aren't responding!"

Serena breathed hard in her helmet, pushing against the harness. Xavier moaned as the g-force spiked.

Still staring at Xanthe over Madison's twisted form, Troy said, "I formally cede command to Xanthe Waters. Deputy, you have the conn."

"Athena, route all primary descent controls through my link." Her vision blurred, then sharpened. The ship's pitch tugged her ribs; yaw twisted her jaw; drift knotted her gut. Thruster heat pressed at her fingertips. Athena surged through her neural pathways, hunting the virus.

"Routing complete. Link engaged," Athena announced over the ship's comms.

Xanthe's fingertips prickled with thruster heat—not the warmth of metal, but a live pressure under her nails. Her whole body electrified as Athena surged, hunting the Condor patch and regaining control of the descent controls.

"Radar lock. Five hundred metres. Descent rate twenty-one metres per second." Athena's voice was calm.

Xanthe panted, the pain like fire in every neural pathway. "Slow it down, slow it down…Madison?"

"Got it," Madison said, stick easing.

Thrusters hammered. The ship groaned.

"Jonas—pulse left thruster," Xanthe said.

"Firing."

The ship steadied.

Xanthe's mind seemed to detach from her body. Athena's control of the ship burned a highway of energy through her brain tissue. She closed her eyes, responding now to Athena's prompts as if from a great distance. Xanthe's consciousness extended into the ship, becoming the ship.

The crosswind spiked—a slap across her temple—and she pushed back, balancing the tilt.

"Warning," Athena said. "Thruster chamber pressure rising beyond tolerance. Failure projected in forty-five seconds."

"That's a fuel feed issue," Jonas shouted above the roar of the ship. "I can reroute through secondary, but the valve's in aft bay two." He reached to unclip his harness.

Athena flashed the ship's schematics on Xanthe's retinas. The maintenance crawlspace was *behind* the heat shield control panel, requiring manual override because the Condor malware was locking Athena out. The compartment was unshielded from descent heating—skin temperature rising to hundreds of degrees—and it was outside the crash couch safety zone.

Xanthe's eyes shot open. "You can't get there in time—strap back in."

"If I don't, we cook a thruster and lose control. That's worse."

Volkov unclamped, blocking him with a steel grip. "I will go. I am immune to heat stress and crash trauma."

"You're not rated for manual override—" Jonas began.

"Your fleshbag will melt. I won't," Volkov said with a sardonic nonchalance.

"You'll be damaged…" Jonas whispered.

"I am here to help, bag of bones." Volkov clamped to the deck, hauling aft as the hull shook.

"Hurry, Volkov," Xanthe urged. "We've got to burn the last thrusters or we're done."

Xanthe shut her eyes tight again, breathing shallow as the pain seared white-hot through every fibre.

Volkov's voice came over comms, counting off valve turns. "Done."

"Jonas—last burn. Hard." Xanthe experienced her own voice as if disembodied. "Madison, hold the trajectory."

They rode the descent curve, Jonas feeding micro-bursts to the thrusters in an even heartbeat at her command. Her own pulse synced with the ship's surges.

Athena counted down their approach.

Dust slammed against the viewports with a choking red haze. She sensed the flatness beneath with the drop in oscillation. A bone-deep rumble rattled her ribcage.

"Fifty metres," Athena said.

Xanthe screwed her eyes shut, straining to stay conscious, a shallow pant fighting the darkness that bloomed behind her eyelids.

A jolt.

"Touchdown confirmed," Athena said. "Lateral drift zero-point-two. Structural integrity nominal."

Silence flooded the chamber but for the ticking of cooling metal.

"Welcome to Mars," Xanthe heard Troy say before everything went black.

⁊

Someone was shaking her. Calling her name. "Troy?"

Xanthe winced, her head throbbing, her chest aching against the harness.

"You blacked out," he said, his hands on her shoulders.

She opened her eyes slowly, the pain like ice daggers. Everything dark.

"Did we lose power?" she asked. "Why are the lights out? Helmet visor blocked?" She rubbed it.

"No," Troy whispered.

She heard the hitch in his voice before the words.

"Xanthe…I think you're blind."

PART THREE

MARS

CHAPTER FIFTY-TWO

"Mars doesn't judge. It's one test: survive or die."

—Lincoln Ellison
MEMOIRS FROM MARS

NYX ODYSSEY, UTOPIA PLANITIA: TROY

Mars Day 1

Troy held Xanthe steady and helped her unbuckle. "What does Athena say about your vision?"

"Nothing. She's gone dark too. Short circuit? Rebooting? Don't know."

"Does it hurt?"

"Strangely, no. My head feels…clear." She leaned back against the chair, eyes closed. "I'm just…exhausted."

He checked the others—slow movements, shallow breaths—all adjusting to the drag of Martian gravity. After nine months of floating, he felt heavy as an elephant.

"Jonas, systems report," Troy said.

Jonas glanced over his shoulder. "Are you in command now, Troy?"

Heads turned. Troy's throat tightened. "I—"

"Wait, Athena's back," Xanthe cut in. She sat forward, eyes wide, unseeing.

"I am online, Commander Waters," Athena's voice came through the ThinkLink.

"What happened?" she said.

Athena's tone softened.

"You've lost all vision, Xanthe. The ThinkLink overloaded your brain's visual pathways during descent—tiny parts of the nerves and processing centres were damaged beyond repair. Some new treatments might help one day, but the chances right now are only about seventeen percent. For now…you need to focus on the mission."

She blinked, squeezed her eyes shut and opened them wide again. Her brows knitted together; her lips trembled.

Troy's gloved hand closed over hers. Around them, the crew shifted in uneasy silence. Xanthe's unseeing eyes remained wide, searching, finding nothing.

Xanthe drew a breath, steadying. "Jonas, systems report."

Jonas hesitated a fraction, then faced his displays. "All functions nominal. Engines cooling. Internal pressure stable."

"Serena, life support for surface stationing?"

Sorrow surged through Troy's chest.

"Affirmative," Serena's voice wavered; she looked at Troy with a pained expression.

"Cleared to remove helmets," Xanthe said. Her fingers fumbled with the latch. She rubbed her forehead, buying herself a moment.

"Xanthe—" Troy began.

"Yes, thank you, Troy." She sat straighter, voice taut but clear. "I cede command to Dr Troy Bruin." Her voice wobbled. "You have the conn."

"Are you sure?" He crouched in front of her, helmet in hand, searching her face.

Her mouth trembled. "Not really. But I'm blind." The words cracked, and two hot tears slid down her cheeks.

The others drew in close, a silent ring of bodies around her chair.

"Athena, route communications through the ship. What help can you give here?" Troy asked, features grim.

Athena's tone was gentle over the speakers. "I can route the ship's radar into Xanthe's ThinkLink and translate it into touch and sound. It's not vision, but with practice Xanthe will navigate as if it is."

Xanthe dropped her head into her hands. Serena's arms went around her shoulders, then one by one, the others joined in, pressing in a tight warm circle.

"We've got you," Troy whispered. "All of us. Together."

Sobs rocked her body, but they held her tight.

Ozone flooded the flight deck, engines hissing as they cooled. Flight deck lights flickered and cast an eerie glow over their pained faces.

Metal clomped up the ladder.

"You do group hug without me?" Volkov said, thudding onto the deck.

Serena drew back, eyes widening. "Holy shit, Volkov! What happened to your face?"

"It's like Silly Putty," Madison said, half horrified, half fascinated.

"An improvement, *non?*" Xavier chuckled.

"Don't worry, he's been worse," Jonas said. "I'll fix you up, buddy. Just glad you survived that manoeuvre." He patted the bot's shoulder.

Troy glanced over. The bot's silicon features had slumped into a glossy, dripping mask, sagging to his chest.

"What is it? Tell me," Xanthe said, a desperate edge to her voice.

A pang ripped through Troy. She couldn't see. "Volkov's face melted," he breathed.

"Oh," she said flatly. "I wish I could see that."

They stiffened slightly then broke away from the embrace.

"Let's begin landing and acclimatisation protocols," Troy said in a low voice.

The moment broke with Athena's voice, cool and urgent… "Commander, I'm picking up radio chatter."

"Patch it through," he said.

A male voice came over, faint and scratchy, then another male voice. And a female one, strident.

Awareness spread across Madison's face. "That's Gareth Barrio!"

"Athena, where are they? Is this coming from the Kunlun base?" Troy asked.

"Negative. The range is further away. Maybe twenty kilometres. My long-distance radar shows smoking remnants—a possible vehicle crash."

"I've got a private hail coming in," Xanthe said. "A ThinkLink, like the ones we were getting in transit. Athena—patch it through to ship comms."

"This is Epiphany, ThinkLink for Dr Victoria Tang, hailing Nyx Odyssey."

"Athena, can we acknowledge?" Troy asked.

"Go ahead, Epiphany," Athena said.

"Dr Victoria Tang is being held against her will by Lincoln Ellison. Together with Captain Gareth Barrio, the three are en route to Kunlun base on foot. Estimated arrival in four hours."

"On foot! They're mad!" Serena said.

"The radiation," murmured Madison.

"Troy, we need to beat them to Kunlun," Xanthe said, waving a glove out in front of her, searching for him. He lurched to grab it and squeezed it reassuringly. "If Lincoln gets there first, we lose the air tech. And Mars."

"We're going to have to speed up our protocol big time," Madison said, pointing at a screen. "There's a dust storm racing straight for us."

CHAPTER FIFTY-THREE

"First impression of Mars? Dust. A lot of dust.
Rocks. Dry. Not a very friendly place."

—**Dr Victoria Tang**
MEMOIRS FROM MARS

UTOPIA PLANITIA: VICTORIA

Mars Day 1

Dr Victoria Tang stumbled over a rock buried in the red dust drift and dropped to her knees. Air rasped in her helmet. She sucked at the mouthpiece; the recycled water gurgled, almost gone.

"On your feet, Victoria!" Lincoln's voice crackled over comms as his gloved hand yanked her upright. Her knees jarred. Always pulling, always pushing. "Storm's closing." He marched on.

Barrio fell in beside her, visor glinting. "Private channel," he said, and the link clicked. "You okay?"

"Running out of water," she panted. "Hungry."

"You and me both." His jaw set under the visor. "Nearly there."

She tried to see through the haze. The storm shredded the horizon into a blur of rusty teeth. Barrio pointed at her wrist display.

"Lose sight of me, follow your telemetry." His helmet light cut a tunnel through the grit.

Hours on foot since the copter went down. The gust had flipped them, an angry god throwing toys. Lincoln blamed Barrio before the wreckage stopped smoking.

"A turtle could fly better than that!"

"Have a go then," Barrio had shot back, slapping the homing beacon to Lincoln's chest.

"Maybe later. Let's move. Nyx will be busy with gravity acclimatisation—we can still beat them to Kunlun."

She'd seen Nyx land as they'd limped in, the fire trail punching ochre sky. Lincoln cursed Claire Edwards and her duplicity, cursed the Condor sabotage flop and cursed all who had failed him. Tang had kept her face neutral, hiding the satisfaction that her encrypted signal had slipped through, Epiphany faking the receipt of an upgrade and sending a pretend diagnostic while hailing Xanthe.

Epiphany had been calling Kunlun since touchdown. No answer.

Catastrophe?

Evacuation?

Wind spat grit against her visor. She wiped it, blinked. Through the murk, a pale glow. Her heart jolted. *Nyx Odyssey. Humans. Not just Lincoln and his henchman.* She shoved away thoughts of those left at the ship, the wrecked copter, the narrow thread of survival. *One foot. Then another.* She pulled at the mouthpiece; a few drops burned down her throat.

"Kunlun base, this is Dr Victoria Tang," she hailed. "Calling Tang Dopplebot. Do you read?"

Nothing but the wind whistling in her ears. Her light caught the curve of Barrio's back as he trudged ahead.

Then—movement. A shadow slid across the beam.

Human?

The pattern was odd.

She slowed. "Barrio...we're not alone."

CHAPTER FIFTY-FOUR

"Mars belongs to all humanity, not to one flag."

—**Xanthe Waters**
MARS MANIFESTO

NYX ODYSSEY, UTOPIA PLANITIA: XANTHE

Mars Day 1

Xanthe remained in her launch chair as the others began moving.

"Jonas, Mad Dog, prep the rover for surface launch," Troy called. Xanthe felt Troy stand beside her as he issued commands. "Serena, Xavier—secure the farm, adjust life support for surface stay, then meet us in storage. Grab the exobraces on your way."

Helmets clicked on.

Visualising the flight deck, Xanthe searched her memory for details to help orient herself. The climb down through the ship would be challenging. Now vertical and in gravity, they had to negotiate a hundred meters of stairs, each compartment with a horizontal rail to step on, treacherous, especially with bodies still learning to stand again.

"I'll help you," Troy said, his comforting hand on her shoulder.

"Give me a moment. Athena's setting up radar."

A surge rippled through her nervous system as Athena linked in.

"The radar will come online once we're on the surface," the AI said. *"I've assigned each teammate a unique sound cue so you can tell them apart."*

Xanthe cycled through the tones until they were second nature. "I'm ready."

Troy guided her to the ladder. Athena counted rungs, describing the spaces they passed. At her cabin, she stopped.

"Can you get Jack's ashes?"

Troy retrieved the pencil case-sized box and pressed it into her hand. She stowed it in her tool pouch.

The descent blurred into a rhythm of grip, step, breathe—until she slipped.

Her hands scrabbled for the rail, heart spiking. Troy's arms closed around her.

"I've got you," he murmured as she trembled against him. Tears threatened as her throat tightened. A breath, another, then she nodded to continue.

The storage bay's solid floor felt alien after months of weightlessness. Four pings in her mind marked her team's arrival.

"Let's get your exobrace on," Troy said.

The powered frame clamped around her legs, waist, back and arms. She flexed and squatted—smooth movement, no pinch points.

"How are you doing?" Troy murmured privately.

"Okay," she lied.

"Then let's tackle the hatch."

A mechanical whirr, then, "Goodbye, fleshbags. I will hold fort. Keep plants and crickets fed."

She listened to Jonas brief Volkov on the maintenance tasks. "Yes, yes, got it," the bot said. "Now go kick Ellison buttock."

Hands led her to the rover and into the cramped cabin. She fumbled for the restraining straps.

"Here, I'll do it." Jonas, his voice gentle.

Next to her, Madison ran through the rover protocols. "Battery full, all systems nominal."

"Seal the hatch," Serena said. A whirr, then a thud.

"*Putain!* Is that the outside temperature?"

Xanthe's head swivelled. Xavier was on her left. Madison on her right.

"Forty-five minutes to the base. Heat's on, no pressurisation—we want a quick exit," Madison replied.

"The storm is in full force." Jonas, on the other side of Madison, Xanthe guessed. "Don't expect much of a view." A pause, then Jonas said with an obvious pang in his voice, "Sorry, Xanthe. I didn't mean—"

"It's alright, Jonas," she replied, forcing reassurance over her despair.

"Nyx, open rover bay door," Troy said.

An alert sounded through the bay, a heavy clunk, a whining groan. A roar as the storm shoved its head through the opening. A forward movement, a tilt that pushed her ribcage against the seat restraints. They rolled down the ramp with a jolt, then eased forward.

"Wheels on ground," Madison announced.

They cheered. They were on Mars!

Radar pings erupted in Xanthe's mind.

Dial it back, Athena.

The tones softened. Athena explained the sweep: jagged peaks, dunes, scattered boulders…then a low triple thud.

"What's that?" Xanthe asked.

"*Pinnacle* crew, maybe—they're pinned down," Madison said.

Another triple thud, closer.

Troy's voice was low, sharp. "Then what the hell is that other thing out there?"

CHAPTER FIFTY-FIVE

"When it comes to survival, every life counts equally."

—**GARETH BARRIO**
MARS MANIFESTO

UTOPIA PLANITIA: VICTORIA

Mars Day 1

THE WIND CLAWED at them, tugging at boots and helmets, every step an argument with Mars, God of War. They ducked behind an enormous boulder, standing silent sentry in the dust. Victoria leaned hard into the boulder's lee, the grit in the air so thick it rasped in her throat filters.

"We wait here," Barrio said, crouching low, his broad shoulders creating an eddy in the wind for her.

Lincoln's voice was tinny with impatience over the comms. "Wait? We're a hundred metres from the base. I can see the perimeter on my HUD."

"You can't see a damn thing in this," Barrio yelled. "Storm will strip you raw before you reach the door."

"Why isn't anyone answering our hail?" Lincoln grumbled.

Victoria turned her head toward Lincoln, her visor scraping

against the rock. She shrugged, dust clinging to every crease of her suit. "Glitch. Or they're screening visitors," she said. "Or the base is dead."

"Either way, we're going in," Lincoln said.

Barrio muttered something she couldn't catch, just as a flicker of movement crossed her peripheral vision—low, fast and then gone in the swirling grit.

She straightened. "Did you see—?"

Victoria pressed her back to the lee of the boulder, visor turned alongside the rock's pitted face, searching for the figure. The storm's roar filled her helmet, every gust slapping dust against her suit in stinging bursts. Barrio leaned over her, shielding her from the worst of the wind. Lincoln sat a few metres away, knees tucked, helmet light flickering in the haze.

Her helmet beam swept the ground—and froze on two legs, planted inches from her boots.

"Holy crap!" She scrambled sideways, boots skidding on grit.

Barrio sprang upright.

Lincoln jerked to his feet.

"Dr Victoria Tang?" The voice over comms was flat, almost swallowed by the static hiss of the storm.

"Yes?" she shouted.

She blinked against the grit scouring her visor. The figure squatted beside her, lifting her wrist, its visor dark.

"Authentic bio signature confirmed," it said.

She squinted into the shadows. "Who are you?"

"I am Dopplebot Tang," the voice intoned, matching her own cadence almost perfectly. "Welcome to Mars, Dr Victoria Tang."

Her name, in her voice. It sent a ripple of unease down her spine.

"What are you doing out here?" she asked, almost adding, 'Why didn't you respond to my hail?' before she caught herself.

"Security."

"The base is functional?" Lincoln said, now on his feet. "Let's go. Take us there."

"Only authorised personnel are allowed on site."

"Bullshit. I am Lincoln Ellison, CEO of Spaceward Bound, foundational pioneer of the space sector, and you will allow us access—immediately." Lincoln stepped chest to chest with the bot. The dust hurled between them.

The bot's head swivelled towards Victoria with slow, insect precision. "Dr Tang, you can follow me."

"You can't leave us outside!" Lincoln jabbed a finger into its chest plate. "That's inhumane!"

A gust slammed her sideways; Barrio's hand shot out to steady her.

"I can't move in this wind," she said.

The bot stepped away from Lincoln. "I can carry you," the bot said, and without waiting for assent, scooped her up, a dust-spattered bride. The Dopplebot turned without a word, striding into the gloom with mechanical certainty.

Over its shoulder, she watched the glow of Barrio and Lincoln's helmet lights shrink, then vanish into the storm, regret and relief swirling with the dust.

CHAPTER FIFTY-SIX

"Deploy the redemption formula: Earn forgiveness. Grant forgiveness."

—**Madison Floyd**
MARS CULTURE CODE

UTOPIA PLANITIA: SERENA

Mars Day 1

THE ROVER SHUDDERED to a stop, dust hammering the hull like hard rain. Serena sucked a mouthful of warm water through her suit mouthpiece, tasting metal and grit, eyes on the ochre void.

"It should be right in front of us," Madison said. "I can't see a damn thing."

Serena's eyes widened and she nudged Madison with a gesture towards Xanthe. Madison bit her lip and raised her hand in silent apology.

Together, they peered into the haze. No lights, no shapes—only Nyx's unanswered hails. On one channel, desperate voices broke through the static: Ellison and Barrio. Serena shivered. He deserved whatever he'd got. But still. Humans. On Mars.

It could have been them out there…

"Jonas, we'll head out," Troy said, unbuckling and moving

towards the exit. "We'll tether to the rover and look for an airlock entrance."

Serena, Xanthe, Madison and Xavier remained in the rover, the heater's hum battling the faint hiss of dust forcing its way through seals. Two suit lights passed in front of the beams, then vanished into the storm.

Dread made Serena jumpy, her thoughts circling to the *Pinnacle* crew. On the radar, two dots sat motionless. Dead? Injured? Two others crept closer. Serena rocked in her chair, anxious for news.

"We've found an airlock." Troy's voice crackled. "Going in."

Serena held her breath. Moments stretched like a river, dust rattling like dry rice on the hull.

"We're in."

Serena exhaled and hugged Xavier who chuckled in relief.

"It's locked," Troy said. "No power."

"I'll come," Xanthe said. "Athena can hack it."

"Xavier, guide her in," Troy replied.

As they slipped into the storm, tether lines trembling in the crosswind, Serena stared at the radar.

"Commander," Serena said. "Request permission to retrieve the others."

Madison peered at her in the dull glow of the console lights.

"Denied. I don't want to split up our team. Too dangerous."

"We're leaving them to die, Commander," Serena said.

"They tried to kill us," Madison snapped.

"Let the *salaud* reap what he planted," Xavier added.

"Then bring him to justice," persisted Serena. "Since when do we just let people die?"

Static on the channel.

"Fifteen minutes," Troy said. "No more."

"Thank you, Commander."

Madison shook her head and plotted a course towards the blips.

The wheels bumped over unseen rocks, dust hissing past the

viewport. Serena kept her eyes on the scan. "Whoa—those two moving dots just disappeared." Serena and Madison exchanged glances. A creeping dread inched up the back of her neck. "Head for the other ones—the stationary ones. Hopefully we're not too late."

Minutes laboured. Her throat dried again. Serena sipped at lukewarm and faintly bitter water. She snuck a look at Madison, whose face was set like granite.

"Mad Dog?"

"Yeah?"

"I'm sorry."

Madison swiped a screen and checked a gauge. "For what?"

"The data stuff. Sneaking messages from Max. It was—"

"Irresponsible? Unprofessional? Criminal?" Madison blurted.

Serena winced. "It wasn't malicious."

"Selfish."

Serena leaned forward, head hanging. "Yes, selfish." Shame rippled over her, heat flooding her body so that a trickle of sweat rolled down her back.

"It nearly cost us our lives. The Condor patch—"

"If I'd known—"

The rover groaned as it bobbled over a rock and jolted again. Serena leaned back in her seat, staring at the grey ceiling of the rover.

"You could have talked to us, Serena. I know what it means to be separated from a loved one, especially someone who is sick or injured." Her voice softer, she added, "You were all so good to me when my Mom—" Her voice quavered. "Point is, we could have done that for you."

"But there were always data dumps, mission critical stuff—"

"We could have found a way." Madison adjusted the fingers of her gloves, checked the cuff seals. "Serena, you're family to me. You and Xanthe, like sisters I never had. When you hurt, I hurt."

Serena's eyes widened. This was Mad Dog, the irrepressible, stalwart, hard as nails fighter pilot flying ace.

"I always wanted a sister," Serena said and put an arm around Madison who patted her knee in response.

A figure burst into the beams. Serena's heart jumped. Madison braked hard; the rover skidded, wheels grinding.

"This is Captain Floyd. Identify yourself."

"Mad Dog, let us in."

Madison's jaw tightened. "Lincoln. Goddamn. Ellison."

"Play nice," Serena said, already moving to the hatch.

They wrestled the airlock open, the storm punching inside in a swirl of grit and cold. They hauled Ellison and Barrio inside, dust crusting their suits and visors.

"Floyd," Barrio said, breathless.

"Barrio." Madison's voice was flat steel.

He offered a wan smile. "Good to see you. Glad you made it."

"Enough chit-chat." Ellison waved a limp hand, dust falling from his glove. "Take me to your leader. We have business."

CHAPTER FIFTY-SEVEN

"One commander, one clear chain of command—anything else is chaos."

—Lincoln Ellison
MEMOIRS FROM MARS

KUNLUN BASE: TROY

Mars Day 1

Troy whirled as the airlock door sprung open, the storm raging in. He pressed into Xavier and Xanthe to make room for four more bodies, covered in red dust, helmet lights blinding as the door creaked shut.

"Greetings, Earthlings."

He knew that voice—Lincoln Goddamn Ellison, his bravado Everest-sized.

"As the first human on Martian soil, I claim territorial rights over this base and all other man-made facilities, as per Mars Accord protocols."

Troy bristled and readied a response, but Xavier beat him to it.

"Trou du cul," Xavier spat. "Should have left you in the dunes."

Troy shuffled forward, gently nudging Xavier aside. "Ellison.

Good to see you again." Bitterness laced his words. "You're welcome for saving your life, but we don't recognise your claim."

"I don't give a rat's fart what you *recognise*, Bruin. We were the first on Mars by a long shot. Now make way."

Ellison jostled towards the door and assaulted the handle with a flourish. It clunked but refused to budge.

"No power, Ellison," Troy said. "Now stand back as we work the problem."

"Like hell I will." Lincoln shouldered his way in front of Troy. "I claim right of first entry, as well as command of this base."

"*Espèce de con!* You and how many of your friends? You and Barrio are outnumbered." Xavier shoved his way towards Lincoln again. "You piece of *merde*—you tried to kill us. You command nothing and no one, not here, not anywhere."

Troy put a restraining hand on Xavier's shoulder. Xavier was still a fierce presence, thin as he was, his eyes wild.

"Ellison will have his day of reckoning, *mon ami*," Troy said, "but first we need to get inside this base."

A female voice blared over the airlock speakers. "This is Tang Dopplebot."

Gasps.

"None of you is cleared for access to Kunlun. Please depart immediately."

"Wait, wait—" Another voice, much like the first.

"This is Dr Victoria Tang. Stay where you are—let me discuss this with the others."

Others? Who was in there? Troy wondered.

The minutes ticked by, and they grew restless waiting.

"Um, okay." Dr Tang again. "It's a bit complicated. Just sit tight while I work this out."

Troy frowned and his mind raced. Barrio and Ellison stood shoulder to shoulder with the rest of them in the tiny space, standing like penguins as dust struck the habitat like shrapnel.

Troy tapped his wrist comm discreetly, alerting the crew to a private message on their heads-up displays. He made a show of pretending to wipe his helmet screen while whispering a message to them: *"Follow my lead in negotiations. Shield Xanthe's blindness from them—give them no advantage. Use this channel for crew discussions. Stay alert to sabotage."*

Minutes stretched to an hour and then another. Jonas worked at the door, trying to engineer a solution that would not destroy the airlock.

"I can't do much without tools," Jonas said over the crew comm. "Maybe we send for Volkov?"

Troy shifted uneasily on his swollen feet, suit pressurisation working overtime to help his body adjust to gravity. With no food apart from the suit slurry, he felt lightheaded.

While Lincoln remained standing stubbornly alongside Jonas and Troy, the others had sunk to the floor, knees touching in the tiny space.

"Okay, listen up." They jumped as Dr Victoria Tang's voice whistled on the speaker. "Uh, I'm in charge now." She cleared her throat. "I've negotiated to let you in. But the Dopplebots don't recognise your authority here. Especially you, Lincoln Ellison, you son of a bitch. Kidnapping, attempted murder and God knows what else." She paused.

"That is outrageous slander—" Lincoln began.

"*Ferme ta gueule!*" Xavier said. "I swear I will kill you myself, you arrogant—"

"If you're quite done in there?" Victoria interrupted. "Me and the Dopplebots are going to let you in. But all of you are going to be locked up in the crew common area while the base's life support systems come back online."

"I can help with that," Serena volunteered. "I'm the life support engineer for the *Nyx Odyssey.*"

A pause.

"The Dopplebots have it covered. Just do as I say."

"This is bullshit!" Lincoln said. "Robots running the show."

"You'll need to go through the decontamination chamber," Victoria said, ignoring Lincoln. "There are lightweight suits to change into. Make sure you keep the helmets on for the time being—quarantine stuff."

A whirr and cheers.

"What's happening?" Xanthe asked.

"The lights came on," Troy said. "The airlock is pressurising."

"Captain Troy Bruin, you first," Victoria said.

"I'm the first man on Mars—I go first," Ellison raged.

"I'm in charge now, Lincoln," Victoria said, voice quavering. "You will do as I say, or you can go back in the storm."

Troy nudged in front of Lincoln, holding his glare until the other man backed down.

"This means nothing, Bruin," he hissed.

Troy smiled.

The chamber door cycled open. Cold air slapped Troy's visor, carrying the faint tang of ozone and metal. He placed Xanthe's hand discreetly on his waist and guided her through to the decontamination chamber. They lined up in front of the unit, a standing coffin-sized cabinet, where Xavier placed a hand on Xanthe's shoulder, taking over when Troy stepped into the decontaminator.

The hatch sealed with a metallic thud that reverberated through his boots. Red lights pulsed across the chamber walls: *DECONTAMINATION IN PROGRESS.*

A low hum vibrated through the floor. The electrostatic grid discharged with a crackle, and suddenly the red dust that clung to his suit lifted in a shimmering haze. Gas jets hissed, scouring every seam and joint, sweeping the cloud into vents along the floor.

Then came the mist. Fine droplets of hydrogen peroxide spattered across his visor, fizzing white against the orange grit caked into the seals. He held his breath as the faint tang of ozone filled the air, sharp and metallic. The chamber bathed in ultraviolet light, a cold bright glow burning against his eyelids.

"Neutralisation complete," the base A.I. announced from the overhead speaker.

Troy stepped forward into the next spacious chamber. The base had been built for future inhabitants, large enough for twenty astronauts to store their suits.

He removed the exobrace and then shuffled backwards into one of the waiting suit cradles. With a hiss of disengaging locks, his armour peeled away, the rigid backpack staying sealed to the port. He climbed out in his sweat-darkened underlayers, shivering as the last blast of sterilising light seared the chamber.

Glancing around, he identified the lightweight suit storage unit across the room. The heat fan blasted the chamber, but the atmosphere was still thin. His breath crystallised in front of him. He felt dizzy and hurried to pull on the suit. Once he'd secured the helmet and fired up the internal gauges, he breathed more easily, the suit warming him immediately. He snapped the exobrace back on, relaxing into the mechanical assist gratefully.

He tested the helmet comm and announced, "Clean and clear."

Xanthe was next. He waited until the unit finished its cycles, then guided her through the port and into the lightweight suit. He shut down his helmet comms and spoke to her directly as they waited for the others to come through.

"Xanthe, does Athena have a read on what's going on with the base—what's the situation with the Dopplebots?"

"We've got the base schematics, but Epiphany and the Dopple-bots are not responding to her. Yet." Her voice was muffled through the helmet, and he strained to hear her.

Troy chewed his bottom lip, mind racing.

"Once we're through to the main base, I'll get the crew to form up, helmets off, store gear, then—"

"Troy, no. Athena says those are closed-loop quarantine

corridors while the life support systems are loading up. Breaking seal protocol will trigger an automatic purge. That procedure will lock us out."

"Damn it," he said. He half-turned, irritation flaring in the set of his jaw. "I'm managing crew safety, Xanthe."

"Exactly why I'm saying stop," she shot back. "The corridor's in quarantine mode. Break seal now, the bots dump the atmosphere and we're decompressed."

Silence for a beat, just the hiss of the ventilation. Then he let out a breath, adjusting. "Alright. Helmets stay on. We wait for base clearance."

They needed a strategy, and fast.

CHAPTER FIFTY-EIGHT

—Troy Bruin
MARS CULTURE CODE

KUNLUN BASE: TROY

Mars Day 1

THE CORRIDOR ALERT turned green. The door swung open and harsh white light spilled inside.

Madison stepped into the decontamination chamber, the last of their crew. Jonas, Xavier and Serena, lined up in their new suits, were waiting and alert. Barrio and Ellison were next.

Troy's mind raced back to the landing, ceding command to Xanthe, the sacrifice she'd made.

"Does the ThinkLink still hurt?"

She shook her head. "When it burned through my visual receptors, it seems to have severed any pain response pathways. Athena's been processing a lot and I'm good."

"Is she able to guide you in here?"

"She's setting up a haptic response in the suit to give me a sense of the environment. She can also talk me through the base floor plan and direct me that way. I went through the decontamination okay with her guidance."

"Good. Keep your helmet light dim so Lincoln isn't clued in."

"Athena's adjusting it now."

Troy swallowed, heart thumping. God, she was remarkable. "Here's what I suggest. I want us to co-lead."

A long pause.

"Are you sure?" she whispered.

"With Athena, you've got a quicker action response time. I can lead negotiations while you do background assessment and strategy. If we need fast action, you'll have insight before I do. Agreed?"

"Alright then, let's do it."

Troy announced the co-lead on crew comms and they whispered agreement.

When Barrio and Lincoln were clear, the airlock alert turned green and the door swung open. Beyond, the corridor glowed with a clinical white light, the edges of the space clean, precise— machine-tended. Two Dopplebots stood in perfect stillness, metal mechanical frames. Their visor slits glowed faint amber.

"They're so creepy without faces," Serena said. "They make Volkov look like the dad next door."

The Dopplebots stepped aside in perfect unison, motion so smooth it was almost fluid. From the far end of the corridor, a human figure approached. Troy saw her face was damp with sweat under her helmet, her eyes sharp despite the exhaustion.

Dr Victoria Tang.

"Um, okay," she said. "Follow me." She led them through a long, immaculate tunnel with low-level strip lighting along the corridor floor. The Kunlun design was based on the Chinese moon-base, Red Star that Troy remembered: a spider web that allowed for modular additions with the capacity to shut down each section in case of a breach.

The crew common area sat at a major intersection with

command comms, crew quarters, life support systems and the farm branching from its hub.

Victoria ushered them into the common room, a sterile white circular chamber with storage cupboards, a rectangular central dining table and chairs for twenty. All of it unused. The Dopplebots had no need of amenities. Their charging dock must be in the workshop, thought Troy.

His mind filled with questions, the mystery of the Dopplebot silence after Dr Tang's disappearance itching to be revealed now they were here and the bots had clearly survived. Something else had driven their silence.

"The base should be cleared from quarantine and life support systems soon," Victoria said.

Troy saw his chance. "Can I suggest you take Jonas and Serena to double-check the systems for you? No offence to the Dopplebots, but they have less at stake if there is a system gauge that is not calibrated properly."

Victoria shifted her weight from foot to foot, rubbing an arm. "Um, alright." She looked at Serena and Jonas who stepped forward. She waved them to follow her. The Dopplebots stepped in behind, herding them away down the corridor, their chest servers humming in eerie harmony.

Troy turned to the rest, who had settled onto chairs: Madison, Xavier and Xanthe on one side of the table, Lincoln and Barrio on the other.

Game on, he thought.

CHAPTER FIFTY-NINE

"No colony of masters and servants: only partners."

—TANG DOPPLEBOT
MARS MANIFESTO

KUNLUN BASE: SERENA

Mars Day 1

SERENA PANTED, VISOR fogging, and scrambled after Victoria and Jonas, the exobrace only just keeping her moving. Lord, she was hungry! She dwelled on what the storage cupboards back in the crew commons might hold.

Two Dopplebots trailed after them—Victoria's muscle. Serena almost smiled despite the tension.

They shuffled through one hatch and into a small hub packed with monitors blinking lights into the dim corridor. This was familiar territory.

Victoria waved at the displays. "Take a look. The Dopplebots tell me all systems nominal."

Serena stood next to Jonas, and together they worked their way through the systems, confirming full function of each.

"What's this?" Serena asked, pointing at a briefcase.

Victoria smiled and stood a little straighter. Serena swore if she hadn't been wearing a helmet she would have tossed her hair with a flourish.

"That," she said pointedly, "is the scrubber we've all been looking for."

"No way!" Serena bent over to peer at the unassuming box. "That is going to terraform Mars and save Earth's atmosphere?" Such amazing tech!

Her stomach growled. Visions of a sandwich filled her mind.

"Well, not just that one unit, no. But a bunch of them, yes." Victoria's smile beamed under her helmet light.

Jonas stared at her. "That's incredible engineering. Serena's Breath Domes gave us a fighting chance at filtering air, but this… to manufacture breathable atmosphere out of virtually nothing… amazing!"

"Thank you." She blushed. "Let's go back to the others and double check the decontamination specs."

Serena glanced at Jonas, who was still studying Victoria. Almost gawking, Serena thought. Good, at least she was human this time. She stepped in beside Victoria. "So, are you on our side?" she ventured.

Victoria frowned. "I'm not sure I'm on any side right now. Definitely not with Lincoln, that asshole. He kidnapped me and coerced me to come to Mars. That and that twobit terrorist Claire Edwards."

Serena and Jonas exchanged glances as he came alongside her. "You must be on our side," Serena persisted. "You tried to warn us about the Condor patch."

"I didn't want to see you burn up and die." Victoria opened the next hatch. "Until I speak with Elena Fischer, I'm considering all of you as potentially hostile."

"We came to stop Lincoln from claiming rights to the base and your amazing tech," Jonas said. "We're here at the behest of the

Lunar Commission, under the direction of Gaia Enterprises and in full compliance with the Mars Accord."

"You sound like a politician," Victoria said as she ushered them through into the next corridor.

"Well, I—"

Serena put a hand on his arm. "What do you need to know to be sure of us?"

Victoria stopped and turned to look at them both, hands on hips. "Xanthe Waters. I need to talk to her. Where is she?"

"Back in the common room with the others," Serena said.

"Oh! I didn't recognise her." A shadow flickered over her features.

"Dark helmet," Serena said. She hesitated, then pressed, "Why have the Dopplebots been silent all this time?"

Victoria's visor tilted toward her, as if weighing how much to share. "They suspected the sync-link back to Earth was compromised. So they cut it. Isolation was safer." She resumed walking.

"And the skin interface?" Serena asked quickly. "Why strip it off?"

"They weren't syncing with humans anymore. Didn't need lungs or warmth. They preserved the skins, kept working in the tubes."

"They just stayed in the tubes?"

Victoria's stride didn't falter. "More secure."

Serena jogged to keep up. "One more thing. I've never seen Dopplebots move that in-sync. Usually they're…independent."

"They stopped syncing with their humans," Victoria said flatly. She paused, boots heavy in the corridor. "Now they sync with each other. A hive mind."

Serena's stomach dropped. Machines weren't supposed to *evolve*.

They weren't just machines anymore—they were a single mind. An army.

CHAPTER SIXTY

"No one will be denied shelter."

—SERENA FOX
MARS MANIFESTO

KUNLUN BASE: TROY

Mars Day 1

TROY LOCKED EYES with Lincoln. This man had tried to kill them, had stolen helium-3, had stoked violence to disrupt Po Secco—and if Claire Edwards's testimony was true, had done worse on Earth.

Lincoln broke the silence first. His voice was smooth as oil. "Bruin, it's obvious we're going to have to cooperate."

"Is it?" Troy said, genuinely surprised.

Xavier scoffed. Madison folded her arms, jaw tight. Xanthe remained impassive, her visor reflecting the pale overhead strips.

"Of course. The Martian Commissioners can settle Kunlun's ownership." He waved an imperial hand, his Ozymandias ring gleaming. "In the meantime, we have a year and a half to survive. Together."

Troy ground his teeth, jaw aching, and glanced at Xanthe. She gave nothing away.

"Or…" Lincoln leaned forward, visor glinting. "You could leave early. *Pinnacle* has a helium-3 booster. We don't need to wait for orbital alignment."

Barrio shifted in his seat, his eyes fixed on the table.

The words jolted through Troy. Back to Earth early. Green grass under bare feet, making amends with his daughter Gemma, air that didn't scrape the lungs… Tempting. Too tempting. He tilted his head, making a show of casual consideration.

Lincoln's gloved finger tapped a steady rhythm on the metal tabletop. *Tink. Tink. Tink.* "The *Pinnacle* has extra O_2 tanks, med-kits, food packs. And my seven crew, who could be a tremendous help here."

Barrio finally looked up, gaze fierce.

Madison cut in. "And how are they getting here? Your copter's toast." Her eyes flicked from Barrio to Lincoln.

Lincoln leaned back, smile thin. "Then we fix the copter. Fly out. Bring them in."

"Barrio?" Madison urged.

The grizzled pilot raised tired eyes to hers. "It's possible. With a lot of work."

Troy calculated it: hours of labour, parts they couldn't spare, the storm howling outside like a mythic wolf. "We could use the rover—"

Xanthe's voice sliced through, cold and flat. "Not enough food. Even if they survived the ride out, you'd drag corpses back."

"Nonsense." Lincoln flicked a hand. "Plenty of food."

Barrio clenched his fists.

On Troy's HUD, Xanthe's private message pulsed: *He's bluffing.*

"You left them to die, you *putain de merde*!" Xavier said, menace low in his throat.

The hatch hissed. Frosted air rushed in as Victoria entered with Serena, Jonas and two Dopplebots.

"Decontamination complete. Helmets off," she announced.

Locks clicked. Troy tugged his helmet free. A gasp of thin, bitter air filled his lungs. White clouds puffed and drifted in the cold, catching in the shards of frost that glimmered on the bulkheads.

Lincoln smoothed his greasy hair into something like a coif. "Dr Tang, perfect timing. We were planning the *Pinnacle* retrieval."

Victoria's eyes burned. "Were you? I've already hailed Earth. The Commission will decide. There's food in the cupboards. Xanthe Waters—come with me."

Xanthe pivoted, and a flicker of tension darted across Troy's chest. *I'll keep you posted,* her HUD message flashed.

Lincoln rubbed his hands together, grin wide, a vulgar white in the dim light. "Think it over, Bruin. The *Pinnacle* crew will be an enormous help. Plus, you don't want to be known as the Commander who let seven people die on your watch, would you?"

He leaned back as though the matter was settled.

"Now, what's for dinner?"

CHAPTER SIXTY-ONE

"Authority must serve, not rule."

—Tang Dopplebot
MARS MANIFESTO

KUNLUN BASE: XANTHE

Mars Day 1

Xanthe trailed Victoria step by step, guided by Athena's haptic pulses along her sleeves and collar. Each vibration tugged her into the shape of the room. Every step was a leap of faith into the dark. The air rasped metallic on her tongue, fans whining behind the walls like they were about to fail.

The footsteps stopped. Xanthe froze, head cocked, every nerve straining for the next sound.

Victoria's voice came low, tentative. "Epiphany—my ThinkLink—wants to know why Athena locked her out during transit."

Xanthe tilted toward the sound, brows knitted together. "We thought it was a virus. We were right."

"We were trying to warn you," Victoria shot back, a defensive edge to her tone.

Static crackled in the vents.

"We know that now. It took Athena a long time to decrypt the code."

"Must be an older ThinkLink model. When did you get yours?"

"Six years ago." Memories of the surgery on the Moon flashed to the surface.

The power surged, fans humming like trapped bees.

A hesitation. "What's wrong with your eyes?" Victoria's voice had thinned to a whisper.

Xanthe let the silence stretch before saying, "I'm blind."

Victoria sucked in a breath. "How?"

"Athena seized control during descent. Saved us from Condor. The surge burned my optical receptors."

"My God. Could that—could that happen to me?"

"Do you get pain?"

"No. Not really."

Xanthe shrugged. "You're fine. For now." She had no words of reassurance for her.

"Can they fix it?"

"Not here."

"Oh."

The air cycler groaned as if it were choking on dust.

"Anyway," Victoria forced a positive note into her voice, the sound brittle as glass. "Let's…focus on the base. The Dopplebots, the hive mind, they're beyond me. I need help." She explained how the Dopplebots were syncing with each other.

Xanthe's mind reeled. Dozens of bots, each loaded with their human counterpart's knowledge, now sharing insights, memories, decisions. Operating as one. Friends—or rivals? A frisson of fear surged through her.

Xanthe tilted her head to listen better. "Tell me, what it's like syncing with a Dopplebot? They get your visuals, but do you get theirs?"

"No. Technicians thought it might send humans a little mad

managing two lives, one robotic, the other human. The sync gives the bots more sensory input. My Dopplebot acts like an extension for me—doing tasks, gathering intelligence, then summarising."

An idea crystallised for Xanthe. Could it work?

Victoria drew a shaky breath. "Epiphany thinks you should run things. You and Athena."

Xanthe's mind reeled. "Why do you want to give up control? After all you've been through."

Xanthe sensed Victoria's anxiety.

"To be honest, I don't know what I'm doing. I'm a scientist, not a leader. I barely survived a colleague who had it in for me. Greg Johnson, that unmitigated prick, tried to claim the ALVEUS was his design! I'm no good at politics."

"Greg Johnson?" Xanthe snapped to attention.

"Yeah. Total snake."

Xanthe filed that intelligence for later. "And what about the Dopplebots—they seem to respond only to you."

"They're more likely to accept you as leader because you have a ThinkLink."

"Would I have to sync with the hive mind?" Xanthe swallowed hard and felt her pulse bound. What more damage could be done with such a process?

"No, I don't think so. They'd just want to consult Athena."

In the background, Athena was running analysis and scenarios. She prompted Xanthe with the next question. "What about comms back with Earth? They'll be desperate to get updates from us, from the Dopplebots. Would they accept a transfer of governance like that? And what about Ellison's claim?"

Xanthe heard Victoria exhale and fidget as she considered these new challenges.

"Epiphany says getting comms back with Earth is easy. There was nothing damaged—they just stopped broadcasting. In terms of governance, full command is with the Dopplebots. Uh, I guess they can cede that themselves. We might have to check though. As for Lincoln…"

Xanthe jumped in. "I suggest we detain him and Barrio. Keep them supervised by Dopplebots. There are some serious accusations by Claire Edwards happening on Earth. We can refer sovereignty claims back to the courts there." Xanthe tapped a finger to her chin, already mapping out the message back to Earth.

"What do you think about the *Pinnacle* crew?" Victoria said. "They're not all bad. They were good to me on the transit over. Took pity on me really. Don't get me wrong, though. They were all in on the scheme for glory and riches, as Lincoln promised. This trip has set them up for an empire of crazy wealth. Still, we should try and rescue them, don't you think?"

Victoria's voice was a mess of doubt and guilt.

"We should rescue them," Xanthe answered, "but that means we are going to have to work with Barrio and Lincoln. There're too few of us, even with the Dopplebots, to manage the base, set up for human habitation and mount a rescue. Those seven people would be very useful. Plus, it's the right thing to do."

"You see! You are the right person for the job, Xanthe. We need you in command here. Honestly, I don't know how to deal with Lincoln. He kidnapped me, forced me to come to Mars. I'm scared of what else he might do to me. Us." Victoria grabbed Xanthe's arm. "You're the best choice. You've got a ThinkLink, so the Dopplebots can work with you. And you've got so much more experience! The Moon, this mission…"

Back in charge? Xanthe felt a shiver of hunger rise inside her. Command. It pulsed like old muscle memory. But Troy's face intruded, the pact they'd made. She tugged at her collar where it bit into her neck. "Troy and I co-lead the team."

Victoria gave a small, disbelieving laugh. "That can't be easy."

Xanthe smiled. "It's not. We're working our way through it."

"So, who do I go to for decisions?"

"Either of us. But for simplicity, go to Troy for personnel, Earth comms and base operations. I'll handle governance, Dopplebots." She tapped her chin, thinking. "Athena will need system access. Will they allow that?"

A pause. "Maybe. They're…guarded."

"Do they have a voice? A spokesperson?"

Victoria hesitated. "I suppose…that's me. I'm the only one they're syncing with."

Xanthe thrust a hand out, and Victoria shook it. "Then you're the voice of the hive. That makes you essential. And very vulnerable."

The silence that followed gave voice to the base, whining and straining as its systems cranked the life support.

"We'll get comms with Earth and get it all signed off." Xanthe felt the surge of power and authority flooding her spine. "Next we need to set up the base so we can actually live here."

Finally, Victoria asked, quieter still, and with a tremor of anxiety, "What about Lincoln and Barrio?"

Xanthe smiled with more malicious glee than was gracious. "Oh, we'll put them to work. The kind that makes no room for subterfuge."

CHAPTER SIXTY-TWO

"No throne is permanent: leadership rotates."

—**Xanthe Waters**
MARS MANIFESTO

KUNLUN BASE: TROY

Mars Day 1

Troy asked Serena and Xavier to organise a meal—Barrio and Lincoln could fend for themselves—while Jonas tugged him and Madison into a corner.

"There are people out there?" Jonas's face was chalk white. "We can't leave them, Troy."

Troy saw what Jonas was really seeing: the Moon, the bodies left behind, the months of silence Jonas had endured.

"This is Lincoln's mess, not ours." Troy's head throbbed. His stomach rumbled. "Our mission is to secure and fortify this base, not play rescue party for the *Pinnacle* saboteurs."

Madison folded her arms, lifted her chin. "We don't know how involved they were. Lincoln could have hidden Condor from them."

Jonas leaned in, voice rising. "There are seven humans out there, Troy. We have a moral obligation—"

"My obligation is to this crew," Troy snapped. He pressed his palm to his forehead, pulse hammering. "We're low on food. The farm's half-dead. Everyone's running on fumes. A rescue could get more of us killed."

"You're not thinking clearly." Jonas jabbed a finger at him. "Seven people. We can save them. Let me take Madison and Volkov—just to assess the copter." His eyes begged, raw and shining.

Madison hesitated, her gaze flicking sideways. "Maybe we should ask Xanthe and Athena—"

Anger prickled the back of Troy's neck and a retort rose in his throat before he caught himself. "I think—" he began, then turned as Xanthe and Victoria stepped in with the bots at their heels. Metal giants, mute and watchful.

"Here's what's what," Victoria said. She repeated what she and Xanthe had arranged.

Troy's gaze slid to Lincoln, who bristled but kept his mouth shut. For now.

Then Lincoln stood and approached Xanthe with a wary look. He waved a hand in front of her face. Xanthe pulled back.

"You're blind," Lincoln said flatly.

"I may be blind, but I *see* you, Lincoln Ellison," Xanthe hissed and stepped towards him, vacant eyes fierce.

Lincoln leaned away instinctively in alarm while Troy shot to his feet.

"Victoria," Troy said, pitching his voice to steady. "We'll do base familiarisation after we eat. Tomorrow—rest, rehab and setup. Then a crew to *Nyx* for supplies. After that—"

"What about the *Pinnacle* crew?" Jonas cut in.

Xanthe's message flashed: *We need to save them, Troy.*

Troy exhaled hard through his nose, forcing down the surge

of anger. His gut growled again. "How about we eat first," he said, every word measured, "and finalise a plan after?"

"Nice work, Bruin," Lincoln chipped, still studying Xanthe. "Let the others eat dirt while you feast." He tore open the Kung Pao chicken wrapper Barrio had slipped him, chewing with relish.

"Ellison, you left them to die. Playing hero now isn't fooling anyone!" Troy's jaw clenched, a slew of curses bubbling to the surface. He swallowed it whole, trying to maintain composure.

Serena pressed a heated packet of sweet and sour pork strips and a fork into his hand.

"Eat," she ordered with a pointed look.

He dropped into a chair, cracked the seal and dug in. The sharp tang of vinegar cut through the sweetness, the sticky sauce clinging to the rehydrated meat. His head eased with each bite, though the silence around the table was heavier than the storm battering outside. Only the scrape of forks and the hiss of heating packs broke it.

The bots stood behind them, watching, impassive.

When the packet was empty, he balled it up and pushed it aside, dropping the fork on the table with a clatter.

"First: rest. Then orientation and rehab. Once the storm eases, Madison and Barrio check the copter. Until then, no one leaves the base. Understood?"

Nods circled the table.

"Victoria," Lincoln said suddenly, wiping his mouth, his voice smooth. "I'll need access to Earth comms to liaise with my team for our next pioneer mission."

Victoria's lips curved, white teeth flashing without warmth. "Oh. You haven't heard."

Lincoln froze.

"Claire Edwards is now head of Spaceward Bound."

CHAPTER SIXTY-THREE

"I don't seek redemption through power. I seek responsibility. Spaceward Bound needs a conscience, not a king."

—CLAIRE EDWARDS
TRANSCRIPT FROM LUNAR
COMMISSION DEPOSITION

GAIA HEADQUARTERS: MAJA

Mars Day 3

MAJA GARCIA CLENCHED her jaw as she stared out the floor-to-ceiling window of the Gaia Enterprises's boardroom. For once, the air con was silent. A hailstorm battered the glass, thimble-sized ice balls rattling like gunfire. The launchpad lay deserted, drowned in a curtain of grey rain.

Behind her, voices clashed around the long mahogany table. Claire Edwards sat at its head, flanked by the Lunar and Martian Commissioners, their debate sharp as hail against tin. They hammered at clauses and caveats for Spaceward Bound's new governance structure, once seized by the joint committee, now shaped to crown Claire as its Chief.

How the tables have turned, Maja reflected bitterly. Claire, once her protégée, once even named her successor—had betrayed her, poisoned her, led ecoterrorists to wreck the Moon mission, kidnapped the crew, shot Xanthe's son…

Was there to be no reckoning?

She thought again of Xanthe's last message. The poor woman was blind now, coleading the expedition with Troy as they wrangled Ellison and secured the future for Mars.

Xanthe had been stoic despite it all. Though she could not understand how Maja and Aryanna had embraced Claire and brought her into the fold. Maja berated herself for her own failings. She'd let Xanthe down so many times: Troy's appointment for the lunar rescue, then again as Commander for this expedition, though Maja knew Xanthe was the better choice.

At least she'd been able to convince Aryanna to support Troy and Xanthe as coleaders on Mars.

"They're the ones on another planet," Maja had railed against Aryanna. "They know the conditions best, know the crew best. For God's sake, let them lead the way they see serves best. It's a new world. It needs new leadership. We are not doomed to repeat past wrongs. Let them be leading lights."

Aryanna had remained unmoved, holding Maja's gaze with an intensity that might have set curtains on fire.

"It sets a dangerous precedent." Aryanna had pointed a finger at Maja. "Reckless independence. We've seen that in Xanthe before."

Sighing, Maja had pulled her woollen shawl around her narrow shoulders. "It might just be careful collaboration. Let them create the future we've imagined."

Then Aryanna had relented.

After all, they were fighting on so many fronts: Po Secco, the air scrubbers, dealing with Claire's evidence and confession. They could allow the Martian crew latitude to manage their own survival and governance.

Maja forced herself back to the table, tea bitter on her tongue as she swallowed the last dregs. She'd endured every session of Claire's testimony, each disclosure like a knife: Lincoln's labyrinth of criminal scheming, Earth First's operational blueprints, the sabotage that had almost ended them all. The sabotaging spy Greg Johnson, now in custody as well. Claire had held nothing back—no loyalty, and no mercy for former allies.

And why would she? The Commissioners had promised immunity for the truth.

But this deal—it was galling.

Maja had argued with Aryanna to no avail.

"How can you put Claire at the head of Spaceward Bound? It makes no sense. It vindicates her crimes."

Aryanna had rolled her eyes, brushing the words away like lint. "Claire's goals align with ours: air filters, water purification, energy grids—all shared human assets. And her freedom depends on complete transparency. One wrong move and she's locked away for life. We don't have that kind of leverage over anyone else."

Aryanna had steepled her long fingers. "Besides, for many, Claire is a warrior—a Robin Hood figure. With this appointment, we bring objectors into the fold instead of leaving them outside to sharpen their knives."

"We reward terrorism," Maja had said flatly.

"We reward atonement." Aryanna had dropped the word like a stone in water, ripples spreading through the room. Atonement: the creed of Gaia's world designers, who saw redemption as the highest calling.

Didn't she once believe the same?

Now bile rose in her throat as she studied Claire. The woman sat with hands folded, gaze lowered, her stillness unreadable. Humility? Or the practiced composure of a survivor who had bartered her way back into power?

Revealing the Condor patch, surrendering herself—those had

been enormous leaps of faith. Perhaps they were genuine. Perhaps this really was a woman turning full circle.

Perhaps.

Maja's chest tightened. Could Claire change?

More dangerous still—could Maja?

CHAPTER SIXTY-FOUR

"How do you really know anyone? Words and deeds tell you a little. But the heart guards its secrets, sometimes even from its keeper."

—MADISON FLOYD
MEMOIRS FROM MARS

NYX ROVER: MADISON

Mars Day 4

THE STORM HAD eased, leaving only a whisper of dust against the hab. Madison suited up in silence, aware of Barrio in her periphery, their long history circling like an eagle and ready to feed on her resolve. A flash of his soft eyes, leaning in, a memory of the surf rolling azure in the distance.

He caught her glance and gave a tentative smile. She looked away, sealed her gloves, locked her helmet and stepped through the decon chamber. The electrostatic grid snapped and fizzed as it discharged.

Barrio followed her out.

The rover sat half-buried, dust still rustling across its flank. They pulled shovels from the rack and dug out the treads, sharp as metal teeth. Sweat soaked Madison's liner as she worked, half-starting a dozen lines in her head, rehearsing what she'd say. None sounded right.

When they finished brushing off the viewport, they cycled into the rover, dusted down and strapped in. Conscious of Barrio's gaze, Madison busied herself with systems checks, setting radar and telemetry for the copter. Treads bit into sand, churning up more dust.

Outside, the haze reduced the world to a handful of boulders, black scabs on cracked red skin. The heater roared. Her thoughts swooped like carrion birds until finally she blurted, "Why didn't you tell me?"

Barrio blinked at her. "Umm, tell you what?"

"That you signed up for Mars with Lincoln?"

He exhaled heavily. "It all happened fast. You remember how things were."

"You couldn't have called?" Anger sliced through the hum.

"We were on strict comms lockdown."

"Even Lincoln would've allowed family calls. You were going to Mars, for Chrissake!"

"We're not exactly family—"

She flinched.

His voice broke. "I didn't mean—"

Heart hammering, eyes burning, she whispered, "What was Florida then? Did it mean nothing to you?"

His gaze, grey and clouded, softened. "Of course it did," he mumbled. "Then the Mars thing happened. We couldn't talk. I thought…it was easier to let it go."

"That's a shithouse excuse." Madison whacked him on the shoulder. "You risk your life flying through space, but you can't talk to me about a long-distance relationship? Lame ass."

The rover pitched over a boulder. He chuckled, then the smile slipped. "Nailed it…And for what it's worth, I'm sorry."

"You've got a lot to make up for, Gareth."

"I do indeed," he muttered.

Madison stared out the viewport, the hiss of sand on the hull filling her helmet. The world outside was marmalade dust, a brand-new planet.

She turned back. "Why back Ellison? And Victoria —kidnapping?"

Barrio tugged at his harness. "Lincoln's tactics are…rough."

"Are you kidding me? He's a criminal!" Madison spat.

"What do you want me to say, Madison?" he shot back. "I made a choice. Maybe it was wrong, but here we are."

The heater whined. Madison punched the controls and it dropped to a low hum. The radar pinged.

"We're close," Barrio said, voice turning brisk.

Madison eased the rover to a halt. They cycled through the airlock, back into the swirl.

Barrio clambered into the cockpit while Madison knelt by the engine, mind stewing on Barrio's words. A rotor blade lay snapped, the missing piece half-buried metres away. Fixable. She swept dust off the engine, purging anger with each aggressive stroke, and squinted at its guts.

"Engine looks good," she rasped over comms. "Needs a clean—"

A sudden gust tore her from the ground. Pain lanced her leg as her calf caught on the engine's jagged edge. She spun away, tumbling over rocks.

Her HUD shrieked. Suit breach. Left calf.

"Madison!" Barrio's voice cracked. "Report!"

"Puncture—" She rolled onto her back, vision blurring as oxygen bled away. The auto-seal crawled over the tear but couldn't close it.

She clawed at the wound, gasping, but strength drained out of her. The world shrank to a tunnel, the last image a blurred figure sprinting towards her through the storm—then Barrio, his grey eyes fierce with panic, before everything went black.

CHAPTER SIXTY-FIVE

—Jonas Seaborn
MARS MANIFESTO

KUNLUN BASE: SERENA

Mars Day 5

Serena cranked a bolt in the Kunlun farm's hydroponic wing. You had to give the Chinese credit, she thought. They did nothing by halves, and this farm was enormous. She wiped her brow with her suit sleeve, looking down the long rows.

The station was built to house one hundred and fifty initial settlers before they moved to the lava tubes. She couldn't wait to see those. Victoria had been talking up the design, the grand window built in the main atrium with a view to the surface, which they still hadn't seen because of the infernal storm.

Xavier carried in a tray of drippers to be installed, Lincoln trailing along behind like a bad smell.

"Any news from the copter yet?" she called out as they approached.

"Madison's decompression bruising is a concern. They're

watching it closely. She and Barrio are holed up in the rover while they wait for Volkov to arrive with the hauler."

Now that's got to be a fun party, she mused. Barrio and Madison in a confined space for hours. Serena knew Madison was prickly about Barrio, but she had never revealed why no matter how much she needled and prodded for info.

Mad Dog's one cool customer, she thought.

Ellison was badgering Xavier with questions about the air filtration, CO_2, filters. Xavier was handling it alright, his hatred for Lincoln tempered by his love for plant cultivation.

"The farm needs to be kept at warmer temperatures than the rest of the hab. We'll get more CO_2 in here naturally once the plants grow. But in the meantime, we need to filter it from the Martian air."

"We use Claire's tech for that?" Lincoln asked.

"*Non.* That's not been plugged into Kunlun. Just old-fashioned scrubbers for now."

"One intake or multiple access points?"

"Multiple intakes, of course," Xavier said, exasperated. Xavier placed the box on the metal workbench with a clatter and turned to Lincoln. "Basic safety for Moon or Mars. How do you not know this?"

Lincoln shrugged. "I have people…"

"Of course you do. Or *did, eh mon vieux?*" Xavier laughed, suddenly delighted with the reminder of Lincoln's corporate emasculation.

Lincoln's face darkened. Serena thought to chide Xavier, but bugger it, this was Lincoln Goddamn Ellison. Let him stew in his own poo.

"My lawyers will tear that injunction to shreds." Lincoln blazed with fury.

"Sure they will." He clapped Lincoln forcefully on the back.

"For now, you can scrub these drippers until every speck of dirt and grit is gone. So clean I could shove them up your *cul*, understood?"

"Xavier—gross." Serena made a face at him but smiled inwardly.

He waved a conciliatory hand.

They worked in silence, Xavier breaking out into the occasional hum, while Lincoln quietly fumed, scrubbing vigorously.

Her back aching, Serena stretched and sighed. "Ellison, come with me. We'll seal off the sections ready for Volkov to bring the *Nyx* plants in."

Lincoln threw the last dripper down gratefully and rose stiffly to join her. One by one, they drew the plastic dividers across the segments until they had a unit big enough to handle crops for the existing crew—*Pinnacle* team hopefully included—as well as the next team, due to arrive in eighteen months.

They left Xavier to install the drippers while they moved to the next hub to check the water cyclers.

"This is Martian water?" Lincoln actually sounded genuine in his curiosity. She trained a careful eye over his features, searching for malicious intent.

"Yup. The Chinese chose this spot because they could mine and filter the ice directly underneath, reducing the need for vehicle EVAs and all that entails. But you should know that." She frowned at him.

He feigned innocence then resumed peppering her with questions. She caught herself leaning in.

Watch yourself, Fox, she reminded herself. *There's nothing more disarming than a flattering listener. He's blowing sunshine up your skirt.*

They finished their task and headed towards the common area.

"I need to use the facility," Lincoln said, stopping outside the lavatory.

"Be my guest," she said, and held the door open for him.

"It might take a while," he said with a grimace.

She was not meant to leave him alone. Standing sentry while Lincoln voided bowels did not sound like a fun time.

Serena rolled her eyes. "I'll wait in the kitchen." She could see down the corridor straight to the door.

She joined Troy, Xanthe and Victoria, who were planning the *Pinnacle* rescue, assuming the copter was serviceable. She sank into a chair, weary.

"Where's Ellison?" Troy asked suddenly.

"In the loo."

Three heads, including Xanthe's, swivelled to stare down the corridor.

Serena's heart jumped at their concern, and she craned her neck too.

Nothing.

She lurched to her feet, shoving the chair aside, ready to bolt when Lincoln slid the door aside.

"That's better," he said, moving towards them, wiping hands on his suit. "Didn't need an audience though."

They all watched him in silence as he swanned into the kitchen, grabbed a rations pack, and split it open with a sigh.

Worry burrowed its head like a tick between Serena's brows. What had she missed?

CHAPTER SIXTY-SIX

"I used to believe in loyalty. To the man. To the company. The reward was opportunity. But the cost? Paid in blood."

—Gareth Barrio
MEMOIRS FROM MARS

NYX ROVER: MADISON

Mars Day 6

Pain lanced up Madison's thigh the moment she shifted in the cramped rover. Barrio leaned close, dabbing sweat from her brow with surprising gentleness.

"How bad?" he asked.

"Eight out of ten." She gasped.

He readied another painkiller. She took it gratefully, hand trembling.

He checked her readouts, then pressed a palm to the patched fabric itself.

She gave a faint nod.

The ground shuddered.

"Volkov," Barrio confirmed, eyes flicking to the radar. He

picked up the radio handset. "Volkov, this is *Nyx* rover, do you read, over?"

A hiss of static, then a voice thick with a Russian burr: "Who is that?"

"Captain Gareth Barrio. We read you loud and clear."

"Traitor assho—"

Barrio raised his eyebrows. "He's gotten feisty."

"Hand it here," Madison said, reaching for the comm.

"Volkov, this is Captain Madison Floyd. You right to manage the retrieval?"

"I'm here to help, Mad Dog."

"Listen, I'm injured, so I can't do a physical assist. I'm sending Barrio out instead."

A long crackle. Then: "I try not to drop copter on his head."

Barrio grimaced, and Madison grinned despite the pain.

"Thatta boy. Great team spirit. I'll monitor from here."

Barrio donned his helmet and gloves and headed out, red grit twisting in lazy spirals.

Madison kept her eyes fixed on the viewport, heart thudding as he guided the hauler's retrieval hook down to the buried copter, securing it to the skids with quick, precise motions.

"Go," he signalled.

The crane took the weight and the copter tore free of the sand with a shudder—and slipped. The skids swung wide. Barrio dove flat as the frame missed his helmet by inches. Metal shrieked against metal.

Madison's breath caught. Her pulse hammered in her throat.

"I'm alright," Barrio's voice rasped over comms, dust-warped.

Heat flooded her face. Her eyes stung. She didn't want to lose him. She hadn't forgiven him—God, not even close—but that truth dug deeper, more raw than the pain in her leg.

The hauler steadied. The copter swung, then lowered onto the tray with a heavy thunk. Barrio clamped it down and trudged back, dust trailing him like a cloak.

"Follow me, fleshbags," Volkov intoned over comms. "I need an oil job and a good lie down."

CHAPTER SIXTY-SEVEN

"Our head and heart make us human.
Everything else is just accessories."

—**Xanthe Waters**
MEMOIRS FROM MARS

KUNLUN BASE: XANTHE

Mars Day 6

Xanthe lay awake on the bunk, eyes open to a darkness that never lifted. She knew from Athena that it was morning and soon the sounds of the crew readying for the day would echo in the hallway.

Six days since they landed.

Six days since light abandoned her.

Six days of a darkness thicker than space itself.

A darkness absent of shape and form.

But lit with memory and imagination, her only solace.

It felt like an eternity.

Every nerve strained as her senses sought data and orientation in her new state, on this alien planet. The rest of her body was slowly gaining strength as she, along with the others, worked their way through the painstaking rehab protocols. She still grew breath-less even in the exosuit.

What she found the hardest was missing out on what was unsaid. The looks between people, the smiles and nods. She felt behind in most conversations, even when she trained herself to listen to the gaps, the breathing, the tone that gave life to much of the communication. There was always something missing: the rustle of someone's movement she couldn't interpret, a pause that might be a nod, or a frown.

Athena was helpful, of course, narrating instructions to help her find her way through the base unaided. But it was exhausting, having to pay constant attention to Athena's voice and every sound around her.

She'd allowed herself a few private moments of grief, weep-ing quietly into her pillow. Her chest ached with a pressure she couldn't release. All that she'd lost…all that she would never see again. Mostly, she worried that she would not remember what Jack looked like. Her son's face hung like a haze in her memory. She'd only had a few precious moments with him, in person, before his life had been snatched away.

And always, at the edge of that memory, the name that burned like acid: Claire Edwards. Now in charge of Spaceward Bound.

Xanthe rolled on to her side before the anger, a familiar searing red light, surged through her body. She did not have the luxury of indulging vengeance or frustration or any other emotion at the moment. Too much of her energy was needed just to move from one place to the next.

Even with help—and the crew were nothing but helpful—it was still taxing.

She hated their suppressed guilt laced with relief. Guilt that her sacrifice had saved their lives. Relief that they were not the ones disabled.

Xanthe sighed and pushed herself to sitting on the bunk. She groped for her trousers and the shirt she had discarded on the floor the night before. She managed a wry smile: Troy hated her sloppiness, but at least she knew exactly where her things were the moment she awoke.

She traced the seams to find the front of the shirt and pulled it on. She wriggled out of her pyjamas and pulled on her trousers. On hands and knees, she swept the floor for her shoes.

She made her way to the ablutions module. Navigating toilets in space was always a challenge, and now more so. She grimaced at her own helplessness, rather than the task itself, as she felt her way into the cubicle, hoping her colleagues had been vigilant with cleaning things up.

She felt around the space, finding the vacuum unit, funnel and wipes. When she was done—and hoped she was clean enough— she left the unit and made her way to the kitchen mess, counting steps, one hand on the wall.

"Xanthe, let me help you." Troy's voice came from behind her and so she waited. He took her arm in his and together they walked slowly towards the main hall. It was quiet, no one else yet awake. Soap and a faint whiff of cloves drifted off his skin. She breathed it in, enjoying it as discretely as she could. The warmth of his body next to hers was comforting. Her eyes prickled.

"How are you feeling about today?" he asked.

Xanthe sighed. "Just another sync. What could go wrong?"

Troy didn't laugh.

"I'm fine. Syncing with a Dopplebot will give me more data."

"As long as you're sure…"

"I'm not sure about much, Troy! This is the most unsure experience I've ever had. But something has got to be better than nothing, right?"

Troy grunted. He led her to a chair at the dining room table and she slid onto it, grateful to be stationary again.

He bustled around her, fetching breakfast and tea.

His hand went to her shoulder as he leaned over and placed the porridge pouch and a spoon into her hands.

As he was pulling away, Xanthe said, "Troy…"

"Yes?"

"Thank you. You've been really helpful. And kind." Her eyes pricked again. "And you're doing a good job leading the team…I'm glad you're here."

His hand squeezed her shoulder, and she pressed her cheek to it. His face came alongside hers and he whispered, "We're leading together. And I couldn't have done this—any of this—without you. I'm glad you're here too."

It was a long, luscious moment, just the two of them, cheek to cheek.

Then Xavier clomped into the room. "*Bonjour!* What's for breakfast?"

Troy moved away hastily.

"Make sure you don't bite too hard, Mr Sexy Pants! I didn't see 'Xanthe' on the menu." Xavier chuckled as he heated a coffee pouch.

Xanthe tucked into her porridge, smiling despite herself.

Xanthe perched on the edge of the medbay surgery table. The whiff of antiseptic and clatter of surgical instruments stirred unsettling memories.

"Are you sure about this?" Troy asked her, strong warm hand on her shoulder.

"Uh huh. I haven't had any pain at all since I lost my sight. And Athena assures me the Dopplebot sync won't add any extra processing for me. The work will be on the Dopplebot side."

"The Dopplebot is ready," Victoria advised.

Xanthe nodded and a bubble of excitement added to her jitters, her hands running cold. "Thank you, Dopplebot," Xanthe said. "I look forward to working in partnership with you."

"It's a pleasure." The Dopplebot's voice was melodic, humanised.

The bot had diverted its human-sync persona, ready to interface with Xanthe. Once the sync had occurred, the Dopplebots' data would be archived and Xanthe's would run on the bot's system instead.

Xanthe heard footsteps from across the room.

"Perfect timing, Jonas," Troy said. "All set?"

"Yes. We'll do the face cast first, and then the sync can get underway."

Troy guided her to lie down on the gurney. Jonas applied a cool, wet gel to her face and then guided a scanner to capture the details. She listened as the 3D printer whirred into action, printing the silicon replica.

"Let's start the sync now," Troy said. "Xanthe, we're going to run a sedative for the data transfer. With Athena running the patch, it shouldn't take too long."

The drug hit her veins, dragging her through a blue haze. Minutes seemed to drag, and she shivered. Troy covered her with a blanket, then resumed holding her hand.

"Sync complete," the Dopplebot voice announced. Xanthe's voice now.

Xanthe stirred as the blue haze receded, her senses sharpening.

"Oh, my God!" Victoria said.

"What?" Xanthe said. "Tell me."

"The face…well, it's just like you! Jonas, you're a genius."

"Uh…thanks."

Troy squeezed her hand. "Don't worry, Xanthe, the bot has brown eyes. She'll never replace you." A catch in his voice.

He helped her sit up.

"Athena? You there?" Xanthe asked.

"I'm here."

"Tell me."

"I can see through the Dopplebot's eyes. You look a little pale."

Xanthe gasped. Her world had become a little less dark.

"Thank you," she whispered. Then louder, "Let's get back to work."

❧

Xanthe still couldn't 'see', but Athena could, so the guidance was more nuanced, and she found she could move a little more easily. Combined with the haptic suit, radar and suit pings, she felt more confident in walking through the base, the bot alongside her.

With Victoria, Jonas and a bevy of Dopplebots leading, they headed from the medical bay straight to the vehicle bay where Barrio and Madison were arriving. They needed the copter repair analysis.

"Troy keeps staring at you."

In what kind of way, Athena?

"Unsure. One part affection, one part freak out."

"Stop staring at me, Troy," Xanthe said.

"Uh—sorry. It's just…weird. Two of you."

"That was all freak out."

"We'll get used to it." She hoped.

They stopped at the airlock while Barrio, Madison and Volkov went through the decontaminator. With a ping and a whoosh, the door cycled open.

Tell me.

"Double takes, as expected."

"Hey Xanthe. And…Xanthe?" Madison asked.

"You can call me Dopplebot Waters," the bot said in Xanthe's voice.

"Doesn't really roll off the tongue, does it?" Jonas said. "How about 'Xanthe Twin'?"

"That's fine with me," Xanthe Twin said.

Gasps and mechanical steps.

Athena, what's happening?

"The Dopplebots are examining Volkov like dogs on a playground."

"Get away from me, creeps," Volkov said.

"You are very ugly," one bot said.

"Yes, I am," Volkov snapped. "But tomorrow Jonas will print me a new face, and you—you will still be stupid."

CHAPTER SIXTY-EIGHT

"Mars rewards cunning, not conscience."

—LINCOLN ELLISON
MEMOIRS FROM MARS

KUNLUN BASE: TROY

Mars Day 7

TROY CRAWLED OUT of his bunk and slumped on the floor, head pounding. The air felt heavy, stifling. He sucked in big breaths like a guppy.

Where was he?

He took a moment to orient himself.

Kunlun. Bunks. The crew back together—Barrio, Madison, Volkov.

Staggering to his feet, he made his way through the crew quarters, unlocked the hatch to the commons and fell to his knees as cool, fresh air with its ozone tang washed over him.

"That's quite an entrance, Bruin." Lincoln looked up from his coffee, seated across from Barrio, who rubbed his stubbled face in his palms.

Troy heaved himself to a sitting position, back against the

kitchen wall, head clearing slowly. He checked his wrist display: oxygen saturation low, CO_2 spiking.

"Barrio, check the air cycler," Troy wheezed. "Hurry."

Barrio's head snapped alert, bolting down the corridor.

Troy pulled himself to his feet and hauled the hatch wide open, forcing fresher air into the crew quarters. "All crew, evacuate!" His shout rattled the walls.

No movement.

He slammed his fist against the bulkhead. "Move!"

Xavier careened through his door, catching himself against the wall, wheezing. Jonas followed, ashen. No sign of the others.

Barrio reappeared at Troy's side. "Carbon dioxide levels critical in crew quarters."

"Get them out!" Troy gasped as Xavier and Jonas stumbled into the kitchen.

Barrio dashed past, eyes fierce. He reappeared with Madison slumped in his arms.

Troy lurched for the first doorway and found Xanthe. He shook her—no response.

"Athena—can you wake her?" he gasped.

Xanthe groaned. Still too weak.

He dragged her upright, staggered, legs trembling, vision tunnelling. He wheeled with his burden, lightheaded, and careened towards the hall. Perspiration ran down his forehead as he strained, his legs wobbling even more. He made it through to the kitchen and sank to his knees, slipping Xanthe gently to the floor then rolling her onto her side.

"Lincoln, grab the O2 masks. Sound the alarm for Victoria and the bots!" Troy wheezed as he checked Xanthe's vitals—stable— then moved on to Madison, still unconscious.

Lincoln hit the distress button. A siren wailed through the hab.

Barrio returned with Serena, limp as a doll. Jonas crawled over and sagged beside her, checking her pulse.

"Here you go," Lincoln said, handing masks to Troy.

"Hand them around, you idiot," Troy barked as he snatched one to slip on himself.

Victoria barged in, mask already strapped on, hair wild, Dopplebots at her heels. "Oh my God!" A hand flew to her mouth, bounced off her mask. "Status?" she asked Troy, waving at the three women lying on the floor.

"Unconscious but stable. Atmosphere readings are off the charts."

"Take them to the medbay," Victoria directed the bots.

The bots scooped up their patients with smooth mechanical precision.

Troy rose unsteadily to his feet but felt his head clearing with the oxygen flowing through the mask. "Jonas, come with me and Victoria to check the air filters. Xavier, watch these two." He jabbed a finger at Barrio and Lincoln.

They threaded down the corridor to the life support hub.

"Epiphany said an alarm should have gone off," Victoria said as Jonas studied the settings. "The alarms are tied to O2 variance."

Jonas pointed at the hab schematic, one section pulsing red. "Problem's isolated to the accommodation wing."

Troy's jaw set. He'd woken by chance—or instinct—before they'd all suffocated. Not all of them. Barrio and Lincoln had been just fine in the commons.

A black stone of dread lodged deep in his gut.

"These wires." Jonas leaned in, frowning. "They're pulled loose."

Victoria hovered. "Couldn't they have degraded? Frozen, brittle—"

"Unlikely. Look here." He tapped the scratched metal. "Something's scraped them."

"From installation?" Her voice wavered.

"Maybe. But it looks…fresh."

Troy's gaze drifted to the schematics. "How does CO_2 choke just one wing?"

"Ventilation damage," Jonas said. "A blocked scrubber, jammed filter—"

"Serena checked all of that when we landed," Victoria cut in.

Jonas's mouth flattened. "Then someone forced it."

A muscle twitched in Troy's jaw. "Check the vents."

Jonas climbed up, pulled the shower grid free. His voice echoed hollow. "Oh, crap." He dropped back down.

"Well?"

"The tubing's collapsed in on itself. Coiled like rope."

"Deliberate?"

"Hard to say."

Troy's jaw hardened. "Jonas, sort this out." He pointed at the ventilation shaft. "Victoria, have Epiphany audit all the alarm systems and review any data for when CO_2 accumulation began in this wing." He tugged at the mask pinching his nose. "And I want Dopplebots watching Barrio and Ellison. Every move."

The bots turned their blank heads in unison, lenses glinting as they waited. Watching.

CHAPTER SIXTY-NINE

"Mars is not a partner. It's a prize. And
prizes are to be taken, not shared."

—Lincoln Ellison
MEMOIRS FROM MARS

KUNLUN VEHICLE BAY: MADISON

Mars Day 10

Dust squall warnings had shrieked across the base; they needed more hands to haul the copter back before the storm buried it.

The test flight had gone well—Barrio in the pilot's seat, natural as breathing.

Damn, he was good.

Now he was in the hangar with Troy and Volkov, dragging the half-tonne machine onto its sled.

The lock pinged green. Madison stepped out. Dust hissed across her visor like angry bees. Her boots found the guide rail, magnets kissing metal under the sand. The tether tugged at her hip, linking her to Jonas ahead.

"Troy, status?" she murmured.

"Workshop doors at 30% open. Volkov and Barrio are

manoeuvring the sled. Wind speed increasing to twenty-six knots. Visibility less than two metres."

Orange haze boiled around her. Dust devils spun like mad dancers over a crater rim.

"Dig in and haul!" Barrio barked.

Madison strained against the tether behind Jonas, and the sled jarred.

"Again!"

She leaned into it, vibrations shuddering through her feet and up her spine.

"Damn it! Hold up." Barrio dropped out of line to check the tracks on the sled. "Dust is jamming the magnets."

Another voice cut through comms: Lincoln.

"Troy, you're shorthanded out there. Let me assist."

Madison stiffened. She could almost see Troy's scowl.

"We don't need you," Troy said drily.

Barrio cut in. "Extra pair of hands won't hurt. Half a tonne in this squall? We'll take the help."

Madison ground her teeth. Barrio always defended Ellison.

But then Barrio had turned out to be a good team player, pitching in beside them. A tender nursemaid with her injuries.

She shook her head. He was a complex man. Hard as a steel rod, soft as a cat.

Besides, Ellison was a powerful force, a charismatic persuader. Hadn't she herself fallen under his spell all those years ago when she too worked for Spaceward Bound? Madison had found herself flying one too many sketchy assignments before she'd finally pulled the pin. It was tough leaving the glow of the wonderkid genius self-made man and visionary. It took guts to see through the shiny bluster.

She'd done it. Maybe Barrio would too.

"Fine," Troy said at last. "Suit him up. He tethers to Volkov."

Minutes later, Lincoln's bulk pressed the line beside hers, comms alive with his feigned camaraderie.

"Don't worry, Mad Dog, I've done more EVAs than half your crew."

Madison ignored him, watching Jonas's line ahead.

The storm hit. Wind slammed her sideways, dust hammering like buckshot.

A figure loomed through the red swirl—a knife-sharp flash at the rope, a sawing motion. Her breath froze.

Then the gust swallowed it. Blind again.

The tether jerked, then went slack.

"Hold!" Troy's voice.

"Jonas is loose!" Madison clawed at the tether, reeling it in, but her gloves found only air.

"Reel him in!" Troy shouted.

"I've lost him!" Madison cried. Her knees hit sand. She swept frantically with her gloves. Nothing.

A hand clamped her shoulder—Volkov.

"Fall in behind me, Mad Dog," the bot said, clipping a tether to her suit's belt and hauling her to her feet. She pressed into the bot's broad back, letting it plough a path. They found Troy, then Jonas limp and bloodied, who they hauled across Volkov's shoulder.

Step by step, they shuffled as one. Madison's world shrank to Volkov's belt in her fist, Troy's tether at her waist, the choking red pressing in.

At last, her boot struck metal—the sled. Relief washed over her.

Barrio's voice cut through the storm, back in range. "We've got to move this copter and close the bay door before the dust makes it impossible." His outline appeared against the hull.

"Jonas is unconscious. I'm taking him to the airlock," Volkov intoned as he reclipped Madison's tether to the copter's sled.

Barrio was beside her, his face just visible as the dust swirls eased. "You okay?" He peered at her, grey eyes flooded with concern.

"Yeah."

As they grabbed handholds on the sled, dark silhouettes flooded around them.

Dopplebots!

Victoria's voice came through the comms.

"Troy, the bots have reattached a line to the sled and are ready to heave. Direct them when ready."

"Roger. On three." He counted down and the sled ground forward, metal screeching on the tracks and shuddering over the dust.

Madison dug her boots through the sand; they secured to the magnetic tracks. Her muscles ached as they heaved alongside the bots, her legs and arms quivering with the strain. Barrio grunted ahead of her while Troy stepped in close behind.

"Nearly there!" Troy muttered.

Two more laboured steps and Troy called 'halt'. She leaned against the copter, panting, limbs burning.

The bay door groaned behind them and then suddenly, mercifully quiet, the storm was blocked. Dust filled the bay in a haze.

"Bay door secure," announced a Dopplebot.

"Volkov—how is Jonas?" Troy asked.

"Awake. Bump on head but otherwise okay."

"Where's Lincoln?" Barrio asked.

Volkov appeared through the dust swirl. "In the airlock. He hurt his hand."

"How?"

"I might have stepped on it," Volkov added, voice dry.

"That damned bot tried to kill me!" Lincoln fumed on the comm.

Troy pushed close to Madison, jaw tight. He held out a tether—severed, ends ragged.

Madison's stomach dropped. She stared at the frayed line, memory of the sawing flash burning behind her eyes.

"I think I saw…" she began.

Barrio cut her off. "Could have rubbed against a rock in the storm." His voice was hard, defensive.

Troy's face was slick with sweat, fury in every line.

She met Troy's eyes, then looked away, biting back her words. The red haze still burned in her memory—a flash of a blade. Maybe the squall. Maybe not.

"Let's get out of this storm," she said.

And into another.

CHAPTER SEVENTY

"Mars is a ledger. No excuses, only debts paid in blood and bone."

—Xanthe Waters
MEMOIRS FROM MARS

KUNLUN BASE: XANTHE

Mars Day 12

Xanthe made her way to the comms room with Troy at her side. She hardly needed Athena's prompts now; the haptic suit twitched like whiskers, her ears and nose mapping the corridors.

She was a mole on Mars.

Not that she didn't miss her sight.

She did—every single minute.

But there was too much to do, to focus on, while the base was being established: plants were being transferred to the farm the next day, fuel manufacturing was underway for their return journey and a thousand tasks pressed on them in an environment that forgave nothing.

And then there was the *Pinnacle* crew.

She followed Troy inside, the ping of a waiting message prickling her attention.

Athena, read it to me.

"It's from the Pinnacle. The resource update you requested. 43 days of rations left. The water cycler has lost a seal and leaked into the hold. They have 50% water remaining. All other systems still nominal."

Xanthe's mouth went dry. *They're screwed if we don't get them out.*

"Lincoln knew that the moment he abandoned them."

Internal pings flared—Victoria, Lincoln, Barrio arriving. She reached for a chair; Troy guided her hand to its back. Air pressure shifted, boots scuffed in the corridor—others entered.

Troy opened the meeting, reading the *Pinnacle*'s report. Xanthe let his voice fade while she and Athena ran rescue scenarios. Her mind drifted in calculations then returned sharply to the conversation.

"Using the copter for shuttle rescues is a bad idea," Madison said. "It's still storm season, and that's our only bird."

Lincoln's voice oiled in. "Correction—it's the *Pinnacle*'s copter. Not a collective resource."

Serena snapped, "We did the repairs. We fuelled it. That makes it ours too, Ellison."

"No matter who owns it, or who flies it," Madison said, "seven people need moving. That means multiple runs, over fifteen hundred klicks of storm-raked terrain."

"What about the *Pinnacle* rover? Barrio?" Jonas asked.

Barrio dragged a foot under his chair. "What's left? Not much. One wheel hub's dead and locked straight, so she's dragging herself forward on just two drives. The main batteries and converters are gone, which means brownouts every time they push her. And the scrubber system? Gutted."

"Can they rig something?" Jonas asked.

Xanthe imagined his engineering brain going into overdrive. Meanwhile, Athena whispered jury-rig solutions.

Barrio let out a long breath. "Yeah, they can rig it. Strap spare battery packs on a sled and feed them in with patched cabling, maybe get two wheels pulling steady. For air, they can lash suit scrubbers into the cabin, swap filters till they're spent and hand pump when the levels creep up. It'll move, but every kilometre'll be a fight."

Jonas's voice dropped. "That's not a rover. That's a coffin on wheels."

"We could send our rover to meet it halfway," Serena suggested.

"That risks our crew," Troy countered. "Fifty days there, fifty back."

"We can't just leave them!" Jonas's voice tightened.

"Exactly," Lincoln said smoothly. "We have a moral duty to save my crew—our fellow human beings."

The audacity of him. Xanthe's nostrils flared.

"What about the bots?" Serena asked.

"They'd drain the batteries and stall in the first storm," Jonas said.

Madison spoke again, deliberate. "Here's what we can do. *Pinnacle* rigs their rover and starts moving. We launch ours toward them. We track the weather. When there's a gap, we send the copter to shuttle two at a time to our rover, which carries fuel for the bird."

Troy shifted beside Xanthe. "That plan's risk stacked on risk."

"We do nothing and they die, Troy," Jonas said, pleading now.

"Who do we send?" Troy's voice dropped.

Madison cleared her throat. "We need engineering, life support, supply here to prep for more people. This one's for the pilots."

Athena ran through the scenarios, but Xanthe already knew the outcome: not all would make it back.

CHAPTER SEVENTY-ONE

"The red God of War makes the law. We only negotiate the terms."

—JONAS SEABORN
MARS MANIFESTO

NYX ROVER: MADISON

Mars Day 25

MADISON RAN THROUGH the checks in the rover and settled back in the chair, already bored brainless. It was the eleventh day on their way to meet the *Pinnacle* crew, eking their way across the pitted landscape. The dust storms taunted them, making the journey even more boring than it already was. No views—just the endless red haze.

Barrio was stuck at Kunlun with the copter until the weather cleared.

More than once, she wondered if this was a fool's errand.

Still, they had to try.

Didn't they?

The soldier in her knew there were risks in every mission. And costs.

The comms filled the silence. In bored voices, those on the

Pinnacle rover passed the time with quiz questions. She laughed along, even managed some reading, an old Western. Sleep kept tugging her under, sending her dozing in the chair as the rover rocked over the rambling landscape.

An alert jolted her awake and she dropped the tablet.

"*Nyx* rover, this is *Pinnacle* rover. Come in, over."

She fumbled for the receiver. "Go ahead, over."

"We've got a situation developing."

Her heart lurched. "Go ahead."

"CO_2 alarms were noisy overnight. Scrubbers are clogging faster than expected. Looks like we'll be stalled for a while, while we sort it out."

"Copy."

Damn. They'd fall behind again. And their supplies were getting thin quickly.

Damn dust! They'd have them all out in two days if the weather broke.

She updated Xanthe at Kunlun before staring at the weather radar. No change. Hours crawled by. She stared at her tablet, trying to read, but her eyes glazed over the text without registering the words.

Madison delayed her lunch as long as possible. Meals were welcome relief to the boredom.

The radio crackled, and she grabbed it mid-swallow of a bite of her chicken wrap.

"Go ahead."

"Hey, Mad Dog. We had a bit of a fright here. Brownout. Lights and fans cut out. We swapped a battery, but Matt burned his hand. Air's still really heavy. We're on manual pump duty."

Madison hesitated. "Copy. Still moving towards you. Barrio's on standby, ready to jump in that copter as soon as it's clear enough."

"Yeah. Thanks."

"Give me an update in an hour, okay?"

"Will do. *Pinnacle* rover out."

Madison sank back in the chair. She imagined what they were facing now: thickening air, a limping rover, rescue still thirty-nine days away. At least.

The silence between calls was worse than the dust. She cleaned, worked out, meditated. Nothing dulled the image of them choking in their own breath.

The storm hit hard on Mars day 27. Dust battered her rover. Then the radio crackled again, Jim's voice thin, laboured:

"Tracks buried. Dug out. But scrubbers spent. Theresa, Ivan… gone. Passed out. Didn't wake. Hypoxia. Exhaustion. They're done."

Madison squeezed her eyes shut. "I'm sorry, Jim."

"Still moving. Just gotta…make it through."

Madison's heart sank and she searched for comforting words. "Jim—good luck."

"Thanks, Madison. Looking forward to meeting you in person real soon."

"Likewise."

Madison kept herself busy while keeping one eye on the radar as the storm approached. She scrubbed the entire inside of the rover, did a stocktake of supplies, moved the human waste bucket to the airlock, serviced the spare air scrubbers, did her body weight routine, meditated, and played solitaire and word puzzles on her tablet.

The storm persisted. Dust swarmed over her vehicle. The tracks shuddered but kept churning through the sand, still on their target as it manoeuvred around craters and boulders, bumbling along as the wind growled.

"*Nyx* rover, come in."

"Go ahead, Jim," Madison said breathlessly as she stood up from a set of pushups.

"Tracks caught in a drift, rover half-buried. We've been out digging. Got it loose but scrubber cartridges spent. Our suits are running low."

The sand scoured the viewport and the tracks whined as the rover climbed a hill.

Madison winced. "I'm sorry, Jim."

"Yeah. We just gotta make it through the storm. We're moving again, at least."

"Conserve your air, Jim."

"Will do."

Madison replaced the receiver and pounded a fist on the dash. So close, but not close enough.

She relayed the news to Xanthe.

All Madison could do now was wait.

✦

She must have dozed off again and woke with a start. The air in the rover was stifling. She checked the gauges—time to change the scrubber. She rubbed her face and shook her head to wake up. The radar showed the storm easing and a blip on the rim of the screen—*Pinnacle* rover. She'd intercept them in five days, assuming the rovers held together.

"Hey, Mad Dog…"

"Jim—go ahead." Madison leaned on the dash, conscious of the smell of sweat wafting up from the neck of her suit.

"Pat…Pat didn't make it. We left the bodies at a cairn. To lighten our load."

"Jim…"

"Scrubber's really struggling. Air is bad. Real bad." A long pause. "We've drawn lots. Susan and Cassius are walking out. They've made recordings for their families."

"Oh, Jim…"

Two left.

Madison buried her face in her hands.

❧

"*Nyx* rover, this is Kunlun base."

Xanthe.

"Go ahead, Kunlun."

"Barrio is loading the copter—spare scrubbers, supplies. There's a break in the storm—enough for one run."

Relief punched through her chest. "Tell him to drop the scrubbers first at the *Pinnacle* rover, then search for the walkers—their beacons are still on."

"Will do."

"And tell Barrio not to be a hothead—no stupid risks. One run, that's it."

"Roger that."

She studied the radar for hours until she saw the copter's dot appear on screen. As it neared her position, she strained to catch a glimpse out of her viewport. Still too dusty.

"Mad Dog, this is Barrio—do you read, over?"

She broke into a huge smile. "Barrio! So good to hear your voice!"

"How are you doing in that old tin can?"

"Need a shower. Otherwise, alright."

"Hang in there, Madison." His voice hitched. "We're all rooting for you."

❧

Hours crawled. Barrio was back on the radio.

"I've got Susan on board. She's critical. Scrubbers have been dropped. I'm heading back to base. Another squall blowing up on the horizon."

"Cassius?" Madison asked.

"Didn't make it."

"Copy."

❧

The radar blip loomed close. Madison's heart thudded. She scanned the rover beams through the red haze.

And there, at last, the rover.

"Jim, I've got you in sight."

"Roger that. We see you!"

"Stay on board until I say. Minimise dust."

Madison pulled on her helmet as the rover drew alongside the other crippled craft. She hit the brakes, crawled into the airlock and hit the cycler. Air pressure vented and the door slid open.

She jumped to the surface as the two survivors tumbled from their vehicle. She rushed to them, slipping under an arm, the other barely standing, spent. Once she helped each of them into the airlock, she salvaged the remaining supplies in the other rover and closed the hatch behind them.

The airlock cycled. They staggered into her cabin. Helmets off. The stench of sweat, sour breath and waste hit like a wall.

"I've had less fragrant passengers," Madison said, "but God, it's good to see you."

❧

Mars Day 114

Madison drove the rover into the bay to cheers over comms. The rescue had taken one hundred and one days. Relief crashed over her body, louder than the fatigue grinding every muscle.

She helped Jim and Matt from the rover—they could clean it later—and together they cycled through the airlock, stripped through decontamination, peeled their suits and stood in their thermal layers: scruffy, hollow-eyed and stinking to high heaven. Applause burst as the hatch slid open.

Serena hugged her first, face wet with tears. Then Jonas, Troy, Xanthe and Xavier.

"*Mon Dieu!* You are as ripe as the swamp!" Xavier patted her back.

Barrio stood quietly waiting his turn, after having greeted his own teammates. "Well done, Madison," he murmured as he folded her in his arms. "Great to have you back."

He smelled of soap and grease. His beard tickled her neck, secret thrills flooding her exhausted body.

Volkov stepped forward. "The eight who build for billions are happily back together." He thrust the rubber chicken into her hands. "Betty says she missed you."

Madison smiled at the bot's new face. Jonas had done a good job. "Thanks, Volkov."

Troy put a hand on her shoulder. "Madison, we all know how much you love confined places. Your courage and willingness to face down this fear, for over a hundred consecutive days, is remarkable. You are an inspiration, Mad Dog."

"Thanks," she mumbled, eyes shining.

And then Lincoln—scrubbed, hair combed and set with who-knew-what—raised his arms. Dopplebots flanked him like guards.

"It's with great delight we welcome you to Kunlun base," he boomed. "Your bravery and commitment are testimony to the strength of character you've displayed in the most harrowing of circumstances. As we mourn the fallen, we honour their sacrifice by continuing our mission: to expand settlement on Mars."

Madison listened in disbelief. A flash of Matt and Jim falling from their rover, gaunt, spent. Four of his crew had died because of his obsession with claiming Kunlun. Yet the *Pinnacle* team's eyes shone, their faces alight with pride. Only Barrio remained impassive, features stony.

Troy cut in. "Matt, Jim—Serena will help you settle in. No doubt you'll be wanting a shower and a decent meal. Medical checks to follow. Madison—same goes for you. *Nyx* crew, we'll assemble after the evening meal. Mad Dog—we've got a surprise for you. The lava tubes are ready."

Home, safe, mission accomplished.

Time for a good long sleep.

CHAPTER SEVENTY-TWO

"Home is what we build together."

—**Serena Fox**
MARS MANIFESTO

LAVA TUBES: XANTHE

Mars Day 115

Xanthe trailed behind Victoria, who chattered excitedly as she led the *Nyx* crew to the Dopplebot tunnel habitat. Dopplebot Tang remained at Kunlun to monitor the *Pinnacle* crew lounging in the commons.

This was Xanthe's first trip to the tunnels. Jonas and Victoria had done most of the work there, assessing the bots' progress. The entrance was a scavenged lander hatch from ten years back. Inside, the bots had sealed the lava tubes with rinsed sand and mined clay, then wired the entire network with salvaged cabling. A nuclear generator powered it all.

The tunnels undulated and branched like fingers, the floor uneven beneath her boots. Athena counted steps while her haptic suit buzzed, helping Xanthe map the terrain. Periodically, the tunnel swelled into caverns, like a natural caving system.

"Here's where we could have a communal gathering place, like a town hall or recreation area," Victoria said excitedly. "Down through here, Jonas and I thought would be good for the life support hub—smaller and more contained."

They moved forward again, Xanthe shuffling behind. The air smelled fresh here, earthy, not metallic like Kunlun, though ozone still clung to her throat.

"There are three tunnels like this," Victoria went on, "where the lava bulges gave us room for enclaves. The bots carved shelves and platforms for bedding. We can add privacy screens or doors later."

Sanitation, plumbing, greenhouse farm, private quarters, communal areas, small kitchens, large kitchens—the bots had built it all. Enough sealed space for a hundred people, with a neighbouring system still being mapped. Safe, stable, shielded from storms and radiation.

Something swelled in Xanthe's chest that she hadn't felt for a long time…

Hope.

"And here is the best part." Victoria's voice brimmed with excitement.

The crew gasped and moaned with delight.

"*C'est beau!*" Xavier sighed.

"Oh, my word…" Madison said.

Xanthe reached for Troy beside her. "What is it?"

"An enormous plexiglass window," Troy whispered so as not to interrupt Victoria, who was expounding on the manufacturing process. "Floor to ceiling, twice human height, with a view out to the surface. A cosy common room where you could just sit and stare."

Xanthe smiled sadly. She would have loved to have seen that.

"The bots even made some benches." Victoria's voice moved

away, and Xanthe followed it, suit buzzing. "They're not comfortable—we can add amenities later—but it's good for now."

"Let's take a seat," Troy said to the team, hand on her back guiding her. "We've got a few things to discuss."

The seat was cold, the air still underheated. Jonas, Victoria and Serena had only warmed the tunnels enough to protect infrastructure.

"After discussing the logistics with Serena, Victoria and Jonas, I propose we move into the tunnels," Troy said. "It doesn't have all the pre-fab cupboards and kit of Kunlun, so it will be rough until we build stuff. But it's a lot more secure and stable."

"What about the farm?" Xavier asked. "A lot of work to move it, *non?*"

"We can keep both farms. Just move some crops," Jonas suggested. "That way we have some redundancy in our food supply. And we can test the moisture impact in the tunnels in a contained way without risking all of our food supply."

"What about the *Pinnacle* crew? What do we do about them?" Serena said. "There's almost the same number of them as us now."

Xanthe flinched at the sharpness. "I don't like the 'us and them' overtones," she began. "We're all in this together now."

"I don't know about that," Madison said. "I saw how they looked at Lincoln during his little speech today. They're still buying into his bullshit."

Xanthe considered this for a moment. "Then maybe they need to buy into ours."

"How?" Serena asked.

Xanthe let the silence gather, felt their attention tip toward her. "A manifesto."

❧

They spent some time discussing the major theme of the manifesto and eventually settled on a message they could rally behind.

On the walk back to Kunlun, the crew chatted easily, but Xanthe's thoughts raced ahead to the harder question—how to merge the tribes.

As they entered the commons, Lincoln's voice carried, full of triumph.

"You'll each have your own dome, all mod cons. As the first on Mars, you'll get priority shipments from Earth. First mineral rights. And your own full company of bots once the next manifest lands. When the scrubbers finish terraforming, this will be the most prized real estate in history!"

Xavier muttered a curse under his breath. Xanthe nudged him gently to keep it down.

"That's a nice fairytale, Lincoln," Serena snapped, "but you're persona non grata and Claire Edwards runs Spaceward Bound now."

"That's tied up in the courts," he shot back. "I've got resources. And a long line of customers waiting for their slice of Mars."

Xanthe lifted her chin. "Mars is not for sale, Lincoln. It's not being cut up like spoils of war. The Dopplebots settled and built this place, and we work with them, for everyone's future, not the chosen few."

A chair scraped hard across the floor. The heat of sour coffee breath washed over her, and she felt Troy draw close at her side, a solid wall of presence.

"I am the first man on Mars—" Lincoln's voice rumbled, with menace.

"Only because you shoved Susan aside."

Barrio's voice startled her. He'd never confronted Lincoln before.

"Being first means nothing," Jonas said, steady and earnest. "It's what you create that matters."

Lincoln scoffed. "Exactly. I offer wealth. Prosperity. Abundance.

A frontier where anyone with grit can rise." He hesitated, catching himself. "Man or woman."

"And the last frontier worked out so well," muttered Madison.

"We offer something different," Xanthe said evenly.

"Oh?" Lincoln stepped back, the movement a shift in air.

"A world worth living in, for a world worth belonging to."

His humourless laugh grated close to her ear. "Still the same hippie nonsense, Xanthe. We live in the real world."

"We live in the world we create," she countered, steel in her tone. "And we start right now. We need to decide how we'll live together until resupply. Our Manifesto is Mars for All."

"How very Three Musketeers of you," he sneered. "As the first man on Mars, I've already claimed the base." His words hit hard, almost a shout.

"Repetition does not make it real, Lincoln," Xanthe continued. "You are under guard until you return to Earth to face the charges against you."

Lincoln huffed. "Me and the *Pinnacle* crew do not recognise your authority."

"They can decide for themselves," Troy cut in, calm but firm. "Join us in the tunnels. Safe air, growing food, working comms. Together we can keep each other alive. Our rescue shows our intentions are genuine."

"What's the catch?" Susan asked warily.

"No catch," Troy replied. "Work with us. Share the load. Share the benefits."

"And help us draft the Mars Manifesto," Xanthe added.

"Mars for All. It's got a nice ring to it, doesn't it?" Serena said, a smile in her voice.

A silence followed, heavy and unbroken. Lincoln's breath sawed in and out, jagged with restraint.

The rubber chicken squeaked in Serena's hands. "And we can teach you how to play chook tag."

CHAPTER SEVENTY-THREE

"Our bonds are stronger than the void."

—Troy Bruin
MARS MANIFESTO

KUNLUN BASE: TROY

Mars Day 117

Troy followed Xanthe and Madison into the vehicle bay airlock to suit up. They were hauling bedding and kitchen gear to the tunnels, the others having gone ahead to work on the new farm.

Barrio and Lincoln were packing up the comms with Jonas while Xavier did a final sweep.

"Can we trust the *Pinnacle* crew, Xanthe?" Troy asked, snapping his gloves closed.

Xanthe shrugged. "They've got to earn it, right? People live up to expectations as much as they live down to them."

Troy wasn't so sure. The *Pinnacle* crew had wavered even as they started talks on the Manifesto. They set up a common drive on everyone's private tablets, and suggestions were coming in. A good sign.

He locked his helmet. The grooves felt slick, too greasy. He adjusted, unease rushing through him.

An alarm blared. Decompression warning.

"Helmets not sealed!" Madison yelled and lurched towards the hatch, groping for the manual override.

"Athena—help!" Xanthe staggered towards Madison.

A hiss exploded in Troy's ears as he careened towards Madison and Xanthe. Cold roared across his skin, stabbing through his sinuses. He stumbled, ears bursting with pain, lungs clawing at thinning air.

Xanthe crumpled beside him.

Through the viewport—Lincoln's face. A flash of teeth, triumphant.

Troy slammed the override button. Madison wrestled the hatch controls, gasping.

Whistling filled his helmet, a shrill keening. His vision narrowed.

Then—movement.

Barrio burst into view, crashing into Lincoln with a roar that rattled the chamber. Xavier pounded on the window, yelling, eyes flashing.

The last thing Troy registered was the hatch groaning in its frame, Jonas shouting, and the taste of copper as his sight collapsed to black.

CHAPTER SEVENTY-FOUR

"Justice must be swift but never reckless."

—Xanthe Waters
MARS MANIFESTO

KUNLUN BASE: TROY

Mars Day 118

TROY GROANED AS the world stitched itself back together. A rattle in the vents, the rough weight of a blanket, the metallic dust taste in his mouth. His head throbbed like a chronometer. He blinked; a face blurred into focus.

"Xanthe?" he murmured.

"Xanthe Twin," the bot corrected.

Another face leaned towards him, real this time, eyes distant.

"I'm here." Xanthe squeezed his hand.

"What happened?"

"Decompression. Helmets jimmied so they wouldn't seal."

"Madison?"

"Feel like I've been boiled, frozen and fried, but otherwise I'm okay."

Madison sat up on the opposite bunk, weary, her eyes raw. Beside her, Xavier lay pale and still.

"What happened to Xavier?" Troy pushed himself up on elbows to study his friend.

Xanthe took a deep breath then said, "He jimmied the airlock open before it finished de-pressurising to get to you. It snapped shut on his arm. I had to amputate below the elbow."

Troy inhaled sharply. Concern for Xavier cut through the fog.

"How did you do that?" Troy's gut dropped. The image of a sightless surgeon removing his friend's arm hit harder than the headache. Blood, buzz of the saw, disposing of the limb…

Xanthe Twin handed him a water bottle and he sipped gratefully, hand trembling.

"Athena and Xanthe Twin did the procedure as I directed, Jonas and Serena assisting."

"Status?" Troy asked, sitting up.

"He's sedated. Stable for now, but we'll need to monitor for shock and infection."

"Lincoln?"

"Currently detained in his room, guarded by Dopplebots, until we sort out what to do."

"Where were they when he hit the decompression button?" Troy spat. "They were supposed to be guarding him."

"Unclear. He might have slipped away when they were recharging."

Xanthe found his shoulder and stroked his back. His mind whirred into action.

"What are we going to do about Lincoln?" he said.

"Communal decision," Xanthe suggested. "Too big an issue for us to decide alone."

Troy nodded. "Let's call the *Nyx* team together first. And Xavier?"

"Let him rest for now," Xanthe said. "We'll need him later."

❧

They met in the farm along with Victoria and a few Doppelbots while the *Pinnacle* crew waited in the common room. If the lead in his gut was anything to go by, the meeting would be arduous, the decision portentous. The air in the farm was heavy too, laden with moisture, thick with the ripe smell of growing things.

"I know we don't believe in punishment," Serena began, "but I sure as hell want to punish his ass." She leaned against the lettuce trays, arms crossed, her face the picture of fury and vengeance.

Madison's answer was flat and cold. "No punishment would change that son of a bitch. He is beyond redemption. I say we send him back to his ship. Let him fend for himself."

"I say we walk him out the airlock without a helmet," Serena said. "A taste of his own medicine."

"That's all a little violent, don't you think?" Troy tried to rein in the vitriol.

"I agree," Jonas said. "God knows I am entertaining plenty of punitive experiences for Lincoln. He's tried to kill us multiple times now. Condor patch, the EVA tether." He twirled a piece of irrigation tubing. "I'm sure he's behind the atmosphere failure too. He could have sabotaged the vents from the toilet cubicle. And now Madison, Xanthe and Troy almost died. Xavier missing an arm…"

Jonas pulled at the tubing as he itemised Lincoln's crimes. "But hurting him like he's hurt us won't solve anything."

"It will make us feel better," muttered Serena. She sat up and tapped the table. "But it's not just that. It's survival. Lincoln has tried to kill us multiple times. Claire bloody Edwards testified to that, for goodness sake! Lincoln Ellison is a direct threat to all of us."

Heads nodded. Troy knew acknowledging their revenge

fantasies would soften the anger. But Serena was right: Lincoln was a direct threat to their survival.

"What did you do in Olympus?" Victoria said, breaking the silence. She sat on a potting table, jotting notes on her tablet.

Xanthe turned to Victoria. "In the SimHub, we ran an atonement protocol. On the Moon, we secured and sedated Lincoln and his crew and returned them to Earth for consequences."

"Which he managed to escape in the end," Serena said. "He manipulated his way out of arrest and ended up spearheading the helium-3 mining operation."

"I don't think atonement is an option," Madison said. "How many chances are we going to give this asshole? Who has to get injured or die next to allow him an atonement program?"

"Redemption, atonement, rehabilitation are all options," Troy said, trying to bring the process back on track. "What else might we consider?"

"Confinement," Jonas said.

"For another four hundred days?" Serena gasped. "Imagine bringing him meals and watching him all that time, while the rest of us slave away running the base and expanding the lava tubes. No way."

"Well, we can't send him back to Earth. The *Pinnacle* can't operate with so few crew." Madison tapped fingers rhythmically on her thigh as she worked the problem. "He's stuck here with us."

Xanthe's voice dropped, low enough to flatten the leaves. "There is another option."

Dread crept through the room, a panther stalking prey.

"Tell us," Troy breathed.

The words fell like a guillotine: precise, cold and final.

⁂

Troy glanced at the sombre faces around the Kunlun common table. Victoria sat at the head, all twelve Dopplebots lined up behind her like silent judges, chest plates whirring. *Pinnacle* crew and *Nyx* crew sat side by side. Even Xavier was there, having insisted, despite the agony in his arm. His face was pale and sweaty, resolute.

"Lincoln Ellison," Victoria began. To Troy, Victoria sounded brittle, as though the words were cutting her throat. Had they asked too much of her? "You are accused of three counts of attempted murder—"

"Cut the kangaroo court hysterics, Vicky." Lincoln lounged back, arms folded, chin high. "This accusation is yet another bullshit attempt to discredit me."

"It's *Victoria*." The snap in her voice startled even Troy; Lincoln flinched, a flicker of surprise. "Eye witness testimony from Barrio has you initiating decompression before the crew was clear."

"Nonsense. I was there to wave them off."

"They didn't need you, Lincoln," Serena said. "Departing teams cycle themselves."

Lincoln threw his hands up. "I didn't do it. I just peeked through the viewport. Then Barrio tackled me out of nowhere."

"*Salaud*," Xavier muttered, the contempt oozing from every pore.

Barrio leaned forward, muscles bunching under his thermal wear. "I saw you, Lincoln. You hit the decompression button."

There was a menace in Barrio Troy hadn't seen before. He sat up straight, alert for potential violence, heart thudding.

"My twin saw you too." Xanthe's voice was icy, her unseeing eyes like lasers boring into Lincoln. Troy shivered.

Victoria coughed lightly. "Base logs confirm activation from *outside* the airlock."

Lincoln held Xanthe's blank gaze, still as ice. "Could have bumped it."

"That's not all." Xanthe Twin spoke with a darkness that made them all shudder. "I've checked the logs and base cams. Lincoln passed through the life support bay at the time of the ventilation alarm tampering."

Lincoln scoffed. "I'm always escorted. Never alone."

"Except for that particular day when your Dopplebot guard had a malfunction. A strange glitch. From a rigged miniature EMP," Xanthe Twin continued, tension building.

"Conjecture. I mean, how ridiculous." Lincoln drummed fingers on the table.

"You did it, didn't you? The ventilation sabotage? From the toilet cubicle vent!" Serena's face was pinched purple like a grape, Jonas seething beside her. "Very convenient how you and Barrio were up so early that day, safe in the commons."

Barrio raised his hands in a 'not me' gesture.

Lincoln rolled his eyes.

"You cut Jonas's tether," Madison said, "in the storm."

"I don't think so." Lincoln appeared bored.

"You have been trying to kill the other humans since you arrived." Xanthe Twin was clinical, dark.

Troy studied the faces around the room: disgust, alarm, fury, confusion—especially from the *Pinnacle* crew.

Victoria glanced at Troy. He nodded. "We'll take a vote. Guilty or not?" Victoria pointed to each human in turn, each replying 'guilty'. Susan, Matt and Jim abstained. Barrio paused, then said in a low voice, "Guilty."

Victoria turned to each Dopplebot. In unison, they replied 'guilty'.

Lincoln gave a brittle laugh and straightened Ozymandias on his finger. "What are you going to do—make me walk the plank?"

Troy leaned forward, taking over from Victoria as agreed. "We've decided to leave you here, at Kunlun. There are supplies, crops. Enough until the next ship. Plus comms to Earth."

"If they'll bother to talk to him," muttered Xavier, cradling his bandaged stump.

"Me and my crew will be just fine, thanks. It's what I suggested from the start."

Troy turned to the *Pinnacle* team. "You can stay here with him or come with us to the lava tubes. Either way, you're welcome."

The words hung heavy.

Troy peered at each of them.

Barrio broke first. His eyes never left Lincoln. "I've followed you across three worlds: Earth, the Moon and Mars. I've seen what you are capable of. What you did. I'm done." He stabbed a finger at the table, then sat back hard.

Lincoln's face reddened.

"Susan?" Troy prodded.

The woman kept her eyes down, squirming in her chair. Then, "Go."

"Jim?" Troy asked.

"Go."

"Matt?"

Matt hesitated, sweat glistening at his temple. "Stay."

Barrio considered his colleague then. "Matt, just so that you're clear, Lincoln ordered me to abandon you—all of you except Tang—knowing the chances of us mounting a rescue were second to none."

"But we did mount a rescue!" Lincoln cried with smug satisfaction.

"Only because we helped, you slimy bastard!" Serena jumped to her feet.

Troy pulled her back again.

Matt shrugged. "Tough leadership decisions. I respect that."

"Your 'leader' tried to kill the people who came to save you, Matt." Xanthe spoke this time, her voice loaded with compassion. "Are you sure?"

Matt stared at the table then up at Lincoln. "Who knows what the future will bring."

Silence slithered alongside the hum of life support.

Troy felt his stomach twist. This was no longer a trial—it was exile.

"It's settled then. Lincoln and Matt will stay here."

"Jim? Susan? Barrio…" Lincoln's tone was equal parts threat and reprimand.

They remained silent.

"You'll lose privileges. No habitat, mining rights—nothing. You're making a big mistake. No settlers' rights—"

"We're not settlers, Lincoln." Xanthe's face had grown still as a Roman statue. "We're stewards. We're not here to exploit the planet. Mars is our partner, not a prize."

"What bullshit, Xanthe." Lincoln slapped the table, making everyone but Xanthe jump. "People want money, riches, a better life. Nothing else is worth the sacrifice. That's what I promised you—" Lincoln narrowed his gaze and pointed at his recalcitrant team members. "And I always deliver. Always." He sat back. "Stay."

Barrio kept his arms crossed, muscles tense under his shirt. Troy could almost taste the animosity oozing from the man's pores.

Barrio leaned forward and said through gritted teeth, "No."

Lincoln sucked in a breath as though the air had been torn from him. He glanced at Susan and Jim who avoided his gaze.

"Traitors," he hissed.

Troy's stomach roiled, but he forced the words out. "It's decided. We leave now. We'll be back every seven days to check the farm. And you."

Lincoln's bravado sagged. "Leave us some bots. I don't know all the systems."

"Don't worry, Lincoln," Serena said with a dark smile. "You'll work it out. Manual's in the cupboard. Farm, sanitation, life support, comms. Plenty to keep you busy."

They rose, ten humans and twelve Dopplebots, suiting up in

the rover bay. Lincoln followed, voice shifting from defiance to pleading.

Through the viewport, Troy watched him shouting, fists on the glass, sound swallowed by the hiss of air cycling.

Troy hesitated, one breath, two. His gut churned like eels in a bucket.

Then he pressed the control.

"Goodbye, Lincoln."

CHAPTER SEVENTY-FIVE

"Unity over faction; collaboration over control."

—**Xanthe Waters**
MARS MANIFESTO

VESTA LAVA TUBES: TROY

Mars Day 259—Commander Troy Bruin, log

The days on Mars feel elastic. They stretch and snap, longer than they should be. Twenty-four hours and thirty-nine minutes doesn't sound like much until you live it, until the light refuses to fade and the shadows refuse to move. Every rotation feels like two.

Base progress

Routine keeps us sane. Or gives us the illusion of sanity. The crew moves through checklists like monks reciting prayers. Serena still insists on logging every micron shift in the air filters. I told her precision was her superpower. She didn't laugh. Just said, "My scintillating wit is my superpower, Sexy Pants." Still, she's the reason the oxygen mix sits predictably at 20.8 percent. Predictability is a gift here.

Victoria's team of Dopplebots pulled another seventeen litres from the ice bore. The drill head keeps clogging with dust—Jonas improvised a mesh filter from EVA netting and a coffee strainer. Ingenious, if temporary. That's the story of this mission: nothing elegant, just enough to keep us breathing. The condensers hum all night now, a low vibration through the floor that's almost comforting—until you remember that if it stops, so do we.

The delay with Earth stretches to twenty-one minutes. I can feel it in the silences. We send our updates, our polite smiles, our "We're doing fine" faces, and then we wait. By the time Mission Control replies, the moment's gone. Their words float across millions of kilometres—encouragements, congratulations, gentle suggestions.

"You're making history."

Sure. History on Mars feels more banal than bodacious on most days.

Crew health and dynamics

Xanthe insists on the daily vitals, though no one wants to sit still long enough to be monitored. Her own recovery is slow but steady; she navigates by sound and discipline now, the Xanthe Twin an ever-present shadow. She rarely smiles. I suppose I wouldn't either if I'd lost sight of the world. My longing for her, what we had, only seems to grow. But there are signs, however minuscule, that her heart is thawing towards me.

Xavier's working hard at his own therapy. I know his stump is painful and he swears a lot more than usual, especially at the little things, as he struggles to do what came easily with two hands. But he's pushing harder than anyone else.

Jonas seems remarkably well. Being on the ground, with lots of people and bots, he's never alone. His head injury is monitored carefully by Xanthe, but so far there've been no lingering issues from the freezer *incident or the rising cranial issues that nearly killed him in transit. Space might actually be agreeing with him! If we could all be so lucky.*

Average sleep time across the crew is down again—five hours, if that. Fatigue seeps in like the dust: fine, pervasive, impossible to scrub out.

Madison and Barrio are a funny pair. They bristled and sparred for the first few months here, but lately there's an easing, a growing intimacy. Almost sweet. If you can call two hard-nosed pilots 'sweet'.

Serena is as effervescent as ever. She has taken the Pinnacle crew under her wing and made it her mission to indoctrinate them in Gaia philosophy and practice. Susan and Jim are now highly competitive chook tag players, much to Jonas's chagrin, who had hoped to win bets off the newbies. He's back to being bottom bunny on the tally. Truly, I am impressed by Serena's turn around: from suspicious and defensive to being the glue that holds us all together.

The grav gym feels more like penance than training. Jonas lifts like he's punishing something invisible. Xanthe moves slowly and deliberately, eyes closed, lips counting the reps under her breath. I try to lead by example, though half the time it feels performative. Leadership sometimes does. Still, if I stop, they might too—and that's not an option.

Supply

Xavier's plants are the only things growing here that aren't breaking down. The hydroponic trays are a green miracle against the rust-red monotony. He talks to them as usual, whispers things in French. Maybe it's prayer. Maybe confession. Today, he spotted the first tomato sprout. The entire crew gathered round like it was the birth of a child. For a minute, the base was alive with laughter and colour. Then the alarm beeped for water usage, and we went back to rationing hope.

Meals are a form of déjà vu. Rehydrated lentil stew, reconstituted protein paste with added crickets, which are thriving. Thank goodness. Our protein deficiencies are less of a concern with them. Serena called the stew "Martian dhal". No one laughed at first. Then everyone did— too loud, too long.

Culture

Tensions simmer under the surface. Jonas and Xavier clashed over grav gym scheduling. I diffused it with humour, my usual cheap trick. It worked for now. But the cracks are showing: exhaustion, grief, boredom. Xanthe isolates more than she ever did, which breaks my heart. Athena keeps her company, but an A.I.'s empathy can only stretch so far.

Lincoln and Matt

Since the separation, we've had only limited exchanges with those two, on purpose. We get updates through Maja as they are monitoring all comms out of their station. Lincoln is pressing hard for his case to be overturned. He rails against anyone and everyone. He still has fans on Earth, and plenty are protesting in his support. But Claire is still running Spaceward Bound and all his companies. That must truly piss him off. Especially as she's also adopted his dog, Mr Puffkins. That makes me happy. It's small of me, I know. But hey, Lincoln deserves it.

Matt finally ditched Lincoln and came begging. Not surprising—I did notice a certain emptiness in Matt the last time we made a visit there to fix something or other. I can imagine conversation with just Lincoln would be taxing after a while. Serena has really made an effort to welcome Matt, once she got over suspecting him of spying for Ellison. Turns out Matt hates the guy as much as we do.

Mars has a way of stripping things down—systems, habits, people. There's no pretending here. Every weakness gets exposed to the light. Every strength gets tested past reason.

We survive by checklist, by stubbornness, by small mercies.

Day 259. Another sunrise—if you can call that pale smear a sun. And yet.

We are still alive, still holding a candle of hope for the future, what we're creating. That we can create a new Earth here with the ALVEUS scrubber. I am proud. And grateful to call this place home, these people family.

❧

Troy closed the journal and tucked it away, out of sight, maintaining a sliver of privacy. Leadership had its challenges, desperate and awful at times, but it was also such a privilege and joy to be part of a thriving team. He left his personal alcove in the lava tubes and made his way to the common room with its giant window.

Troy savoured the chatter of the crew, the quiet whirr of the Dopplebots' chest plates filling the pauses. He sighed, content. 'Vesta' was the perfect name for their lava tube habitat: goddess of the hearth and communal fire. He traced a finger around the sculpture Xavier had made for him a lifetime ago on Nyx.

Romans didn't get it all wrong, he thought.

"Listen up," Victoria's voice cut across the room. "Time to make this official."

Troy smiled at the scientist. She had done a spectacular job as the Dopplebots' spokesperson and conduit.

"The Dopplebots formally offer shared governance of Kunlun and Vesta to Earth's Martian Commission and all Martian inhabitants. They formally endorse the Mars for All Manifesto as the governing principles for current and future custodians."

They cheered and lifted cups of Xavier's special apple cider, freshly brewed. By God it was good, thought Troy.

"Xavier, this is the best batch yet, *mon ami*." Troy smiled at his friend.

"Nothing but the best for the Sexiest Human on Mars."

The old joke sent them into laughter again—a nickname resurrected when Troy's thermal wear had split in all the wrong places.

"*Excusez moi,*" Xavier began, standing before the group. "I'd like to say a few words before we watch more movies from Earth." He waved his stump, and they grew still, listening. "Since I had this bit of pruning, it's been hard…adjusting." His voice grew gravelly and he cleared his throat.

"Turns out you use a hand and an arm for many things. Drinking, eating, washing—these are okay with one arm. But zippers—they are the worst! I want to thank all of you who have helped me with trousers. Except for Volkov. You don't have the delicacy required for this task."

"Fleshbags have weak points, I've discovered," the bot intoned.

"We'll keep you away from my 'weak point', if you don't mind!"

They chuckled along with him.

"Since I can't do everything myself, I've noticed how much I rely on each of you. But it's more than just opening meal packets and little things like that. All of you are brilliant and essential for life here. I don't think I truly appreciated you geniuses. Serena, I think I have been the hardest on you. If not for you, we'd be frozen rats in a tunnel. Xanthe—you saved my life. Again. Jonas, you can fix anything. Madison, you are the best pilot. Yes, better than Barrio."

Barrio feigned being insulted.

"And the *Pinnacle* crew, I admire your courage. Losing people, it's hard. And Mr Sexy Pants, you've done okay as Commander. You and Xanthe make a great team. She keeps your head from swelling bigger than this chamber."

Troy beamed at him and raised his glass.

"Each of you—you make my life, all our lives, better. I am so honoured to be in your company. Thank you."

Cheers and hugs.

Jonas dragged a stool and propped the display for them all:

movie night, starting with messages from Earth from the latest data dump. They'd shared these communally, unless the message was tagged 'intimate'. They left those to the individuals, with a nod and a wink.

The business messages came first. Victoria had made her scrubber tech open source. Troy raised his cup as news scrolled across the feed: Breath Domes springing up worldwide, factories rolling out industrial units, millions saved. Each mention of air scrubbers drew another toast until Troy's head buzzed pleasantly. Xanthe's leg brushed his, a live wire from toes to crown.

Serena's message from Max was up next. She sat up close to the screen, beaming as Max's image came to life, the oxygen clip held tightly in a bunched fist.

"Hiya, babe! How is my Martian Queen? Things here are hunky-dory. We had a win at Terra Verdi this week: seven days in a row with no climate refugees. Plus, we exceeded food harvest quotas by seven percent. Tell Xavier I'm the one to beat now. They're talking awards, medals, a Nobel…"

"*Ta gueule!*" Xavier heckled, earning another round of laughter.

"Oh—and one piece of important news. Two actually." Max's eyes twinkled. "Xavier's cat, Sophie—"

"I hate that thing," Jonas muttered. Madison punched his shoulder, and he rolled his eyes.

Max scooped up a little grey striped kitten and held it up to the camera. "Sophie had a litter of kittens. This little fella kinda adopted me." He buried his face in the kitten's soft belly fur. "I'm calling him Calvin. And me and Calvin"—Max leaned into the camera lens in a conspiratorial tone—"we're coming to Mars. On the next supply ship.

"Turns out they need the second-best life support technician, and his cat. So, babe, get ready for a hot and steamy reunion. Then we're climbing Olympus Mons." He blew a kiss. "We are T-179 days. Love you, babe!"

Serena reached out a hand to his frozen image on the screen, tears bright. Applause and whistles.

Another face jumped on screen. "Sorry to video bomb, but I wanted to say 'hi' too."

"Dave!" Madison and the others whooped.

"They need a pilot for the supply mission. And after Aryanna got down on her knees and begged"—guffaws—"I said okay. Someone needs to look after Max, no? He's not so good with landings. I have asked for extra spew bags." Max thumped Dave who pretended injury and giggled. "See you Mars-side!" Cheers and clapping.

Xavier jumped up. "We watch it again and drink every time he says 'babe'!"

More cheers.

A message from Gemma was next. Troy straightened and he braced himself.

"Hello there, Troy," she began, auburn hair cascading over tanned shoulders. "I hope things are good on Mars. I've been thinking of you." A lump grew in Troy's throat. "So, some news. I've met a fella. It's serious. Dad's met him." Troy blinked, envy burning. "But I'd really like you to meet him too. Get your blessing and all that. It would mean a lot to me. Can't wait to see you back on Earth." She blew a kiss. "Love you!"

Troy's lips trembled.

Xanthe reached for his hand and squeezed.

The crew sighed in empathy.

Troy let it wash over him, his heart swelling. Madison and Barrio leaned their heads together, talking quietly, pretending to everyone that they weren't an item. But all of them knew they shared a cubby down the far tunnel.

Then there was Jonas, besotted with Victoria, muddling his way through an awkward courtship that Troy and Xavier coached good-naturedly in the background. There they were now, sipping steaming hot chocolate in mugs Jonas had printed a few days ago.

And Xanthe…still a work in progress. But they were sharing leadership. Not only with each other but with the whole crew. A collaborative governance. Not without its challenges, but a culture worth belonging to.

He caught Victoria's approach out of the corner of his awareness—her face taut, joy gone.

"It's Lincoln," she whispered.

Troy's buzz soured. "What does he want now? We unclogged his toilet just two days ago."

"He's missing."

CHAPTER SEVENTY-SIX

"Mars for All."

—**XANTHE WATERS**
MARS MANIFESTO

VESTA LAVA TUBES: XANTHE

Mars Day 260

KUNLUN'S RECORDS HAD shown an airlock cycling the day before, after sunset. Lincoln must have left the base. Xanthe and Serena monitored the comms while Troy led the ground search party. The pilots took to the sky. Madison had finally had a chance to fly the copter alongside Barrio. Together, they followed the suit telemetry signals until the geolocation tag cut out.

There was no sign of him, the wind having blown over any footsteps.

Had Lincoln killed the geotag, or had the battery simply died?

Xanthe wondered what had gone through Lincoln's mind as he trudged into the darkness.

A twinge of guilt prickled at her. They'd checked in on him every seven days, as promised, for the last one hundred and forty days. He'd been everything from belligerent to pleading. Demanding and conciliatory.

Matt had left Lincoln for Vesta when he'd had enough of the ranting. Things had come to a head when Earth-side had advised that all human transport to Mars would be suspended until Earth's atmosphere had stabilised. They'd fix one planet at a time.

Lincoln had gone ballistic, ripping the comms displays from its bracket and smashing furniture. When Matt told Lincoln he was leaving, he'd chased Matt into the airlock, throwing cutlery after him. Matt barely had enough time to hit the manual override while Lincoln pounded the airlock door and yelled obscenities.

Matt had arrived, shaken. "The man's unhinged."

And alone.

Xanthe reminded herself each time of his crimes, the multiple attempts to kill them.

The man was a manipulative psychopath.

He had no remorse. No compassion. No capacity for redemption.

Still, he was human.

Exile was a brutal sentence. Silence, worse.

Xanthe rubbed her temples, her mouth dry and her heart heavy. She imagined his tread into the endless dark. She knew that dark—lived in it daily. But unlike her, he had chosen it.

"Checking the far corner of Vesta now," Troy's voice crackled on comms.

"Roger," Madison replied.

Serena put a hand on Xanthe's.

"It's not our fault," she said quietly. "Lincoln was a weapon waiting to fire."

Xanthe's throat tightened. "He was someone's son." Memories of her own son bobbed, his ashes tucked away on her alcove shelf.

"You give that man far too much kindness."

"Isn't that what we agreed? Kindness first?"

"Not the kind that gets us killed. You know he'd have tried again."

Static hissed. Then Barrio's low voice: "We found something. I'm bringing it in."

✌

The crew stood silent as Barrio laid the helmet on the table. Xanthe traced the scuffed surface, dented deep along one edge. Dust caked the seals. He'd found it at the lip of a crevasse, half-buried.

They'd checked the stores. Every suit accounted for but one.

They'd rummaged through the entire base, searching for clues, finding only a tatty journal, his own counter to their Mars Manifesto. The entries had become more and more volatile, erratic. It left them with two hypotheses: he'd left the base to wreak vengeance, or he'd left the base to surrender to fate.

Either way, Lincoln Ellison had walked into the void.

And the void had kept him.

CHAPTER SEVENTY-SEVEN

"We live not as strangers, but as kin."

—Claire Edwards
TERRABOUND GLOBAL MANIFESTO

GAIA ENTERPRISES HEADQUARTERS: MAJA

Mars Day 272

LINCOLN'S DISAPPEARANCE FILLED Earth's feeds day after day. Conspiracy theories multiplied like mould: he was alive; Nyx astronauts had shoved him into a crevasse; the Dopplebots had executed him; Claire Edwards—new head of the freshly rebranded *TerraBound Global*—had even sent an assassin to Mars.

Meanwhile, quieter stories scrolled by, updates on the shared governance of Kunlun and Vesta.

Maja joined Aryanna at the boardroom window overlooking Gaia Enterprises's launchpad. The hulking clock marked time in booming ticks. The *Bellona*, the next supply ship to Mars, stood gleaming while engineers swarmed its flanks.

"We've done well," Aryanna said, her voice low, almost tender. She smoothed the sleeves of her silky white kaftan.

Maja let out a long breath. "Have we? Too many have died to get us here." She traced the contours of her owl and heart necklace charm.

"And many will live because of what we've built. Because of what the crews endured—on the Moon, on Mars." Aryanna turned to her, eyes searching. "You can see the good, can't you?"

Maja's mouth twisted. "I can. But I see the costs too."

The boardroom doors banged open. Huw Chan strode in, one arm hooked around a champagne bucket, glasses rattling in the other.

"Ladies! Thought I'd find you here." He dumped his cargo on the table, popped the cork with a grin and poured fizzing streams into waiting flutes.

"What's the occasion?" Aryanna asked, slender fingers already reaching for hers.

"Occasion?" Huw laughed. "Only this—we live, we love, we push the world forward, inch by inch. We build better worlds. To a life worth living!" He raised his glass, clinking theirs.

Maja sipped, the tightness in her chest loosening. "I'll drink to that."

Maybe that was all any of them could ask: to live and leave the world a little better.

Yes, perhaps that was mission enough.

CHAPTER SEVENTY-EIGHT

"We came to Mars to build a future. Somewhere along the way, I learned how to reclaim my past."

—**Xanthe Waters**
MEMOIRS FROM MARS

VESTA LAVA TUBES: XANTHE

Mars Day 482

Xanthe stole a moment for herself and made her way down one of the tubes toward her personal nook. She let her fingertips trail lightly along the cool polymer walls, feeling every vibration of the murmuring machinery beneath them. Athena whispered subtle guidance in her ear, and the Dopplebot twin paced silently at her side, its presence a comforting shadow.

She lowered herself onto the thin mattress and exhaled. The nook was quiet, but from the hub she could still hear the faint clatter of utensils, the hum of the air scrubbers and the warm rise of laughter—crew finishing their evening meal together.

Four hundred and eighty-two days on Mars.

They had earned the right to call themselves settlers.

They had survived the planet's fury, Lincoln's sabotage, the staggering losses that still lived in the walls of this base. And yet they were here—still growing food, feeding one another, coaxing a fragile civilisation from dust and stubbornness towards something lasting, something with strong foundations for the future.

Her body ached. Her legs throbbed with the dull heat of a long day spent marching through the base: systems checks, team reports and a thousand tiny decisions required to keep everyone breathing. Pride warmed her chest, but exhaustion tugged at her bones.

Her fingers drifted to the compass patch stitched to her jersey. So far from Earth. So far from the woman she once was. Her mind slid to the moments that had hurled her life off its axis—the tsunami that tore Jack from her arms, the miracle of his return, the devastation of losing him again. Her years as a Gaia Enterprises world designer. Olympus. The triumphs. The tragedies. Maja's invitation. Troy's steady conviction that she belonged on this mission.

So many lives, fallen like grains of sand in the whispering winds of Mars.

Her hand reached behind her, finding the small box on the ledge. Jack's ashes. She worked not for his future—she no longer had that—but in his name, for the futures of others. That, at least, was something she could still protect.

She breathed in deeply, then wiped the corner of one eye with her thumb.

Footsteps approached in the corridor—unhurried, familiar. Troy. She could tell by the gentle saunter in his gait. Warmth spread through her chest even before he spoke.

"Hey," he said softly.

"Hey yourself."

"Mind if I join you?"

"Of course."

She shifted, making space. The mattress dipped as he perched beside her.

"That was a big day," Troy said. "Glad we got the water recycler sorted."

"Every day's a big day on Mars," she murmured.

"True." He hesitated, then added, "We make a good team."

"Who would have thought," she said with a smile in her voice.

"I'm glad we're sharing leadership. This job…it's brutal sometimes. I couldn't have done it without you."

His fingers brushed hers. She twined her hand with his, and a quiet settled between them—comfortable, steady.

"This has been hard, Troy," she said finally. "Harder than I ever imagined."

"What do you mean? You always seem to take everything in stride."

"I've gotten used to solving problems. There's always another crisis, another fix. But since I lost my sight…" She swallowed. "It's like a corner of me has lost its magic."

"What do you think you're missing?"

"I don't know. I just…wonder what I don't get to see anymore."

"I don't think you're missing anything," he said. She heard him shift closer, felt his breath warm the air between them. "I can describe the world in front of me, but you see far more without eyes. You see with your heart. That's the real magic."

She let that sit, her breath steadying.

"Will you describe things for me, then?" she asked. "Athena is helpful, but it's all technical—'five metres forward, mind the step'—that sort of thing."

"I'd love to," he said. "Though I'm no poet. You'll have to forgive my clumsy metaphors."

"Your voice is the paintbrush," she said. "I hear the magic in it."

He gave a soft laugh. She pictured his lopsided smile.

"You've changed," she said.

"Really? How?"

"You're steadier. More present."

He pressed his shoulder to hers. "I think I've spent my whole life looking for a sense of worthiness. Chasing approval through performance, through medals and missions. I didn't realise how hollow it all was until…" He exhaled. "Until you. You showed me I was enough, Xanthe."

Emotion trembled in his voice. She turned toward the warmth of him.

"Was that humility?" she teased lightly.

He laughed—quiet, embarrassed. "Maybe."

"It's good to hear you laugh," he said. "I've missed that."

"Thank you, Troy," she whispered.

"For what?"

"For giving me hope."

Her free hand lifted to his cheek, finding the curve of his jaw, the roughness of stubble, the warmth of living skin. He stilled under her touch. The faint scent of cloves, always so distinctly him, curled into her senses.

She leaned in. He met her halfway.

Their lips touched—soft, certain, grounding. The taste of him sweet, his lips warm and gentle.

She'd missed this: the tenderness, the desire.

With a realisation that stole her breath, she'd missed *him*.

And in that moment, with the pulse of the habitat humming around them, and Mars whispering its ancient winds just beyond the walls, it felt like coming home.

Not to Earth.

To him.

To herself.

CHAPTER SEVENTY-NINE

*"We dare, we build, we lead: in honour of those
who have left us. And for those yet to follow."*

—XANTHE WATERS
MARS MANIFESTO

UTOPIA PLANITIA: TROY

Mars Day 714

XANTHE AND TROY climbed the escarpment just below Vesta's panoramic window. She'd left her twin behind so they could be alone.

"Tell me," she said, breath catching from the climb.

Troy beamed. He put an arm around her, steering her so that they were facing the expanse below. He loved moments like this, when his words could give her the world again.

"We are standing on a ridge, rocks crimson with slashes of black and blood red. In the hollows, crystals catch the faintest light. The sky is still deep, but at the horizon—it's loosening. Apollo breathing a few strands of gold into the darkness."

He watched her smile, radiant through the helmet, and his heart bloomed. "The ridge slopes to the plains laced with cinnamon. Darker veins crack the surface. Like an old man's skin."

A breeze stirred and the dust swirled.

His voice hushed. "Apollo is splashing the sky azure now, readying for ascension to his throne. It's blue-grey, a watercolour wash—a purification before the moment of dawn," Troy whispered, the solemnity of the occasion moving him. He watched a tear slip down Xanthe's cheek.

"Farther to the heavens, amber, rust, coppery pink." His heart quickened. "The shadows behind us are heavy, almost purple-black. But at the rim—" He faltered, awed. "There's a halo of electric blue, fading into rose and burnt orange, spread over the red desert. Glorious!"

Xanthe's breath caught. She breathed in sharply, holding the moment close.

"And now," Troy whispered, "the sun."

Heat touched their suits as the first rays crept along the ridge.

"Apollo's reaching his fingers along the ridge. Cinnamon dancers swirl around us."

"Now?" she asked.

"Yes."

Her hands fumbled at her belt pouch. She pulled out the small box and cradled it in her palms. For a moment she only held it, gloved thumb brushing its edge, her breath uneven.

"Ad Astra, my beautiful boy."

She opened the case and tipped her son Jack's ashes into the rising swirl. The dust lifted, sparkling in the dawn.

"He's shining, Xanthe," Troy murmured.

Xanthe's lip trembled. She squeezed Troy's hand tight.

They stood a long while, hand in hand, sun streaming over the land, full of memory.

Full of promise.

The End.

NOTE FROM THE AUTHOR

Thank you so much for following the adventures and tribulations of the Gaia crew on Earth, the Moon and Mars. It's been a pleasure exploring the lives and ambitions of these daring leaders in a world rife with challenges.

The series started with the question, "What kind of leadership do we need now for what's next?" Then, the imagining of what a future world might look like began. Its people emerged from that haze, bringing their hopes and aspirations, their wounds and worries, and their longing for a better future.

Wherever we end up as a species, we take ourselves with us. We will still have egos to wrangle and differences to bridge.

One truth remains steadfast: the future can only be better when good people take courageous action in building a world worth living in.

These characters live with me, their stories emerging from the pain and triumphs of friends, colleagues, family and my own world. Like Xanthe, I've known the devastation of being sidelined by another female leader with authority. I've been the cocky leader tripping over themselves as Jonas has been. I've searched desperately to fit in and find belonging, as Serena has. I've seen great people, great leaders, struggle with their own self-belief, but get up and fight another day because they believed in building a better world.

If that's you, I'm here for you.

I'm always developing my work to serve big thinkers with big hearts who want to make a big difference: through books, workshops, events and community. The themes of my work gravitate toward power, fairness and overcoming self-doubt for a courageous life.

If that calls to you, and you'd love conversations with others who are building better worlds, then come join us at *www.zoerouth.com*. I have a regular blog/newsletter I've been writing for over twenty years. It's a starting point for imagining a wiser and more compassionate world.

I always offer plenty of value: a free ebook, *Terra Blanca Insurrection*, the prequel to this series, as well as in-depth thought-provoking articles, podcast interviews, book reviews and recommendations, and a place to connect with other leaders and readers.

Come join us! You are welcome and wanted: a place to belong.

Please rate and review *Olympus Dawn*

If you enjoyed this book, and even if you didn't, I'd love it if you'd leave a review on Goodreads or Amazon. This encourages other readers to take a chance on this series. Courage is contagious, so even if you've never left a review before, know that taking a moment to share your thoughts may inspire others to find their voice too.

ACKNOWLEDGMENTS

I'm deeply grateful to you, the reader, for joining me on this odyssey! Thanks for diving in and exploring the Gaia universe.

I couldn't have pulled off this epic series without the amazing Darren Nash, my developmental editor. I am so grateful for his help in wrangling this beast into a workable story. He challenged me on key plot points and character arcs and made some excellent suggestions.

A huge thank you to Meredith Anderson for passing a fine comb over these words to pick up weird author ticks, typos, and other random things that escape an author's eyeballs.

A big thanks to my friends and family who have asked me about the books and celebrated my progress.

And of course, huge gratitude to my husband, Rob, for believing in me, and for needling me to submit the books for movie production. And if you know someone in that department, let me know!

A.I. Assisted Artisan Author

Joanna Penn coined this phrase and practice, and I think it's apt for the modern creative. I see myself as a creative director, bringing to life the characters, their world, and their development in service of the story.

I use A.I. to boost my writing process. I use ChatGPT for research, ideation, brainstorming, writing critique. Sometimes its suggestions are fantastic, sometimes 'meh'. I also use Google for searches, *thesaurus.com* for language options, ProWriting Aid for editing suggestions, and Midjourney and Canva for marketing images. I also have two human editors and proofreaders and a human A.I. Assisted book cover designer.

ΛBOUT THE ΛUTHOR

Zoë is a leadership futurist, multiple award-winning author, strategist and podcaster. She shows CEOs and their teams how to navigate the future.

She has worked with individuals and teams internationally and in Australia since 1987. From the wild rivers of northern Ontario to the remote regions of Australia, Zoë has spent the last thirty-five years showing teams how to navigate the wilderness of leadership.

Zoë is the author of five leadership books and an award-winning speculative fiction series. Her fourth book, *People Stuff – Beyond Personality Problems: An advanced handbook for leadership*, won 'Book of the Year' at the Australian Business Book Awards 2020.

Zoë is the host and producer of The Future of Leadership Podcast, a show about what leadership we need now for what's next.

Zoë is an outdoor adventurer and enjoys telemark skiing, has run 6 marathons, is a onetime belly-dancer, has survived cancer, and loves hiking in the high country. She is married to a gorgeous Aussie and is a self-confessed dark chocolate addict.

www.ingramcontent.com/pod-product-compliance
Lightning Source LLC
Chambersburg PA
CBHW050956210726
48287CB00004B/1246